Ellen Warner Olney Kirk

Walford

Ellen Warner Olney Kirk

Walford

ISBN/EAN: 9783337001254

Printed in Europe, USA, Canada, Australia, Japan

Cover: Foto ©Andreas Hilbeck / pixelio.de

More available books at **www.hansebooks.com**

WALFORD

BY

ELLEN OLNEY KIRK

AUTHOR·OF "THE STORY OF MARGARET KENT," "SONS AND DAUGHTERS,"
"QUEEN MONEY," ETC.

" A little child, a limber elf,
Singing, dancing to itself ;
A fairy thing with red, round cheeks,
That always finds, and never seeks. "

BOSTON AND NEW YORK
HOUGHTON, MIFFLIN AND COMPANY
The Riverside Press, Cambridge
1890

To
MY MOTHER

CONTENTS.

WALFORD.

"A little child, a limber elf
Singing, dancing to itself,
A fairy thing, with red round cheeks,
That always finds and never seeks."

———◆———

I.

EVELYN.

IT was a saying with Walford people that Mrs. Rexford was jealous of the sun that shone and the winds which blew on her little daughter. It is certain that she liked to perform every possible service for the child with her own hands, felt aggrieved at the briefest separation, and could not endure to miss the least of the wise utterances which issued, at times somewhat mystically, from the baby lips.

One day in October Evelyn was solacing herself for the prospect of a long, uncongenial afternoon without the child, by herself dressing Bessy for a visit to her godmother. Each button, each knot of ribbon, was an apology for a snatched kiss, sudden, swift, and tender as a lover's. Although Bessy was now almost three years old the miracle was always fresh to the young mother; the upward glance of the child's blue eyes, the arch or wistful smile, the veins on the temples, the

soft whiteness of the throat, the curve of the round
shoulders, the dimples on the knees, stirred the insatiable maternal instinct to possess, to enfold, to guard.
Such caresses were so much a part of the daily phenomena of Bessy's little life that she accepted them
with the same resignation as the infliction of hooks,
buttons, and pins.   Meanwhile a flash of sunlight
across the mirror was a wonder to watch, and the buzz-
ing of a fly on the window-pane stirred some recollection, and she babbled on to herself about a bee in a
morning-glory.   The bee was eating honey, such a
greedy, hungry bee he forgot to finish his meal in due
season, and the morning-glory, keeping hospitably open
as long as it might, finally could keep open no longer,
so shut up, imprisoning its visitor in its corolla.

"And the bee called 'Buzz, buzz, buzz,'" said the
child. "Bessy could hear him say 'Buzz, buzz, buzz,'
all inside the morn' glory."

"What did Bessy do?" asked Evelyn.

"Buzz, buzz, buzz," repeated the child from the
depths of reverie. "Buzz, buzz, buzz."

The idea of the bee humming in the shut flower-cup
was evidently something to linger over. So Evelyn
carried on the story.

"Bessy heard the bee, and called, 'Where is the
buzz, buzz, mamma?' She put her little hand on the
morning-glory all shut up and gone to sleep, and felt
the bee inside. Then Bessy gave a loud cry, papa
came, opened the morning-glory, and out flew the bee
and went home to his mamma. *So* glad."

"*So* glad," murmured Bessy, with a dreamy smile.

"Mamma's little girl will be glad to come home to-
night," said Evelyn. "Bessy must not get shut up in
a morning-glory."

" Buzz, buzz, buzz," repeated Bessy, perhaps with some straggling idea that the bee's experience might be worth undertaking.

" How much does Bessy love mamma ? " demanded Evelyn.

" Mor 'n tongue c'n tell," responded the little maid, with cheerful indifference.

Ten minutes later Evelyn was leaning over the gate, watching Bessy go down Walford main street with Jenny, — the bright-faced English nurse. Fido, the old collie dog, stood beside his mistress, looking yearningly up into her face and uttering a feeble complaint that he was not permitted to follow.

" No, Fido, no," said Evelyn. " You 're too old, you 're getting far too old. Poor fellow ! I 'm sorry for you. But Madam Van does not want you, — she does not want me either, she only wants our precious baby."

It was the twenty-fourth day of October, but the sun was warm, the air soft, and the mellow autumnal tints still showed a gemlike delicacy and brilliancy. The beauty of the world seemed to Evelyn wholly wasted since Bessy would not be at home until sunset. She walked up the lawn followed by Fido, and when they reached his kennel she chained him lest he should contrive to slip away and follow the child. He submitted, but did not at first lie down, and looked pleadingly into her face ; then, as Evelyn shook her head, he stretched himself out with a deep sigh, while his eyes followed her as she went to the flower-beds to pick some chrysanthemums. " Poor old Fido," she said to the dog as she passed him again. She too felt lonely, smitten ; a limb lopped off, a dull ache at her heart. " Perhaps Roger will go

to ride with me," she said to herself, and went to the
gate once more to see if he were coming. There he
was ! She flew down the street to meet him. Walford
people regarded Mrs. Rexford as the embodiment of
whim, caprice, and fastidiousness. Thus there was
nothing phenomenal in the glimpse of domestic life
she now offered to the public, — putting up her face to
be kissed, then strolling back to the house with her
hand on her husband's arm, looking, as was her way,
happy, proud, above the world.

Roger Rexford watched her approach with a brightening aspect. He was in no soft mood, and his habit
in these days was reserved and rather taciturn, but his
delight in his wife's beauty was almost more passionate
than it had been when he married her four years before.
She wore to-day a gown of some white woolen material,
with a collar and cuffs of black velvet, so simply made
that not a line of her figure was lost. The sun shone
on her chestnut hair, burnishing it into reddish gold.
Her complexion was like the inner leaves of a blush
rose, and her brown eyes were full of a pure, wonderful
brilliance.

" Where 's Bessy ? " he inquired.

" It is Thursday, — she has gone to Madam Van,"
said Evelyn. " I hate Mondays and Thursdays."

Roger laughed. " You do begrudge poor aunt Lizzy
a sight of that child."

" Of course I do," said Evelyn. " Particularly when
aunt Lizzy not only wants Bessy all the time, but dic-
tates, finds fault, and above all does everything she can
to spoil her. I do want my own baby to my own self.
Roger, I have an idea ! Why should we not spend this
winter in New York ? "

He shrugged his shoulders. "How am I to get away from this treadmill?"

"Mr. Spencer will be here," said Evelyn, ready to insist on a scheme born of a momentary fancy. "Besides, you have partners. I am sure that in your father's day the works used to run themselves from October till May."

"The times are different," said Roger, rather curtly. "There is no chance of my getting a holiday."

They had entered the house and presently sat down to a half-lunch, half-dinner, which was their midday meal.

"I have heard," said Evelyn, her mind still running on the scheme she had proposed, "that men become bound up in their business, — that money-making is an infatuation which grows like any other. But when we were married, Roger, you did not expect to devote all your life to the works."

"You know exactly as much about my business as Bessy does," Roger observed.

"I know as much as this," said Evelyn, archly, "that you think of nothing else and care for nothing else."

"I take it," he retorted, "that the difference between a man and a woman is that she is always thinking about what she likes to do, whether she must do it or must not do it; while a man is obliged to consider what he must do, whether he likes it or not."

There was a hint of savageness in his tone, and Evelyn's eyes dilated with surprise.

"Men say such clever things about us," she replied, "but I don't think that clever things are invariably true." She was silent for a moment, evidently turning his words over in her mind; then she went on: "And it seems to me that we women accept grievous burdens and complain of them very little. There is hardly a woman in Walford who does what she wants to do: she simply does what she can."

Roger was amused by her evident desire to argue seriously on his pettish outburst. He was sorry he had spoken roughly, but he considered that his wife was criticising, almost judging him. Few men like to live with their critics and judges, and more than most men Roger was jealous of any one's dictation.

"My dear," said he, smiling, "you are the sweetest woman in the world and by all odds the most beautiful, and certainly you ought to bear no burdens. You should have married a millionaire, had a house in New York, fronting on the Park, a cottage at Newport, trips to Europe and " —

She sprang up, ran round the table, and nestled against him. "Don't say such things. Don't fancy I had any such meaning in my mind," she murmured, putting her cheek to his. "You know that I am perfectly happy, — indeed, sometimes when I have you and Bessy within reach I feel almost too happy! It frightens me."

He kissed her, pushed the soft curls off her forehead, and sighed.

"I must go," said he.

"I was in hopes we could have a ride this afternoon," she ventured.

"It is out of the question. I myself feel ridden."

"What do you mean ? "

"Black care is on the crupper, and I have got to go her pace."

Evelyn looked at him with apprehension.

" Do you mean that business is bad? "

" Is business ever anything else, nowadays ? "

" Has anything new happened ? "

" Oh, dear, no. The same old story. Don't talk about it. I hate any mention of it at home. By the way, Rex is here. He can ride with you."

" Rex here! How nice! I suppose he is at Mrs. Goodeve's ? "

" Yes. He told me to tell you he was coming to see you. I 'll send him word that you want a ride. Just put out my things for him. Lewis shall bring the horses round by half-past two."

When, half an hour later, Evelyn ran down the stairs in her habit she found Rexford Long waiting for her. He was a friend older even than her husband, and it was indeed through Long that the two had met. Evelyn had been an orphan from an early age, and had lived with her mother's uncle, who was at the head of the publishing house of the Synnots, in which Rexford Long had a position. He had been a good friend to the young and lonely girl, and she was cordially fond of him. She was especially glad to see him to-day when she experienced a longing for companionship, — felt a beat of her pulses and a desire for expression, expansion, action, beyond what Walford possibilities offered. Evelyn was a little afraid of trespassing on her husband's patience, but Long never counted with her as a man to be propitiated, humored, made much of. Roger Rexford always knew definitely what he himself wished and what he considered best for his wife. Evelyn had sometimes put out her hand, expecting to find his clasping hers with eagerness to carry out her wishes, and had instead encountered a check

which brought sudden blinding tears of disappointment.
But she never felt the least hesitation in assuming
that Rexford Long was ready to do exactly what she
asked of him.   She talked to him with more freedom
than to her husband, and on a wider range of subjects,
counting on his insight and sympathy even when her
revelations were not only feminine and foolish but individual to herself.   Physically the two cousins were
very different : Roger having fine proportions, with a
square head solidly put upon a powerful pair of shoulders, a profusion of dark brown hair, fine eyes of blu-
ish gray, a heavy mustache shading a firm mouth ;
altogether he was an unusually handsome man ; while
Rex was too slender for his height, had a rather ugly
but speaking face, hair so fine and soft as to appear
scanty, and a mere line of blond mustache on his
upper lip.   Then in manner Roger was impressive and
occasionally imperious, while Long, although his tone
with his intimates could take on a caressing sweetness,
was too quiet and rarely asserted himself.   He was a
better listener than talker, and neither by word nor look
let out his secrets easily.

"Let us go to High Rock," said Evelyn, as they
turned out of the gate.   "I long to get on high ground.
Oh, Rex, I am so thankful you are here.   I wanted
somebody to talk to.   Don't you remember Eugénie
de Guérin's saying, ' Everything is green, everything is
in bloom : all the air has a breath of flowers.   How
beautiful it is !   I will go out !   No, I should be alone,
and all this beauty when one is alone is nothing ' ? "

"Alone," Long repeated in a tone half of irony.
They were ambling their horses along the main street
of Walford, and Evelyn was nodding and waving her

hand to men at the doors of shops and stores, and matrons and girls at windows. Walford was always an active place, but to-day showed an unusual stir; all the farmers and their wives for miles about seemed to have come to town; there were heavily loaded vans, carts, wagons, and chaises; the merchants were selling over their counters; but in the midst of all the movement and bustle every one was ready to be observant of all that could happen before his eyes, and the moment Evelyn's trim figure was recognized on one of "Roger Rexford's bays" (for in Walford one knows not only his neighbors but his neighbors' dogs and horses) and Rexford Long's on the other, there was a general suspension of private and personal interests until the riders had passed by, and had turned in at Mrs. Goodeve's open gate.

"Oh, there you are," said Mrs. Goodeve, coming out into the porch. "I hoped I should have a glimpse of you."

It was a large, generously built house, belonging to Walford's best period, and Mrs. Goodeve, a tall, handsome woman of fifty or more, made up a part of the impression of hospitality which belonged to the whole aspect of the place.

"We are going to High Rock," said Evelyn. "It is such a pleasure to feel the horse under one. As soon as we are out of the street, we shall gallop, may n't we, Rex? I long to drink in the wind."

"I am glad you have got Rex to look after you," returned Mrs. Goodeve. "Rex is a useful fellow. I 've been telling him he ought to marry, but perhaps we could not spare him."

"Indeed, Rex must not marry," said Evelyn. "When

a man marries, his troubles begin. Look at Roger
buried in his business. Look at your husband in a
morass of manuscripts. There is no telling what sort
of a monster Rex would turn out if he had a wife and
children. What do you suppose it is in married life
which makes a misanthrope of a man? Is it bills?
Or is it that, having got what he wants, man delights
not him nor woman either? No. I want Rex to be
happy and not to lose his illusions. I insist that he
shall not marry."

"I thought you were planning that he should marry
your sister Amy," suggested Mrs. Goodeve, enjoying
the younger woman's smiles and laughter, her bright
eyes, the symmetry of her figure. She considered Evelyn a bewitching, half-spoiled child.

"No, indeed, Rex shall not marry Amy. Roger says
her idea of life is that everybody shall keep in a con-
tinual state of perspiration. Besides, Amy has made
up her mind never to marry. She considers men a
great interruption and clog to the best ambitions of
women. Rex could n't live up to Amy's ideas. Possibly in twenty years or so, I may allow him to marry
Bessy, but nobody else."

"I have got a son of my own whom I am saving
up for Bessy," said Mrs. Goodeve. "Well, good-by!
Take care of yourselves."

The horses had been pawing restlessly, and now,
with a wave of the hand from Rex and a blown kiss from
the tips of Evelyn's fingers, there was a sharp pull at
each bridle and the animals set off at a good pace.
They turned at the next corner, and leaving the village
behind Evelyn had the gallop she was longing for. It
was not until they were toiling up Stony Hill that she

drew rein again. As they reached this part of the road the outline of the low mountains which surround Walford became clear and distinct, and it could be seen that the village lay as it were in the centre of a huge saucer, which sloped upward to a jagged ruin of domes and serrated ledges. The afternoon sun was flooding the whole landscape : it was still the early autumn sunshine, which seemed to saturate the foliage and burn in every leaf instead of glinting off and keeping itself remote and alien as is the way of November sunlight. It had been a calm, dry season, and the leaves had decayed slowly. A few hours of rain and wind would scatter them, but to-day they hung out their gorgeous banners with almost a summer-like luxuriance and amplitude. The chestnuts showed a pale gold, the hickories a rich russet, the oaks a dull, burnished red. Evelyn had a quick eye, and she caught a glimpse of each fringed ruff of the hazels, each scarlet hip of wild-rose along the hedgerows. In this rarely traversed region nature had been despoiled of but few of her summer treasures. Dense bowers of clematis were still over-hung with the feathery carpels where once the starry masses of flowers had been. Bittersweet trailed in and out, its seed vessels ready to burst at the first hard frost. The hawthorn and buckthorn had been visited by flocks of migrating birds, who had providently left an ample store of berries for their return. Barberries were heavy with the fruit which would soon ripen into flame. Frost-grapes displayed their clusters. Some broad cymes of scarlet berries like waxen beads, and others of lustrous purple, roused Evelyn's curiosity, and she at once assailed Long with questions about their names and uses.

"I want Bessy to know everything she sees," she explained. "A child is learning all the time, and she may as well learn facts as foolish false substitutes for facts."

Long had a habit of answering all Evelyn's questions, whether about botany or social economy. He had first met her as a school-girl of fifteen, and it had seemed to him a promising scheme to interest her in himself, to teach her to depend on him and love him. For the next two years he had coached her, directed her reading, had a care for her music, and had been indeed the most stimulating of all the influences which were forming her. Then when she was seventeen Roger Rexford encountered her. The two instantly fell in love, and a year later they were married.

Probably Roger suspected that he was snatching the honors of victory from the man who had toiled for them, but the idea had never occurred to Evelyn that Long's devotion meant more than kindness to an ambitious schoolgirl whom he liked to drill in his favorite studies. Long himself was no egoist, and many things in the universe appeared to him more important than his own private happiness, — for example, Evelyn's welfare. He still watched over her jealously, for he was frequently at Walford. It had troubled him that she had spoken to-day of feeling lonely. It seemed to him, who was actually one of the loneliest of men, that Evelyn was surrounded by a care, a tenderness, a worship, which filled and answered all need of companionship; and, besides, she had multitudes of friends and was flattered and caressed by all the world.

However, as they rode on he decided that her words had meant nothing deeper than some momentary impatience. As they climbed the hill her spirit as well seemed to open into wider horizons and to gain fresh lights. She found wonderful beauty in the rows of stacked corn, with golden pumpkins scattered here and there among the yellow stubble ; the glowing colors of the tier upon tier of wooded hills satisfied her eye : she liked the fruity smell in the air, occasionally emphasized by a clear, cool whiff from a cider-press beside some stream. By the time they had reached High Rock, the air had grown clearer, and the distances were swept free of haze. For miles away the mountain outlines rose distinct, each ledge sharply defined. East Rock had lost its blue and stood up steep and rugged, while the chain to the north looked as if almost within reach. Towards the east the horizon was extended for many miles, and spires rose out of remote towns and villages. Here and there sparkled a watercourse, and, listening, they heard a sound like that of breakers on a beach.

"It comes from Roaring Brook," observed Evelyn. "When it sounds so loud, it is sure to rain. The wind has gone to the east, I fancy. The air is actually keen."

"The afternoons are short now," said Long. "The sun is almost down."

"We must go back at once," exclaimed Evelyn, startled. "I told Jenny she must not keep Bessy out a moment after the sun had set."

They began the descent at once, and as long as they were compelled to walk their horses Evelyn talked about Bessy, pouring out a recital of the child's droll sayings and doings. Along with the story of her happiness came the young mother's rebellions.

"It seemed very natural," she said, "to name Bessy

after Madam Van when she desired it. She is a rich, childless old woman, and it was a pathetic sort of plea which it would have seemed an inhumanity to disregard. But I did not know that I was giving up half my own child. Nothing satisfies Madam Van. I send Bessy to her every Monday and Thursday, but that is not enough. Whenever Roger and I go away, I leave Bessy in her charge. Last summer she kept the child five weeks, and I supposed such a concession would make her more reasonable. On the contrary, appetite came with eating. Having had Bessy for five weeks, she now wants her all the time."

"Don't begrudge poor aunt Lizzy a little joy this side of eternity," said Long. "She is sure to leave Bessy all she has."

"That is where the sting comes in," returned Evelyn. "Roger constantly tries to pacify me with that argument, and it makes me ashamed. I hate to have him seem not disinterested, bending himself double to conform to her whims. I don't want her money."

"Roger may see the advantage of it more clearly."

Evelyn made a little grimace. "I was accusing Roger at luncheon of caring for nothing but money-making," she exclaimed.

"I am afraid it is not making money that he has a chance to care about," observed Long with a shrug. "What he has to bear is losing money."

"Losing money?" repeated Evelyn. "I asked him if anything new had happened, and he said it was only the same old story."

"There has been over-production, — the markets are glutted. There have been failures, and there are panic prices. Everybody has grown timid, — there is general stagnation, and unless something happens, — why, I am afraid something will happen."

Evelyn experienced a sharp pang of remorse for having seemed for a single moment to be lacking in sympathy. Her mind, with tense realistic energy, took in a full sense of her husband's position, and a wave of unutterable longing to be everything to him in any possible emergency rose and broke, as it were, leaving tears in her eyes.

"You know," she said to Long with a half sob, "Roger will never tell me anything that can possibly pain me. He wants to bear all himself; there was never anybody so noble, so generous, so great."

"Roger is a strong man."

"Oh, he is. Let us ride fast; I want to get home."

The sun would not be down for a quarter of an hour, but at this moment it vanished behind a long, low purple cloud lifting up the edges into an intolerable radiance. Instantly the air grew sharper. The horses felt the goad of a longing to reach their stables and their supper, and they settled into a free, bold stride flank by flank almost as close as if they were in harness. The mountains all about took on a dark indigo blue and loomed up like sentinels. Just before it was to sink below the horizon the sun emerged, and for three minutes shone brilliantly, lighting up every fold of color on the wooded hills, the stubble of the fields, the piles of corn-ears, the hips and haws in the hedgerows, the thistle-down in air. Then it sank, and the glorious light was seen only in the clouds, which looked for a time like mountains on fire. In turn they too faded, passed over, and vanished. The low western horizon still glowed with a delicate salmon color tinged with rose, deepest when the sun disappeared, and fading upwards. This gradually dimmed. At one stride came the dark. When they reached the house Evelyn was too impatient to wait for Long to dismount to help her. She flung herself down.

"Bessy?" she called. "Bessy! Is not Bessy at home yet?"

II.

LITTLE RED RIDING-HOOD.

It was just one o'clock when Jenny, holding Bessy
Rexford tightly by the hand, turned the corner, and,
leaving the main street of the village behind, they
reached a quiet part of Walford, commanding a view
of the Quinnipiac River, beyond which pretty stream rose
an undulating country, stretching to high, wooded hills.
Pursuing this road they soon came to the high gate of
Madam Van Polanen's place, abbreviated by Walford
people into "Madam Van's." The house, set off by
many gables and bay-windows, stood far back from the
street, surrounded by lawns and gardens bordered by
shrubberies full of dim nooks and recesses, the haunt
in summer of innumerable birds. The side lawn, sloping toward the west, ran down to the water-side, for
the little river cut through the estate, forming just here
a broad basin. Where the stream entered and left this
miniature lake large willows bending over each bank
interlaced their branches and almost closed the vista.
Towards the farther shore grew all sorts of aquatic
plants, and to-day among the broad lily leaves and
pads myriads of late insects were skimming and dart-
ing, sending up bubbles and ripples which broke the
clear, sunshiny mirror into a thousand lines. A drowsy
breath of sweetness and a soft sound of flowing water
were wafted up together. Bessy uttered a cry of delight,

and said that she was going down to the river to sail a boat.

"Your mamma said you must not go near the river, Bessy," said Jenny with decision. "Don't you remember you promised your mamma, Bessy?"

The child first looked meditative, as if examining her conscience; then said, with Spartan firmness: —

"Bessy go near the water? No!"

They were within the tall iron gates. The glass doors of the house opened upon a veranda from which a flight of wide steps descended to the graveled path. Sitting inside in full view was an old lady in a wheel-chair, and the moment child and nurse had reached the foot of the steps, at her orders a man came out, nodded to Jenny with a swift, admiring glance from his black, velvety eyes, and lifting Bessy, much against her will and although her sturdy legs and arms fought him all the way, he carried her up and did not set her down until he reached the hall.

The child shook herself free with angry scorn of the Italian servant.

"Bessy like Nino?" she screamed with indignation. "No! No!"

Nino smiled darkly, shrugged his shoulders, and retreated, while Madam Van Polanen covered the little one with kisses. Madam Van regarded most spectacles with a grim humor, and it always amused her to observe the child's hatred of the Italian.

"Why does not Bessy like Nino?" she asked.

The child gave her a full, candid glance out of her blue eyes, and seemed to consider; then waiving the question, said cheerfully, "Bessy likes gamma."

"Nino," said Madam Van, "wheel us into the dining-room."

A delicate dinner awaited the little guest. Bessy sat in a high chair opposite the old lady, and it was evident that the child's tastes had been catered to from the white soup to the cream ice which was moulded in the form of a bird. Nino waited on the table assiduously, and constantly received orders to mince Miss Bessy's chicken, to give her more marmalade, to fill her mug, and the worse the grace with which he performed these menial services and the more repugnance Bessy showed to his proximity, the better Madam Van seemed to be pleased. It was well understood in both households that Nino was jealous of Madam Van's little favorite. He was an Italian, not of the sunny sort, but petulant, jealous, fantastic in his requirements in any matter which touched his dignity. He hated to be considered a servant; he had entered the service of Baron Van Polanen, madam's third husband, as courier, but as Van Polanen's health declined had gradually assumed the duties of nurse and valet. Since Madam Van Polanen became a widow Nino had held an anomalous position, dividing the functions of nurse, companion, and butler.

Madam Van was by this time seventy-six years of age. She had passed a varied life in different parts of the world, and among other hazardous adventures had married three times. Her first husband was John Rexford, the brother of Roger Rexford's father and of Long's mother. He was the founder of the Rexford Manufacturing Company, and left his widow a large fortune. Her second experience of marriage was of the briefest, her husband being killed by a railway accident while they were on their wedding journey. Lastly she married Baron Van Polanen, a Dutch gentleman, somewhat her junior, whom she met in Italy. He was an amateur in several arts, and with him she was very happy. But Van Polanen, always delicate, finally became a hopeless invalid, and his wife brought him back to her old home in Walford, where he died about nine years before the opening of our story. From the moment of his death she declined from the vigorous health and tireless energy of middle life into an infirm old woman. When a little daughter came to her nephew Roger, she asked that it should be named after her. The only child born of Madam Van's three marriages had been a Rexford. The little creature had lived but five months, but had remained an imperishable memory, and the lonely old woman seemed to have transferred all her pent-up passion of motherhood to Evelyn Rexford's little girl. From the time of Bessy's birth there had existed a singular jealousy between the mother and the great aunt. Each longed for exclusive possession, each felt defrauded by the other's claims, and each felt that the other was victorious in the conflict. Roger had, however, never permitted his wife to oppose Madam Van's imperious demands concerning the child. It was well known that the latter had made her will, leaving the bulk of her property to Bessy, and it was a simple matter of justice that the child should brighten the remaining fragment of her life.

More than once in Bessy's short existence she had been left with Madam Van for a month or more while Roger and his wife went on a journey. Days enjoyed by the desolate old woman, looked forward to, and tenderly remembered ! To have the little one's last sleepy kisses at twilight, to be able to watch the cherub face on the pillow, the pale gold of the hair, the peach bloom of the skin, the crimson of the dewy lips, the whole night through if she liked, — that was a compensation which counterbalanced a long monotony of desolate griefs. Her arms ached for the child's embraces ; her lips hungered for her kisses. It was an obstinate grievance that Evelyn Rexford came back, claimed her little girl, and would permit her to leave home but a few short hours twice a week.

Dinner removed, Madam Van was left to the unspoiled enjoyment of her visitor. Nino was not allowed to go beyond call, being summoned periodically to wind up an animated toy, to put a peripatetic doll in motion, to set out Noah's Ark, to wheel the invalid chair into a new place, to draw up or lower the window-shades. He had for years been essential to Madam Van's comfort, and she missed him if he were not about her. She allowed him to discuss subjects as if on an equal footing, even to dictate to her ; but he never sat down in her presence, and she took a high, brusque tone in issuing her commands to him, not unfrequently giving him a downright scolding which he accepted with the grimaces of a rebellious child. Yet when occasionally he got into a dangerous temper she evinced unwearied anxiety to propitiate him, even when he slighted her and neglected his duties. She herself had a temper, and perhaps appreciated the force of character which actuated temper in others. She enjoyed pitting Bessy against Nino, and Nino against Bessy, admiring the easy disdain with which the child met his advances, and feeling diverted by his shrug and gesture of indifference when she knew him to be consumed by pique and envy.

With all these fillips to intercourse, the afternoon

soon waned. The sun declined, the air seemed to Madam Van to grow chilly. She was tired, and her spirits ebbed at the thought of losing Bessy. She had gone back to the red couch where she spent the greater part of her time, and ordered Nino to put the tiger-skin over her.

"Tell Bessy about little Red Riding-hood," said the child, clambering up beside Madam Van. This story was their frequent entertainment, for the tiger's head with fierce, snarling mouth and sharp fangs easily took the part of the wolf to the baby mind, filling her with shuddering delight and terror. An air of intelligence and intense seriousness was apparent in the little creature as she listened. Not a smile touched lips or eyes. The narrative after being twice repeated assumed a dramatic form, Bessy taking the part of Red Riding-hood, while Madam Van personated the wolf.

"Gamma, what big eyes you 've got !"

"The better to *see* you, my dear."

"Gamma, what big ears you 've got !"

"The better to *hear* you, my dear."

"Gamma, what a big mouth you 've got !"

"The better TO EAT YOU, my dear."

The tiger's head bristled up at this point and played an important rôle in the catastrophe.

Jenny was already standing at the door with the child's white cashmere cloak and muslin cap. Nino was out of sight, but he was, in fact, holding the hand of the pretty nurse, and talking to her in a low tone while this diversion was going on. Madam Van was, however, far from suspecting that Nino had a love affair, and now, while the two were exchanging whispers and glances, she was gazing insatiably at the little girl, dreading to part with her.

" Please, madam," Jenny now interposed, " Mrs. Rexford said Miss Bessy must be at home by sunset."

" Oh, my sweetest one, must you go ? " said Madam Van. "Ask mamma to let you come to-morrow."

" Yes, Bessy 'll tum to-morrow," said the child, sleepily submitting to the close folding embrace.

Jenny approached with the wraps.

" Is that all your mistress provided for her little girl this cold weather ? " said Madam Van, sharply. " Nino, go out and see how the thermometer is."

Nino obeyed, and coming back, said that the mercury stood at fifty-four ; that the wind had gone to the east.

Nothing pleased Madam Van better than convicting Evelyn of some neglect towards her child.

" That is a summer garment," she said. " It is entirely too thin for this time of the year. Nino, bring me the box which came by express yesterday."

He produced the box, and at her further order drew forth a little seal-skin coat and cap. They had been intended, Madam Van remarked, for the child's Christmas present, but they were clearly required for the chilly night. The long coat was buttoned over the frock of embroidered lawn ; the cap was drawn on the pale gold hair. Still, this was not enough. " Nino," said Madam Van, " go to my dressing-room and get the lace scarf lying on the table."

Nino lounged off with a clearly perceptible shrug, and brought back a square of valenciennes lace, fine as a cobweb. This Madam Van tied about the tender little throat which no harsh wind must be permitted to touch.

. All these delays could not make the parting less

inevitable. Jenny led the child away, and, left alone, Madam Van huddled forlornly on the lounge, hiding her face in her hands.

"If madam has no objection," said Nino, "I will go to the post-office. Phœbe will answer the bell."

Madam Van made an impatient movement which the man took for assent. He told one of the maids that he was sent to the post-office, and leaving the house he lounged slowly down the walk to the kitchen gate, which he closed behind him with deliberation. Once on the street he glanced up and down, saw no one, and ran swiftly along the path screened by the high hedge, until he came to a gap in the fence. He crawled through this and was again in the grounds, but at a point far below the house and near the river. Although well out of sight of the windows his precautions did not relax. Every shrub, every trailing bough helped to hide him until he reached the willows which grew on the banks of the stream, their great roots jutting out and overhanging the water. Here he swung himself across, and, gaining the opposite shore, he ran rapidly up the meadow to the bridge, and with the ease of long habit, clambered up the side, jumped over the rail, and found Jenny waiting for him. Bessy was sitting on the planks with a pile of pebbles which the nurse had picked up for her, and was talking and singing to herself, evidently finding entertainment of a high order in throwing the stones through the lattice-work of the parapet into the water. Nino drew Jenny away from her charge, and at once began a voluble discourse about certain grievances for which he demanded her sympathy. He had been trying to influence Madam Van of late, and had received a repulse which had made

him savage. The doctor had told her she must winter in a warm climate, and Nino had attempted to persuade her to go to Italy. The only answer she had
vouchsafed was that she should never leave Walford
again, but that if he was anxious to get back to his
beloved country, all he had to do was to give a month's
warning and go.

"As if I were her servant," cried Nino shrilly, "like
the maids in the kitchen, or the gardener in the stable."

He bemoaned his fate in having exiled himself from
Italy ; he had made the sacrifice for a sentiment ; he resigned his country from a magnanimous sentiment toward Baron Van Polanen, whom all the world had loved.
The baron had said, "I need you, Nino, but I shall not
need you long." So, sundering all the ties of national-
ity and of kinship, Nino had followed the baron to this
wretched place, this wilderness, this desert, this abomi-
nation of desolation. The baron had lived two years ;
then, when he was about to die, he observed, "Madam
will reward you for your faithful services to me, Nino."
Madam, becoming a widow, said, "You will not desert
me, Nino. Whom have I left but you?" Thus always
the victim of his own generous impulses, Nino had
stayed on. He had remained nine years, in the bloom
of his youth, the flower of his middle life, and now,
when he alluded to his deprivations, when he uttered a
faint aspiration for a sight of his own country, he was
told that he could go if he gave a month's warning!
He, a man of education, of culture, who knew the arts,
who could speak nine languages, who had been the
daily companion, almost the bosom friend, of the highest aristocrats! He, who had carried the purse of a
Russian prince, mapped out the tour, ordered the meals,

and instructed with his inexhaustible fund of anecdotes all the prince's party! For him to be buried in an American village like Walford, a place which contained, it might be said, not an inhabitant with whom he had anything in common, — the sacrifice was monstrous! It was incredible, by the saints; it was impossible!

Jenny listened with a mingling of feelings in which sympathy with her lover had to struggle with fears lest the root of his desire to go back to his own country might be devotion to some old sweetheart waiting for him there. Nino was twenty years older than the bright English nurse, but there were times when he made love to her with all the warmth and passion her romantic heart craved. Once on the subject of his wrongs, however, he kept the lover a little too much in reserve. At the least stab to his vanity he seemed to swell in stature; he puffed up with importance, and exacted the tribute of flattery and devotion which at other times he was willing himself to pay. Accordingly, Jenny, although conscious of her own wounded sensibilities, tried to soothe him with endearments.

"And madam will die one of these days," she added, "and she will leave you a lot of money."

"That baby will inherit everything," Nino responded, with a tragic gesture towards the place where the child had been standing throwing stones into the water. "Madam said to me only to-day, 'She is to have all that I possess.'"

"She did not mean *everything*," interposed Jenny soothingly. "I have heard Mr. and Mrs. Rexford say a dozen times that you were sure to get some money from Madam Van. You have only to be patient, Nino. It will all come out right."

"She may well do something for me," exclaimed Nino. "I have sacrificed everything for her. She has had all my service for thirteen years. I have been like her son, and if she is not grateful I shall have wasted my life. I am no longer young. I am forty-three, my poor Jenny; you will have an old husband if she does not die soon. And I sometimes think she means to live forever. Why does she want to live?. What pleasure does she get out of life? She says that child, that lump of flesh, that little machine of tyranny is all the comfort she has on earth. A proud little doll, whose foot she plants on my neck until sometimes I long to cry out, 'I am not a'" —

"Hush!" said Jenny. "There comes a carriage. Here, Bessy!— Nino, turn away, you look so fierce; seem to be looking in the water."

A covered buggy, rapidly driven, crossed the bridge at this moment going towards the west, for this was indeed Westbury Turnpike bridge. When the interruption was over, Jenny, looking into her lover's face, told him he must smile at her, and with a true woman's pleasure in the signs of her power she beguiled him into some show of fondness.

"You are sure you love me, Nino," she said.

"If I did not love you, I should love no one but myself," Nino responded tragically.

He was evidently in no mood for further concession, and Jenny with some pique drew back and said :—

"I ought to have been at home long ago. I shall get a scolding, and all on your account, Nino. The sun has set. Come, Bessy, mamma will be looking for you."

"We are both under the thumb of that child," said

Nino. "It is Bessy here, Bessy there, Bessy every-where. I hear nothing from morning until night except 'Bessy.' I sometimes wish she was dead."

"Oh, Nino, dear, you 're cross to-night," said Jenny. "Come up a little later and I 'll meet you out at the gate. We must go now. Come, Bessy. Why, where is she? Bessy, Bessy, come this moment. You 're very naughty. Don't dare to be playing me any tricks. It's getting dark." Jenny, half incensed, called from one side of the bridge and then from the other, at first softly and then at the top of her lungs. No soft voice answered, no little figure was visible. A moment before it had seemed to Jenny to be just sunset; now all along the banks of the river night had descended like a curtain. At the west the yellow sky showed above the long white highway rising gradually to the hills. Everywhere else the trees shut out the landscape.

"If madam had n't put that brown coat on her I might find her better," said Jenny. "I can always see her little white frock. She is just up the road, perhaps, or do you think she could have gone back to madam?"

"I do not know; I cannot think," said Nino, bewildered. "I did not see her go off the bridge. You called her when the carriage came; do you feel sure she was there?"

"Sure! I supposed she was close by me," said Jenny. "I 'm thinking she got tired and has run on, and I 'll overtake her. But you 'll go back to Madam Van's, Nino."

They were staring into each other's faces, vague ideas of the answers they must find for possible reprimand forming in their minds.

"Go on, Jenny," said Nino sharply. "It is late. Perhaps she has sat down somewhere and fallen asleep."

Apprehensions began to swarm. Each felt the necessity of haste, and they parted at once, Jenny to run on towards home and Nino to search the grounds. A thought striking him, he called Jenny back that he might if possible elicit something definite as to the time she last saw the child. Jenny, with worse terrors assailing her each moment, found it a difficult matter to be sure of anything.

"Was it before or after the carriage went by that you saw her?" Nino said. "We must both be sure."

"It was just before," said Jenny with instant conviction. "Oh, Nino, you don't think they've stolen her?"

"Stolen her?" repeated Nino contemptuously. "People want to get rid of children, not to run off with them. Now, then, go on. You will overtake her."

One fear did not, could not enter their minds, namely, that Bessy might have fallen from the bridge into .the water. This was a private bridge built many years before by John Rexford in order to open a short cut to Westbury Turnpike. The structure spanned the river crossing the entire narrow roadway, and the high fences on each side ran up the incline and joined the parapet. The rail of the latter was higher than the head of the child, and the supports were filled in with fine lattice-work.

Three gates opened into Madam Van Polanen's place, which stood on a corner. Nino ran first to one about a hundred feet above the river, which was a sort of door cut in the high board fence that screened this side of the grounds. It was with some relief that he found it closed, bolted, and padlocked. Evidently Bessy could not have crept in at that entrance. He then went to the heavy iron gates in front of the house. They also were shut, and, being so massive as not to be easily handled even by a tall person, for the child to have opened them would have been an utter impossibility. The third was the little back gate by which he had left the grounds. That was so far away from the bridge as to be out of the question. In all probability Bessy did not know of its existence. It was clearly a matter beyond dispute that she had not come back to Madam Van's. Doubtless Jenny had found her long before this. Yet in spite of this clear conviction Nino was goaded by the necessity of looking all over the place. He went down to the river, where the water had grown black and rippled on with gurgles and murmurs, and made his teeth chatter with a thousand nameless horrors. He peered into the shrubberies, and almost swooned when once his invading touch disturbed a flock of sparrows that flew out with cries and then settled into the nearest thicket.

He could stand no more such ordeals. He went indoors. Phœbe was lighting the lamps in the vestibule.

" Sure now, — something has happened," she said, the moment her eyes fell on him.

" I do not understand," said Nino.

"You look as if you had seen a ghost. You are pale and your eyes are big."

" I have seen no ghosts in all my life," said Nino.

"Where are the letters and papers?" demanded Phœbe."

"The mail has not come in. The train is late," said

Nino. He walked past the girl, tiptoed along the hall, and looked in at the open door of Madam Van's room. There was no light, except from the fire, which tinged the ceiling with a vermilion flush, and gave an added gleam to the white hair and the clearly-cut features of the woman on the lounge.

"Nino," she called, "is that you?"

"Yes, madam."

"You were gone a long time."

"The train was late."

"Did you see anything more of Jenny and the child?"

"They went home by the other road," said Nino. "How should I have seen them?" Something in his voice sounded to her quick ears like intense exasperation.

"Nino!" she exclaimed, suddenly sitting up and shaking her forefinger at him, "you are jealous of that dear little girl; you hate her; you are ready to do her some mischief. I should be afraid to leave her alone with you."

Already strung to his highest note, every nerve feeling the strain of suspense, Nino uttered a cry.

"What is the matter?" said Madam Van, startled.

"You accuse me of horrible things," he exclaimed. "You make me out a murderer."

"It is your own evil conscience which accuses you," said Madam Van. She uttered a peevish moan. "How violent you are!" she muttered. "You have given me a turn; lay me down. Take the upper pillow away. I want to lie flat on my back."

He was used to lifting her, and now adjusted her cushions, and settled her anew with the utmost gentleness.

"You can be good, Nino," she murmured after a time. "You might be a great comfort to me if only you were not so jealous of Bessy."

"Shall I light the candles, madam ?" he asked.

"Yes, light the candles."

He was glad to expend his nervousness in some labor. When the room was lighted, however, and she saw his face, she was startled. His look seemed to suggest a dangerous mood. She observed that he kicked aside every obstruction in his way as he went from window to window to close the shutters, and when he drew the curtains he twitched them with a roughness which twice tore off their rings.

"Nino !" she called, "come here." He approached her slowly and reluctantly. "Nino," she said with energy, "you are a fool, an utter fool."

He shrugged his shoulders. "Madam has often told me so."

"Well, lay it to heart. What are you jealous of that child for ? I have got enough for her and for you. If you are a faithful friend to me and to her as long as I live you will find after I am dead that I have left you enough to take you back to Italy, and allow you to live in comfort with a little house and garden and vineyard of your own."

She expected to see the cloud roll off his face at this definite realization of his clearly defined hopes, but to her surprise the contraction of his brow and the wildness of his eyes seemed to be intensified.

"Of course," she went on, smitten by a desire to talk about Bessy, "I shall leave the greater part of my property to the child. I should adopt her if her mother was not in the way. I don't see," she added querulously, "why a healthy young woman like Evelyn Rexford should not have a baby a year as they did in my time. If she had two or three other children she would not begrudge me Bessy."

Nino had been listening with some semblance of attention, but now gave a violent start and, turning, seemed to be straining his ears to catch some distant sound.

"What is it?" she demanded nervously.

"A person is at the door," he faltered, and something indescribable in his face of shock and alarm startled her. "I will go and see what it is," he said, and at once ran out of the room.

Left alone, the old woman was overpowered by a vague terror. Twice she made an effort to touch the bell which lay within easy reach, but found herself unable to lift a finger. A confused sound of different voices gave evidence that all the servants had gathered; distant doors in all parts of the house were opened and shut violently; heavy feet went up and down the stairs. Now and then a deep groan was audible, and again a sharp exclamation. Twice it seemed to Madam Van that she heard Bessy's name called. She herself tried to shriek, but no sound came to her lips. Her senses were no longer clear. She heard nothing except her own heart-throbs. She could not tell how much time had passed when gradually she became aware that somebody was in the room, and, opening her eyes, they fell on Nino who was kneeling beside her on the floor. His face was ghastly, his eyes frightened and dilated.

"What has happened?" she said, by a desperate effort.

"Oh, madam, oh, madam," he whimpered, "I had

nothing to do with it. By the wounds of Christ I am in no fault."

"What has happened? It is something about Bessy."

"She is lost," said Nino. As he spoke his voice broke into sobs, he threw himself prone on the floor, and cried with the abandonment of a child.

"Lost? What do you mean?" Her stifling apprehension of some strange and undefined catastrophe could not take in the foolish possibility of Bessy's being lost. She called Phœbe, who came in followed by the Rexfords' cook and housemaid, and between them all the story was told. Jenny, on her way home, had turned to look at a passing carriage, when all at once she missed the little girl whom she had supposed to be close beside her. She took it for granted Bessy had hurried on, and expected, if she did not overtake her, to find her at the house. When Jenny heard that nobody had seen her she had gone into violent hysterics. Mr. Rexford had arrived at the same time and had at once sent Lewis and the cook back to find Bessy. They had looked through the house here, and the men were searching all through the grounds and up and down the streets with lanterns.

"Preposterous! Ridiculous!" shrieked Madam Van. "Nino, get up this instant or I'll have you taken away to an insane asylum. Go and find Bessy Rexford. You know perfectly well where she is. I read in your eyes that you have done something to her. But no, no, no!" she exclaimed, seeing the horrified expression she had brought to the faces of the women; "I don't mean that, Nino. You are as harmless as a mosquito. You never could have had the wit to do anything.

The child is hiding somewhere, just for mischief. She is full of pranks. She has fallen and hurt herself. She has lain down on a stone and gone to sleep. She was heavy with sleepiness before she went away. The idea of a child being lost here in Walford! Under one's very eyes! It is a world of fools! Go, every one of you, find Bessy Rexford and bring her to me. Don't give her to her mother, a giddy, spoiled thing who takes no care of her. I'll keep the child in future. Go, I say, don't stand gaping at me. If you do not bring me back that child, Nino, you shall never have a penny of mine. Go, I say, go, go!" She was sitting up, waving her hands excitedly; her eyes were glittering; a faint color had risen to her cheeks; her thin white hair had fallen, and floated about her face. Every member of the household knew better than to waste a word in expostulation while she was in this mood. Nino gathered himself up and crawled out, not once raising his eyes, and the women followed him.

III.

AT the same moment Evelyn Rexford — who had been for half an hour trying to obey her husband, who bade her sit with the nurse and try to gain a connected story of what had happened — was herself setting out to seek Bessy. She had gained little from Jenny except the admission that she was on Westbury bridge when she first missed her charge, and this suggestion of the river had filled Evelyn with horror. She could no longer waste time in listening. The news had been kept from her until the last moment. At her call as she rode up to the house Roger had run out, led her in and up to her room, when he had told her that Madam Van had kept Bessy to tea. It was not until the sound of Jenny's sobs and lamentations reached her ears that she was permitted to know what had happened, and even then she had gathered little beyond the idea that Jenny had come home and left the child at her godmother's. It was only when she sat in the deserted house beside the girl whose hysterical outbursts alternated with fits of unconsciousness, that the grim reality fairly dawned upon the young mother. With the first kindling of her imagination that somewhere out in the darkness and cold her baby was perhaps weeping and calling for her, Evelyn seized a hat and cloak hanging in the hall, and was about to leave the house.

"Where are you going, Mrs. Rexford?" a voice asked out of the darkness the moment she opened the door.

"Oh, is it you, Mr. Spencer?" she said. "I am going to look for Bessy. I am getting worried about her."

"We are all troubled about her," said Spencer, an active, bright-eyed young man, who was the superintendent at the works. "Here are Mr. Peck and Mr. Mumford, Mrs. Rexford. They have come to ask a few questions about the child."

Evelyn felt impatient of the interruption, but as the three men had entered the hall, she was forced back step by step into the lighted parlor, whither they followed her, closing first one door, and then the other. Mr. Mumford, a short, stout, dark-complexioned man, with a deep, husky voice, was the deputy-sheriff of Walford. Mr. Peck was chief constable, and, as if by law of opposites, he was slight, thin, and pale, with a pair of prominent blue eyes. He was a little overpowered by the occasion, and stood looking at Mrs. Rexford, hat in hand, raising himself on his tiptoes, and breathing loudly through his nostrils.

"What is it?" whispered Evelyn, looking from one to the other of the group.

"There are some very singular circumstances about this disappearance," observed Mr. Peck in a high voice. "I may say they are unusual."

"I call it mysterious, very mysterious, indeed," said Mr. Mumford in his deep bass.

Evelyn turned to Spencer and put her hand on his arm.

"Tell me what they mean," she said imploringly. "Why do they come here?"

"They want to ask a few questions," said Spencer. "Mr. Rexford is telegraphing everywhere, and there are certain details"——

"Telegraphing? Telegraphing about my child?"

"It is necessary to know, it is even important," said Mr. Peck, rising on the tips of his toes and sniffing loudly, "how the little girl was dressed."

Spencer had led Evelyn to a sofa and forced her to sit down. It seemed to him that she was fainting. "Try to remember how she was dressed," he said with gentle persistence.

"She had on a white embroidered frock, a white cashmere coat, and a muslin cap," said Evelyn.

"All in white, pure white," observed Mr. Peck, sentimentally. "I should have expected it of Mrs. Rexford."

Evelyn looked up in Spencer's face, her own pale and drawn.

"What do they think has happened to her?" she faltered.

"The girl said the last she saw of her was just before a carriage, rapidly driven, crossed Westbury bridge."

"Oh, the river, the river!" cried Evelyn, and rose to her feet.

"Don't be afraid of the river," said Spencer reassuringly. "She could not have fallen into the river. The railing is too high for her to have clambered over it, and the lattice-work is too close for her to have got through it. There is no way for her to have got into the river except through Madam Van's grounds, and both gates were tightly shut. The little one near the bridge was locked by five o'clock. Birdsey says. I must go back and tell your husband how she was dressed. Mr. Long has already gone to Westbury. Try to be patient, Mrs. Rexford. You had better wait here, you had, indeed. She may be brought in at any moment."

Spencer went out at once. Evelyn was so bewildered that her thoughts could not fasten upon the full meaning of his words and the imperious instinct again welled up to go and look for Bessy herself. But Mr. Peck and Mr. Mumford hemmed her in.

" I should like," said Mr. Mumford, in his preternatural bass, " to put a few questions."

" There are some very singular circumstances connected with the affair," said Mr. Peck, sniffing loudly between each word.

Evelyn looked from one to the other of the men like a creature at bay.

" If you have anything to say," she cried, " say it. Why should you waste time in this way? "

" My wish is," said Mr. Peck, " to ascertain, if possible, what character your nurse has in general maintained in your family."

" She is a good girl," said Evelyn coldly.

" You have trusted her ? "

" I have trusted her."

" I should also like to ask," continued Mr. Peck, " that is, to inquire what your opinion is of Madam Van Polanen's Italian man ? "

" I can't wait," said Evelyn forcibly. " Nino ? Nino is a silly, spoiled creature, worn out attending to an old woman full of whims. I must go. Tell me what you want. I can't stay any longer."

" We wish," said Mr. Mumford, " to see the nurse."

"She is in the laundry, lying on the lounge," said Evelyn.

She opened the door, made a gesture towards the rear of the house, then, as if fleeing for her life, she herself ran out into the darkness. It was something gained to be clear of the two officials who had oppressed her like a nightmare. The logic and reason of their untimely visit she could not even waste a thought on. In fact, at this moment she seemed to understand nothing; straight-minded and clear-headed as she usually was, eager to know the truth and reality of things, and to face them, she now stood still one moment and tried to decide what course to pursue. She remembered that she had some hours before chained Fido to prevent his following Bessy. The first thing to be done was to loose him, for he was devoted to his little mistress, and old and worn out although he had lately become, he possessed astonishing sagacity in following the child anywhere. Evelyn went to his kennel, but found it empty; either he had been unfastened or he had slipped his collar. She ran out of the gate and down the street alone. Her only thought now was that she must painfully traverse every inch of ground which Bessy could have gone over between her house and Madam Van's. The moon, just past its full, had risen and began to light up the skies. The blurred outlines of trees and bushes cleared every moment. Along the village street the lamps burned brightly. Evelyn turned down the alley to the river road, her eyes searching everywhere for the gleam of Bessy's white raiment. Where any shadow fell she crouched close to the ground, feeling the whole place over. Arrived at Madam Van's gate, she remembered somebody's mention of Westbury bridge and crept down the narrow road to it. It was not enough to cross it and recross it once, twice, thrice. To satisfy herself that Bessy could not have clambered over the rail or through the lattice-work, she needed painfully to go over all the intersections, cutting and bruising her hands. And she tried the high board fence on each side of the road to discover if there were any gap which would have permitted the child to enter the open meadow to the north opposite Madam Van Polanen's grounds. She had not known of the existence of the little gate, and when she now came upon it to find it wide open, as if this were a corroboration of her worst fears, she uttered a loud wail. Some nameless terror seemed to strike at her very life. She did not define it to herself, but stood just inside the gate staring down the lawn into the blackness which hung over the river where, as yet, no ray of the moon penetrated. Again that deadly presentiment, that feeling of stark, staring horror crept over her, chilling her to the very marrow. She had to fight it off like a physical enemy. She asserted herself against her dread.

"I remember now," she said aloud, "Mr. Spencer said that Birdsey had locked this gate."

This effort to reason in face of the emergency helped her. Hitherto she had been acting by instinct; now she tried to reinforce her powers of mind by summoning all sorts of fancies and suggestions. She believed she was thinking coherently and sensibly. She remembered how many times Madam Van had said that she wanted to keep Bessy and let her grow up in this house and play over this place. Her mind could fasten on nothing so probable as that the wicked old woman was detaining the child and hiding her away from her mother.

Evelyn ran up the lawn with a surge of passion, a beat of intense anger all through her arteries. The door of the house stood wide open, for none of the servants had thought of ordinary precautions in the general excitement. Evelyn walked straight in at the side entrance, through the hall, and entered the room where the old woman had been for an hour watching alone, waiting for news to cheer her or to bring a climax to her misery. This blank of expectation seemed to be terribly filled up as she saw Evelyn come towards her like a fate.

"Oh, Bessy is dead, then!" she cried with mournful eagerness. "She is dead. I felt it. I knew it."

"*Dead?*" faltered Evelyn, shrinking and cowering. "What do you mean?" She crept towards Madam Van, trying to resummon her resolution. "Aunt Lizzy," she said beseechingly, "you know where Bessy is. I am certain that she is hidden somewhere here. You always wanted her and now you are keeping her from me."

"I keep her from you?" said Madam Van. "Evelyn, you have gone mad! You look as if your brain were unhinged." They gazed at each other a moment in silence. "If I could but know she was alive and well," continued the older woman, with suppressed vehemence, "I should be content never to see the little dear face again." She broke into deep, tearless sobs which seemed to rend her from head to foot.

Evelyn pressed a palm to each temple. "Where is she, then?" she asked abruptly. "It came over me that you might have kept her. Where is she, then?

Father in Heaven, where is my child?" Her voice had risen into a shriek as facts again pressed upon her inexorably.

"Hush, hush!" said Madam Van. "See that dog! Is it your dog?"

For as if at the sound of Evelyn's call a huge collie had dashed into the room, and with a joyous bark and wagging tail began to paw his mistress' gown to gain her attention. She looked down, half impatient at the interruption.

"What has he got in his mouth?" said Madam Van.

Mechanically Evelyn stooped and tried to draw something from the animal's closely locked jaws.

"Let go, Fido, let go," she said, and after repeated soft urgings she made him relinquish his grip upon what she at first took for a handkerchief, but which on examination proved to be the torn half of a Valenciennes lace scarf.

"See," said Evelyn, holding it listlessly toward Madam Van Polanen, who snatched it with a faint exclamation, examined it, then with a trembling finger pointed to the jagged end.

"I put it on Bessy's neck," she faltered.

"To-night, — you put it on Bessy's neck?" said Evelyn, as if experiencing a half comfort in establishing some clear link between her and the child.

"But who tore it in two?" whispered Madam Van, impressing into her words a meaning to freeze the blood.

Evelyn had not fully relinquished her hold on the lace, and now, as madam sank back on her pillow relaxed and trembling, she carried the scarf to the light, while Fido stood by panting feebly, wagging his tail, and looking up eagerly as if awaiting commendation or perhaps some action on Evelyn's part.

"Who tore it?" she repeated, as if trying to follow out the undefined dread expressed by Madam Van's words. She tried to supply the link between the jagged scarf and the soft little neck it had protected. She could not think consecutively. The persistent thought came again, "Where can she be?" She was pulsing and palpitating from head to foot. She went back to Madam Van's couch. "To think," she gasped, "that at this moment my little darling may be reaching out to me, — may be calling for me."

A sharp cry came from the old woman. The impression from the words burned into her consciousness. For a few moments there was no sound except of stifled sobs.

Madam Van, in spite of her age, had the fine ear of a greyhound. After a time she lifted her finger.

"There comes your husband," she said. "He brings news."

In another moment Roger Rexford was in the room. He had been searching for Evelyn, and at sight of her he held open his arms, and she tottered towards him and clung to him with a convulsive cry. He folded her close.

"Roger," said Madam Van, breaking imperiously upon this scene, "suppose you tell me if there is any news."

He lifted his head.

"Rex has telegraphed from Westbury that a man and woman, the latter carrying a sleeping child, took the 6.14 train."

"It may have been any child. How was she dressed?"

" Just as Bessy was, in white from head to foot."

" Bessy was in seal-skin," said Madam Van. "I put a new coat and cap on her."

Evelyn uttered a groan. " I looked for something white," she murmured in an agonized voice. " I was sure she was in white. I may have missed her, — I may have passed her by."

Roger clasped his wife's face between his two hands: he tried gently to explain that the moment Jenny brought news the child was missing half a dozen men had searched every inch of the road, every part of these grounds, even the river itself, by the aid of lanterns. Finding no trace of her, the only reasonable hypothesis seemed to be that Bessy, having wandered away from Jenny, had been picked up by some person or persons unknown, and at once carried off to some point, probably Westbury.

He impressed his listeners. He rarely talked idly, and when he offered an explanation it was always clear and seemed to be founded on facts and clear logic.

" But now that you tell me Bessy was dressed in dark clothes," he added, " it is fortunate that I have had another clue followed up. It seemed safest to let nothing escape. I heard from Chauncey that a man and woman, leading a little girl of about three years old, dressed in brown, took the 5.58 up train."

" That was Bessy," said Madam Van with conviction. " Offer a reward, telegraph it everywhere, — a thousand, five thousand, ten thousand, twenty thousand dollars, anything to get her out of the clutches of those vampires before they kill her. Roger, look at that lace scarf, — it is mine. I put it on Bessy's neck. The dog brought in this fragment of it. He picked it up on the

road, no doubt. That man and woman whipped it off
her neck, tore it in two and gagged her, — there is not
the least doubt of it! They gagged her with the other
half to stifle her cries."

Evelyn was at the end of her strength. She slipped
from her husband's arms to the floor.

IV.

MADAM VAN'S WILL.

No coroner's inquest and no trial by jury gathers particulars, sifts evidence, and balances probabilities as does a group of village loungers at the post-office or on the platform of the railway station. And when, a fortnight after Bessy Rexford's disappearance, no clue had been followed up to any result, Walford public opinion was far from being favorable to the sagacity of the chief parties who had set the detectives in operation. It is proverbially an easier task to ask questions than to answer them, and not a few wiseacres put queries which staggered every hearer. For example : Why was it Nino, the Italian, if he had had nothing to do with the child's disappearance, came in that evening looking, as the girl Phœbe said, " white as a sheet?" Where had the collie Fido found the lace scarf? By what sort of strange coincidence was it that the dog died a few hours later, and was next morning found cold and stiff on Madam Van's porch?

Public opinion had long been averse to Nino, the like of whom had never before been seen in the New England village, and who was beyond not only Walford experience but Walford imagination : a mixture of man and lady's maid, who carried the old woman about in his arms and obeyed her least whim, yet assumed fantastic airs of superiority to every one else he came across. He was handsome, according to some feminine critics ; but men declared him hideously ugly. Very odd stories were told of him : that he played the guitar and sang, — Heaven knows what more.

Circumstances for a time looked black for Nino. Mr. Peck had felt it his duty to arrest him, at eight o'clock on the evening Bessy was lost ; but then at midnight, as both he and Mr. Mumford were quite worn out, they let him go, thanking God they were "rid of a knave," and majestically bidding him be ready to be taken up again as soon as they found any evidence against him. It was impossible to discover any evidence except that he had told lies and exhibited signs of abject cowardice. For example, he had said that he had been at the post-office, on the evening of the twenty-fourth, and that the mail was late. He had not been at the post-office and the train had not been late. He had declared he had not seen Jenny and the child after they left the house. Jenny herself falsified him on this point. It was she who came finally to her lover's rescue and made it clear that he was in no wise concerned in the catastrophe. The shock had prostrated the girl, and it was not until a fortnight had passed that Dr. Cowdry declared her well enough to give her testimony. She then confessed that she had for a year been betrothed to Nino, but that he insisted their engagement should be kept a secret, as he was afraid of rousing Madam Van's displeasure. On that last day he had told Jenny he wanted a chance to talk to her, and asked her to go down to the bridge and wait for him there. It had been their habit to meet in this place, which was quiet, rarely intruded upon, and safe for the child, who loved the water.

Jenny said that she had left the house at five minutes
past five by the hall clock; the sun was still some distance above the horizon; she went out of the little gate
which opened into the road near the bridge. She was
sure that she closed it after her. She picked up her
apron full of stones as they walked on, and gave them
to Bessy to fling through the lattice-work into the
water. Nino reached the bridge a moment later. He
at once began talking earnestly, and she was interested
in what he said; but she felt certain the child was
close beside her the greater part of the time. She
called to her when she heard the carriage, but received
no answer, and the moment the carriage had passed
discovered that Bessy had vanished. No amount of
cross - examination could shake Jenny's statement.
She had left the house at five minutes past five; the
sun was well above the horizon, the side gate was
unlocked, and going through it she closed it behind
her.

Birdsey, the gardener, had testified that he entered
the grounds by this same side gate, which he found
wide open, just as the sun was setting. Looking at
his watch it was not quite five o'clock. As his regular
custom was, he padlocked the gate and kept the key in
his pocket until an hour or more later, when he opened
it for the convenience of the men who were searching
the grounds. This evidence clashed slightly with
Jenny's, but as Birdsey confessed that he had been to
the Woodbine and taken two glasses of beer there, his
accuracy was not to be relied on. Naturally, men who
befuddled themselves daily, and never had a clear idea
whether the luminary in the heavens was the sun or
moon, had a fellow-feeling for Birdsey, and declared

that two glasses of beer cleared rather than obscured the perceptions, while a girl going to meet her lover had no sense of time or place. There was a close cross-examination on the subject of this little side gate, but it was felt to be time wasted on an unimportant detail not worth all this circumstantial evidence. It was not probable that the child would have wandered back into the grounds. Had she done so, she would not have got into the river. Had she fallen into the river there must have been struggles and cries. Had she been drowned, her body would instantly have been discovered, for the river was searched at once, and next day, and for many days after was dredged and sounded inch by inch for half a mile upstream and two miles below to the dam. The summer had been dry, and the stream, always shallow, contained very little water. It was proved beyond all cavil that Bessy had not been drowned.

The presumption was that she had exhausted the pile of stones Jenny had given her, and then had gone back to the road to pick up more. While loitering here out of sight — for the alder bushes would have hidden her from Jenny — she had been seized, gagged, and borne off. Whether the covered buggy which crossed the bridge carried her away, or whether she had been taken in a different direction, was a question yet to be answered. The dog Fido had held the only clue, and in the excitement of the evening this had been irreparably lost. Where did he find the fragment of the lace scarf? Doubtless had any one bidden the sagacious collie, "Go find Bessy," he would have led the way to the precise spot where he came upon this clear trace of the child. Strange to say the old dog was next morning stretched out stark and stiff on Madam Van's porch. Some wiseacres, as we have remarked, pretended to find more than met the eye in the sudden death of so important a witness. However, no signs of violence could be discovered upon the animal. He was known to be sixteen years of age, and had long been feeble. Probably excited by the commotion and hearing Bessy's name called on every side, he had contrived to break his chain and follow the search. This had been the expiring flicker of the old strength; his zeal had killed him, and the only thing to be regretted was that the secret of the lace scarf had died with him.

The fifteenth day after the little girl's disappearance came a striking confirmation of the theory that she had been stolen. A small wad of lace was picked up by some children playing in a bed of leaves by the roadside, near the railway station in Chauncey, a large manufacturing town, five miles to the east of Walford. Two experienced detectives engaged in working up the case were ready to turn everything to account; after following up a dozen false trails, here at last was a valuable clue. The lace proved to be the missing half of Madam Van's Valenciennes scarf, which she had tied round Bessy's neck. It was now impossible for even the most skeptical to doubt that the little girl had been picked up, the scarf snatched off, torn in two, and half of it thrust into her mouth to stifle her cries. As they approached Chauncey, having by this time frightened Bessy into silence, perhaps overpowered her by a drug, they had dispensed with the gag, which had been thrown away, or more probably dropped by some carelessness. Nothing could well be more clear and circumstantial than the story up to this point. If some shook their heads and declared oracularly that the closest chain of evidence is no stronger than the weakest link, and that a mistaken judgment on the least detail may upset the conclusions of the most cogent reasoning, they were asked to provide some better theory. It is true that Mr. Peck and his deputy, Mr. Mumford, found it embarrassing to answer inquiries as to why that man and that woman and that child had not been found on the train when, on its arrival at Springfield, it had been searched by the police.

"There are a great many very mysterious circumstances connected with the whole affair, I might almost say peculiar," was Mr. Peck's stereotyped answer, as he impressively rose on his toes.

"And if," put in Mumford, "if you wake up in the morning and find there has been a burglary in your house, do you go searching high and low for the thieves, expecting to find them close by? No, you don't; you feel sure they have taken pains to get out of the way."

This illustration, it was conceded, gave the gist of the matter. Naturally, the people who carried off the child had not left their own safety to the chapter of chances, and waited to be overtaken. A fox knows how to brush over his own tracks. The true course to pursue was to make it desirable for the thieves to give up the child. All were agreed on that point. If Bessy were still alive she was worth more than any amount of money. The mother's life had been in jeopardy ever since the child was lost: it still hung on a thread, and all the doctors could say was that she had youth and a good constitution on her side. As for Madam Van Polanen, it soon became clear that she was never to rally from the shock. A reward of a thousand dollars

had at once been offered for the safe return of Bessy
Rexford. In a fortnight the amount was raised to five
thousand, and a month later to ten thousand. This
inducement was held out for any information concerning the whereabouts of the child.

Before now, winter, always a hard season for Madam
Van Polanen, had set in. This year the first chill
shook her like a leaf. She shivered and shuddered
perpetually. Nino was always with her ; he heaped up
fires and brought wraps. She had scarcely addressed
a word to him since the night of Bessy's disappearance,
but her eyes often met his with a silent question which
he always understood and always suffered from, and
sometimes answered by his characteristic gesture, turning both palms outward. She never put it into words
until the night before her death, which came early in
the New Year. For ten days she had been painfully
weak, kept alive seemingly by powerful cordials and
hot applications. Nino had nursed her with a jealous
attention which had excluded even Phœbe from bearing any share of the watch. Madam Van had dozed
almost constantly, and could hardly be roused from a
heavy slumberous state in which she seemed always to
be seeing visions and dreaming dreams. This night
she awoke suddenly in a bright, alert mood, and, finding the man bending over her, she said with a glint of
the old humor in her eye : —

"Nino, what do you expect to get for all your
pains ?"

"Nothing, nothing the least in the world," he replied. "Once madam felt kindly towards me, but that
is over."

She stretched out a little skinny hand which fastened

like a claw on his arm. "Nino," she said shrilly, "what became of Bessy Rexford?"

"She was carried off. All the world says she was carried off," answered Nino, with his quiet gesture.

"Nino," Madam Van pursued in a voice fine and clear as an accusing conscience, "you had something to do with the affair."

Her glittering eyes searched his face.

"Madam," said he, with a sort of pathetic dignity, "before the saints in Heaven, before the Blessed Mother, before the Holy Child, I am wholly innocent."

"Nino," she said in a suppressed, suffering voice, "it is borne in upon me that you know what became of Bessy."

Again he made a gesture as if throwing off the accusation.

"It is in your eyes," she persisted. "It has been in your eyes ever since that night. You have never looked at me in the same way that you looked before."

He shook his head mournfully.

"Your great fault used to be your vanity," she went on. "If the wind struck your nose you were afraid it meant something derogatory to your dignity. You were always trying to impress people that you were a nobleman in disguise. You suffered if you were told to bring in the coal-scuttle. In one hour you were changed. You have become a different man. Now what changed you in the twinkling of an eye? You may as well tell me. In a few days I shall know everything. I am going to die. If there is another world I shall either find Bessy holding out her little arms to greet me, or the Almighty will impart some of His knowledge and let me see where she is on earth."

"You will find out that I am innocent, madam," said Nino, shaken with emotion. "You may discover that I have been timid, afraid of my own shadow, but you will never discover that I have done wrong to anything alive."

She gazed at him steadily. "But I see it in your eyes," she muttered. "You have not a good conscience."

"Madam," he said, "I will tell you everything."

"Yes, tell me everything," she said sharply, then blanched as if afraid of the revelation she had invoked. But he began a long rambling recital about his ancient jealousy of Bessy, his envy of her privileges, his fear lest her enticing childish beauty should utterly rob him of Madam Van's love. Then, too, the child's every whim had been humored, her least caprice became the law of the household, while he was repressed, scolded, thwarted, and his ambitions ridiculed. He had so often said to himself that he wished something would happen to the little girl, — said it without any real malice, or any clear meaning, — that when the event came to pass, he was frightened out of his wits at seeing his maledictions bear result; he was filled with bitter repentance. He cried out with sobs and tears that he would not have injured a hair of that little head to gain a kingdom for himself.

Madam Van listened while Nino tried to prove by incontestable arguments that he had everything to lose and nothing to gain by his ill-will, and that he was aware of it, and that Jenny was trying to put him in a good humor about the child at the very moment she disappeared.

"What were you and Jenny talking about that night on the bridge?" madam inquired coldly.

"I was telling her I wanted to go back to Italy," answered Nino.

"Did you expect to take her with you?"

He shrugged his shoulders. "It was a dream — it was a homesick dream," said he. "It came and went. How could I take her to Italy?"

"When did you see Jenny last?" madam went on.

He put out both hands. "Oh, weeks and months. I count time no more," he said.

"Where is she?"

"She is in New York."

"They sent her away from the Rexfords."

He nodded.

"Does she write to you?"

"She has written."

"Do you write to her?"

"Not yet."

"I remember, you were always a lady-killer. I suppose she made love to you like the rest of them. Are you anxious to marry her?"

"I have no heart for woman," sighed Nino. "I am a *mee-ser-a-ble* man, of many sorrows. And she — she is a good girl, but she reminds me – of – *what – I – want – to – forget.*"

"You want to forget, you want to forget," cried Madam Van shrilly. "I knew there was something you were hiding."

Nino shook his head and made a gesture as if washing his hands of the matter. Madam Van lay very quiet the rest of the night, evidently brooding over some thought. Her eyes did not close. Early next day she directed that Squire Graves, the lawyer, should be sent for, but when he reached the house it was already too late. Madam Van Polanen had been partly dressed and bolstered up in bed to receive him, then had lost consciousness. She had in fact suffered a slight stroke of paralysis. It was at first believed that she might rally, but later in the day a second came, and she died the following morning at daybreak.

Roger Rexford had been with her from the time of her last seizure, also Mrs. Goodeve. Evelyn was still very ill. Madam Van Polanen had made many wills, Squire Graves said. The last had been drawn the preceding July, and she had added important codicils four weeks after Bessy Rexford was lost. The lawyer requested that the two nephews of Madam Van's first husband, that is, Roger Rexford and Rexford Long, should be present at the reading of the will ; also Giovanni Reni, the Italian, the servants in the house, and Mr. and Mrs. Orrin Goodeve, to represent their son, Felix.

The chief provisions of the main instrument were as follows : Madam Van Polanen bequeathed a thousand dollars to each of certain charities which she had liberally endowed years before at the time of Baron Van Polanen's death, and in his name. Her house, its furniture, its grounds adjoining were given to her first husband's nephew, Roger Rexford. Three quarters of her entire estate, both real and personal, were left to Roger Rexford in trust for his daughter, Elizabeth Hazard, until she married or came of age. In the event of the child's dying before she came of age or married, these three quarters of the estate, real and personal, passed to the college of surgery of —— University to be used as a perpetual endowment for a Children's Hospital.

This will was dated the July before, and as the lawyer explained, although signed and witnessed, left a considerable sum of money unappropriated. Madam Van Polanen had remarked to him at the time, " I have not yet made up my mind what to give to my man Nino, or to Rexford Long." She had once showed him some memoranda she had jotted down, but had added that she did not intend to die just yet, so preferred to think over the matter. That was shortly before the child was lost. Later when he was sent for she had produced this memorandum, torn it into bits, and put it in the fire. He had then received her directions for these codicils, which had been signed and sealed the twenty-second of November.

To Rexford Long she left without reservation the sum of ten thousand dollars.

In case that the death of Elizabeth Hazard Rexford was clearly proved, the testator, as bound by the foregoing instrument, gave, devised, and bequeathed three quarters of her whole estate, both real and personal, to found the Children's Hospital under the trusteeship of the college of surgery of —— University. Her present place of residence, — the house, the furniture, and the lands adjoining, — were to be transferred absolutely, in consideration of his generous services, to Roger Rexford.

If, however, within two years from the date of her disappearance, Elizabeth Hazard Rexford should be restored to her parents in sound health and intellect, Roger Rexford was, as in the previous instrument, appointed trustee of the whole estate until his daughter married or came of age, when the entire property was to pass into her exclusive possession.

" Also," the codicil proceeded, " in the event of Elizabeth Hazard Rexford's being restored in sound health
and intellect to her parents before October 24, 18 —, I
direct my executors to pay to my companion, servant,
and friend, Giovanni Reni, the sum of fifteen thousand
dollars, free of legacy duty, for his faithful services to
my husband, Baron Hugo Van Polanen, and to myself."

Many small sums were bequeathed without reservation to each servant in the household, and to numerous
outside dependents on Madam Van's bounty. The
estate was to be settled within three years from the date
of her death, and Roger Rexford and Felix Goodeve
were appointed executors.

V

"HERE I AND SORROW SIT."

WHILE Evelyn Rexford's life for many weeks was hanging in the balance, two women watched over her, feeling, even while they tried every expedient to save her, that if she came back to renewed consciousness she came back to torture; that death offered at least deliverance and peace. They almost dreaded to see her again taking up her pilgrimage, creeping on bruised and aching knees to a new Calvary, for the sacrifice had only begun.

One of these watchers was Mrs. Goodeve and the other Evelyn's sister, Amy Standish. The two had been orphaned in their infancy, and having but a scanty inheritance had been separated; Evelyn to be brought up by her maternal uncle and Amy by her father's father. They had occasionally spent a summer together, but the intimate link of sisterhood which use and habit make had had no chance to form. They had always loved, admired, and wondered at each other. Amy was fourteen months the elder, and the years Evelyn had spent in married life she had devoted to study in England and on the continent of Europe, where she had taken degrees we shall not venture to name, lest our readers should compel her to live up to them in the face of Walford hindrances and privations. Her grandfather had for several years resided

with her abroad, promoting all her wishes, but died
while she was at Leipsic, leaving her, if not a great fortune, enough money to secure her independence.   For
the past six months she had been devoting herself to a
study of life among the poor in New York.   She had
found so much that appealed to her sympathies and
energies that it had not been easy to decide what should
be taken and what left in the way of work and duty.
What she wanted was a sharp grapple with the verita-
ble facts of human misery.   She had become absorbed
in her labors, but at the first news of her sister's sore
loss had come to Walford.   She was a skillful nurse,
having spent several vacations in a training school for
nurses.   Thus she was able to take the responsibility
of a critical illness which left Evelyn's powers of life
at their lowest ebb and demanded unerring skill combined with swift insight and tenderest sympathy.   The
doctors told Roger Rexford that Miss Standish's nursing had saved her sister.   Mrs. Goodeve, who was
used to helpless folk, who knew not their right hand
from their left, regarded the girl as a revelation from
heaven that a new dispensation had dawned for women.

Amy had thrown herself into these duties with intense energy, also with clear knowledge, but above all
with a sudden passion of sympathy.   Her actuating
principle had hitherto been to live in close relation to
the absolute facts of life.   She was a clever, many-sided
girl : had written essays on the problems which con-
front modern society, and had reviewed books in the
line most interesting to her.   Whatever man has known
or done she longed to know and to do.   But we may best
express her, perhaps, by remarking that, besides being
a clever girl, she was a remarkably pretty one.   She did

not resemble her sister except in an instantaneousness
of smile and vibrating sympathetic ardor of glance.
Evelyn was fair enough to be called a blonde; Amy
had a delicate, imperious face with hair and eyes of the
darkest, and a pale, olive skin. In repose one admired
her features like those of a cameo finely cut, but she
was rarely in repose. The moment she was dominated
by an idea, — and she was always dominated by some
ideas, — she flashed and glowed with a distinct purpose. If events pleased her, she expanded into life
and charm, mirth and tenderness; when she was not
suited her eyes seemed to hold lightnings in reserve
which flashed dangerously on an opposer. But even
her frown could not repel; rather, it piqued and fascinated. She was of a pretty figure, slim as a nymph,
and with an airy movement: "swift as a huntress"
had been said of her.

Amy had never seen her little niece. What represented the child to her mind as she watched Evelyn
was the subtracted capacity of this stricken one to
gather strength. The shock which the loss of Bessy
entailed had given almost the first intimation that Evelyn was, in a way again to become a mother. It was
hard to tell, whether she herself had any clear knowledge that a freshly budding life had been cut off with
Bessy's; that she was thus doubly desolated. By the
time of Madam Van Polanen's death Evelyn had been
pronounced out of actual danger: all apparently
needed was that she should be nourished and stimu-
lated back to life. The ebb of strength was, however,
followed by no flow; her faculties seemed to be held in
suspense; each function waited until the heart, fluttering like a candle in the wind, should decide whether

to take up its tasks or throw them off forever. She lay in her bed like a waxen image, staring at the ceiling, and apparently taking no notice of her surroundings. When her husband asked her if she knew him, she would reply with a half smile, " Oh, yes, I know you are Roger." And if Amy pressed the same inquiry upon her she said, " Why, of course, it is Amy. Why should I not know my own sister? I am not out of my mind." But she answered only urgent demands upon her consciousness. She kept an unchanging face and seemed to have no thoughts. She accepted nourishment, but after a few teaspoonfuls threw her head on her pillow, refusing to take more. Her pulse did not gather volume ; and in truth what was at first regarded as a hopeful convalescence soon excited almost more apprehension than the most critical period of sharply defined danger.

" She must be roused," said Amy to Mrs. Goodeve. " The intellect does not act. She needs to use her reason and to see the importance of rallying her powers."

" We must not rouse her too suddenly," said Mrs. Goodeve. " It is Heaven's mercy which keeps her from remembering too much."

" But she does not gain," said Amy. " She will have to suffer sharply, and then perhaps she will be able to adjust her mind to these altered conditions. She has lost her child, but she has her husband, — she has me. Women have such griefs to bear all the time, and they bear them with resignation."

" If the poor girl could only have gone on and had her baby," said Mrs. Goodeve. " There is nothing like a new baby for comforting a mother."

Mrs. Goodeve was the woman to whom beyond all

others in Walford every one looked for advice, and for
her to be in doubt, hesitate, go forward and back, and
urge delays, showed that she was afraid of adopting
ready-made panaceas. She was a woman of fifty-four,
of unusual height, with a commanding figure, and a
face so expressive, so lofty and noble, she might have
inspired awe had she not been so wholly permeated
with sweetness. Her clear gray eyes seemed to look
into the very heart of the mystery ; her lips had a lovable curve ; her smile was serenity and peace. But
when she folded Evelyn's hands in hers, and looked
into the soft, pale face, in spite of all her strength and
insight, she knew not what to say except, "God is
good, Evelyn. Believe me, God is good."

The stricken creature smiled back at her and murmured, "Yes, Aunt Laura." That was all. No hint
of what was going on in the brain ; no suggestion of
curiosity, alarm, hope, or dread.

"She must be roused," Dr. Cowdry began presently
to say, half irritated at being compelled to come upon
Amy's ground. "She loses instead of gaining. She
must be roused."

By this time, Mrs. Goodeve, urged to action, saw light.

"Leave her to me," she said. "I will rouse her."

She went out and returned presently with little Rose
Martin, the child of a neighbor who had sometimes
played with Bessy.

Evelyn lay with closed eyes when Mrs. Goodeve approached the bed and lifted the little girl to the pillow.

"Evelyn," she said, "here is little Rose come to
see you."

Evelyn opened her eyes and stared at the sudden
apparition of a bright little face peering into hers. A

flicker of something resembling color came to her cheeks ; then she paled, a shiver ran over her, and she made a gesture as if the child was to be taken away.

" Bessy loves her very much, you know," said Mrs. Goodeve, pressing the soft cheek against Evelyn's and folding the little arms about her neck.

" I cannot ! I cannot ! I cannot ! " gasped Evelyn. A fit of shuddering shook her from head to foot ; tears began to stream from her eyes.

Mrs. Goodeve sent Rose away ; coming back, she closed the door, and sitting down on the bed, drew Evelyn into her arms.

" Dear child," she said, " since Bessy is not here to be a comfort, I thought you might like to see little Rose."

Evelyn was convulsed with sobs.

" Bessy is dead, I suppose," she faltered.

" We do not believe that she is dead. Great rewards have been offered ; and half a dozen times your husband has heard of children who might be yours, and has gone off sometimes hundreds of miles to see them. Your little darling has not been found yet, but she will be. I do feel almost certain that you will have her in your arms again. Some time, sooner or later, she will be brought back. I want you to try to get well, Eve-lyn, so that when she does come, you may be ready to welcome her."

Evelyn seemed to drink in this assurance as if it were a cordial, and from that hour she improved slowly.

Day by day Mrs. Goodeve would bring Bessy's things to her, — toys, clothes, shoes, little torn books, — and Evelyn would put one article after another to her cheek and lie thus for hours, tears welling from her eyes. If anybody approached her she looked up with painful eagerness to read the expression of the face. When she saw Roger she would ask, "Any news?" "No, dear, no news yet," he would say cheerily.

When she began to sit up she still seemed to find a sort of satisfaction in surrounding herself with everything which could remind her of Bessy. She arranged and rearranged all the little playthings as if to put them in their most attractive shape.

Amy Standish, looking on at this dumb show of preparation for the child's return, dreaded the awakening from such delusions. "I can't help thinking you did wrong," she observed to Mrs. Goodeve, "to persuade Evelyn she will have Bessy back again."

"I wanted her to live," said Mrs. Goodeve. "She had to have something to live for."

"But it becomes, week by week, more and more an utterly irrational hope."

"An irrational hope is better than none," Mrs. Goodeve replied.

"It is dreadful to see her wasting her time in this way," said Amy.

"What could the poor child do?"

"One can always learn a new language, or a new science."

"She is learning a new language,—a new science," returned Mrs. Goodeve. "You may learn them, too, one of these days, my dear."

"It seems to me that one should accept the facts of life," persisted Amy.

"What facts do you know? You are a lucky girl if you know many. I have a husband and three children. I hope and believe that all are alive and well at this moment. I can, by five minutes' walk, ascertain Mr. Goodeve's condition. He is pretty sure to be tearing his hair because he cannot put his hand on the right manuscript. But my daughter is hundreds of miles away; my son Orrin is in Chicago, and my son Felix is in Colorado. I have to take it on trust that these dear ones are to be restored to me. I have to comfort myself by thinking that they cannot be where God is not. So I feel as if Evelyn ought to be free to gather what comfort she may. Her child is somewhere."

It was June when Evelyn first sat up; it was autumn before she could leave her room. All the second long, cruel winter she sat day after day in the vacant nursery, dressing her little girl's dolls, setting out little tables with china tea-sets, pasting pictures in books. That is, she used her feeble strength in these occupations; then, when it was spent, she threw herself down and wept.

VI.

ROGER REXFORD.

MADAM VAN POLANEN'S will was generally considered to be a singular document — a regular woman's will, which promised, tantalized and denied in a breath. Had there been needy heirs-at-law it must have found contestants, but there were absolutely no heirs-at-law. Even Roger Rexford and his cousin were only nephews of her first husband, who had left his fortune to her without restrictions.

Ever since his father's death, some six years before, Roger Rexford had been Madam Van Polanen's man of business. She had herself disliked all responsibility about investments, and had blindly intrusted all her affairs to her nephew, as through her brother-in-law's life she had imposed them on him. .

Roger Rexford was not, as his father had been, a prudent, far-sighted man, but he would not have been willing to confess it. His quarrel with destiny was that he had always been hurried by events, tyrannized over by some pressing need. He was never able to be himself. At the time of his aunt's death, with his child strangely snatched away and his wife's life hanging by a thread, it was a galling mortification that he must needs be feverishly anxious to know the provisions of the will; that it was a vital matter to him that he should be appointed executor. He breathed freely only

when he found that for the present, at least, affairs were
left in his hands. Felix Goodeve would not for some
nîonths be ready to come East, and by the time this
coadjutor appeared, affairs were likely to be on a better
footing.

A strange fatality seemed to Roger to have attended
his business career; and it was his unique misfortune
that his troubles began a week after his marriage and
had thwarted and limited him ever since. He had confided his embarrassments to no one; the mask had
grown with his face, and he looked to all the world a
calm, strong, imperturbable man, with deep feelings
which he resolutely held in reserve. He had been passionately enàmored of his young wife, but had never
been free to give himself up fully to his domestic life.

To love and to dream of love; to feel her heart
beating and her brain developing; to study, to divine,
to understand her husband, was the sole thought of the
eighteen-year-old bride. Roger realized only too keenly
the discords and dissonances of his own moods. His
thoughts were preoccupied with his unspoken apprehensions, his impatience, his suspense. He was
tortured by the delays with which his crying needs
were answered and the over-haste with which events
progressed when they led towards disaster. At the
time Roger succeeded to his father's interests in the
Rexford Manufacturing Company, business had for
years been buoyant, and every enterprise had floated.
John Rexford had founded the concern more than half
a century before, at a period when he had almost no
competitors, and when railroad interests were extending
all iron industries. He had soon contrived to heap up
riches for himself. After his early death his younger

brother, Roger, and Orrin Goodeve took his place in
the company. Neither of these new managers was a
pushing business man, and their policy, although safe,
had been timid. Both disliked the aggressive methods
which stimulate and at the same time keep a tight grip
on trade. Thus the Rexford Manufacturing Company
soon lost the monopoly it had enjoyed in John's time.
Until the death of his father Roger had had the control
of the Western branch of the concern. When he succeeded to his father's position he came to Walford with
a clear determination to initiate a new policy ; to seize
every advantage the situation could offer and turn it to
his own interest. His father's and Orrin Goodeve's system he believed to have been over-cautious and short-
sighted. He wanted a new company with fresh blood
in it, a new administration of affairs, new buildings,
and new machinery. He had his way. The Rexford
interests were not only larger than the Goodeve, but
the Rexfords had always been the working members of
the firm. John Rexford had left the plant, machinery,
business, and good-will to his brother, who already had
a considerable capital in the company, and all these
became his son's. Orrin Goodeve had never been an
active business man, and after the death of Roger Rexford, senior, declined into a mere silent partner. Mr.
Lowry, also a partner who held a fair amount of stock,
pleaded infirmities of age and rarely appeared at the
office, saying that so long as he received his dividends
promptly he had no reason for interference. Orrin
Goodeve, junior, became manager of the Western branch
of the works. Thus Roger, without any dangerous usur-
pations, had been as well able to carry out his views
as if he had owned every share represented in the

books. He congratulated himself on his almost irre-
sponsible position. He felt sure of his capacity, and
declared himself willing to make the success of his innovations the measure of his intellect and the tally of
his powers, — a dangerous vaunt. For six months all
progressed fairly ; then he married, and his ill-luck began. He had enlarged the concern when he might
have better contracted it. The conditions of trade became unfavorable and had so remained ever since. All
these four years Roger had found himself bound hand
and foot in knots which no skill could undo and which
had constantly to be cut at any sacrifice. His talent for
bold and skillful combinations remained useless, and
his clever methods of domination had been exerted, not
in leading his subordinates to victory, but in keeping
them from murmuring against the possibility of defeat.

And the chief trouble was that he stood absolutely
alone : to confess his position was to admit his incom-
petence ; not somehow to coin money was to be obliged
to have old Mr. Lowry come prying into his affairs.
Roger had appointed himself the rôle of a strong man
armed at all points. If not strong he was at least
bold in devices. We have said that he had been for
six years Madam Van Polanen's man of business.
Every six months he had presented a statement which
she had signed without even glancing over it. More
than once when she was in good humor, she had remarked, " It is all yours ; that is, it will soon be all
yours in trust for Bessy."

In these years of unexampled financial depression
the temptation had been irresistible to use this money
in his hands to tide over successive embarrassments.
It was, of course, a mere temporary expedient to cover

the expenses of the new buildings and the new machinery. He would have denied indignantly that his in-
tegrity or his sagacity was at fault; the worst that anybody could say, he told himself, was that his methods
were unbusiness-like. Let only those who have been
tempted and have stood firm against the solicitations
of makeshifts which promise the happiest results call
Roger by the worst names. Although he would not
admit to himself that it was fraud, he hated his own
course. The longer it went on the baser it seemed to
him. More than once he tried to free himself by some
lucky speculation, and more than once he lost heavily.

He had never breathed a word to his wife of his real
troubles. In his theory, what a woman loves in a man
is not his confession of fatigue, hunger, and thirst, but
his health, power, energy. He was, besides, always
looking forward to the time when his lavish output
should bring in golden returns. He still remained invincible in the belief that he had been born under a lucky
star and that any adverse fortune was a mere accident.
It is, nevertheless, a curious fact in human experience
that what we regard as accidental and casual, the result
of circumstances which might easily have been avoided,
is apt to remain in some shape the law of our existence
from its beginning to its close.

We can see that with such a state of affairs it was
essential that Roger should be appointed executor of
his aunt's will. This had come to pass. Unless, however, his child should be restored and thus be able to
inherit, in two years the entire property, except the
Walford house, would pass out of his hands, and he
would stand on a perilous margin.

When he had carefully followed up every clue to the

possible fate of his child and offered great rewards for her recovery, it would have been his logical decision that she was dead. He could see no reason why, if Bessy still lived, she should not, with such inducements offered, gladly be given up. The ordeal had been cruel, and he soon grew to hate the half-vistas which hope opened to the mind only to disappoint and exhaust it. In his secret heart he longed to know that somewhere on this wide earth a grave had closed over his little bright-haired one. He loved her, and that certainty alone could quiet the fang of apprehension, ready to bite venomously and poison days and nights. Having once caught sight of the spectre which confronted him if he believed his little girl to be in the hands of unscrupulous people, he wanted to rid himself of such a terror by denying that she could possibly be alive.

One afternoon late in the May succeeding Madam Van's death, Roger was sitting in his office when Henry Spencer, the superintendent of the works, came in. In the absence of working partners Roger had thrown not a little responsibility on this ambitious young fellow, who, during the past six months especially, had made himself more and more useful, until he held a position which could hardly have been fixed within any definite limits. He had now returned from a trip to New Jersey, whither Roger had sent him to look up a child whom a detective had traced to a remote place. It was but one of the many fruitless quests which had been undertaken ever since the event of the preceding autumn.

Roger sat at his desk with his head on his hands when Spencer came in. They exchanged the briefest greetings, and then the superintendent remarked, " Of course you got my despatch."

" It came last evening. I knew all the time there was nothing to be gained by the journey. She is dead ; it is borne in upon me that she is dead."

" I would n't say that," said Spencer, straightening himself against the door he had closed behind him.

" You would want to say it yourself if you were in my place," said Roger with irritation. " This damnable uncertainty " —

" Is better than a damnable certainty," said Spencer.

" I don't at all agree with you."

" It seems to me clear. If the child is found, a large property is left at your entire disposal ; if she is not found, it must be handed over to a lynx-eyed set of trustees."

Roger uttered an exclamation of disgust.

" I certainly do not wish to go on believing that Bessy is alive," he said sharply, " because her return might be profitable to me."

" That was not what I meant," Spencer returned smoothly. " If I do not express my sympathy with your feelings it is only that here we are in the habit of looking at everything from a business point of view. That will of Madam Van Polanen's is the most galling instrument that ever was drawn. If the child is re-stored, you have everything ; if not," —

" I know the terms of the will quite as well as you can," said Roger curtly.

" All I want to say is that the child must be found."

Roger sprang up. " Spencer," he said in a deep voice, " it is the wildest chimæra to believe that she is still alive. We have to nurse the poor mother's hopes, but we, as men, must look the situation in the face."

" The facts are all in favor of her being alive," said Spencer. " I tell you, Mr. Rexford, she is alive ; the thing is, to find her."

" The thing is, to find her, no doubt," said Roger.

The superintendent turned into the outer office, and then exchanging a word or two here and there with the half-dozen men at the desks, he went on into the whirr and dust-cloud of the works to make his afternoon round. Roger, sitting at his desk, brooded over Spencer's allusion to his affairs, wondering if it were his own uneasy conscience which had for a moment startled him with a suspicion that his secrets were not wholly his own. It was hardly possible that Spencer could have spoken except in a general way about the embarrassment of losing Madam Van's money. But if things drifted on as they seemed at present to be drifting nothing mattered. He could at least be sure of Spencer's faithfulness, his quick understanding. The young fellow had been a protégé of Mrs. Goodeve's, and at her request had been taken into the office when but eleven years old. He had been advanced from one position to another with a rapidity which did credit to his quick-witted intelligence. No one could help admiring the boy who, in spite of every drawback, had continued to study doggedly in his hours outside his business and now at twenty-seven was fairly well educated. The Rexford Manufacturing Company might count on an absolutely canine fidelity from Spencer, for his interests were bound up in theirs, and as they succeeded or failed, he was likely to succeed or fail. He was ambitious. Walford was his world ; he had mapped out the territory he was to conquer.

Walford is a thriving town lying in the hollow of intersecting ranges of high hills, or mountains as they

are called, in the mid region of Northern Connecticut.
It is a busy place ; it feels its own life, and is not a little
given to glorifying its own importance in the universe.
Its inhabitants are the reverse of cosmopolitan.   They
believe in Walford ; they are the mainspring of Walford
prosperity, and every inhabitant likes to measure his capacity by the vastness of Walford enterprise.   No Walford man can be unimportant.   He vindicates his claims
to consideration by showing a bustling interest in larger
men, by a definite knowledge of everybody else's affairs.
In these respects the least is bigger than the greatest.
The Rexfords had always been useful to the town ; indeed, John Rexford had developed the place from a
sleepy village, with a stage-coach plying between New
Haven and Hartford, into a thriving centre on the
direct line of transportation.   Roger Rexford was now
one of the most important citizens, and he had often
felt as if his public responsibility was so much better
recognized than his individual liberty that he was the
mere chattel of the town.   Probably, Spencer, in seeming to dictate his course, was merely using Walford
off-hand and downright ways of speech.

We have said that Spencer had been a protégé of
Mrs. Goodeve's.   In those days Orrin Goodeve, senior,
had been one of the acting partners.   But both he and
his wife were very rich people, at least for a country
place ; and as soon as his old colleagues died and re-
tired, Mr. Goodeve made up his mind no longer to endure the uncongenial duties of office or counting-room.
He had better work to accomplish before he should be
called hence.   He had always been a studious man,
and of late years had been writing a history of the
Connecticut Colony under Sir Edmund Andros, having

found some authentic documents which threw a flood
of light upon the charter conspiracy.   It was Mr. Goodeve's delight to bury himself in his study, surrounded
by his books of reference, folios, maps, the first manuscript of his own work, his second type-written version,
his third copy with the addenda, notes, modifications,
and amplifications.   There was such a fatal superabundance of material that the work had by this time
usurped the whole large library.   It covered two desks,
the secretary, and the davenport.   The centre table
groaned under huge quartos ; the table in the south window was taken possesion of by manuscripts, and three
or four little stands trembled beneath the weight of conflicting authorities on the great subject.   The lounge
had long since become a mere receptable for books of
reference, lying open, or turned down on their faces ;
every chair was usurped by a volume or a bundle of papers.   The greater part of Mr. Goodeve's time was spent
in walking from one bundle of manuscripts to another,
with nervous, outspread hands ; for these treasure-
houses overflowed each into the other, so that when he
wanted to put his hand on the Massachusetts Colony he
took up the Connecticut Colony instead.   At such times
it was his habit to emerge and search through the rooms
for his wife, putting his hand to his forehead, as was his'
way when puzzled.

"Well, dear, what is it ? " Mrs. Goodeve would ask.

" I was thinking," the historian would murmur dream-
ily, looking about the room covetously at the sight of
so many unoccupied pieces of furniture, " that if I had
a light table it would be an easier matter to know just
where to put my hand down when I want a thing."

Not to have answered any human being's least claim

upon her would have seemed to Mrs. Goodeve a waste
of her most precious privilege. Walford people do not,
as a rule, illustrate their descriptions of people by clas-
sical allusions, but still they had a clear conception of
large goddess-like qualities in Mrs. Goodeve. She was
like Juno, Ceres, Pomona ; she was a giver, a dispenser, an unfailing source. Bounty overflowed from
her. She gladly found tables for her husband ; she
contrived all sorts of receptacles for his precious manuscripts. Although she was the soul of order, too, she
bore with the confusion of the library. If the room
ever knew broom, duster, or mop, Mr. Goodeve was
unaware of the intruding angel, which he would have
believed to be an angel of destruction.

The Goodeve house stood on the main street in Walford. It was built of brick, in a solid, old-fashioned
way, and presented a wide, high façade to the street,
with a square porch in the centre ; and the great oaken
door, made with a hatch, was decorated with an enormous brass knocker. On the north side the house was
only one room deep ; on the south side it ran back to
the depth of eight rooms. In the middle was the dining-room, with a door opening directly upon the garden.
In Mrs. Goodeve's garden every flower that one loves
grew in such profusion that, although she cut bouquets
from morning until night, blossoms seemed always to
run riot over the place. The first crocuses and snow-
drops were always seen there, peeping out of the rich
mould ; daffodils, jonquils, hyacinths, tulips, narcissi and
primroses ; Maypinks, crown imperial, iris, and lilies ;
until chrysanthemums rounded off the floral year. One
might quote Homer in describing the Goodeve place :
" There grew tall trees blossoming, pear-trees and pome-

granates, and apple-trees, with bright fruit, and sweet
figs and olives in their bloom. The fruit of these trees
never perisheth, neither faileth, winter and summer, enduring through all the year. Evermore the West Wind
blowing brings some fruit to birth and ripens others.
Pear upon pear waxes old, and apple on apple, yea,
and cluster ripens upon cluster of the grape, and fig
upon fig." Making due allowance for the rigors of
New England latitudes, this may answer for a picture of
the Goodeve orchards and gardens ; and what store of
good things climate denied was made up by the per-
ennial plenty inside the house.

Mrs. Goodeve kept two capable women and two men,
but with no object of indulging any love of ease on her
own part. Thrice a week, summer and winter, she rose
at dawn and swept every room on the ground floor with
her own hands. She experienced an actual æsthetic
pleasure in cleanliness, and liked to prove by knowledge, and not by faith, that things were clean. Twice a
week she spent an entire morning in the kitchen, baking
bread of all sorts, rusks, puddings, cakes, pies ; above
all, "cookies," in quantity like stars in the Milky Way,
made of every delicious compound, with currants, with
caraway seeds, with ginger, with cinnamon, and with
citron, — cut, too, into every shape, some like stars,
flowers, birds, others simple and round as Giotto's O.
Every child in Walford knew the taste of Mrs. Goodeve's
cookies, and made errands to her house to secure a
pocketful of them, bringing her wild flowers, honey-
suckle-apples, berries, and nuts. A steady stream of
men, women, and children flowed through the Goodeve
place from morning till night, and not one went away
empty-handed. She provided, it might have seemed,

for half Walford. Yet her ways were frugal as well as large. Waste was abhorrent to her. There was nothing which had not its use. In her creed no gown could be said to be worn out until it had been turned at least twice, and to buy a material which could not be used on both sides was, to her thinking, wicked unthrift. Ready-made clothing she held to be an apology for indolence, an excuse for living from hand to mouth. She liked intrinsic worth, durability, permanence. She carefully preserved all that had been bequeathed to her, and liked to feel that she could pass it on to her successors in almost as good a shape as she had received it.

Rexford Long's father had been Mrs. Goodeve's half-brother, while his mother was the sister of John and Roger Rexford. Ties of family, of sympathy, and of long neighborly habit connected the Rexfords and the Goodeves, and both families had for generations been identified with Walford. Orrin Goodeve had been taken into John Rexford's company as soon as he was through college. Indeed, the Rexford Manufacturing Company had been from its start a sort of family trust. If the enterprise could not be said to have founded the family fortunes, it had at least solidified and quadrupled them. All Walford was proud of the staunch concern, founded, as they declared, "on a rock." The Rexfords enjoyed the highest reputation as financiers; an almost unique prosperity had attended them, one after another, throughout their careers. It was a great piece of good fortune to secure a position for a boy in the works, and it had always been an object to choose recruits carefully. It was felt that Mrs. Goodeve stretched her influence a trifle when she asked Roger Rexford, senior, to give Henry Spencer a place. She was interested in his mother, and the boy was a bright fellow. "Too clever by half," was the verdict after two or three slight deviations from the established code, more than one of which might have cost Spencer his place if Felix Good-eve had not taken the blame upon himself.

Spencer was, however, too intelligent to go on making mistakes which he saw would spoil his whole future. He had an aptitude not only for ideas, but for applying his ideas to life, and, as we have said, he soon justified the choice of his patroness by making himself indispensable at the works, and especially to Roger Rexford.

One day, about a fortnight after the interview which we have recounted in the beginning of this chapter, Roger was sitting at his desk writing letters when he heard some one enter the door behind him, and asked, —

"That you, Spencer?"

"No, sir," was the answer, in a voice and accent so startling and unexpected that Roger turned sharply and said sternly : —

"Nino Reni! What are you doing in Walford? I told you I wished never to set eyes on you again."

"I know that you said it," replied the Italian with pathetic dignity. "But a man in a passion speaks words which he regrets. I hoped you had come to feel that you had done me injustice."

Roger had been looking over his shoulder at his visitor, who stood behind him. "Come round here," he said briefly, and Nino with his soft, slow movement crept round the desk and stood by the window with the full light on his face. Roger looked at the man with keen, curious eyes. He had grown thin; his face was sallow and showed deep lines. His hair, formerly jet black, had become streaked with gray, and his soft, velvety eyes looked larger in their orbits.

"I don't think I was unjust to you, Nino," said Roger. "Naturally I was indignant. My child would be safe at home in her mother's arms if you had not been making love secretly to my servant, a young girl, twenty years your junior."

Nino made a gesture with both hands.

"I was an exile," he said gently. "She cared for me; no one else cared for me. I accepted her free offering."

"That is all very well. I have blamed myself far more than I have blamed you. It seems strange to me now that we could have trusted the child out of our own sight. But I have no wish to discuss the subject. What is your business here?"

"I came to say good-by," said Nino. "I am going back to Italy. I have engaged with a party of Americans going to Europe for the summer."

"Oh, you want me to give you a character."

Nino made a magnificent gesture.

"I have credentials the most distinguished," he said. "I have letters and papers from an English duchess."

"I am glad you have found a good position," said Roger. "Americans are no longer as dependent on couriers as they were twenty or thirty years ago."

Nino shrugged his shoulders as if his ability to secure a place was easily beyond question. "I came, Mr. Rexford," he said, in his plaintive way, "to ask a favor."

"Very well. Speak out."

As Roger gave this sharp command he observed that

his visitor's face changed. The light went out of his eyes; they became opaque; the lines about his mouth deepened.

"I want to say this," said Nino with singular intensity. "I did the child no harm. I swear it before the Blessed Virgin. I did her no harm. We had talked. Madam had made me angry and I was telling Jenny. The child was one minute close beside us, talking, singing to herself; then we turned and she was not there."

"Look here, Nino," said Roger, "you don't quite understand me. Had I supposed for one instant that you had touched a hair of my little girl's head, do you think you would be going free to-day? If the law could not have interfered and taken care of you, I should have taken your punishment into my own hands."

Devoid of ruddy tints although the Italian's face already was, he blanched at these words and the stern glance which accompanied them, until he looked like a piece of parchment.

"But Madam believed it," he said petulantly. "That is why she did not give me the money."

Roger was silent for a moment, then observed, "She was very old; she was terribly broken after the thing happened, and that suspicion was a part of her malady. I told her I had sifted the whole matter to the extent of my ability, and that I could not find a grain of real evidence against you."

"I was frightened when the child vanished," said Nino, "because I—I had been jealous, and everybody knew it. Madam had eyes and heart only for her. She made me,—her friend, her companion, her son, —a mere servant. It cut me deep. I was loud in my complaints, but I never could have done that accursed thing. They say we Italians are revengeful, but I am not revengeful. I hate trouble, I like an easy conscience. I "—

"Enough of this," said Roger. "You would have been a fiend incarnate if you had thought of doing the child harm. What favor were you going to ask of me?"

"It is about Madam's legacy."

"You get nothing, nothing at all, unless the child is restored in a little more than a year's time," said Roger impatiently.

"I know. When the lawyer read out the will, it was as if I heard Madam say, 'Nino, you know where Bessy is. Bring her back and you shall have the fifteen thousand dollars to buy the little house and vineyard you want near Sorrento.'"

"The blow had affected her mind," said Roger thoughtfully.

"But she had left me no money by the will she made in the summer."

"She had spoken about it to Mr. Graves, and in former wills which were destroyed she had left you in one five thousand and in another eight thousand dollars. She said to me once that she paid you good wages, and that you ought to have laid up a competence."

"She gave me fifty dollars a month," said Nino. "For thirteen years I had this and all expenses paid. She knew that I sent it to my father and my mother at Sorrento. Now," he went on with an eloquent gesture, "I have no money to send to my father and mother; they are suffering. I go to work, to aid them. I shall have no more money except my wages, unless the child is found." He gave a swift glance into Roger's eye.

" Every possible measure has been taken," said Roger, feeling a terrible depression. " But it all seems wasted effort."

" Nothing is done in a day," said Nino impressively, and in a reassuring vein. " The time will come."

Something crafty in the man's look and tone startled Roger. He had felt irritated by Nino's persistence in harping upon a subject which had become simply perturbing and hopeless, but now he was roused by a sudden sharp suspicion. He sprang up, ran round his office table, and seized Nino by the throat.

"You villain!" he exclaimed; "I believe you do know something about the matter. You were in league with the thieves who carried her off." He shook the man as if he would have throttled him. At sight of the ghastly pallor and chattering teeth Roger's mood changed and his clutch relaxed. "What did you mean ? " he demanded.

" I meant nothing," said Nino shrinking and cowering.

" Why did you say *the time will come?* " thundered Roger.

" I meant perhaps, — who can tell? who knows? I have not mastered the language," faltered Nino. " I hope it, that is all I am sure of. I have nothing else to hope. I know nobody in this country. I have not a friend. I want to go back to Italy and live among my own people."

Roger gave him an impatient glance while he poured out these incoherent asseverations. They were of no effect, for Roger would never have accepted the man's unsupported testimony on any subject. But he had sifted every jot and tittle of available evidence against the Italian, and was convinced that he had been only accidentally concerned in Bessy's disappearance.

"What is it you want of me?" he said, feeling that he had foolishly allowed himself to be carried away.

"Just this," gasped Nino, clutching at the desk and looking half dead from fright. "I want to feel sure that even if I am out of the country, I shall not lose Madam's legacy, — that is, if the little girl is brought back."

"You need have no fears on that account," said Roger.

"But I will leave an address that I may be found," said Nino. He fumbled in his pocket, and brought out a scrap of paper with a printed heading.

"Pietro Bianchi, Pearl Street, New York," Roger read out; then added, "You just told me you had no friends in this country."

"He is not a friend; I have seen him once. It is this Bianchi who sent my money to my parents. He is a banker. He can communicate with my people; they will know where I am."

Roger had made a memorandum in his diary, and turning to the address-book which lay on his desk he entered it there as well.

"There it is secure, in case of accident," said he. Then as a new idea struck him he went to the door, opened it, and called across the row of desks, "Spencer, are you there?"

Spencer entered at once, nodded at Nino with no air of being surprised at seeing him, and waited with an air of interest.

"I may as well say before you, Spencer," said Roger, "that here is Giovanni Reni, who intends to go back to Italy. In case of his ever inheriting under Madam Van Polanen's will, he may be communicated with through Pietro Bianchi, Pearl Street, New York City. I have made a note of these facts in my address-book under this date. Are you satisfied?" he asked, turning to Nino.

Nino made a broad, expansive gesture.

"Very well, then, good-day, I wish you all the luck in the world." Without looking again at his visitor Roger resumed his work, and did not raise his head until the door had closed. Glancing about him then he saw that Spencer had apparently left the room with the Italian. He did not see the superintendent again for some hours; then happening to meet him he asked: —

"Did the fellow say anything to you, Spencer?"

"He seemed anxious to get away; inquired about trains."

"I wish I had asked him what he has been doing during the past few months," said Roger. "I wonder if he has seen Jenny."

"Franklin and Davis say that Jenny went to England in January. I dare say they have had an eye on Nino," said Spencer.

"For a moment," observed Roger meditatively, "I actually was under the conviction that he knew something about the affair. But it was a mere passing thought. He is innocent. I know men, and he is not the sort of man to do more than talk and bluster."

"He wants his money badly," said Spencer, in a tone of peculiar significance.

"Did he tell you so?"

" Yes."

" I thought you said he only spoke about the trains."

" There was nothing in particular," said Spencer. " Of course I made a few remarks. It would be very profitable to him if the child came back."

" You are always harping on that string," said Roger impatiently. " It would be very profitable to me, but that does not alter the facts of the case." .

"I know if I were Giovanni Reni," pursued Spencer with a little laugh, " I would find the child if " —

" Stop it ! " said Roger. There were clear signs of anger on his face, and Spencer desisted.

VII.

WHEN Amy had come to Walford she had supposed that she was to answer only her sister's temporary need; but weeks had run into months and months into seasons, and there could, for a long time yet, be no possibility of her leaving the little New England town and resuming her work.

She had tried not to be impatient. She said to herself that she was working with nature and must be content to take nature's own time. The mother's heart was almost broken: that was no mere sentimental statement, but a plain fact. Amy herself might be able to reason that the loss of a child ought not to be a cause of hopeless grief. Statistics prove that only half the children born into the world live to come to maturity, and even with this regular diminution of their numbers, many philosophers grumble over the dangerous increase of population. Still Amy realized that statistics, even precepts and exhortations, were not yet to be thought of in Evelyn's case. She carefully chose books to read to her which might be useful, it is true. She talked, too, about the urgent interests of real life. Even when she sang to her she tried to infuse into her music something beyond the passion and pain of hopeless regret.

She acknowledged that all these sisterly efforts were so far of no use. But perhaps it seemed to Evelyn a treason to accept any thought or occupation which separated her from the memory of Bessy.

There was, besides, a serious complication in the way of Evelyn's recovery. This was a trouble of the eyes, at first considered unimportant. It began with an abhorrence of light, and on searching for the cause the doctors discovered severe inflammation; this was not necessarily dangerous to the sight, but, under the incessant irritation of tears, it soon became acute.

While Evelyn lay on the lounge possessed by some fresh shivering of doubt and fear, or in the evening in her bed restless and starting and with no hope of going to sleep, Amy would draw a thick screen between the lamp and the white face with its burning eyes, and read on for hours till Roger came in.

"Thanks, sister," Evelyn would say; "you are very good to me."

"You are not good to us," Amy would answer, "else you would try to listen and not cry. It is wicked for you to cry."

"I know," said Evelyn. "The doctor tells me I shall lose my sight if I go on crying. I try not to cry, but"—

From Evelyn's few distracted words they all realized that she knew not how to repress tears. In the pleasant weather she had wept, remembering; when the snows came down, when the March winds blew, she had wept, remembering; at the thought of the first crocus, the little rifts and cracks of the upheaved flower-beds into which the child had once peered curiously, awaiting miracles, she was all tears. Bessy had so loved everything, babbled of everything: snows, sheets of rain, plashing showers with rainbows in the east, breaking clouds, the sun, flowers, everything with wings that darted, skimmed, flew, between earth and sky.

" Is not my loss as much as yours, Evelyn ? " Roger
would say sometimes when she sobbed all this misery
out on his breast. " A father loves his child as well as
a mother can, yet I cannot give myself up to grief."

At such words Evelyn was assailed by a realization
of her own weakness and selfishness. She tried to take
up some occupation, but any use of her eyes was for-
bidden. She endeavored to go about the house in the
old way, but every nook was full of cruel reminders,
and she flew back to the solitude of her own room or of
the nursery where there could be no fresh shocks of
feeling.

Rexford Long came to Walford occasionally, and it
was he who could do most for the unhappy mother
sitting in the nursery with Bessy's things around her.

" I can talk to you, Rex," she said to him one day,
" but I do not dare say anything nowadays to Roger,
or to Amy. Amy is like Mrs. Chick; she wants me to
make an effort. She tries to induce me to talk French
and German with her. She reads aloud to me. I know
Wordsworth's ' Ode to Duty ' by heart, and also ' Rabbi
Ben Ezra.' "

" So Amy reads Browning to you," said Rex with the
flicker of a smile in his eyes.

" Oh yes, she goes on and over the verse : —

" ' Then, welcome each rebuff
    That turns earth's smoothness rough,
    Each sting that bids nor sit nor stand, but go !
    Be our joys three parts pain !
    Strive and hold cheap the strain ;
    Learn, nor account the pang ; dare, never grudge the throe !' "

Evelyn repeated the lines with some spirit, then added
with a little soft laugh, " I sometimes long to give back
to her —

"'Irks care the crop-full bird? Frets doubt the maw-crammed
        beast?'

if only one could mouth it! I wonder if Browning knew
he was only repeating Job, and for the worse. Job says,
'Doth the wild ass bray when he hath grass, or loweth
the ox over his fodder?'"

Then came tears again.

"You see, Rex," she went on presently, "they don't
know how much I have lost, how little I have left to
live on. Mrs. Goodeve, she knows; but a girl does not
know, and a man cannot know. One begins to love
a child, — to love it with an ache and a longing, for
months before it is born. One day, a little while before
Bessy came, I stopped and spoke to a woman who was
carrying a wee baby, and as I happened to make a gesture towards the child its little hand twined round my
finger. I could not get the idea of that little hand out
of my head. I used to dream that a baby was holding
my finger, and when I woke up I felt as if, unless I had
that little hand in mine that minute, I should die of
the longing for it. Then once I saw an engraving at
Madam Van's of one of Correggio's pictures of a sleeping baby; the moment my eye fell on it I was so happy
I wanted to stay and look at it always. When I had to
turn to speak to people the wrench hurt me. I kept
making little errands back, to stare at the tender curves
of the little dear body, the legs, the arms, the round
face. Madam Van, — she was a clever old creature, —
she found me out, and said, 'Here, take it home with
you!' It hangs in my bedroom now, but I should n't
dare look at it even if I could see with my poor blind
eyes. A mother's love is made up of such foolishness
and tenderness: it is a yearning to touch, to hold, to

minister to. She feels more than she can explain of it. Don't you know they say that when a man loses his arm or his leg, the nerve still throbs at times; he dreams of the lost limb being there, and it causes him suffering."

Long said nothing. What was there to say?

"Do I bore you, Rex?" she asked after a time. "It is so easy to talk to you, and I never minded boring you as I mind boring Roger."

"You cannot bore Roger. Don't accuse him of lack of sympathy."

"He gets very impatient with me at times," Evelyn murmured.

"Because he feels how important it is for you to put away your sorrow and regain your health. Roger loved his child, but he loves you better. Love has jealous distinctions. It must hurt him now to see that you have never held him first, that you loved Bessy better."

Evelyn put her hand to her forehead. "Don't accuse me of loving anybody better than my husband."

"You have him left, yet you are most unhappy, most miserable!"

Evelyn stretched out her hand and touched Rex's arm. Her face had a strange, troubled look.

"I love Roger," she whispered, "but Bessy is so little, so tender. Anything could hurt her. She needs warm clothes of all sorts, — she outgrows her things so quickly, and who – can – tell – if"— A violent shivering seized her. Flinging her head down on the arm of the sofa she burst into terrible sobs.

It was easy enough for Rex to gather a clear suggestion of her state of mind from these few distracted words. Who could give her comfort while her imag-

ination shrank back in fear from the phantoms it created? It might be easy for any one else to accept the
mystery, to say that there could be no clue to the un-
knowable, but Evelyn could not rest while her soul was
blurred and troubled by these sudden terrors, these
involuntary convulsions of anguish. While the uncertainty lasted, the grief, the conflict, the unvoiced regret, the bitter complaint, the restless presentiments,
unrealized dreams, and vague sufferings must go on.
What wonder if the mind fed morbidly upon itself?
What wonder if tears were never far from the eyes?

Amy could not help being profoundly moved by the
tragedy of her sister's sorrow, but we must not blame
her if she could not enter into the mother's feelings,
even if she sometimes looked on at this changeless
sorrow with a sensation of stupefying ennui. Amy abhorred emptiness, negation. The young blood was stirring in her veins with a longing for movement, action,
and the excitement of the congenial work from which she
was cut off. Evelyn divined this, and begged her sister
not to stay in the unnaturally darkened rooms to which
she was condemned, but to go out, find companions, occupation, and interests of some kind or another. Thus
set free, Amy soon threw herself into energetic action.
She established clubs, a cooking and a nursing school ;
she was introduced by Mrs. Goodeve to all the latter's
protégés, and undertook in particular to regenerate the
family of a ne'er-do-well, named Sam Porter.

It was through her more public enterprises that she
first found out how practically useful Henry Spencer
could make himself. She had necessarily seen him
more or less intimately ever since she came to Walford,
and had gradually come to associate his animated and

rather handsome face, with its bright gray eyes and clearly cut features, his crisp, short hair, his well-knit, alert figure, with practical help, and a wonderful executive ability in carrying out all her schemes. Like all ardent enthusiasts, Amy had suffered from the torturing delays and hindrances caused by the indolence and the apathy of her coadjutors, and she now found something miraculous in the ease with which difficulties could be smoothed away so that she was free to spend her strength on her prime objects.

She was gratefully anxious to do something in return for Spencer's good services, and when she discovered that he had taught himself to read French and German, but could not speak either language, she offered to help him. This intercourse soon became a chief interest in Amy's present life. He was candid with her ; he described his career of struggle ; his determination while a mere boy to overcome circumstances, not to be ignorant and not to be inferior. Amy was clear-sighted, and she saw in Spencer a man of average faculties, but immense abilities for turning to account every talent he possessed, indefatigable in labor, and capable of any practical effort. His mother had died when he was sixteen, and fighting his way, inch by inch, he had missed more fortunate people's opportunities to look at the finer and better side of life. The poetic, the philosophic, and, in particular, the highest moral sense was deficient in him, she argued, and here she could help him. From the literature these French and German studies opened up, useful lessons might be gleaned.

There was many a debateable ground between the two intellects, but their widely differing individualities gave a clear zest to discussion. The instinct which

with Spencer had shaped every effort had been born of
hunger, thirst, greed, covetousness, the desire not to be
looked down upon by his fellow-men, but to possess all
they had in their power. Amy, on the other hand, to
whom everything had come easily, longed to atone for
her privileges of wealth and culture by sharing them
with the poorest. For Spencer not to have dined on
twelve courses and drunk Chambertin and Tokay when
other men had satisfied their hunger and thirst so ex-
pensively, was to have a definite ambition ; he meant
some day to do the same. Amy had more than once
been ready to declare, when she saw depths of poverty
and degradation of human misery, that she would never
know luxury or joy again. She had had to silence these
casuistries of conscience, or to deaden them by the
conviction that she needed to be strong and happy
in order to have courage for action ; that to carry out
the work she had appointed for herself, she must accept human conditions in a simple and childlike spirit,
disregarding differences, and putting her belief in a
Providence which allows reparation and progression.

Amy might have been called a socialist, while Spencer was, in all his views, prejudices, and ambitions, a
stiff aristocrat. She saw in him all sorts of false tendencies which she longed to straighten. An experience
like his ought to have broadened instead of narrowing
him. He had suffered ; he ought to have understood
the pain of the world. She plunged deep into the
vortex of argument. She was carried away. Her heart
beat, her eyes flashed. In her involuntary abandonment to her theme, the hint of austerity, the frequent
touch of hoar-frost in her manner, melted. Such topics
may seem impersonal, but when a young man and a

young woman talk together on any subject it will suffice
to interpret one to the other with more or less com-
pleteness.   Spencer was dazzled, more than dazzled, —
he was charmed.   He saw himself in most attractive
colors at these signs that she singled him out and distinguished him.

Amy would have considered it a horrible caricature
of her feminine privilege, had she been told that the
effect her soft, persuasive eloquence had upon Spencer
was to show her beauty in new lights, now flashing
upon him like a jewel, now withheld, just long enough
to make him long for it.   Beginning with the attitude
of a Juno, she was sure soon to melt and glow, turning
to him in an appeal which was directed to his intellect,
but instead only touched his emotions.

She had more than once told Spencer that he was
deficient in imagination, and she little suspected to
what flights she instigated the fancy she had called
limited by sordid and practical considerations.   Amy
had received two offers of marriage, one from a cousin
and the other from an English professor, but it might
be said that she had never had a lover.   She regarded
her cousin Dick as a hobbledehoy, and the professor as
an academical abstraction.   She had besides identified
herself with a work which detached her from the interests and hopes which other women hold dear.   She
wished to help Spencer, and probably found him a
trifle more piquant than the Porters, for example, on
whom she spent far more pains and more actual
thought.   Spencer gave her a sense of mental freedom
which enabled her to discuss all subjects with verve,
while the Porters irritated and hindered her.   Spencer
was everything the Porters were not — energetic, ambi-

tious, and self-respecting; but her self-imposed thrall-
dom to the necessities of the Porters occupied not a
little of her time.   Sam Porter was a hopelessly incompetent man, who had made his outlook in life all the
more hopeless by marrying an incorrigible slattern.
Mrs. Porter, who had four children under the age of
five, and another momentarily expected, could hardly
be expected to profit by the educational privileges
which Amy's sewing and cooking schools held out;
accordingly, Amy sewed for her, cooked for her, nursed
for her, and when the baby came, promised to stand
with Mrs. Goodeve to support the father, who was, for
the first time, to be sponsor to his offspring.

   Amy hated a shirk, and Sam Porter was a shirk.   He
had in early life been taught to read, but by disuse of
his intellectual powers reading had become one of his
lost arts.   He bore the deprivation philosophically.
He was humble-minded, and liked to reflect that he
was only Sam Porter, and that what he did was of no
consequence.   To make people discontented with their
own inferiority was to Amy the first essential of any
hopeful work.   She labored hard to show Sam, as by a
flash of lightning, how poor he was, how dirty, above
all how densely ignorant, hoping that in some moment
of irresistible intuition of the joys of a promised land
he would begin to improve.   Her initiative step must
be to invest him with the responsibilities of a parent.
This was his first-born son, the other four children were
daughters, and he should stand godfather to the boy
and read the responses in the service.   By this time
Sam regarded his benefactress much as he looked upon
the weather, something which had to be borne, and
which, in spite of buffetings, freezings and meltings,

lightnings and thunderbolts, occasionally brought intervals of blue sky and sunshine. Ever since the boy's birth Amy had been drilling Sam in the responses in the baptismal service, and it had been with some pleased surprise that he discovered that the letters, particularly the capitals, were not so unfamiliar as he had supposed, and that after a week's incessant practice he could get through his portion, partly by the aid of his eye and partly by dint of memory, to his own admiration.

The baptism was to take place in the middle of the afternoon service the first Sunday in April. From early morning Amy had been at work in the Porter household. If order had been evolved out of chaos, it was not the divine, grandiose, cosmogonic order of which she had dreamed, but the compulsory order which comes from a sharp tussle with each and every detail. However, at half-past three o'clock Amy had marshaled her forces to the vestry-room, where they were to wait and be joined by Mrs. Goodeve. Mrs. Porter looked very pretty in a suit of Amy's clothes. The baby was in spotless cambric and fast asleep in its mother's arms. Sam was astonishingly well-dressed, well-washed, clipped, shaven, with a broad smile on his lips; and the two eldest children, who were to swell the procession on this great family occasion, were fittingly arrayed; and Amy had done it all.

But the task had been no light one, and a fever made up of impatience, disillusion, and indignation, had burned in Amy's veins all day. With all her sweet charity, her boundless benevolence, it was painfully irksome to her to have to deal with stupid, incompetent people. Could she but have shed a few tears, the nervous tension might have relaxed, but as it was, it reached its crisis when on entering the vestry, instead of finding an ark of refuge in Mrs. Goodeve, she came upon a tall, broad-shouldered young man.

"Is this Miss Standish?" he said to her. "I am Felix Goodeve. My mother sends her very particular love. My father is not well to-day and she dislikes to leave him. Accordingly she asked me to become her substitute and help Sam out. I have helped Sam out before at a pinch, have n't I, Sam?"

"I beg you will not interfere with the service to-day," said Amy petulantly.

"I thought I was to hold the child, name it, make the responses, and bring it up in the way it should go," said Felix. "Tell me, however, exactly what I am to do, and I will do it or perish miserably."

There was a gleam of mischief in the young man's face which Amy resented.

"Please do nothing, — nothing at all except to walk up the aisle to the font," she said with some haughtiness. "I particularly request that you will not help in the responses. Samuel is to take the whole duty on himself, and any interruption might put him out."

"Very well," said Felix. "I am to be absolutely dumb."

"Absolutely," said Amy coldly. "If you will walk on we will follow."

Felix marched in, and held the eyes of the congregation for five minutes until Amy, leading a shrinking and cowering girl by each hand, followed by Mrs. Porter with the baby, and Sam with his prayer-book, took their places below the chancel steps.

Mr. Neal, a mild young priest with a melodious,

melancholy voice, began the service at once. Sam, it
was evident, was doing his best to follow the clergyman
conscientiously, but was at some disadvantage, and
unless Amy had twice, or thrice reminded him to kneel
or to rise, he might have missed the minor details of
the function. Amy had informed Mr. Neal that Sam
was to be the chief and only real sponsor, and therefore when he began pleadingly, —

"Dearly beloved, ye have brought this child here to
be baptized," the full weight of the exhortation was
addressed to Sam, who, with his eyes glued to the
prayer-book, was toiling manfully after the clergyman.

"I demand, therefore," said Mr. Neal, and here
Amy with a touch upon Sam's arm directed his attention to the exact place where he was to find the responses, and then stepped back a few paces.

"I demand therefore," said Mr. Neal, "Dost thou,
in the name of this child, renounce the devil and all his
works, the vain pomp and glory of the world, with all
covetous desires of the same, and the sinful desires of
the flesh, so that thou wilt not follow, nor be led by
them?"

The priest paused and waited for the response, but
no response came. Sam's eyes were fastened on his
book, his features were working, his lips opened and
shut, but no word issued. Amy knew the signs; the
action of his mind and of his tongue were both a little
stubborn, but the answer would be forthcoming in another moment. She might have prompted him, but
was conscious that Felix Goodeve was looking into her
face with eyes widened by amused interrogation, and
a quick current of indignation ran through her at the
incredible impertinence of this stranger's being in the

place at all. As he continued to gaze at her, she turned upon him fiercely with a shake of her head. Felix at once put his prayer-book in his pocket, folded his arms, and withdrew half a dozen steps.

By this time the pause had grown long, and Mrs. Porter herself nudged Sam. He nodded with an air of understanding the whole subject and disliking any interference. His eyes gleamed and his features worked, — still no syllable came.

Mr. Neal was much perplexed: he liked precedents, and felt this situation to be without precedent. He grew nervous, and all he could do was to go on to the next question.

"Dost thou believe all the articles of the Christian Faith as contained in the Apostles' Creed?"

"I renounce – them – all," said Sam at the top of his lungs, " and – by – God's – help – will – endeavor – not to – follow, – nor – be – led – by – them."

It was a terrible moment to Amy. The whole church seemed to be swimming round. She heard Felix Goodeve say in a deep, full voice, "I do," and she could bear no more. She retreated to the vestry, and sat down blinded by tears. It had certainly been a most miserable performance. She was as a rule exempt from the dread of ridicule, but she had a clear perspective of Mr. Felix Goodeve's thoughts regarding her imperiousness and self-assertion, for his eyes had a glint which suggested that the comic side of things was far from being lost on him. She had heard a good deal of the young man from Mrs. Goodeve, of whom she had grown very fond. She had expected to like him, and regretted to find him so detestable. He had come like a thief in the night, apparently. She sat with her hand over her eyes through the short afternoon discourse endeavoring to tranquilize her nerves, and when at the benediction she mechanically rose, she saw that he had entered the vestry by way of the chapel and was standing near her. His presence had to be endured through the hymn and prayer.

"I am sorry your trouble was not better rewarded," he said, approaching her as the congregation rose inside with a rustle and began to stream out. "I took the Porters home. Sam is immensely proud of the way he stood up to the parson, as he expresses it. Pray don't undeceive him, Miss Standish."

"He as an incorrrigible shirk," said Amy. "He has been drilled for weeks in his part — " She finished with a gesture of angry disdain.

"He was like a balky gun," said Felix, "primed and loaded, but takes its own time and goes off at an awkward moment. Don't lay it to heart, Miss Standish. Personally I feel grateful to Sam. I shall have such a good story to tell my mother."

"If you have no feeling of the sacredness of — " she began.

"Don't make me out a scoffer and an infidel," put in Felix, "at least until you have tried and tested me. I am going to walk home with you, if you will permit me."

"Many thanks," said Miss Standish with all the grandeur of which she was capable, "but I see Mr. Spencer, and I wished particularly to ask him a question ; so I must beg you to excuse me."

And not a little to the surprise of Felix Goodeve, she singled out the one individual in Walford whom he really disliked and walked away with him.

VIII.

THE postoffice at Walford was, so to speak, the club, the exchange, the forum. The chief mail of the day came in towards evening, and a full half hour before the time a group of men was seen to gather, not with impatience, but with the air of generous leisure which belongs to lookers-on in Vienna or in Walford. They dropped into chairs and benches by the fire in winter, and in summer sat on the bench outside. Personal interest in the contents of the mail-bag they had little or none. Letters to their womankind were accepted with a shrug, and indifferently consigned to their pockets with a suggestion of being buried in at least temporary oblivion. They glanced at the newspapers, and greeted the news of the world with an air of having predicted it from the beginning. One or two among them were used to pose as wise men: their verdicts were final. No subject was too great, and at the same time nothing was too trivial, for discussion.

The Monday evening following the incident in the last chapter the usual group had gathered at the postoffice, and were talking about the late cold snap which had cut off the hopes of an early spring by nipping buds and killing all the new-born lambs on the mountain farms.

"I 've allus heerd," observed Caleb Wooden in his

high, piping voice, "that when March comes in like a lion it goes out like a lamb, but this year it come in like a lion and went out like the devil, and took all the lambs with it."

"There's no truth in proverbs," said Mr. John Weeks. "It is said a peck of dust in March is worth a king's ransom, but I don't think the inhabitants of Walford set any particular store on the bushels and bushels of dust which go flying up and down betwixt the Baptist and Presbyterian meeting-houses. And it often is so in March."

"I see that sister o' Mrs. Rexford's a-strugglin' agin the blarst," observed Ben Wooden. "She's the neatest-footed woman in Walford."

"Yet it's said she's a blue-stocking," observed Mr. Weeks, "and has been to all the colleges in Europe and taken more honors than could be counted. She could be a lawyer, or a doctor, or anything she liked to be."

"Instead of which she comes here nursin' her sister, which is a sensibler thing to do," said Ben Wooden.

"I myself don't want no female doctors and no female lawyers," piped Caleb. "Women are useful in their place."

"No doubt, no doubt," said Mr. Weeks with magnanimity. "Women are a curious sex, now," he added, as if the subject loomed before him inexhaustibly.

"Curious is the word," said David Coe emphatically. "They're curious in themselves and curiouser still in the effect they have on a man's ideas. Now if I'm a workin' for a man, I go straight along: ef he says anythin' out o' reason, why I know my own trade; and ef *he* hain't no common sense, why *I* have an' he sees it. But a woman is always expectin' a carpenter can contrive to do what can't be done. A man may think that two and two make five, even six, but you can show him he 's wrong. Now a woman ez likely ez not expects that two and two makes a hundred and fifty, ef not, why then it ought to and somebody is wrong. Then the female mind jumps at conclusions. Just for example : I was a doin' odd jobs over at Mrs. Lowry's, and came to repairin' her little boy's rabbit-house. As it happened, a hen had managed to make a nest in the hutch and laid three eggs in it. Mrs. Lowry, who was standin' by givin' me directions, looked at me with eyes as big as saucers when I found the nest. 'Why,' says she, 'I never heard before ez rabbits laid eggs.' Now that just shows the operations of the feminine mind."

"It 'll be a queer world when women get the upper hand o' things generally," said Dennis Bristol reflectively. "They say that time 's fast approaching."

"Who says as woman is a goin' to get the upper hand o' things?" inquired Caleb Wooden skeptically.

"You read it everywhere," said Bristol authoritatively. "And if you keep your eyes open, you 'll see that there 's no place where they 're not creeping in. Every man has a weakness for a woman ; I suppose it 's the result of long habit. So when she puts her foot down, he is charitably inclined, stands aside, and yields. I have n't heard of a woman managing a railroad yet, but she runs factories, publishes papers ; she is a lawyer, a doctor, a minister ; she keeps store, teaches school, writes books ; is postmaster, school committee. In short, she seems ambitious to do everything that man has ever done, and she will do it, sooner or later."

"You don't really suppose," struck in Caleb Wooden's shrill voice, "that here, — here in Walford, women will ever run factories, publish papers, be postmasters, and keep store ? "

" The indications all point that way," said Bristol, with an air of scientific accuracy. " There 's hardly a store in town that has n't got a girl perched up on a stool."

" I never thought of it before," observed Mr. Weeks ; "it is so."

" What I want to be clear about," said Caleb solemnly, "is what this thing leads to."

" It seems to me easy enough to predict what it will lead to," said Bristol.

"What 'll become of us men ? " asked Caleb, showing unmistakable signs of apprehension.

" You 've kept bees, hain't you ? " asked Bristol gravely.

" Why, yes."

" Did you ever see many bees of the masculine persuasion cluttering up the hive ? "

" That 's a fact, they do die off," said Caleb with an expression of profound astonishment. " But then," he added hastily as if to escape the fate appointed for his sex by irrefutable logic, "we are not insects."

Dr. Cowdry had come in for his mail, and, attracted by the fire, approached to warm his stiffened fingers, nodding to one man after another of the group.

" Any news, doctor ? " inquired Mr. Weeks.

" Well, no, — no particular news."

" Much sickness ? "

" A good deal of sickness in different parts of the town, but no very bad cases just at present."

" I heerd," said Caleb Wooden, " that some New

York doctors had been up to look at Mrs. Rexford's eyes."

"It seemed best to have a specialist, as she does not improve," said Dr. Cowdry, "so Dr. Light came to-day."

"What did he say?"

"He says she must not cry any more; that she is worn out," said Dr. Cowdry dryly.

"Tears won't bring the child back," observed Caleb.

"Nothing so unreasonable as a woman's tears," said David Coe.

"Dr. Light ordered a course of treatment," said Dr. Cowdry, "but he says the nerves are at fault, and that she needs a quiet mind, to get well. He told Mr. Rexford he had better take his wife to Europe. That's the fashionable remedy, but it would not answer here. Of course Roger Rexford can't go, and I doubt if she would go. There is hardly a week when there is not a report of a child's being found somewhere who might turn out to be Bessy. It will be so as long as the reward is offered. I tell him he had better give up advertising a temptation to thieves and liars. I wish with all my heart we knew for certain that Bessy Rexford is dead. Then the trouble would come to an end. As it is, it has to be lived through every day. There can be no relief from it. Nothing can be settled. It's a horrible state of things for a delicate woman, and unless the child is found I am afraid nothing can save the mother."

"Bessy Rexford 'll never be found now," said Caleb Wooden oracularly. "They didn't go the right way to work. They lost time — they — "

"I consider there is a good chance of the child's

being found," said Dr. Cowdry irritably, and with a curt good-night he went out.

"It is a very singular case," said Caleb. "As my wife was a-sayin' yesterday, the Lord is above all; so we know that dispensations is sent. And when we reflect they are not sent to you or to me, but to people who set themselves up, as it were, an' purtend to be better than their neighbors, why, it is pretty clear what is thought on high of such pride an' vanity."

"I never accused Mrs. Rexford of setting herself up," said Bristol. "If there was ever a woman in Walford ready with a smile ánd a word it used to be Mrs. Rexford."

"Not another woman in Walford rode horses," Caleb insisted. "She kep' three girls to do her work, an' one of 'em was tricked out in a white cap an' apron to look after the child. Nobody else in Walford ever put on such airs, and such judgments as have come upon Mrs. Rexford never happened to anybody else."

"I 've heard," timidly ventured a man named Gideon Finch, who had hitherto sat silent but deeply attentive, "that it 's their way at the Rexfords. to change their plates every time they take a fresh helping o' victuals."

"Knives and forks too," said Caleb in corroboration; "so my wife says. Such people may flourish for a season."

"But I should hate to think that pretty creetur was goin' to be blind," said Ben Wooden.

People had been coming and going, and there had been a momentary lull in the conversation while inquiry was made at the boxes; observant eyes had noted the number of letters allotted to each; then when the outer door clanged again the talk went on as if it had not been interrupted. But at this moment a young man entered, at whom each one stared in eager curiosity.

" Felix Goodeve ! " Dennis Bristol ejaculated, and as if the others had only waited for somebody to take the initiative, each repeated the name in every variety of intonation and pressed forward to shake hands with the new-comer, who returned the greetings warmly : —

" How are you, Caleb? I heard your voice in the street ; it drew me as 't were a nightingale. Ben, too, — I 'm glad to see Ben. How do you do, Mr. Weeks? You have not grown a day older, nor you, Dennis Bristol. When I used to go to school to you I supposed you were a hundred, but now I see we are much the same age. There is nothing like sitting solidly down in Walford and not allowing one's self to be bullied by the outside world, if a man wants to keep young."

" Now, you 've grown older, Felix," said Caleb Wooden, admiringly.

" Older ! I should think so," said the young man. " Life does not stand still out in Colorado, nor is it all beds of roses and amaranthine bowers."

" I hear you have found silver on your uncle's lands," observed Bristol. " They say there 's no end of mineral wealth in a part of the tract you have been least hopeful about."

" Many a man's heart has been broken by finding a vein of ore," said Felix philosophically. " We don't intend to break ours. The fight has been to hold our own. Things had got a little mixed, and there were other parties who wanted to ' prospect.' "

" How do you manage ? "

" We reëstablish the survey, and next we stake our boundaries," said Felix. " Then up jumps a fellow and says, 'This is my claim.' 'You'll have a lively time getting me off it,' I answer. 'Do you know who I am?' he asks. 'No, and don't want to,' say I. 'I'm Mountain Tim, they call the Invincible. I've killed my sixteen men easy, and I'll just trouble you to vacate.' 'Do you know who I am?' I thunder back. 'I'm Felix Goodeve, the Colorado Terror, with a record of twenty-five, and you will make the twenty-sixth unless you skip in ten seconds.' And he skips," added Felix with a twinkle in his eye.

"You don't really mean, now," began Mr. Weeks deprecatingly, — "you don't actually intend we should understand that " —

"That I've killed anybody? No. I never had to," said Felix. "You see I am tall and I am broad. I rise up slowly, and by the time I reach my full height and look down on my adversary he is apt to wilt."

Something in the young man's appearance made this account of himself plausible. But the secret of his strength lay probably as much in his glance and the charm of his smile as in his muscle. He had grown up in Walford, and every man of them knew every scrape of the boy whose love of fun had sometimes done him more mischief than his talents had done him good. They assailed him with questions. When had he come? Had he come back to Walford to stay? Had he decided to settle down? Had he got a wife? Was he going to get a wife?

"I reached Walford at sunset Saturday night," said Felix. "I meant to have stopped a week in Chicago, but once started, I wanted to see my mother, and I could n't wait. When I saw the river here and the valley and the hills and the evening sky beyond, I made up my mind I had come home to stay, never to go away any more. Everything I left behind, the noise, the hubbub, the smoke, the stamping and crushing mills, the smelting works, the sluicing and washing and turning earth inside out, seems like a horrible nightmare. I like this better. I have not got any wife, not a single one. Going to have one? Of course, I 'm going to have one, without loss of time. I 'm going to marry all the prettiest girls in Walford. That is the way we do things in Utah."

" Saw you in church yesterday," put in Mr. Weeks with a chuckle.

" Teaching Sam Porter to deny the Apostles' Creed and all the articles of the Christian faith," said Dennis Bristol.

They all began talking about Miss Standish, Miss Standish's enterprises, Miss Standish's inexhaustible patience with the Porters. From this topic they went on to Henry Spencer, whose affairs roused a critical spirit in those he had passed and left behind in his upward path. They told Felix that Alonzo Sloper was everywhere bragging that his daughter was to marry Spencer, but that the young man himself was running after Miss Standish. From these topics they passed to the Rexford troubles, and every man had his theory concerning little Bessy's disappearance to impart to the new-comer.

Felix had been little in Walford for the past ten years, but it was easy to see that the man had not outgrown the boy who had been in touch with every interest in the place. He was Felix Goodeve still, they all said to each other after he had left them ; experience had not tamed him, success had not spoiled him, and he had kept his heart in the right place.

IX

MOTHER AND SON.

"You are twenty-seven, almost twenty-eight, years old, Felix," said Mrs. Goodeve. "That is not very young."

"I don't consider it altogether kind of you to throw my old age in my teeth," Felix retorted.

"But you said that you were too young to marry."

"Perhaps, after all, the difficulty is that I am too old."

"A man should not live for himself alone," said Mrs. Goodeve. "He should feel that he belongs to the state and to the world, above all that he belongs to some sweet woman, who without him, as he without her, misses all that is best in existence. Should you not like to have a nice little home where you could settle down and find out what you liked best and needed most, and share it all with some lovely young wife who adored you and lived for you?"

"Should n't I just!" said Felix, with a twinkle in his eye.

"Can it be possible you have never thought of any woman?" Mrs. Goodeve proceeded. She was sitting at her work-table in the "middle-room," repairing some of the garments her son had brought home, and perhaps the thriftless way in which good flannel and linen had gone to waste for lack of a stitch in time lent earnest-

ness to her views on the undesirability of man's living
alone in the world.

"Never thought of any woman!" repeated Felix as
if with indignation; "I never think of anything else."

"Do you mean to say you have been in love and
never told me about it?"

"Well, perhaps not what you would call actually in
love," said Felix, "but I've seen some very taking
women."

"Not probably in Colorado."

"Oh, yes, in Colorado and Montana," said Felix.
"There was Kitty Macdougal. She ran a ranch, and
raised I can't begin to say how many thousand head of
cattle. She had an army of cowboys, whom she kept
in order like a drill sergeant. You should have seen
her riding a fiery mustang. She never used a side-
saddle."

"Do you wish me to understand that you were intimately acquainted with this woman?" asked Mrs.
Goodeve, with some asperity.

"Well, rather," Felix returned imperturbably. "She
bought a few hundred acres of me, and naturally I saw
a good deal of her. Besides, 'Kitty's Ranch,' as it is
called in that region, was a general rendezvous. She
was a handsome woman: bright red cheeks, plump,
cheerful, always with a smile on her face. She always
reminded me a little of you, mother."

"Thank you. The way you describe her is not
exactly my notion of myself. The least imaginative
woman has an ideal. But no matter, go on. What
became of Miss Kitty Macdougal?"

"*Mrs.* Kitty Macdougal. She was a widow — perhaps several widows in one. All went on smoothly

until some of her cowboys got into bad company and were fleeced by some gamblers over at Eagle's Brook. This roused Kitty's ire. She mounted her mustang, rode over to Eagle's Brook followed by her cowboys, and entering the gambling den she covered the dealer and banker each with a six-shooter and demanded the money they had won of her men. The gamblers flung up their hands, confessed the cheat, and offered to refund. In fact, they were trembling for their lives, as the cowboys had brought ropes and threatened to lynch the rascals. Kitty saved their lives, took all the money into her own possession, and the sharpers were chased out of Eagle's Brook without a cent in their pockets."

" She is evidently a woman of executive ability," remarked Mrs. Goodeve, feeling that something must be conceded. " Still, I should not like to have her for a daughter-in-law."

" I was afraid you might object," said Felix, " so I never asked her to marry me. Besides, just at that time I had to go to Idaho, and I fell in with the Kansas Nightingale."

"What was the Kansas nightingale ? "

" It was a remarkably handsome young woman, so handsome and captivating I could have sat and smiled at her for a week. Her name was Isabel Prince, or so she said. She had a voice like a bugle. You should have heard her sing ' Annie Laurie.' The unlucky thing about her was that she had a temper." ·

" Did she fall out with you ? "

" Fortunately it was another man she fell out with. He attempted to criticise her singing, and she shot him dead."

" Felix Goodeve ! You don't mean to say you ever had anything to do with a woman who killed a man ! "

"My dearest mother, you don't begin to realize the capabilities of your sex for taking care of themselves. You are cribbed, limited by a conventional two-inch rule. You consider that a woman is a tender flower, an exotic. Once I was going from Fair Gulch to Evan's Dam in a stage-coach, which carried only one other passenger, the prettiest woman I ever saw in my life, with a soft, sad smile and beautiful gazelle-like eyes. She was well-dressed, too, and talked capitally. I had not seen an attractive woman for six months, and I was charmed, — charmed? I was fascinated, carried away, bewitched. She was going on, and nothing but the direst necessity could have forced me to leave her at Evan's Dam, except that I had been sent for to stop some trouble at the mines, so was compelled to bid her adieu. I told her how heart-broken I was, and she gave me a tender glance and a sweet, sad little half smile, and confessed that she, too, was sorry. 'Besides,' I went on chivalrously, 'it's a rough region you're coming to; I hate to think of your being alone and unprotected. Don't you feel a little timid?' At this she whipped a pair of revolvers out of her pocket and put one at her right hand and the other at her left. 'No, sir-ee,' she replied. 'I'm not afraid. I know how to take care of myself, you bet. I'm a crack shot.'"

"You got over your sentimental regrets at leaving her, I hope."

"She was a deliciously pretty woman, nevertheless. You must not be prejudiced. You see you have not had to battle with a hard world. You ought to feel for unluckier women. While I was coming East last week, I fell in with a handsome young creature, who confided to

me that she was going home to Missouri to get a divorce. She added that she had twice before obtained
a divorce, and in each case had married within twenty-
four hours after the decree was granted. I politely
remarked that I could easily predict the same result
would happen the third time. She gave me a soul-
stirring glance, and said with a clear note of regret in
her voice that no, there was nobody now, and she did
not feel sure what her family would think of her breaking off with her present husband without having first
secured another."

"What did you say to her?"

"What could a fellow say except that he was at her
disposal?"

"Felix, you did not say that?"

"Well, no, — you were at the end of my journey, so
I put on a stiff upper lip and resisted temptation."

Mrs. Goodeve had dropped her work, and was looking at her son with a mingling of pride and anxiety.

"I never realized before what I meant when I prayed
for all who travel by land or water," she said devoutly.
"I feel all the more keenly that you must have a good
little wife."

Felix leaned towards his mother and kissed her.

"Find me just such a woman as you are," said he,
"and I 'll marry her."

"We are too much alike. There ought to be a little
incompatibility between husband and wife. Suppose I
was just like your father."

"Heaven forbid!"

"There is Mrs. Root. She is modest, economical,
and never feels that she deserves a new dress or bon-
net, and her husband is also modest and economical

and never has the grace to insist that she shall be well dressed, so the poor woman never makes a decent appearance. You see they are too compatible. Then there are the Porters, also of one mind in a house, both lazy shirks, both putting off everything until the morrow."

"You have convinced me," remarked Felix. "I am big, disorderly, extravagant, say more in a minute than I can stand to in a month, accordingly I require a diminutive, neat, thrifty, precise woman, who holds her tongue from one year's end to the other."

"I am not so sure of that," said Mrs. Goodeve anxiously. "What kind of a woman do you like best in your secret heart?"

"One exactly like my mother."

"I mean next best, you flatterer!"

"Next best? I fancy that must be a clinging, helpless, pretty creature."

"No tyrant on earth so despotic as a clinging, helpless, pretty creature."

"Then I won't marry one. I don't want a tyrant. I prefer to do the tyrannizing. I crave softness, infinite sweetness, in a woman."

Mrs. Goodeve looked at her son with eyes widened by speculation.

"Felix," she asked, "how do you like Miss Standish?"

"Can't bear her," said Felix.

"Oh, don't say that."

"Never in all my life was I snubbed, browbeaten, trodden upon, as I have been by that girl!"

"It was unlucky that you saw her first when she was put out by the Porters. Confess, at least, that she is handsome."

"No doubt of that," said Felix. He jumped up and strode about as if excited. "The question to my mind would be whether such good looks could redeem her temper, or whether such a temper would spoil her good looks."

"I have known her eighteen months, and I am in love with her."

"I have known her a week, so you cannot expect me to be in love with her," said Felix, resuming his seat. "If she were like Mrs. Rexford, now, that might be an easy matter."

"Amy is not like Evelyn," said Mrs. Goodeve thoughtfully, "but she is just as sweet and just as womanly. She is fond of children, not alone the clean, prettily-dressed ones, but of dirty, ragged little creatures, whom she delights to take hold of, wash, comb, smooth out, and make happy with a toy or a bit of candy."

"Poor things!" said Felix, with a mischievous glance. "I know she rubs their noses the wrong way when she washes their faces."

"Nothing of the kind. She is born with an irresistible knack. You should have seen her go into Jimmy McCann's house one day. She and I were out together and met the seven McCann children all in a string, and one of them asked her for a penny. 'I'll give each one of you a penny,' said Amy, 'if you will go home and wash your faces.' They trooped off on the instant, serious as could be, and we followed to see what would come of it. We found them entreating their mother to give them a basin and water and a towel. Mrs. McCann was scolding them for the fine airs they were putting on when we appeared. She complained to us of the trouble she had in keeping them clean. ' Now, Mrs. McCann,' said Amy, ' let me show you how to manage.' She found a basin, and she herself scrubbed the basin, then managed to provide something for a towel. She did not content herself with washing the children's faces; she cleaned them from head to foot. Then she insisted — just to show Mrs. McCann how easy it was — on making the Irish stew herself, setting the table, and making ready for Jimmy to come home. Jimmy McCann enjoyed his dinner so much that he insisted on his wife's going to the cooking-school, and the children's chief delight ever since has been to show Amy how clean and shining their faces are."

Felix had listened intently. " How does she happen to know Henry Spencer so well? " he asked.

"Yes, that troubles me. For after all it is the merest accident. She undertook to teach him French and German and other things."

" Yes, other things, no doubt of that. Spencer treads on air when he is with her. It is amazing to come back and find him the elegant individual he has turned out. Is Miss Standish going to marry him? "

"Marry him? Never. Besides, Henry Spencer has been engaged to Leo Sloper for years," said Mrs. Goodeve. " I should like Amy to know the fact, but it was confided to me as a profound secret. She would be indignant if I told her she was monopolizing a man who ought to be wrapped up in another girl."

"Ought to be, perhaps, but he is actually wrapped up in Miss Standish, just as she is in him."

" I tell you, Felix, she only thinks of helping him. She is run away with by the idea of giving every person a chance to live out his or her life," said Mrs. Goodeve, with a note of indignation. "She longs to regenerate the human race, — to have mankind begin over again."

" So she experiments on Spencer."

" Ah, that rankles, evidently."

" Nonsense."

" I only wish it might rankle. I only wish it might go far enough to make you jealous. I hate to see Amy making a mistake and running the risk of enduring a sharp mortification one of these days. I should be delighted if you would cut away the ground from beneath Henry Spencer's feet, take his place with her, make yourself useful and — "

" I should be sorry if I could shrink into any place which he had been able to fill satisfactorily."

" I call that conceit."

" I call it innate consciousness of superiority."

" Show your superiority by pleasing Amy Standish better than he does," said Mrs. Goodeve. "I don't care about the sort of superiority which has to be accepted at the owner's valuation. I like the world's stamp of success on men."

It was plain to Mrs. Goodeve that from the moment the conversation turned on Amy Standish her son had shown not only an intense interest, but a sort of physical disquiet. He was again striding about restlessly. After a short pause he turned, and looking at his mother with an air of taking in fresh bearings of the situation with lightning-like rapidity, he said, —

" You say he is really engaged to the Sloper girl?"

She nodded.

He was silent a moment ; then he burst out : — " If

it were anybody in the world except Henry Spencer I
might like to try a tilt with him. I should like to
see if there is any softness in that proud girl. But I
can't put myself in competition with that fellow." He
·flushed as he spoke, the light in his eyes deepened,
and his lips quivered. He made the tour of the room,
then, returning, pulled a chair close to his mother, and
in a soft voice, as if continuing the same subject, said,
"Mother, do you suppose there is any chance of little
Bessy Rexford's being found? Roger told me yesterday
he had not given up the hope yet."

"I have not given up the hope," said Mrs. Goodeve.
"Still, I sometimes feel nowadays that perhaps we have
killed Evelyn between us by making her believe there
is a chance of Bessy's being alive."

"Oh, poor girl!" said Felix. Tears had started to
his eyes. "It is bitter, it is beyond words. I remember when Roger brought her home to Walford. She
changed all my thoughts of woman in a moment. When
you took me to call on her, she wore a white dress with
pink ribbons. Then you invited her here to tea, and
she came in blue, azure blue, and she had on little blue
kid slippers and blue stockings. I used to lie awake
nights and try to decide whether, if ever I had a wife,
I should prefer she should wear white with pink ribbons or pale blue. When I remembered how the rose-
colored ribbons matched the color on Mrs. Rexford's
cheeks, I wanted the white and pink. But then when
it came over me how the blue silk stockings fitted over
the insteps and ankles, I was ready to choose the blue."

"Upon my word!"

"And now she is stricken, childless, and almost blind."
He started up. "Mother," he exclaimed, "I feel as if

I longed to set out and search the world over for that child."

"Plenty of us have felt the same way," said Mrs. Goodeve. They sat silent, their thoughts narrowed down to the problem of poor Evelyn.

X.

A MAN cannot always remember that the race he runs is for life and not a mile heat. Spencer had at an early age made up his mind to choose only the friends who were in a position to help him on in his career, yet he had been so inconsistent as to make love to a girl with neither money nor family. He could only justify his weakness by arguing that he had never pledged himself irrevocably, and thus might easily break off the entanglement if he found it inconvenient. What he had felt when he made his conditional promise was that if he were ever in a position to support a wife he wanted to marry the prettiest girl in Walford, and at that time he thought his most fastidious demands answered by Miss Leo Sloper.

Her name was Leonora, but "Leo" better suited the sprightly aspect of the young lady. She had a dazzlingly white skin, a brilliant color on cheeks and lips, bright hair of reddish gold, and finely cut features of what had in the days of his infatuation seemed to Spencer the purest patrician type. Her hands were small and white as if cut in alabaster, her slight figure was pretty and graceful. Then, too, a saucy, aggressive quality characterized every article of dress Miss Sloper put on. Her hats, her ribbons, her muffs, her tippets, her clasps and buckles, the bangles on her wrist, the very heels of her boots, seemed as it were to rankle in the imaginations of her admirers. Her hats and bonnets were invariably surmounted by birds; the head of some animal set off her muff; the boa round her throat suggested a sinuous creature itself coiled there. Some people are repelled by such savage ornaments, but to Leo these trophies seemed naturally to belong to beauty. She had heard of a woman whose ball-gown was decorated by two hundred dead canary birds, and the idea had not a little charm for her, only as blue was her favorite color she would have preferred that the sacrifice should be a flock of jays.

The circumstances of her family were depressing, but Leo had never been depressed. "I will rise above them all," she had always said to herself, with a toss of her pretty head, when she encountered any rebuff from her more prosperous neighbors. The dull present was merely a stupid experience, to be endured until some great piece of good fortune should fall into her lap. The moment she met Henry Spencer she recognized the man whose alchemy was to convert her dull lead into gold, her cravings into substance.

Even when Spencer had been most ready to commit himself unalterably to Leo, he had shuddered at the thought of her family. Many a lover has plaintively asked, like the enamored swain in the old ballad : —

> "Can such folks the parents be
> Of such a girl as Sally ?"

Mr. Alonzo Sloper, did not, it is true, imitate Sally's father, make cabbage-nets, and cry them in the street. We regret to explain, he did nothing so creditable. For many a year he had been on the downhill side of life. The descent had been no steep one, rather an easy decline from what was half failure at the beginning. Still Leo inherited her aspirations from her father, who had lost one position after another from his habits of tippling, and now looked forward with irrepressible hopefulness to the triumph of certain cherished communistic ideas. "The present system of society is a failure," he was in the habit of saying, as he fastened his coat over his fat paunch by the one remaining button, "but we shall live to see a better state of things."

Poor Mrs. Sloper had no aspirations, unless perhaps an unvoiced longing sometimes thrilled her to be over and done with a world which had brought her only trouble. Her whole look suggested a half lethargy of despair and impotence. She was thin, colorless, and dispirited, not only in face but in figure. Since her early married life she had never been seen to wear any new article of apparel. It was a Walford conundrum where she could have found such a succession of faded and shabby gowns. Not, however, that she was often seen : she never lifted the latch of her own gate, and if a neighbor came into her house she fled precipitately and sat on the back steps until the visit was over. Fugitive glimpses of the hard-working woman hanging up clothes on the line, carrying buckets of water or armfuls of wood, were all that Walford people gained of Mrs. Sloper. She was nevertheless respected even more than pitied. Not even the narrowest of bigots was inclined to refuse her the Kingdom of Heaven, she had had such an unhappy time on earth.

"Mother is so old-fashioned," was Leo's phrase. There can be no doubt that the young lady herself was

of the very newest fashion.   She and Spencer had first
met at a picnic given by Mrs. Goodeve at Compounce
Pond.   She had duly followed up the acquaintance,
and soon the tumble-down house seemed to expect,
watch, and wait for Spencer.   He could not keep away
from it.   "Heavens and earth," he used to say to himself when he encountered red-nosed, fuddled old Sloper,
anxious to discuss socialism, of which he was a zealous
apostle, "what a father!"   And when in far reaches
and dim vistas he caught sight of Mrs. Sloper's be-
draggled calico, he would murmur, "What a mother!"

The poverty, the unthrift, the meagre possibilities of
such an existence revolted him, yet he was at first moved
to admiration at the buoyancy with which Leo escaped
from the inferiority of her position.   He hated and
scorned poverty : he knew too well what it was.   He saw
in her something of his own spirit which made her ready
to defy and overcome disadvantages.   Although Spencer was a fly with a lively presentiment of the dangers
lurking in the pretty parlors of spiders, he had presently found himself caught.   He insisted that there
should be no positive engagement, saying with most
unlover-like decision that he could not be in a position
to marry for five years at least.   Leo had bewitched him,
yet he was never wholly satisfied about the wisdom of
his decision.   After he had seen Miss Standish Leo's
imperfections, hitherto vague, became more sharply
defined.   A demon of discontent started to life in his
brain as soon as he was brought in contact with a girl
of such widely differing characteristics.

Amy had tried to correct Spencer's false ideas and
tendencies, little knowing what a twist she was giving
to what had hitherto been cherished ideals.   He had

once considered Leo miraculously pretty : she now appeared to him doll-like and inane ; he had fondly believed that she dressed well : it now became evident that she chose what women of taste have a quick instinct to avoid. He had credited her with a sprightly wit : how crude she now showed herself, how trivial, above all, how flippant!

When the half-gods go, the gods appear. Spencer knew very well with whom he was in love now. Had he been free, Amy must soon have awakened to the fact that she had thrown a fire-brand into dry fuel. As it was, he kept down every show of ardor with an iron resolution. He had triumph enough for the present in the conviction that Miss Standish appreciated him at his true value. Events must take their course. He knew how to wait. "I have resolved to run when I can, to walk when I cannot run, and to creep when I cannot walk," might have been said to be his motto. The civilized man, according to his creed, is civilized because he knows how to conceal the ferocity of his appetite. He toys with knives and forks instead of snatching at and tearing his food ; he keeps his hands from picking and stealing ; he pays compliments to a woman, listens admiringly to her most faulty logic, even goes on his knees to her, when his instinct would be to carry her off and impose a grate and veil on her. Spencer was incapable of understanding that a hungry man may be patient of restraints, that a man in love may be humble and disinterested, that a poor man does not long to get at his neighbor's strong box.

But laws and conventionalities do exist, and Spencer knew how to obey. He veiled the gleam of his bold bright eyes before Amy, although he intended to marry her as soon as he was safe from Leo Spencer. Somehow matters would adjust themselves. Everybody knows that until a man is actually married everything in his lot is conditional. When he had told Leo he should like to make her Mrs. Henry Spencer, he had not seen Miss Standish. He was enormously grateful to the latter for offering him new sensations and fresh capacities. Although he had seen her intimately, he had not yet mastered the whole secret, could not fully decide whether she were absolutely candid and in earnest or trying to impress him. He liked to believe that she was subtle and something of a coquette. She stirred his perceptions, and represented for him the acme of civilization. He was eager to attain new refinements.

It had piqued Spencer's vanity not a little that Miss Standish showed a clear preference for his society after Felix Goodeve came back to Walford. He had dreaded this young man's return. The two had grown up together, and had not a few memories in common, some of which humbled Spencer to the dust. The Goodeves had been his own and his mother's benefactors. Felix had been little at home for more than ten years. He had gone through a course at Harvard, and at the law school. Then, soon after he entered a law-office, his uncle had died, leaving Mrs. Goodeve a large property in Colorado and Montana, which for a time at least required vigilant supervision. Accordingly her youngest son had gone West.

Felix, as we have seen, did not like Spencer. Still, it was necessary that a representative of the Goodeve interests, himself a partner in the Rexford Manufacturing Company, should meet the superintendent every day, confer with him, go about the shops with him, look over the books, and, putting away any private feeling and prepossession, look at affairs calmly, and find out why Rexford's was making no money, had made no money for three years.

"You have plenty of orders," he said to Spencer. "You are working full time. Yet you don't make a cent."

"That 's just where business is," said Spencer.

"What is it? Competition?"

"Yes, it 's competition. There 's too much enterprise in the world now — too much supply, too little demand. High-priced materials and low-priced manufactures are the fashion, and there 's no profit."

"I don't understand it," said Felix.

"I do," said Spencer almost savagely. "We ought to be reducing wages, but we don't dare do it. There has been talk among the men of an increase instead. They believe that everything is going on swimmingly. They don't realize that since the enormous expense of new buildings and machinery we have never yet got fairly to work."

"I don't like the situation at all," said Felix. His voice was quick, his accent peremptory, his eye clear, and his whole countenance wore an expression of indignation.

"Who does?" returned Spencer drily. "The only consolation is that most manufacturers stand just where we stand, accepting the least possible margin of profit, content if they can keep good feeling among their men and good credit abroad. There has been over-production. All the markets are glutted, and we have got to wait for reaction."

"It is simply a case of standing out against a siege, I should say," said Felix.

"I have sometimes felt this last year as if it were more like a man in a marsh who, when he finds his footing sinking under him, jumps to the next bog, gaining a temporary safety, even though it, in its turn, will shortly sink under him."

"What can help us?" asked Felix.

"Nothing but time and opportunity."

"Not money?"

Spencer shook his head. "Such matters are outside of my jurisdiction," he said. "As it is, I often feel that I am assuming powers not my own. Mr. Rexford has been terribly preoccupied with his private griefs."

"There is something I have a little curiosity about," said Felix. He had folded his arms, and leaning on the table, bent a square penetrating glance upon Spencer. "I understand the terms of Madam Van Polanen's will," he said deliberately. "Next October, unless the child has been found meantime, which begins to seem improbable, her money all goes to build a hospital. Will the loss touch Rexford's?"

Spencer's eyes wavered a moment, then fell. "Tell me everything you know about it," said Felix. "It will be better. We Goodeves have got a heavy stake in this concern."

"I know you have," Spencer replied smoothly. "As far as I know Madam Van Polanen sold out when the new company was formed. I am sure her name is not on the books. I don't see how her estate can be mixed up with the affairs of the company."

This evasive answer carried no weight, still it gave Felix relief. His intercourse with Spencer had cleared his mind of many of his former impressions; the superintendent had seemed candid, acute, with no reticence,

or equivocations on doubtful points.   Any suspense
would be ended in a few months, and it was as well to
accept patiently the trying conditions.   Since action
must be postponed, it was best to suspend decisive
conviction, and he did not trouble even his mother with
his perplexities.   In old days the Rexford Manufacturing Company had been managed very differently, and
Felix confessed to himself that possibly what at present
seemed lacking were merely the solemnities of self-importance of the old-fashioned president and board of
managers, the hearings, auditings, and resolutions at
the monthly meetings, all of which had been conducted
with a ponderous gravity impressive to his youthful
mind.   Mr. Goodeve and Mr. Lowry, the two survivors
of the old state of things, never entered the works nowadays.   At present it was a one-man power.

"Mr. Lowry says he always has a fresh touch of
rheumatism if he comes into the place, and I suppose
your father gets more amusement out of his history
than he does out of the business," Roger Rexford said
to Felix when the latter alluded to these changes.

"I don't know about amusement," said Felix.   "He
is in the clutches of his Idea, and I fear his Idea is too
much for him.   It swells out like the genie released
from the bottle.   He wants to get it compressed into
three volumes, but let him condense, abridge, cut down,
and erase, he has still enough for seven.   Who, he asks
plaintively, is likely to buy a history of the Connecticut Colony in seven volumes?"

"I wanted to get him to come here one day each
week," said Roger.   "But he said the noise of the
machinery made his head ache.   Then he tried to look
in the first Monday in each month, but even that was
too much of an effort."

"The Goodeves don't like practical matters. My Uncle John was telling me what a tax business is," said Felix. "He feels that he is driven to death. An old friend came and asked him to become a director in an insurance company. 'But I know nothing about the duties or the methods of an insurance company,' said Uncle John. 'That is exactly what we want,' replied his friend ; 'you have no prepossessions, no prejudices. We do not like innovations and new ideas. We desire to go on in the old way.' 'But I know nothing about the old way,' said my uncle. 'It is very simple. We have a business-meeting once a month.' 'I hate business-meetings,' said Uncle John ; 'they bore me to death. I gave up my place on two boards because every month I had to sit three hours at business-meetings, and I could not stand it.' 'But then,' said the other, 'our business-meetings only last ten or fifteen minutes. The last one was something out of the common and ran to twenty, but that shall not happen again.' 'Do you mean to say,' said my uncle, 'that you take all the pains to attend a meeting once a month which is over in a quarter of an hour?' 'Oh, afterwards we dine.' 'Oh, the directors dine together!' 'Yes, we dine, and that is, in point of fact, the chief object of our meetings.' 'I suppose, then,' put in Uncle John, 'that all the business is performed by committees. I detest committees. They always put me on committees and I have to do all the work.' 'We have only one committee,' said the man, 'and we call that the committee on furnishing.' 'A committee on furnishing,' said Uncle John, — 'furnishing what?' 'They furnish the wines.' 'Oh,' said Uncle John, 'they furnish the wines!'"

"'That is your Uncle John Goodeve in Philadelphia. He became a director, no doubt."

"Yes, but he complains of the dinners, they are so long. He says it takes him two days to get over one of them."

"I should like to change places with him for a year," said Roger gloomily, without a glint of answering humor.

Felix spent half his time at the works. Roger gave him a little office next his own, and the two men, thrown together in this way, became, if not intimate, used to each other. Felix had to a certain degree known Roger all his life, and was not slow to detect the absence of just the attributes he had believed to be characteristic of him, that is, a habit of quick decision, boldness in conceiving plans, and steady persistence in executing them. The apathy and inaptitude for affairs which Roger now displayed could easily be ascribed to the uncertainty, grief, and apprehension which the loss of the child had brought upon him. He evidently leaned on Spencer, and spared himself trouble in all ways. The superintendent, Felix was ready to admit, proved himself acute and zealous, but there was a certain commonness of mind and tone about him, a want of dignity in his conduct of affairs, an insensibility to the higher aspects and finer responsibilities of business, which, Felix believed, must lower the standing of the company.

"I wish, Mr. Rexford," Felix said to him one day, "that you would take your wife and go to Europe for six months."

Roger turned his chair round and faced Felix.

"What for?" he asked. "Not but that it is the advice everybody gives me."

"You both require a complete change."

"No doubt of that," said Roger. His face and tone expressed a peculiar bitterness. "How could I get away?"

"Spencer is efficient, and I will do what I can."

"You don't understand," said Roger. "We have to eat, drink, sleep, read the newspapers, and talk of indifferent matters, but we are living through a crisis not ended yet. Sometimes Evelyn brightens up in the evening and makes me almost merry. I go to bed in tolerable spirits and to sleep, then waking up suddenly I find that my wife has gone from my side. I follow her; I know only too well where she is, — she is crouching among Bessy's things, crying as if her heart would break, and murmuring, 'Oh, my lamb, my little tender white lamb, my angel, she is alone, only four years old and alone somewhere, — no father, no mother.'" He broke off almost more at the sight of Felix's emotion than his own. "Don't, don't!" he said. "I ought not to have disclosed the skeleton in my house, but there it is."

"It is killing your wife."

"Don't I see that?" said Roger. "That she is losing her sight is at least no fiction imposed by my dread."

"A change will do her good."

Roger had risen and gone to the open window, and now sat down on the ledge.

"The battle is here," he said. "Here and here only it has got to be fought out. I begin to feel that we are beaten. When all is lost, then we can crawl away somewhere out of sight."

"You have stopped advertising a reward, I see."

" Yes, the detectives advised it."

" They are still at work ? "

" At work, yes ; I have news every day of some sort. I lie awake half the night waiting for the morning to come, eager to have my breakfast, reach my office, and find my letters. Who knows what they may contain? Every time a telegram comes in fate seems to be knocking at the door. When the chances of the morning are passed I look forward to the evening mail. Then I breathe only in the thought that night will be over and daylight break."

Felix shrewdly guessed that some carking financial anxieties lent a sting to Roger Rexford's suspense. No plummet could reach the bottom of such a sea of trouble. Felix did not again try to sound it. He endeavored instead to meet the emergency by showing a faith, a cordial optimism, a fixed belief in some better state of things, and here he found himself working shoulder to shoulder with Spencer, who was doing his best to sustain Roger and keep his hope alive that some news of the little girl would shortly come.

Felix found his prejudices against the superintendent dropping one by one. It was evident that the latter kept himself in touch with whatever was moving the men, and used his influence wisely. One day he overheard this conversation between Spencer and O'Noole, the foreman in the foundry.

" I suppose," said Spencer, " you would n't mind my dropping in."

" Any man 's free to come," returned O'Noole, " but it 's a workingmen's club, — not a sort of gilt-edge workingmen's club, but the rale article."

" I am a workingman myself," said Spencer, " and

by no means a gilt-edged specimen. I 've been below the poorest of you, and if I have risen it is because I have been willing to work harder than any of you. I 'll go to-night and see what you are talking about."

"To-night will be a foine time," said O'Noole. "Beresky is going to spake."

Spencer laughed good-naturedly. "I thought you said you were all workingmen. Beresky is not a workingman. He is a talking-man. I don't believe he has earned a week's wages in twenty years."

"He's above that sort of thing," said O'Noole. "He's got the gift."

"The gift of the gab," said Spencer. O'Noole passed on, and he turned to Felix. "Don't you want to hear a fiery socialist?" he asked. "I like to know how the pulse of the world beats."

Felix assented, and at eight o'clock that evening found himself at Chester's Hall. It was a warm summer night, and it might have seemed as if any sort of idleness out-of-doors would have been preferable to being pent up in the unfragrant room with its flaring lights and stifling atmosphere. Some thirty men had gathered, and were sitting about on the benches in costumes and attitudes suggesting a desire for all the comfort attainable under such circumstances. There were O'Noole, Harley, Davidson, Cook, Macdonald, and MacBean, six of the very best men from Rexford's. There were also O'Fee, Chattus, and Dufour, from Flaxman's, with other men strangers to Felix. He observed that Spencer was in the front row within a few feet of the speaker, and close beside him sat Mr. Alonzo Sloper. This was a somewhat unusual conjunction, since Spencer disliked the father of Miss Leo in a way almost out of proportion to his offenses. Perhaps Mr. Sloper had of late missed the society of his son-in-law elect, and now was making up for his deprivation by establishing himself at Spencer's elbow. In spite of Mr. Sloper's heavy crimson cheeks, his purple nose and his dull, bleared eyes, he evinced a peculiar elation at being in such good company. Disregarding the warmth of the evening, he had buttoned his coat, and while he sat listening to the speaker assumed a critical and judicial air, holding his head a little on one side and seeming to weigh every word.

Beresky, the orator, was mounted on the platform, and as Felix entered had advanced to the extreme edge and with shrill vehemence seemed to be directing an indictment against Spencer himself.

"It is a zystem of ex-teur-mi-na-tion against the poor man," he was saying. "The reech man zays, 'I will pind him hand and foot, — I will make him a zlave. He zall have no land, the land pelongs to me.' But no matter. If the poor man had land he would have no time to gultivate it. The poor man has no time for anyting exzept to make the reech man more reech and more powerful. The poor man moost work or he moost starve. He cannot peg, the laws are against pegging. He moost lif without a ped to lie town upon. If he goes to zleep in the streets or in the fields unter the overarching tome of heafen, he is arrested as a tramp. What can the poor wretch do? Noting exzept to zay to the reech man, 'I haf strength, I haf intelligence, I haf ampition: tak all these and gif me in return a morzel of pread to eat and a place to zleep.'"

Beresky was a small man, with masses of fine dark hair, matted, tangled, and unkempt, shaggy eyebrows and whiskers. His eyes were small, deep-set, and of startling brilliancy. He spoke with a strong foreign accent, which served rather to give each utterance clearness and deliberation than to make his meaning indistinct. He frequently gesticulated, and seemed at times to be stirring up the fount of his own passion.

" And in offering his work," he went on, " he has to gome into gompetition with other men as poor, as unhappy as himzelf. The reech man zays, ' I moost have workmen at the lowest price.' The man with a wife and chiltren has too many mouths to zupport. ' I can't haf you,' zays the reech man. The next one has only a wife. ' One too many,' teclares the reech man, and so he takes the third, who is childless, who has no home, no hope of private joys. What are those who are turned off to do ? If they peg, they are arrested ; if they steal, they are put in prison ; if they murter, they are hanged."

As if conscious of having staggered his audience, Beresky paused, still keeping his eyes on the superintendent from Rexford's.

" Is the subject open for debate ? " asked Spencer.

"Any man is free to speak," said O'Noole. " That's a rule of the club,— if a man jaws at us, we can jaw back again."

" I should like to put one question to the speaker," said Spencer. " He does not make it clear to me whether he is talking about some system of things in Europe or in Walford."

" I am talking apout zoziety eferywhere," said Beresky. " There is no more real freedom for the poor man in America than in Europe. The reech ride in their carriages and the poor starve."

" I should like to have Mr. Beresky made aware that
he is addressing land-owners," said Spencer. " Here
are O'Noole and O'Fee, each of them with a neat house
and an acre or more of ground. Both have gardens,
where they find time to raise the best vegetables in
Walford. There is Harley, also a land-owner, and
MacBean — "

Mr. Sloper had risen to his feet, and turning to
Spencer, said in a husky voice with a raised forefinger :

" But the poor land-owner has taxes to pay. He
helps the rich man to pay his taxes." At this point his
forefinger happened to come in contact with his neighbor's shoulder, at which, with a look of haughty disgust,
Spencer moved to the extreme end of the bench. Mr.
Sloper, somewhat disconcerted, looked over at O'Noole
with a fatuous smile and inquired, "What was I saying ? "

" You were talking about the disadvantages of workingmen, sure," said O'Noole. This pregnant hint at
once loosed the floodgates of Mr. Sloper's eloquence.

" It is an ex-tra-or-di-nary spectacle," he ·began,
" how a man may spend his whole life in hard work
and still, as society is now constituted, make no pro-
vision for his family. And why ? It is because it is in
the interest of the capitalist that the poor man shall
never get rich. Everybody else gets rich except the
poor man. The grocer, he lays up a fortune, — he
trades on our necessities. The tailor, because we feel
the cold and cannot make spectacles of ourselves, he
gets rich. If a hail-storm comes and breaks our window the glazier get rich. If our houses burn down
the carpenters and masons get rich. The doctors get
rich because we are sick. Lawyers get rich because
we have lawsuits. Even ministers of the gospel — "

At this point the speaker's wavering glance encountered that of Mr. Beresky, who regarded his rival with a smile of such ferocity that Mr. Sloper's mind again wandered, and he lost the thread of his discourse. Oblivious of Spencer's rebuff he moved towards him, and nudging him with the affectionate intimacy warranted by their close relations, he said in a voice intended to be inaudible, " What was I saying? I forget what I was saying."

Spencer seemed neither to hear nor to see the fuddled speaker, whose irrepressibly hopeful gaze transferred itself to some one in the next row, who happened to be Felix Goodeve.

" I think, Mr. Sloper," said Felix, " you were remarking you would now bring your remarks to a close and allow the lecturer to proceed."

" That was it," said Mr. Sloper magnanimously and grandiloquently, " I will now bring my remarks to a close and allow the orator of the evening to continue his discourse."

Beresky took instant advantage of his opportunity. He attacked commerce and trade, which robbed society at every point, buying up raw material, governing both production and consumption by raising and lowering prices, taking away the poor man's opportunity of obtaining the least answers to his needs until the price of manufacture, waste, carriage, and handling are added to the original cost.

" He is repeating my very words," cried Mr. Sloper, beaming.

Beresky glared at the interruption, and went on to say that the worth of an article no longer consists in its own intrinsic value, nor in its value to the consumer, but is determined by the requirements of the manufacturer and trader, who have often thrown cargoes of grain and fruit into the sea rather than have the market glutted and the poor man afforded an opportunity to buy at a price within his reach. Then, too, while the poor man is compelled to pay cash, manufacturers and traders carry on their affairs not on their capital, but by means of bills and credit to any extent. Thus power is put into the rich man's hands, wholly incommensurable with his actual capital, to protect himself by controlling markets and fixing prices. All this comes out of the pocket of the humble consumer.

Beresky, believing that he was at last in his saddle with too firm a seat to be ousted, was flinging out both hands with a gesture preparatory to a higher flight of eloquence, when a fresh interruption came. The night was warm, and the audience was growing restless of these glittering generalities.

"I say," said Mr. O'Noole, looking up at the speaker in a friendly way, "what we want to know is how to cure these abuses."

"I will tell you how I gured them," answered Beresky with his fierce dry smile. "Zeventeen years ago I walked out of a cursed fountry where I had peen trotten unter foot, and haf not called any prutal capitalist my master since."

"But then you've got money to live on," suggested MacBean.

"I haf not a tollar in the world laid up," shrieked Beresky. "The first time I went on a strike was twenty years ago. There was a reduction of wages. It came at a time when my young wife was in ped with her zecond child. She lay shifering, with not plankets enough

to keep her warm, no good food to nourish her, no
tender nursing. It was a time, if efer, when she needed
all the money I could earn for her. Yet I felt it was
my duty to go out, and I deed go out. We stayed out
for seex monts, and we fought like tigers inch by inch
for terms, and we got them."

"What became of your wife?" demanded little
O'Fee.

"She deed all she could. She turned her face to the
wall and died. Her baby died first."

"You let her die," said Felix Goodeve with indignation. "I would have worked for ten cents a day, if I
could have got no more. I'd have begged. I'd
have" —

"She died for want of proper care and food," said
Beresky, with tragic emphasis. "Was it my fault?
There are times when the interests of humanity are
paramount to the interests of the intivitual. He moost
do his duty and leaf the gonsequences to God. A
workingman must tink not only of himself but of his
prothers. An injury to one is an injury to all. Because some of you here in Walford are gomfortable and
happy, you must not forget that there are men who love
gomfort and happiness as dearly as you can love them,
who have no gomfort and no happiness, only pitter,
purning wrongs which they look to you to avenge."

Spencer had begun to show signs of being roused.

"Wait a moment," said he, jumping up. "I want
to ask O'Noole and MacBean a question. They are
prosperous; they have houses, wives, children, and the
respect of all good citizens in Walford; they have, I
believe with all my heart and soul, no reason for discontent against their employers. Do they consider

that they are bound to be in sympathy with fanatical anarchists in other parts of the world?"

"We are all brothers, 'sure, we workingmen," said O'Noole.

"An injury to one is an injury to all," said Michael MacCann. "The workingmen is one body, what you feel in one extremity you suffer 'in the — the — the other extremity."

"Do you mean," said Spencer dryly, "that if a man in Chicago has no dinner you go hungry?"

O'Noole rubbed his forehead, feeling a trifle puzzled.

"That's a confounding of things," observed Mac-Bean.

"A man has his duty to do," said Spencer, "and he has to answer before earthly tribunals and before the bar of heaven for not doing his duty, not my duty, not your duty, but his own individual duty. No man on earth can perform the duty of another man. Each makes his own fate here, and earns his own reward and own punishment hereafter."

Spencer was becoming excited. It had been evident that Beresky's arguments had impressed some of the men from Rexford's, and a quick current of irritation ran through the superintendent's nerves.

"I tell you," he proceeded, "what each of you have to do is to lead a good, honest life, have a wife and children to love, and try faithfully to make some little corner of God's earth a nest of peace for those who depend on you. Having done so much you are above the world. No man can do more, be he king, emperor, or capitalist."

"The Saviour of men died for the world," put in Beresky. "He might easily have gontinued to live on gomfortably with enough to eat and trink. But *He chose to die* instead, and who shall zay we haf not peen petter for his martyrdom?"

Spencer could hardly control himself.

"He compares himself to the Saviour of men," he cried. "He let his wife and her baby die for lack of the necessities he should have provided. What became of your eldest child?" he asked, sharply turning on Beresky.

"She was zent to the workhouse. I know not whether she is alife or tead," replied Beresky, who had his pleasure in these signs of Spencer's perturbation.

"You have heard Mr. Beresky's story, my friends," said Spencer; "now I want you to listen to mine. He compares himself to the Saviour, but go into the heart of the matter and you will see that it was his wife who paid the forfeit, not Beresky. 'I want to tell you about myself. You probably know, all of you, that my father was a young man of good family in Hartford, who came here and set up a law practice. He died four years after marrying my mother, who was a poor girl without home or friends. My father died — I might better say, he drank himself to death. I don't remember him. My first recollections are of crying when my mother went out to sew. She was apt to take my sister Jenny with her, and I dreaded to be left alone. But I soon came to understand that we were dependent upon my mother's daily absence, that we were poor, and that she earned every crust I ate. Little Jenny had always been sickly, and as I got older my mother used to put her under my charge. I felt very proud of having the little sister to take care of. She faded away before my eyes, but I knew not what the change meant,

and used to enjoy the thought that she was so weak
I must give her sips of milk every half hour by the
clock.   I was eight years old when she died.   After I
was alone with my mother, it became more clear to me
how miserable it all was, how hard she had to work,
how tired she felt, what a longing for rest.   One day
Mrs. Goodeve said to me, 'Henry, you're getting to
be a big boy.   You will soon be able to help your
mother.'   After that, I used to put it in my prayers,
'Oh, God, let me grow up and earn money for mother."
I began earning money when I was ten years old; by
the time I was twelve I had a place at Rexford's, and
when I was thirteen we were well enough off for my
mother to stay at home, henceforth, as long as she lived;
and she stayed at home, and did as little or as much as
she chose.   It is the only pride I have, it is the best
joy I have ever had or shall have, that for four years
before my mother's death I earned every dollar for her
support."

Spencer had been carried to that elevation of soul
where his usual objects in life dwindled, and ordinary
considerations of reserve and almost of shame for his
beginnings vanished.   It was for him almost a sublime
moment, one of those rare chances in life when feeling rises to its highest flood marks.   The pity is that
reaction from a sublime moment is apt to offer embarrassments.

He had carried his audience, except possibly Beresky,
along with him.   Especially he had moved Mr. Sloper,
all whose paternal instincts were awakened.   The tears
were running down his heavy purple cheeks.   Spencer
was his dear Leo's betrothed husband.   The young
man had spoken nobly.   The story he had related was

most pathetic. A young man who worked so well for his mother ought to be encouraged to go on and work for his wife's father. Such thoughts, oozing out of Mr. Sloper's rich fount of sentiment and emotion, were a call to action. He pulled himself up on his feet, and, fastening his moist hand on Spencer's shoulder said in a voice broken with agitation : —

"Gentlemen, this is my son. Gentlemen, my own son ; " and he bowed right and left.

"Let go my shoulder!" said Spencer with intense exasperation. "Confound you, what do you mean by such a statement?"

Mr. Sloper gazed at him at first as if incredulous that any rebuff could be intended, then, his features broadening into a smile, — "No disrespect intended to your mother, none whatever, my dear boy," he said in his ponderous voice. "All I meant to intimate, gentlemen, is that Mr. Spencer is engaged to marry my daughter, Leonora. A noble girl, if I may say it, the most beautiful girl in Walford, and well worthy of him. I am proud of my son, gentlemen, I am proud of my daughter, I am proud of them both. Pardon the pride of a fond old man."

He looked at Spencer for some confirmatory glance of affection, but meeting none gave him a half pathetic and half haughty bow, nodded to the grinning groups about, and made his way along the aisle and out the door.

It was the signal for the breaking up of the club. Felix, turning to Spencer, asked him if he were going home, and the two went down the hall together. Every phrase of his speech was echoing through Spencer's mind, rousing sensations of rankling shame ; he was not at all satisfied that he had not made a complete fool of himself. He could not trust himself to think of Sloper at all. He was in a fury with him and with Leo, and was ready enough to believe that it was a conspiracy to mortify him, or perhaps rather to fasten chains on him he could never break. As they left the building he gave a tentative glance at Felix, and their eyes met. Felix laughed. He had been not a little moved by Spencer's words, but when he thought of Mr. Sloper's tears he laughed.

"You seem to be amused," said Spencer tartly.

"One might as well be amused by that maudlin ass," said Felix. "His nonsense served its purpose, however, and broke up the meeting in good-humor. I don't like that tricky anarchist. I was glad you circumvented him and had the last word."

"They are all asses," said Spencer, "insensible to reason and a weak prey to sophistical arguments. It seems to them all a pleasure to destroy what others have given their lives to build up. They do not recognize the laws on which their own existence depends, but invoke forces which bring about confusion and chaos. D—— them all, I say. There's not one among them who would stand true to us if we suggested a reduction of wages."

They had walked along the street together, and at this point their roads diverged. "Good-night," said Spencer, hurrying off.

"Wait a minute," said Felix. He put out his hand. "I am glad I was there," he said, with peculiar sweetness. "We were boys together, Harry. I'm glad to have you turning out so well. You do credit to Walford. I shall tell my mother what you said to-night.

I look up to a man who, taken unawares, and speaking out of his heart, rings true, — now you *rang true.*"

Spencer's cheeks stung with the blush which came in the darkness. He knew now that Felix remembered something he had hoped forgotten. He wrung the proffered hand, gasped his thanks, then strode off into the encompassing gloom.

XI

THE KEY-NOTE IS STRUCK.

To applaud a man for showing noble instincts is perhaps to show that he has surpassed our belief in him. Hence, when Felix Goodeve observed that for some days after the incident at the workingmen's club Spencer's manner was touched with acerbity, he was ready to confess that the superintendent might well be indignant at having hitherto been rated below his deserts. It had been not one but many recollections of their boyhood which had tinged all Felix's impressions of Spencer; but this was the one most deeply bitten into his memory : —

One rainy Saturday, when both lads were about thirteen, Felix had gone over to the works, and after strolling through the various departments, talking with the operatives and even trying his hand at the machinery, he had passed into the counting-room to watch George Lowry, who was getting ready to pay the men their week's wages. Henry Spencer was coming and going from the office with slips of paper which required to be certified, and while he waited he and Felix played about, talked, and discussed the amount probably contained in the rolls of money. By some accident, as a fresh bag was opened a heap of loose coin was suddenly scattered over counter and floor. Felix scrambled to help pick up the pieces and replace them before

Lowry. It was all accomplished in the twinkling of an eye. Henry Spencer had been called away the very moment the coins fell, but Felix had happened to see that two silver dollars had rolled exactly under the boy's hand, so that without a change of muscles his fingers had closed upon them. Felix experienced a sensation of blank horror, and stood turning hot and cold, wondering if he ought to speak or to be silent. More than once he had taken upon himself the blame for some merely boyish prank of Spencer's, but this touched the very foundations of things. George Lowry, fastening with the vulpine instinct of an expert teller upon the deficit, eyed Felix and saw the trouble on his face.

"You little rascal!" said he. "Give me those two dollars you pocketed."

Felix stood irresolute. His heart swelled. It was a terrible moment. Then he remembered he had two silver dollars in his pocket. It was his birthday, and his mother had given them to him. He drew them out and flung them down with a quivering lip.

"Of course I knew it was a joke," said George. "But if it had been Henry Spencer, it might have been a pretty dangerous joke for him. Never play tricks where money is concerned, Felix. The way a man treats money touches his whole character."

"I didn't want your money," said Felix, indignantly.

"I know very well your father's son is not in need of money," said George. "But remember what I tell you: never joke about money; it's dangerous." ·

Henry Spencer had returned while this dialogue was going on, but apparently paid no attention to it. Afterwards when the two encountered face to face Felix eyed the other with a scorn which told even on Spencer's callous nerves. The lads never again played together. Felix never alluded to what had happened. Now, after hearing Spencer's story of the yoke he had borne in his youth, he was ready to forgive the crime, if it were a crime and no mere boyish peccadillo, the result of a momentary instinct repented afterwards and possibly atoned for.

Like all people of vivid imagination, Felix was now inclined to make all possible reparation; indeed, to put Spencer on a pedestal. Unluckily, Spencer himself was at some trouble to dispel illusions.

One day when Roger Rexford was absent Felix was sitting in his office writing, when Spencer entered and closed the door behind him.

"Mr. Goodeve," he said without preamble, "I wish to put a question, which you may answer or not, as you think best."

Felix looked up in some surprise at the curt tone.

"Ask your question," he replied, with a quizzical movement of his eyebrows, "then I can tell better about the danger of committing myself."

"You may consider it an intrusion on your personal liberty," Spencer pursued, "for me to inquire into your proceedings; you may say that you are the best judge of what is fair and honorable; you may" —

"Is it as bad as that?" said Felix, throwing himself back in his chair and clutching at his hair with a look of comic bewilderment.

"I don't care to be laughed at," returned Spencer in a quick, irritated way. "There has been too much of that already."

"I'm serious. I'm a yawning grave," said Felix.

"Come, put in your grievance, and let's bury it for good and all."

"I wish to inquire," said Spencer, the blood rushing to his face, "whether you told Miss Standish what happened the other night."   •

"I don't understand what you allude to," said Felix. "What happened?"

"You know very well what happened," said Spencer, as if stung. "You were laughing about it as we came out of the club together."

"Oh, that tipsy old loafer!" exclaimed Felix, staring at Spencer. After a moment's silence he added, "Do you mean to ask me if I told Miss Standish about Sloper's interrupting the meeting?" Spencer's eyes met his a moment, then shifted their direction. It was as quick a glance as well might be. It lasted no longer than a flash of lightning, but it illuminated everything as a flash of lightning can. "Possibly you allude to his announcement of your engagement to his daughter," Felix went on, with an ironical glance.

"I see," said Spencer, "that you have told her all about it. I saw it in her face. I will say frankly, Mr. Felix Goodeve, that I don't call it fair." His voice was low, but his face had grown white to the lips and his eyes burned.

Felix looked back at him with his head on one side and the same half smile.

"Is it true, then?" he inquired blandly. "Are you engaged to Miss Sloper? Is it my duty to congratulate you?"

"No!" thundered Spencer as if in a terrible rage, and turning on his heel he strode out of the office, banging the door behind him.

It was Felix's nature to be contemptuous of accusa‧tion. To have told anything regarding any man alive which could put him in a false light would have been an abhorrent action to him. Certainly Miss Standish was the last person to whom he would have breathed a syllable damaging to Spencer. It had not seemed worth while to resent the imputation put upon himself. Spencer evidently had made a bad tangle of his love-affairs. It was clear he was engaged, or had been engaged, to poor little Leo. How about Miss Standish? It had always seemed incredible to Felix that a girl of that beauty, that elegance, that fire, should care for Spencer. But she talked with him, listened to him, all with a glow apparently born of sympathetic companionship. Evidently she was not a girl to care for the inferences outsiders might draw as to such an intimacy. If she thought of such considerations at all, she would pique herself on despising them. Certainly, so far as appearances went, she was offering Spencer every sort of encouragement. The possible preference of such a charming woman might easily make any man totter in his allegiance to a mere Leo Sloper. No doubt it was a trying situation, and it was not worth while to condemn Spencer until one knew the whole story. Felix smiled to himself, recollecting the burst of impotent rage just exhibited. Reflecting on what had happened, he now blamed himself for not having made it clear that Miss Standish probably knew nothing of what had taken place. It would be a pity if that young lady were to be brought to task for offenses she had never committed.

He jumped up, opened the door, and called, — "By the way, Spencer."

Spencer, however, was not to be seen ; and after in-
quiring where he was likely to be found, Felix walked
through the outside office into the packing-room, and
thence, crossing a little bridge, entered one of the
upper workshops, where he found the superintendent
discussing some matter with MacBean. He turned as
Felix approached, and looked at him inquiringly.

"I simply wished to say, Spencer," said Felix,
"that I ought not to have let you carry away a wrong
impression. I have never spoken of the incident you
alluded to."

Spencer had dropped his glance to the floor. He
was ashamed of his irritation and sore at heart, and felt
at a loss what to say.

"You understand me?" Felix proceeded.

Spencer for an instant looked up. "All right," he
said curtly. "Thank you."

Felix walked on, and descending the stairs, turned
into the main building, encountering the whirr, roar, and
tick-tack of ceaseless belts, pulleys, wheels, hammers,
and saws. He felt no disposition to go back to his
desk. He had experienced a sudden disenchantment,
which he could hardly have defined. He wanted to
worry the thing off. The machinery seemed to make
him feel giddy. He passed on into the foundry, where
the moulds were ready for the casting, and men were
testing the melted iron, which sent forth myriads of
fiery sparks as they poured it out. He stood for a few
moments watching the great crane travel up and down
with its huge ladle, which took up the molten mass and
carried it the length of the place. Then, thinking
to himself he might as well get outside this thrice-
heated furnace, he issued by a little back door at the

very rear of the works, and came into an ugly quadrangle heaped with slag, broken bits of machinery, and
grindstones. A clear intention now began to take the
place of his listless wanderings up and down. He
crossed the quadrangle, skirted a long row of low out-
buildings, and then, passing round the further end,
found himself on a bank just above a meadow which
sloped to the banks of the little river. He jumped the
fence, struck the footpath and followed it. Every inch
of this region was familiar. Memories buzzed about
him like bees. He looked across the middle distance
to the " rye lot," alive to-day with the activities of the
summer harvesting; to the hills beyond, from behind
which floated up the same soft white clouds he had
pondered over as a boy, wondering about their whence
and whither : why sometimes they came out of the west
like a fleet of white swans floating joyously until they
vanished in the eastern horizon, then again changing
into a black and lowering phalanx, holding thunders
and lightnings in their depths. All the tract beyond the
river had been in old days mysterious, romantic, weird ;
the region of possible wild happenings. There was
"Wolf Hill," a name to shudder at. As a youngster he
had had a passion for going to the " Spring lot," where
a source bubbled out of white sands on the hillside in
a basin set in a margin of fine grass, the earliest to disclose the beautiful secret that spring was at hand. Here
he used to find the first blossoms of the liverwort. He
could not have told why of all flowers he loved the
liverwort best. The secret of our tenderness sometimes
lies in the love we give things, and not in what they
give us. But he could remember his deep sense of the
ethereal sweetness of the flower, of how he had more

than once thrown himself down on the ground and kissed the pure petals while his heart beat. There had been a clump of white violets which he had cherished the secret of. Year after year, he had stolen to the corner of the snake fence where they grew, and when he saw that the lovely shy creatures were still there, had smiled and nodded like a miser at his hoarded gold.

Why did he remember these things now when he was a big overgrown fellow, with duties to perform in the world? It was because he felt a little sore, inclined to ramp and fret and fume, and say that he was a fool never to be quiet and sensible like other men, but to put the whole of his heart into things which in return only tormented him. Spencer's apparent appropriation of Miss Standish had perhaps disgusted and disheartened him. Felix was not in general in the habit of complaining of life. He knew that men hate and love beyond reason, and go to strange lengths to gratify their feelings. He had often reflected upon this tendency of humanity. But yet it was a curious fact that he himself should have come home to Walford to be smitten on the instant by a blind attachment, which was all on his own side with no possibility of return. In a general way a one-sided passion might not have been altogether unheroic. There is something grand, something touching, in disinterestedly loving a woman, giving all and asking nothing in return. But to be in love with a girl who liked, who even tolerated Spencer was a nuisance. He wished at the moment he had never seen Amy Standish, and determined to put her out of his head.

He paused on the brink of the Quinnipiac as he reached it, with the old boyish thirst to plunge into its cool depths. It was just here he had learned to swim.

In those days the river had seemed to him very wide and very deep; there had been one pool of incredible depth, where the water, even in summer, came almost up to his shoulders. The Quinnipiac was the Indian name and meant "winding stream," and indeed it had a way of turning so as never to let you see where it was going, vanishing round a corner, as it were, and beckoning you. Felix obeyed its call and followed. All was mute as a dream except for the soft eddying of the current. A great elm-tree on the bank waved luxuriantly over the shining water, each branch and twig and leaf looking down at its own glorified reflection. Here and there were lush growths of bulrushes, cat-tails, and iris. In one spot the bed of the stream widened, and broad leaves of water-lilies floated with their closed buds pressing upwards, which the first rays of to-morrow's sun would open into white flowers with golden centres and a breath like honey. He liked the soft tinkle of the river, the subdued insect hum, the general rustle and murmur. He did not wish to turn away from it, but he had reached Westbury Turnpike bridge which spanned the water, and was obliged to clamber up and cross the road before he could again strike the bank on the other side where the stream meandered through the Van Polanen place, now vacant except for Birdsey the gardener.

Felix had enough of the boy about him to choose the hardest way of getting over the obstacle. He found a crevice in the stone pier where he could plant one foot, then caught hold of the corbels, swung himself towards the centre of the arch, put his foot on the trestlework, and was about to make a flying leap over the parapet when an unexpected vision startled him.

The very face he had been trying to dismiss from his memory suddenly peered at him over the railing. He almost lost his balance.

"Oh, Mr. Goodeve!" said Amy Standish. She contrived to catch his hand, and leaning down flung her arm round his neck, and held him with all her strength until he could reëstablish his footing and vault over the balustrade.

He did not speak at first, but his cheeks glowed and his eyes burned as he looked at her.

"I startled you as you were making a flying leap," said Amy, with the smile which as we have said possessed not a little witchery. "Even professional acrobats sometimes come to grief."

"I am out of practice, to say nothing of being a heavier weight than I used to be," replied Felix. "I am very grateful for your helping hand."

"I am very proud if I actually did help you," said Amy.

Words did not come to him easily; she observed with surprise a trembling of his lip. He had been thinking with a sort of bitterness of her dislike to him, and his mind had run on a dozen instances when she had been at pains to show her preference for Spencer. Then suddenly he had had that wonderful face with its splendid startled eyes almost pressed to his; her warm, close clasp had sustained him resolutely. His whole being was suffused by a perception of the sweetness of the chance which had befallen him. And here she was still, close beside him, and for a wonder smiling. It was enough simply to look at her. She was dressed in sheer white, with a broad-brimmed hat, round which a mass of transparent white gauze was wound.

"You know," she said to him almost in a whisper, "this was the place where Bessy was seen last. I come here sometimes to think about it all."

"She was there, just where you are standing," said Felix.

"Yes, just here, throwing stones through this fretwork. Did you ever see the child, Mr. Goodeve?"

"When she was six months old." He took off his hat and looked up. "Oh, God, let me see her again!" he said suddenly and startlingly. It struck Amy that she had never before heard a passionate prayer. "I wish I had been here at the time," he went on. "Of course, it is mere presumption on my part, but I have always felt that something must have been left undone. How is Mrs. Rexford?"

"She droops. This warm weather is trying to her."

"If she were my wife, do you know what I would do?" said Felix. "I would have a yacht, and we would sail away into the north."

"She could not be on deck; she could not bear the light," said Amy practically.

"All day long, then, she should lie in her berth and sleep, or if she were awake I would read and talk to her. Towards sunset I would carry her on deck, it is so beautiful on the water then. She should have a luxurious chair, and lie stretched out at her ease with pillows, wraps, and rugs, not to feel a breath of chill. She could eat in that air. I would provide all sorts of nourishing things. I am sure she would revive."

"She could not forget," said Amy sharply and regretfully.

"If she were my wife," said Felix forcibly, "I should be first with her. Bessy would have been our child.

She would have had me before the little girl came.
There can be nothing on earth like the love between
husband and wife. Don't you think so?"

He was so fervently in earnest that Amy, although
she had been half inclined to smile, answered with
equal seriousness, —

"It has sometimes seemed to me that the natural
ties are the strongest."

"Natural ties?" he repeated. He looked at her
questioningly. "Oh, you mean that marriage is accidental, provisional, not a tie of blood." He mused
over the idea a moment, then remarked, "I always
took it for granted that I should love my wife better
than forty thousand mothers, but perhaps I could not.
I adore my mother, — I simply adore her."

"And she adores you," said Amy.

"She loves me quite as well as I deserve," said Felix.
"She knows I would do anything to please her. Were
you ever at Père la Chaise? And did you see an inscription from a pious son to his mother? It struck
me powerfully. I have said over to myself a thousand
times, 'Dors en paix, oh ma mère, ton fils t'obéira tou-
jours.'"

Amy's glance rested on him with an expression he
had never before seen on her face. A thought struck
him.

"I wonder if it bores you having me here," he exclaimed.

Her jetty lashes first went down, then were raised, —
she was laughing.

"I don't wonder you believe I am a disagreeable
person," she said. She went a step nearer and held
out her hand. "Couldn't you forgive me all my mis-
deeds?" she asked half mischievously.

"Very easily," said Felix, coloring furiously and barely touching the little fingers she put into his hand, for he was so glad he felt afraid of crushing them. "Why could we not walk on?" he asked, as if in a hurry to get away from more personal subjects. "We can go up this road, turn into the fields, and then strike the woods. Did you ever go through these woods in the afternoon and see the light on Wolcott mountains?"

"No. Is it fine?"

"When I come to die, if the glory of heaven were to shine down on me it could not easily be brighter than the light I used to see on Wolcott mountains," he said. "Where did you live as a child, Miss Standish?"

"Chiefly in New York. We traveled in the summer."

"What a pity! You had no chance to strike roots."

"I consider myself a very deeply-rooted person."

"How can any one have roots who has not lived a large part of his or her life in the country?" persisted Felix. "You remember that George Eliot says a human life should be well rooted in some spot of a native land, where it may get the love of tender kinship for the face of earth, for the labors man goes forth to, for the sounds and accents which haunt it, for whatever will give that early home a familiar, unmistakable difference amidst the future widening of knowledge, — a spot where the definiteness of early memories may be enwrought with affection, and kindly acquaintance with all neighbors, even to the dogs and donkeys, may become a sweet habit of the blood."

"It is a pity to see Orion only over chimney pots," said Amy. "I confess so much. Still, I like the city, and I do not like the country, particularly a village."

" Yet you are a philanthropist, — have humanitarian schemes. Don't you realize that what makes the hopeless problem of city misery is that the wretched people you are trying to benefit live in the city? A city is a disease on the face of the earth : there may be costly forms of mitigation for it, but no cure."

They had gone up the road, and now, leaving the glare and dust of the highway, turned into a field at the right where oats were ripening, these July days. They walked single file along a narrow foot-path under the shade of a stone wall overrun with blackberry vines. He was leading the way, but now looked back at her over his shoulder, and she tried to read his glance, wondering if he were in earnest.

" The city kills life, intellect, and soul," he proceeded, with a half twinkle in his eye. " There is no vitality, hence no possibility of any originality in people who have always lived in a city. The world's work is done, and always has been done, by people who have stored up energy and force in country living and country thinking. Even the money makers, the great financiers, are country born and bred ; so with inventors, scientists, mechanicians. Of course, every one admits that everything worth doing in art has been done by men who found their inspiration in early rural life. For actual knowledge of the world one must have lived in a village, for nowhere else does one have a chance fully to know other people, their habits, ways, idiosyncrasies. The novelists who have written out of experience and not out of phrase-books have always had a treasure-house of early associations in some country neighborhood. For example, the germ of all George Eliot's best work lay in the incidents and impressions of her rural life as a child."

"She *happened* to have lived in the country," said Amy.

"Happened!" repeated Felix. "Don't you see that nature is inevitably and irresistibly behind all great art? Your city life sharpens, narrows, concentrates, exhausts. It makes critics and useful mediocrities."

Amy listened, half vexed and half amused. She was accustomed to be serious herself and to impose a rôle of high seriousness on others. She could not feel certain that the theories he was advancing were not a mere challenge, and if he were not in earnest she did not wish to waste her own earnestness in the desert, for without being moved her mind did not work easily. She tried to think of some clever illustration which should disclose the fallacy of the views he was putting forth as if incontrovertible, but was afraid of uttering a mere platitude.

"The city stimulates," she said, presently. "One feels as if one's heart were beating and one's life were worthily expanded."

"It spends itself on trivialities. The quietest life is the best preparation for great events, the best background for the most varied and beautiful — not to say worthy — thinking."

"I cannot agree with you at all," said Amy, who began to feel that she must assert herself.

"That is simply because you have not thought about it," said Felix. "Ponder the matter and you will see that country life has always furnished the wellspring of character, intellect, morality, philosophy, religion, and, of course, art. Provinciality gives the key-note of all genius."

They had reached the end of the field, and at the stile he paused. "You are laughing at me," she said.

" Do you suppose I am content to feel you are longing to be back in the city at this moment ? " he said,
pointing to the scene behind her. The warm breeze
was swaying the grain, imparting to the ears a perpetual motion like a ripple in a calm sea, seeming to
multiply the beams of light, which took by turns radi-
ations of gold and palest green. " I want you to be
happy here," he said, in a half-aggrieved tone. " I hate
to think you dislike Walford when you are doing so
much good. So much order, energy, light, helpfulness,
come out of you, I want you to have something in return."

His look and tone were so friendly and caressing that
she smiled back at him.

" You want to go on with your work among the poor
people in New York," Felix proceeded, "when the best
service you can possibly render them is to bring them
here. So many foolish Walford men and women have
gone off to cities to make a fortune, sought for work
and found none, despaired, and come to grief altogether. The tide has been sweeping out of New England for years, and the right thing to do is to try to turn
it back."

" You give me an idea," said Amy.

They crossed the stile and entered the woods.

XII.

NEWS.

THE summer had passed. It was the first of September. Rexford Long, the "literary man" of the great firm of Synnots, book publishers, had had his holiday and was again at his desk hard at work one day, when the card of his cousin, Roger Rexford, was brought to him.

He directed that his visitor should be ushered into a little room upstairs which he kept for himself, and presently the two cousins were face to face. Long looked at the other in silence for a moment, then said, " Something has happened."

" The same that has happened over and over again," returned Roger. " I am going to Chicago to see a child whom Orrin Goodeve, junior, believes to be Bessy. I dare say it is another cheat." But as he spoke the color rose to his face and the tears to his eyes.

" Has Orrin seen her ? "

" Yes. A Mrs. Lorenz, who has charge of the little girl, took her to see him. Read what he says for yourself."

Long was white to the lips ; his hands trembled so that he could hardly take the extended sheet. The letter ran thus : —

CHICAGO, *August* 27.

DEAR ROGER, — I hope I am not holding out false hopes, but I honestly believe the child I wired you about is your Bessy. I have seen her twice since. I have questioned the woman closely, and have looked into her antecedents. Her neighbors substantiate her story, that is, they remember that her husband brought the little girl to the house six months ago. Her name is Susan Lorenz; she is English, was formerly a house-maid or waitress in New York. She married Bernard Lorenz, a journeyman plumber, and they came West two years ago, after living at Fair Haven, Connecticut, since their marriage. They left Bernard's sister Bertha behind them there. Six months ago this Bertha became insane, and Lorenz went to Fair Haven to look after her and her effects. When he returned to Chicago he brought this child, about whom he seemed disinclined to speak. Mrs. Lorenz had an idea for some time that she was Bertha's own daughter. But Lorenz now and then dropped a word or two about the little girl's being worth the pains of looking after, and once he said that if he were not afraid of getting into trouble, he might have a fortune for keeping her. Just after this he was killed in a gas explosion. His death, which occurred last April, left his widow destitute, with three children of her own. Mrs. Lorenz was one day complaining to a neighbor about the expense this adopted child would be to her, and she told what her husband had said about a fortune. The neighbor suggested that some time before a child had been lost in New England and enormous rewards had been offered for her. This statement led Mrs. Lorenz to make inquiries, and she was directed to me. I have, as I say, seen the child twice. I should take her to be about four years old. She has very bright golden hair, blue eyes, good features, and a particularly white skin. Her resemblance to your wife would have struck me, even if I had met her casually. She speaks very fluently but not very distinctly, her English, I should say, showing traces of a foreign accent at times. I questioned her, asked if she remembered her mother. She said she walked with her mamma in the garden. I inquired who else was there. She answered at once, *Jenny, Nino,* and *Fido,* the big dog.

My own impressions must go for what they are worth. Of course you must see the child. And, by the by, look up this Bertha Lorenz in Fair Haven. She was an operative in a silk-mill. She had also lived out as a servant. She was always, her sister-in-law affirms, a very excitable woman, and had a terrible grudge against rich people.

Long had not read this without many an exclamation.

"Oh, my God!" he said now, "I do believe she is found."

"Don't talk about it. I try not even to think about it," said Roger. "I am off for Chicago in two hours, and must have something to eat first."

"Have you found out anything about Bertha Lorenz?"

"She died in the State Insane Asylum six weeks ago," said Roger. "I am having her antecedents looked up."

"Of course you have not said anything to Evelyn."

"Oh, no. If — if there is any news, Rex, I wish

you would go to Walford and prepare her. I would
rather feel that you are there. You will be careful of
her, and she is used to you."

"You will telegraph as soon as " —

"Of course."

They went out together and tried to eat a meal, but
Roger was too tremulous to utter a syllable. Long
took him to the cars, went on the train with him, and
sat by his side until it moved. Then they wrung
hands silently as if it were for a hopeless parting.

Within forty-eight hours, Long, sick with suspense,
received this dispatch : " I start this evening with
Bessy. I do not see that any one can find a shadow
of doubt. Go to Walford."

Long slept at Mrs. Goodeve's that night. The following morning at eight o'clock he was at the Rexfords'.
He sent up a note to Amy asking her to come down
quietly without letting Evelyn know that he was there.

She descended almost on the instant, entering the
library where he was waiting, a little pale and flurried.

"You have brought some news," she said, without
any form of greeting.

"Good news, — I hope and pray good news."

"Bessy is found ? "

"It seems as if we might say so. Roger has telegraphed that he feels that there can be no doubt."

"Oh, thank God ! " said Amy, " thank God ! " She
caught her breath painfully ; tears were running down
her face, but she smiled at him. " Roger sent you to
tell Evelyn ? " He nodded. " Is he bringing Bessy
home ? " she asked.

"They started last night." This absolute definiteness when there had been such cruel obscurity was

hard to take in. They stared at each other, finding it almost incredible.

" Don't let us be too sure," he exclaimèd, feeling with sudden anguish of soul that they might possibly be laying up retributions for themselves. " Until Evelyn sees the child I shall not venture to rest on the certainty."

Amy raised her hand. " I hear her moving about her rooms."

The thought of Evelyn's present solitude, the emptiness, the chilling void of her life, had suddenly to be measured against the great boon offered. She was so fragile nowadays it seemed as if too violent a surge of any sort of emotion might kill her. Amy was used to trusting her own powers, but she shrank back in this emergency and left everything to Long. She felt that she was too eager, too precipitate ; she longed to hide herself. He had to school her to the task even of meeting her sister as if nothing had happened. Evelyn must come down, eat her breakfast, gain the full courage and serenity which the day gives, before she was told what was to happen.

Even while they were settling their plans Evelyn was on the stairs. Long braced himself with a kind of agony as he went out to meet her. He stood without uttering a word, watching her descend. She wore a shade over her eyes, and came down slowly, holding by the baluster almost as if she were totally blind. She had on a loose gown of white cashmere, and a fleecy shawl was wrapped about her shoulders. She looked as pale as her dress ; still he observed that her lips were smiling.

" Who is that ? " she said, catching sight of a

man's figure at the foot of the staircase. Her foot slipped as she spoke, and she would have fallen had he not caught her in his arms. "Oh, you dear old Rex!" she exclaimed. "I thought for a moment it was Roger. Where did you come from?"

"I stayed all night with Aunt Laura," said Long. "I told her I should breakfast with you. I heard that Roger was away."

"Yes; he rushed off suddenly on business. He is away so much," Evelyn said, with a little sigh. "I am so glad you have come, Rex." Amy advanced and kissed her. "Well, dear, is breakfast ready?" Evelyn asked.

Amy replied that she had rung for breakfast, and they sat down at table, Evelyn in her place behind the cups and saucers. She leaned both elbows on the table and rested her chin on her two palms. Both Long and Amy watched her with a pang, she looked so frail; the little wrists and fingers were so thin, the veins about her transparent temples were so blue.

"Nobody asks me how I am," she said in a voice just touched with petulance, "but I feel better to-day than I have felt for a long, long time."

"I observed you were smiling," said Long. "I am glad."

"Eat a good breakfast, dear," put in Amy.

"I don't feel very hungry," said Evelyn. "You see," she added, turning to Long, "I have had a dream, — such a wonderful dream."

"Are you going to tell it?"

"If I can. But don't you know, it is never easy to get hold of a dream. When you think you have it all the substance vanishes, — it turns into a cloud, as the old goddesses used to."

"Let us have even the cloud of it," said Long.

"I felt eager to tell it ; that was why I got up early, dressed and came down by myself. And when I mistook you for Roger I thought how nice that he had come back in time to hear it. However, I'm not sure, Rex," Evelyn said, with a touch of her old archness, "but that I like you better for an audience. Roger is forever thinking about something else when I talk to him. Now you must — both of you — listen." She made an imperative gesture, then began with animation : "The first distinct impression I recall is that I was sitting on a hillside, and all the world about me was so beautiful I felt steeped in an intense happiness. I could see far away into wide distances, and the vast horizons were, oh, so lovely ! The sun shone, the sky was of a heavenly color, and the whole visible universe seemed revealed to my perceptions, as if I had never before realized just how beautiful the world was. All at once the thought crossed my mind that this must be the Italian sky and atmosphere. I said aloud, as it seemed, 'Oh, I always wanted so much to be in Italy,' and again I was stirred all through with a sense of keen joy in being alive, in seeing and feeling. I realized too that I must improve this wonderful opportunity and watch and study and drink the meaning of it all in. There was enough to look at, although at first there was nothing save sky, atmosphere, horizons, and the wide empty hillside. All at once my solitude was broken. From everywhere round about girdling me in I saw odd, beautiful little beings approaching. You know how it is in dreams. These creatures were partly like children and partly like birds, cherubs perhaps, and each bore in its hand a censer which it swung to and

fro. 'How odd it is!' I said within myself. 'But
I suppose it is one of the customs of the country.'
I was singularly interested. They came nearer and
nearer. At first it was an exquisite pleasure to see
them close, then I began to divine that they somehow
threatened me. A pang darted through my bliss. I
suddenly realized that what it meant was that I was to
die. And oh, the idea brought such an anguish! I
recognized the summons which told that body and soul
were to be wrenched apart. I cried out, 'Oh, I do not
want to die. I am so young, the world is so beautiful.
I never knew before how beautiful it is. It is such a
waste when I have lived only twenty-four years to have
the rest of my threescore and ten buried up away from
the sunshine and light.' For a minute I seemed to
struggle as against a physical enemy. But all at once,
as if a strong compelling hand were laid on me, I gave
up. My impulse changed. I said, 'Oh, perhaps it is
best. I was a happy child and have been a happy
woman. The world is so full of pain and trouble; perhaps I have had my full share of happiness, — if I had
more it might not be good for me. Let it all go.'
Absolutely resigned, I seemed to float up into the air,
and there midway I rested and looked down on the spot
where I had been sitting. And looking down, I saw,
— I saw, as it were, the other half of me sinking into
earth, and as it sank these little cherubs I told you
about waved their censers, and even while they waved
them bright little flowers sprang up and covered the
place."

She paused, smiling. "What do you think of that?"
she asked, and when nobody answered she went on:
"Why, what is the matter? Are you laughing or crying?"

For the ideas the dream suggested coming into collision with the excitement felt both by Long and Amy had roused a feeling almost too poignant. "Oh, don't cry," said Evelyn. "What is there to cry about? It made me feel happier than I have been for a long, long time." She did not go on to say that as she lay in her bed, moved as she had never been moved before by a presentiment of her individual lot, she had suddenly recognized Death as the great benefactor of mortals: the ender of hard tasks, the dispenser of rest. And since Death was sure to come, since she had only a few years to spend, she said to herself, she must try not to spend them in vain, as she had lately been doing.

"I'll tell you the rest by-and-by," she added, with a little nod. "Now, eat your breakfast." She tried to put hot water in the coffee-cups and laughed at her failure. She could see nothing clearly near at hand, she explained. This horrible stuff Dr. Cowdry put into her eyes every day might be doing good, perhaps they ached less, but she was actually blind. She told about Dr. Johnson's sightless old friend, Mrs. Williams, who used to make tea for his visitors and was accused by some over-fastidious people of putting her finger into the cups to feel if they were full.

She was once more the old Evelyn, bubbling over with talk, far-darting fancies answering one another in her mind. She laughed at Amy, told Long stories about her activities, her plans for regenerating society, and when Amy sat quiet with not a word only grew saucier. Long's silence seemed nothing particular; Evelyn had always been used to his silences.

The moment they rose, she went to the window.

The clouds hung low, and a soft, dripping rain was falling steadily.

"I wish it had been a pleasant day," she said. "I would ask you to take me out to drive, Rex. I feel like going into the air."

"You certainly are better, Evelyn," he answered. He had followed her into the bay-window, and she turned about and faced him.

"I have made up my mind," she said, "that I will be better. I have worn everybody out. I have been horribly selfish."

"Come into the library and sit down for a while," said Long.

He led her in, placed her in a chair before the open wood fire, then went back and shut the door.

"Rex," exclaimed Evelyn, as he advanced towards her again, speaking in a voice which vibrated in answer to some strong inward emotion, "my dream had two meanings for me. It helped to bury my dead. I had never buried Bessy before. Now I feel as if I could say to myself, 'Bessy is dead.' We must all die, and her little day was appointed to end soon. She had a happy time; it was too short for her to have gone deep into life. She was saved much pain. If what they tell is true she is with the Saviour who said, 'Suffer little children to come unto me.' And if Heaven does really exist, and our visions of it are not mere dreams, how happy she must be! Yes, Rex, I have given her up at last. Death no longer seems such an enemy."

Long laid his hand on hers.

"I dare say my old sorrow will come back," she went on with a sudden agitation of all her features, "and that I shall wake up with a feeling of vacancy and emptiness, but hereafter I intend to conquer it."

"I am glad you feel strong," said Rex. "I want you to be wise and sensible. If you bear your grief so nobly, who can tell but that it may be turned into joy?"

His voice sank toward the end, — took a thrilling characteristic note which always touched her.

"Joy?" she repeated. "Amy would say you ought not to talk about joy; she says we are not put here to be happy."

"Nevertheless I want you to be very happy," said Rex. He was bending down towards her, still pressing a hand on hers. . She began to feel stirred by a sense of something in his words beyond the words themselves. She observed that his voice was full of emotion and his breath came quickly and unevenly. She tore off the shade from her eyes and looked at him; seeing nothing clearly, she made a gesture as if to brush away cobwebs.

"Evelyn," he said, "be strong and calm."

She rose up slowly, putting a hand on each of his arms.

"Rex, tell me," she whispered, a flush coming to her face.

"I had a telegram from Roger yesterday afternoon," said Rex.

"Has he found Bessy?"

"He has found a child exactly like Bessy. He is bringing her home."

"Is it Bessy? You would n't tell me if it were not Bessy."

"He thinks, he fully believes, it is Bessy."

"He does not feel sure?" she asked in a suffocated voice.

"It seems best that the decision should be left to you. You would know in an instant."

"Know? I should think so." She seemed to be struggling for breath. "When am I to see her?" she asked.

"If Roger is not here to-night, he will surely come to-morrow."

She turned with a blind motion, feeling for the chair she had left. As he guided her to it he observed that her hands had grown cold.

"I have been too abrupt," said he.

"Oh, no."

"Can you bear it, dear child?"

She turned her face towards him with the old frank, bright smile.

"One can bear joy."

"Don't believe too implicitly. It is almost two years, and children resemble each other; besides—"

"Let me have a moment to hope, to believe once more."

She sat as if tranquil, her hands crossed in her lap. Long opened the door and called Amy, who came in, and the sisters kissed each other.

"You are perfectly drenched with tears, Amy," said Evelyn. "I am not crying at all. I feel as if I could never cry again. And that may do my eyes good," she added with a little laugh, "for the trouble was the tears would come, and when they came they cut like knives."

She sat for an hour or more as if plunged in pleasant reverie. Then the brain, at first stupefied, roused itself, cleared away the mists, and began to work.

"Rex," she called, "where did they find her?"

"In Chicago."

"How did they find her?"

He told her every detail with which he was acquainted. She listened eagerly, putting question after question in logical order. When there came a hiatus which his knowledge could not fill up, she was quiet, reflected for a time, then bridged the chasm by some conjectural hypothesis. Her mind was actively at work in a world of new ideas which it was trying to assimilate. At first Rex had seemed a radiant angel, who had come out of the darkness with a clear message for her. Now she began to remember that he had suggested a doubt, had implored her not to believe too implicitly, as if there might be a half truth and a half falsehood. It had been sweet to have even a transient taste of the sweetness of the fountain, but oh, the unspeakable bitterness of going back to the thirsty desert! She felt roused to an alarmed resistance of his fears. She pressed question upon question upon him as if to discover what was behind the phantoms he conjured up. She wanted facts and realities. It was a clear help to have Mrs. Goodeve come in, to listen to her large, reasonable speech and feel the warm grasp of her hand.

Evelyn clung to her. "Do you believe it?" she whispered.

"Believe it?" said Mrs. Goodeve, — "Of course I believe it. Roger Rexford would not allow himself to be imposed upon, and he is not likely to bring home any child but his own. My son, Orrin, writes that she is the perfect image of you. What is there to doubt about it? We have been looking, hoping, and expecting that Bessy would be found and brought back, and now she is coming. When you have her in your arms again, some of us will be ready to sit for the rest of our lives folding our hands in content and thankfulness. God is good, his mercy endureth forever."

Evelyn looked up. " Yes," she said in a piercing tone. " He is good." She had said she should never cry again, but to feel Mrs. Goodeve's warm clasp stirred the fount of tears.

"Such a night as we had!" said Mrs. Goodeve. " Rex came at ten o'clock. Felix was almost wild with delight. I don't believe he went to bed at all. I heard voices at three o'clock and looked into Rex's room. Felix was sitting on the side of his bed, and they were talking. Rex evidently had had no chance to put out his light or close his eyes. I rebuked Felix, and he shouted at me, ' Night was not made for slumber.' "

Evelyn pressed her hands to her temples.

" If I only knew, if I only dared to feel sure," she murmured.

" Have you got her things ready ? " inquired Mrs. Goodeve.

" No," said Evelyn, startled.

" It is noon now and I think they will be here at 6:42. Let us go up-stairs and see what we can do. The crib must be ready, and the bath and the clothes. Do you suppose she will have outgrown everything you have in the house ?"

Evelyn turned to Mrs. Goodeve with an indescribable gesture ; it told of a passion of gratitude. They went up-stairs together, and it was easy to see in the young mother the reëmergence of something long repressed, the satisfaction of a yearning which had gnawed like hunger.

XIII.

BESSY.

FELIX GOODEVE met Roger Rexford at the train that evening.

"How is my wife?" the latter asked.

"She is taking it very well," said Felix. "This is the little girl, is it?" He lifted her and kissed her. He did not put her down, but carried her in his arms as he and Roger walked along the street together in silence.

Rexford Long stood holding the door open as they entered the gate. "Where is Evelyn?" asked Roger.

"Waiting in the library."

Felix put the child on her feet, and the three men set to work to loosen the wrap, and remove the hat and coat. Not one of them uttered a word, but each gazed in smiling admiration at the little creature thus disclosed. Long's eyes met Roger's, and the two gripped hands. It was surely Bessy and none other, their look said. She was a trifle taller and a trifle thinner than of old, but here was the same beautiful head, with masses of golden hair in large, loose rings, curling away from brow and temple; the same satin white skin, red lips, and tender little throat. The orbits of the blue eyes looked larger and the pupils were dilated. She was evidently frightened, and looked from one to the other as if seeking a refuge.

Roger led her into the middle of the empty library, then dropped her hand, stepped back into the doorway, and waited. The little girl stood perfectly still, looking about her; the smile died out of her face and she uttered a sort of sob. Evelyn at the last moment had hidden behind the window-curtain. This little note of grief went to her heart. She flung back the drapery and stood disclosed; she and the little girl were face to face. There was another moment's utter silence, then the child took a step forward and said in a soft voice, " Mamma, mamma."

" Bessy, Bessy, Bessy ! " said Evelyn. She flung herself on her knees, opened her arms, and the little creature ran into them and clung tightly to her. " My baby, my baby ! " Evelyn gasped, rocking the child to and fro. " My baby, my baby, my precious one ! "

She kissed passionately the hair, the eyes, the mouth, the temples, the little throat. " You are my Bessy," she cried, holding her out at arm's length and gazing at her. " I did not feel sure till now." She rubbed her eyes as if to clear their blurred vision. " It 's Bessy's hair," she said, an exquisite smile breaking all over her face. She looked round as if in triumph. " I 've got a lock of it up-stairs ; I 'll show it to you." Then she turned back, and half holding the child to her and half pressing her away to get her into focus, she murmured, " And the eyes, the eyes ! My precious baby ! Kiss me. Kiss me again. Oh, I 've got you back ! Oh, thank God ! Oh, my God, I thank Thee ! It always seemed to me that Heaven could not be so cruel." Her voice had broken and died away in gasps and sobs, and the little one joined her in loud weeping. Then, as if startled by the child's grief, Evelyn checked her own, laid her cheek against the tearful one on her breast, and said : "What makes you cry, Bessy?"

"I like to cly," said the little girl.

"Who am I? Did you ever see me before?"

"You are mamma," said the child.

"You darling! How do you know I'm mamma?"

"Oh, I know," she said with a little nod.

"How do you know? Where did you ever see me before?"

The child was looking up with round peach-like cheeks, her blue eyes full of mischief and delight.

"I know," she said.

"Who else was there?"

"Jenny and Fido. Mamma said, 'Poor old Fido.'"

"It's Bessy," cried Evelyn sharply, with a new touch in her voice. She turned round to the group at the door. There were Amy, Roger, Long, Mrs. Goodeve, and Felix. "Don't you hear?" she said, starting to her feet; "she said it just in my way, 'Poor old Fido.'" She seemed for the first time to remember that her husband had come. She went to him and looked into his face. "It *is* Bessy," she whispered to him. "You feel sure it *is* our Bessy?"

"Dearest wife, of course it's Bessy," said Roger.

"There is just a little difference," Evelyn murmured. "It is in the voice, I fancy. But don't you think it could be easily accounted for?"

"It would be strange if there was not some decided difference," said Roger. "She is two years older."

Evelyn went wistfully up to Long.

"Rex, *you* think it is Bessy, don't you?"

"I am certain of it."

"She kisses me more warmly than Bessy used to," whispered Evelyn. "Of old, she was a half indifferent little creature. But of course then she had me all the time; I quite wore her out. It would not be strange, would it, if she had grown more affectionate?"

"No, indeed."

"Amy, you never saw Bessy before, so you are no good, nor you, Felix Goodeve," said Evelyn, passing them with a little wave of her hand and going up to Mrs. Goodeve, who had taken the child on her knee. "Aunt Laura, you are sure it is Bessy, are n't you?" she cried, peering into her face with an expression of mingled longing and compunction.

"Of course it is Bessy," said Mrs. Goodeve.

"I'm Bessy! Of course I'm Bessy," said the child gleefully.

"Of course she is Bessy," said Mrs. Goodeve. "What other child ever had such hair or such a cherub face? It is indescribable how exactly it is Bessy."

Amy had followed Evelyn, and kneeling at Mrs. Goodeve's feet looked up at the little girl, moved by the wonder and the mystery of the miracle. All the restlessness, all the pain, the wild and impotent longings, the cruel defeat, were ended here. This little child, who had been dead and was alive again, lost and was found, offered a new dispensation.

"She certainly looks like you, Evelyn," Amy exclaimed. "I wish you could see her as I see her."

"I can see her," said Evelyn. Her voice broke into a half sob, half laugh. "She has grown prettier." She too was kneeling at the child's feet, gazing up. She took the little hands in hers and felt them all over. She spanned the little ankles and legs. These slight tokens of uncertainty, these timid approaches, these tremulous touches, showed not doubt, but the profound need of her soul for an absolute belief. On the verge of decision everything once more trembled in the balance. Hope and faith fluttered one instant before folding their wings.

Nobody except Mrs. Goodeve quite understood the conflict.

"You don't quite dare let yourself go, Evelyn," she said gently. "You can't take it all in. Don't be afraid to love her. At any rate, she is a motherless baby; she needs to be warmed in your breast and fed from your cup."

Evelyn gathered the little creature into her arms, then had a momentary reaction; a last doubt had assailed her. But at Mrs. Goodeve's quiet assurance she felt herself transported into a luminous world, all happiness, as if after stumbling in darkness she had come into effulgent day. The tense chords of feeling snapped again. She burst into tears. Bessy pressed her little finger against her mother's cheek.

"Don't cly, mamma," she said. "Bessy does n't want to cly."

This touch of comfort, combined with something imperative in the childish behest, stirred her tenderness even while it amused her.

"We will not cry, Bessy," she said, struggling with her agitation. "We will be sensible. We will eat our supper. Bessy wants some bread and milk. Think of my not feeding her." She rose with the little one in her arms.

"Let me carry her," said Long.

"No, not to-night."

" She is too heavy for you."

" She is not heavy," said Evelyn. " She used to be such a solid little creature. I do not believe she has been well fed."

She bore the child rapidly down the hall. In a niche opposite the front door, over a fireplace little used, was fastened the mounted head of a caribou that Roger Rexford had shot years before. As Evelyn swept past it with the little girl in her arms, she suddenly checked herself, pointed to the object, and asked, " Bessy, what is that ? "

Bessy nodded, smiled, and stretched out her hand : " Caballoo."

Evelyn turned back triumphantly, " Did you hear it ? " she called in the old ringing voice. " That is exactly what she used to call it."

The whole group watched her as she gave Bessy the hot bread and milk. As each mouthful was offered Bessy smiled and gazed into the face on a line with hers. She soon began to show besides supreme happiness an air of sleepy satisfaction. Presently she shook her head at the proffered mouthful, made a little gesture to have the bowl put away, and transferred her full gaze to her mother, as if that sight alone offered full sustenance.

" She is sleepy," murmured Evelyn with an air of intense indrawn content. " I shall carry her off and put her to bed."

She refused all aid, — would allow no one to go up-stairs with her. Even while they were ascending Bessy's eyes closed, and by the time Evelyn was in the chair before the fire in her own room she was fast asleep. A maid brought a bath of warm water. Evelyn wanted no lookers-on. After all, this was the crucial test. She had said to Mrs. Goodeve that day that there could be but one Bessy in all the world, no other baby had been like her born without spot or blemish on the lily skin. Ever since she first clasped the child she had experienced a passionate yearning to have the little round moist body open to her sight and touch. She drew off the clothes; garment by garment she flung them aside. Bessy should wear them no more. She knew it was her own child: her heart could not go out with this irrepressible love to any other woman's child. Yet she trembled and quaked as she laid bare the neck and shoulders, and disclosed the faint bud of the breasts, the round trunk, the supple arms and legs.

It was Bessy, her own perfect first-born. There could no longer be any possibility of a mistake. God alone knows what Evelyn felt as she sat before the fire rocking her baby. We must not pry with conjecture into that mystery of joy, of repossession.

Roger Rexford, waiting outside, after a time heard a soft lullaby, a lullaby he knew. He opened the door and looked in. Evelyn was putting Bessy in the crib. "May I come?" he asked.

She flung her arms round her husband.

"I'm horribly selfish," she cried. "But, Roger, I'm so happy, I'm so happy. It is our baby, — our baby back again in her own crib. Look at her."

He bent over the little bed. Bessy had half waked as she was laid on the pillow, but now was fast asleep once more, her hair ruffled, her cheeks flushed, her lips apart.

Roger bent down and kissed her.

"Thank God," he said. "It seems now as if she

had never been away. How did we live through that terrible time?"

Evelyn clung to him, weeping. "Roger," she said, "when I was bringing her up-stairs I said to myself, ' If it should turn out not to be Bessy after all, I will tell no one, I will keep it a secret.' For it seemed to me to lose this little soft creature out of my arms would drive me wild."

"But it is Bessy; you need not make any pretense. And you must not cry any more. Give up those foolish, foolish tears, and your eyes will get well."

Mrs. Goodeve came in, followed by the others. Evelyn went up to each, to Rexford Long, and Felix as well as the two women, and kissed each in turn.

"Good friends, best friends," she said, "I am so happy! Come and look at Bessy." She stood pressing her clasped hands to her breast for a moment in silence, then burst out: "I cannot speak of what it is to me. It is beyond description. All I want is to be silent and to feel it."

XIV.

FELIX MAKES LOVE.

"COME and live with me, Bessy," said Felix Good-eve, "and I will give you a white pony with a mane like silk, and a cherry-tree full of blossoms which will turn into plums that will melt in your mouth."

"No," replied Bessy; "I like to live with my mamma."

"But I will give you nineteen chickens just out of the shell," Felix went on, "each as yellow as a canary bird, with a little black spot on the top of its head and ten toes exactly like what you have got yourself."

"Can I take them up in my own hands?" demanded Bessy.

"I don't feel sure about that," said Felix. "But I'll give you a star and the moon, and we will light them up every evening. And then you shall have a bright, golden sun, and each morning we will set it in the east, and send it spinning up the sky till it falls down in the west at night clean tired out."

"I've got a sun and moon of my own," said Bessy, "and stars, too, heaps of stars."

It was now about eight months since Bessy had come into her kingdom. Events had moved on a little. Roger Rexford had given up his place on Walford main street and had brought his family to the house John Rexford had built, where his widow, Madam Van

Polanen, had died. Evelyn was very happy in making the change. This was such a pretty house for Bessy to grow up in. Madam Van had always said that she wanted Bessy's childhood and youth spent here. There were such pleasant nooks to play in ; so many windows opened upon flower-beds and shrubberies ; the glimpses of the river were so picturesque, and the far reaches beyond all so restful. The garden was just such a garden as one loves ; then each of the three lawns was delightful in its way, especially the west one, sloping down to the river bank. Thus Bessy was able to retort to Felix Goodeve when he cunningly set forth his temptations : —

"We have got a wiver, and a wobin's nest in a tree, and mamma says that next week four little birds will come."

Bessy was by this time reëstablished in actual life. She was no longer regarded as a changeling, a fairy child. At first Walford people had examined her curiously, questioning her about her recollections as if to establish some fresh proof of identity. All admitted that it was Bessy Rexford, the duplicate in miniature of Evelyn except for the eyes, which were like her father's. But every one wished to have a logical account of all her experience; to understand the reason and the method of her being carried off. Nothing clear had been elicited concerning Bertha Lorenz's connection with the child, although some of her fellow-operatives at the mills remembered that they had seen a little girl with the woman on Sundays.

The vague ache of longing somehow to throw light on that black interval of absence had, however, died out gradually and naturally. For a time, when inquiries were pressed upon Bessy it was evident that she was straining some sense to grasp ideas which she only caught by snatches as they came and went in her mind. More than once, at some suggestion, she seemed to be listening as if to master some vaguely heard sound, then again put out her hand as if to lay hold of something half seen.

A striking incident was connected with the Rexfords' removal to the old place. They had come in at Christmas, leaving their own household goods behind them, and entering into possession of Madam Van Polanen's. The house had been cleaned, fires had been lighted, but no changes had yet been made, and they found the aspect of the rooms so familiar they were half haunted by the presentiment that the former mistress would be wheeled in by Nino, take her place on the red lounge, and draw the tiger-skin over her. It was this tiger-skin which instantly attracted Bessy's attention, and the evidence thus given of her clear recollection of old times made Evelyn feel that it needed only a clear hint to have the temporary oblivion removed, and the whole current of memory regain its full sweep.

For the child ran to the tiger-skin as if remembering a familiar friend. "Mamma," she called imperiously, "come and play Red Riding-hood."

"How do you play Red Riding-hood?" Evelyn asked startled.

Bessy instructed her as to every detail. She was to lie down on the lounge, and she herself would say, —

"Gamma, what big eyes you've got!"

Then the answer should come, "The better to see you, my dear."

"Gamma, what big ears you've got!"

"The better to hear you, my dear."

"Gamma, what big teeth you 've got!"

"The better to eat you, my dear!"

While rehearsing this drama, Bessy, strongly excited, seemed momentarily in absolute possession of her past self. However, it proved to be like other efforts of memory, an instantaneous flash which fell only on one association; the rest was left in darkness. Yet she had played at Little Red Riding-hood so many times in this room with Madam Van for a fellow-actor, there was something startling, almost uncanny, in the swift and unerring feat of memory. More than once it appeared to Evelyn as if Bessy actually remembered more than she was willing to make an effort to tell. She would say, "I know," and then stop tantalizingly, while only her expressive features showed that there was more behind. And occasionally there had been a hint of the child's having a troubled consciousness of past pain and disaster, and that she disliked questions which roused dim images of what she still half recalled, and wholly dreaded. But it was not long before her little stock of memories began to be utterly swept away. For four or five months, when prompted, she would speak of Jenny, of Nino, of Fido, of Madam Van, with startling clearness. But it could be seen that her hold upon these old associations gradually slackened, and by this April her mind could hardly be stirred into activity concerning past events and people. Evidently her present happiness was swallowing up lesser joys as the ocean swallows up rivulets. She was a charming child, full of energy, full of swift, indomitable impulses, changeable as the wind, at once shy and bold, tenacious and capricious. She had a bright intellect, with more than a touch of humor, was by turns sensible and paradoxical, but wore always the air of being desperately in earnest. In spite of the little creature's merry imperious ways, — her inclination to put her foot upon everybody's neck, and regard all the world as mere auxiliaries and subsidiaries to carry out her whimsical behests, — she had a touch of morbidness about her mother. It was not easy to separate her from Evelyn, and she was never so well contented as when limited to Evelyn's quiet rooms. She liked Mrs. Goodeve and Felix, and was especially fond of Rexford Long. Of her father she sometimes showed signs of jealousy, as if she feared that Evelyn loved him better than her covetous little self. Amy Standish was not one of her absolute favorites. Amy taught her all sorts of things, insisted on her being good, above all resolutely took her away from her mother for some hours each day, for Evelyn's health was far from satisfactory, and she still needed watchful care.

Amy had been hard at work all winter. It was now her idea to take a house, put in plain furniture, and two sensible motherly women to make a home for a dozen delicate, tired seamstresses from New York during the summer. Mrs. Goodeve had suggested that an empty house which she herself owned might answer the purpose, and had offered it rent free, and Felix had come this morning to take Amy to look at it.

"Bessy is to go with us," Amy remarked, as she entered dressed to go out. "Evelyn is lying down, and says that the walk will be good for Bessy."

"I don't like to go to walk," said Bessy. "I like the pony cart."

"No matter what you like," said Amy sweetly. "You

are to walk with us, and mamma says you must be a good girl."

" I shall be naughty all the time," declared Bessy. " I shall say don't, and sha'n't, and won't, and that I hate being good. I shall be velly naughty, velly naughty, indeed."

" Don't you know what I do to naughty little girls ? " asked Felix.

Bessy's eyes danced with eagerness. " I 'll be dreadfully naughty and then you 'll do it, won't you? Please say you 'll do it."

" Just wait till we are on top of the hill," said Felix.

But what latent naughtiness there might be in Bessy died a natural death in the pure, clear air out of doors. It was an April morning, with a brisk west wind which drove before it masses of white clouds, which later in the day might grow black and heavy and bring showers. The girdle of mountains surrounding Walford showed purple and violet, and the uplands toward the north were chased with flying shadows. Occasionally the sun was obscured, then burst out with fresh warmth and brightness. Everything seemed alive and full of joy. Bessy had the two dogs with her, Nix, a snowy Pomeranian, a present from Felix Goodeve, and Sir Walter, a beautiful Gordon setter that Long had given Evelyn after Fido's death. Bessy sang at the top of her voice. She ran hither and thither, followed by the dogs, keeping always in advance. If she lingered a moment the others instinctively paused and waited for her. It showed the vibration of the old note of terror that Evelyn, at the last moment, when Bessy was to be taken out, clutched at the one who was to accompany her, and said in an anxious voice, " Don't lose sight of her."

They took an unfrequented street, bordered by pleasant houses with gardens, just beginning to show signs of the spade and the rake. Felix Goodeve stopped at each fence to exchange a word with the man or woman who was sure to be out sweeping the yard with a broom of twigs, planting the garden, or at least superintending somebody's labors.

"Well, Mrs. Carrington," he said to an old woman who sat on a porch watching a man who was transplanting lettuce, "you keep up your garden."

"Yes, we keep it up after a sort o' fashion," she returned. "Mr. Carrington he says every year he don't want a garden. He says every bean we raise costs a dollar, and every pea-pod two dollars. But I tell him I like a garden, that I can't get along without a garden, and when we get so 'tarnal poor we have to use an oil stove and can't afford to raise our own vegetables, I want to go to the town-house, but till then, I want a real fire and a garden."

Some of the trees still looked bare, but others had their downy leaves tumbling out of the buds.

"Everything is growing and blooming, Mr. Clark," Felix called to an old man planting beans, inch by inch, in a long double drill.

"Yes, sir, it's my happy time of year," said the planter, rising up slowly and leaning on his hoe. "It does me good to get them there beans in the ground, and I say to myself, 'In two months I'll be a-pulling 'em, and a-stringing 'em, and a-snapping 'em, and my wife will boil 'em, and we'll have 'em every day for dinner for a month.' There's no pleasure like it, sir. But to-morrow I mean to get corn in. I know it's early, but there's allus a chance of good weather, and

the earlier it gets started the sooner we can have suc-
cotash. It makes me feel as if things were alive again
when I can get seeds into the ground."

Amy's beautiful dark eyes were full of amusement
and sympathy as they met Felix's glance. She began
to tell him, conscious that she had once undervalued
the privileges of village life, that she understood nowadays that there was no satisfaction like that of getting
at the facts of existence, and that where " oats, peas,
beans, and barley grow," the elementary facts of existence are more palpable than in cities where everything
has to be accepted ready-made. Felix had been away
the greater part of the winter, and now she had a satisfaction in letting him into the secret of her summer
plans. For the germ of her present enterprise lay
in something he had said to her once, — that every
city charity ought to have its rural outlet; that the
greatest mercy to thousands of wretched people would
be simply to lift them out of the crowded streets and
tenements and drop them down among grass and trees.
She entertained a suspicion, which was almost a certainty, that Felix himself was behind his mother's
generous offer of the house they were going to see.
Thus she was to-day frank and trustful. There had
been times when she believed that he was laughing at
her, drawing her out because he considered her theories
irresistibly amusing; but now she frankly and joyously confided all her plans for the " Summer Rest."

" Do you understand it all ? " she asked, finally paus-
ing, with a consciousness that she had hardly given him
time to utter a word.

" I understand a little," Felix returned. " There are
only half a dozen men in the world good enough fully
to understand you, and they could n't."

"I don't know precisely what you mean," said Amy.

"I know exactly what I mean," he retorted. "Amy, you are a lovely woman. You take such infinite pains for others. You seem never to think of yourself. There is not a trace of selfishness in you, nor of coquetry."

"It is very good of you to praise me," said Amy. "I used to think you did not like me." They were entering the gate, and she turned and gave him her hand, which he grasped warmly.

"To tell the truth," she went on, "I am better worth liking now than when I first came to Walford. It seemed such a poor answer to all my dreams of doing some good in the world, to settle down here, cut short my career, and have my energies fall useless. I was narrowed down to one special outlook. Humanitarian views ought to quicken insight and sympathy, but I am afraid they reach so far that they become just a little abstract. They blur one's vision for the sacred little duties and tendernesses near at hand. One generalizes, one wants to grasp the full scheme, and is impatient of the obstacles and interruptions which belong to family life. Mr. Goodeve, I want to tell you that I have improved, widened. Evelyn has done me good, your mother has done me good, and you — you have done me good."

Felix, still holding her hand, looked down into her face with an air of not being fully satisfied with what his eyes saw or his ears heard.

He did not try to answer at the moment. He had the key of the house ; so he dropped her hand, turned, went up to the porch, and admitted Amy, Bessy, and the two dogs. The shutters were already open, and he proceeded to fling wide the windows and let the mild breeze into the disused rooms. Bessy found the place full of echoes, and shouted at them as she ran up and down.

"Bessy, dear," said Amy, taking out her note-book, for she had come to accomplish specific purposes, "don't make such a noise."

"I don't make the noise, Aunt Amy," Bessy replied. "It makes itself."

"Whisper, then listen, and perhaps it will whisper back."

Bessy fell to whispering, but with the dogs looking wistfully into her face and requesting some form of amusement, she soon managed to find other means of dispelling tedium.

No sooner had Amy's plan shaped itself in her mind than she busied herself with exact calculations regarding every piece of furniture which must be bought, and a hundred ingenious minor arrangements for the comfort of the little home. There was one room with two windows opening towards the east, and another towards the north, through which a wide expanse of country lay visible, which she chose for the dining-room. A square alcove lay between it and the kitchen, and for this she began instantly to contrive a miraculous arrangement of safes and cupboards over which she exhibited purely feminine rapture. Felix had never before seen her in just this mood, which invested her with fresh lights and enchanting prettinesses.

A plaintive voice broke into their discussion of shelves.

"I wish I can have a match to light him wiz."

Amy turned. "Bessy," she called serenely, "don't put poor Nix into the fireplace."

"What can I put into the fireplace, then?" demanded Bessy, altogether at a loss. "There is n't any wood."

"My dear Bessy, you must not àt any rate put Nix into the fireplace. He is a dear little dog."

"I wish I can have a match to light him wiz," mused Bessy, studying the effect of the unhappy Nix trembling inside the grate.

"Don't be naughty, dear."

"I'm going to be velly naughty, velly naughty, indeed," said Bessy cheerfully. She ran up to Felix. "What do you do to 'ittle girls when they get velly naughty?" she inquired with lively curiosity.

"This is what I do," Felix returned gravely, and catching her up he set her on his shoulder. Bessy screamed with delight. She could touch the ceiling with her hand, and she was triumphant besides at the wistful glances the dogs gave her, finding her so hopelessly out of reach. Amy went on investigating her pantry with a speculative eye, trying to think of every possible deficiency. She was filling the little blank book in her hand with notes. At each fresh quandary she pursed up her lips and seemed to try to frown, but the way her dark lashes drooped along her cheek and her chin dropped on her breast seemed to Felix to offer fresh opportunities for studying the sweet, clear beauty of each feature.

"I think," she said, turning to him, "there is space for a table in the dining-room accommodating fifteen or sixteen people."

Felix was recalled from certain dreams and hopes of his own to his companion's very different calculations and contrivances. He paced the room, still holding

Bessy on his shoulder, and declared its size to be fourteen feet by sixteen.

"I don't think you could seat more than a dozen," he observed.

"Perhaps two or three of the girls will be inclined to keep quiet in their bedrooms," said Amy, yearning to enfold the largest possible brood under her wings. She led the way up-stairs, finding each moment some fresh demand upon all her energies. The bedrooms were especially attractive, each with an outlook into what to jaded city eyes was likely to seem a paradise. Amy ran about with a quick little thrill of pleasure which probably communicated itself to her companion, for his look was both glowing and restless. She had found his suggestions of practical value, and now appealed to him at every turn to show her the way out of some difficulty. Hers was to be not only the swift prescience of the brain, but the cunning of the right arm and the industry of the fingers. She herself, she declared, would fit up all these many bedrooms in chintz, chintz was so bright and so neat; each room should have a different pattern. The walls too should be freshly papered, as well as the ceilings, in tints at once fresh, cool, and pretty. By this time, at Bessy's instance, Felix had set Bessy down, and he stood listening to Amy with such a fire in his eyes that she said, — "What are you thinking about?"

"I am thinking," said Felix deliberately, "that if you take such pains for a set of working-girls whom you never saw in your life, what would you do for a husband and children?" She did not answer. "Are you angry with me, Amy?" he asked.

She glanced at him, ready to flash out some half

pettish rejoinder, but his face startled her. It was illuminated as if from some joy within.

Bessy, meanwhile, whose energies were as inexhaustible as her aunt's, with less chance for outlet, had dragged the unlucky Nix almost to the top of the sill of the open second-story window as if with the intention of casting the animal down.

"Bessy," Amy cried indignantly, "you must not throw Nix out of the window!"

"What can I frow out the window then?" retorted Bessy.

"You must not throw Nix out."

"May I frow Sir Waller out the window?"

"Certainly not," said Felix. "I see that I shall have to do the very worst thing I know how to do to naughty little girls."

"I 'm velly naughty," returned Bessy, "velly naughty, indeed."

"Here, then," said Felix, "I shall shut you up."

He lifted the child, and with one sweep deposited her inside a large closet they had just been investigating, which was lighted by a small high window well out of reach. The dogs rushed after their little mistress, and shutting all three inside, Felix turned the key in the door and went back to Amy. She was laughing, but there was a little embarrassment in her glance as she met his eyes.

He stood a few seconds mute, his lips trembling, but a smile of rare sweetness and indulgence in his eyes.

"Amy," he said, "I ask you to be my wife." He put a hand on each of her shoulders and drew her to him.

She looked back at him startled or defiant. Yet it seemed to him she wavered. For a moment he was ready to think that his eager arms might draw her closer yet. But she put up her hand with a compelling gesture. " Let me go, Mr. Goodeve," she said. " You ought not to say such a thing to me. I ought not to have permitted it."

He did not quite release her. He clasped one hand and his gaze enwrapped her. " It is the only speech which rises to my lips," said he. " So far as I know no man has ever said such a thing to you before, and so far as I believe and dare hope no man has a right to say it. But I have a right, — I love you, I have loved you from the very first moment we met."

She trembled ; she was blushing from pride or shyness ; the blood rose to her cheeks in waves, each mounting higher and higher. Her eyes had fallen, and he could only see the lids.

" Look up, Amy," he said, in a soft controlling voice.

She compelled herself to raise her glance and meet his look, which was at once tender and stern. He was strongly moved, and was putting a powerful restraint upon himself.

" You do not understand me in the least," she said steadily. " It is dreadful to me to have to explain myself. I feel as if I had done wrong. You speak as if I looked forward to marriage. I am not looking forward to marriage. I do not expect ever to marry."

" It is the unexpected which happens," he said, laughing, as he bent forward with entreaty in his face, trying once more to take the hand she had withdrawn. She retreated a few steps.

" Aunt Amy," said a little voice from the closet.

"Well, dear?"

"Don't speak to me, I'm being put in the closet."

"Have you got through being naughty?"

"No. I'm dwef-fully naughty, and Sir Waller is naughty, and Nix is naughty."

"Then I think the closet is a very good place for all three of you."

"Don't speak to me," said Bessy, and relapsed into silence.

Amy's swift retreat had not intimidated Felix. He took a step nearer.

"Why are you afraid of me?" he demanded. "Surely you are not angry?"

"A little angry. I do not consider that you quite do me justice."

"Justice? Good heavens!" murmured Felix. "Why, Amy, I love you. Do you know what it means when I say that I love you? Why, simply that from the crown of your lovely head to the soles of your little feet I worship you — I — "

"That sounds excessively foolish, Mr. Goodeve," put in Amy, with energy. "I had hoped, — I had believed that no man would ever dare address such words to me."

"Foolish? You don't half begin to understand my folly," returned Felix, nothing daunted. "That is merely the beginning, the cornerstone, something for you to trample on. There is a whole lofty superstructure on top of that. You say I do not do you justice. I revere you, I admire you, I delight in you. You are learned, you are clever, sometimes you are brilliant, you are full of resources and ingenuity. And if I began to talk about your goodness, I should weep. As it is, I am near weeping. It is no light matter to me that I love you. And even if I seem presumptuous, I am not presumptuous. All the more that you are clever and wise and full of a thousand ingenious devices, I believe that you need me to spare you, to keep you from wasting youself, to separate you from what is unworthy and dull and tedious. I want to take care of you, too."

She had turned red and pale by turns under his flood of words. Moved, too, by the magnetism of his glance, she tried to shut herself away from it. She put up her hands to her face.

"I despise myself," she burst. out. "I never despised myself in this way before. It is all so new, so unexpected."

"New, unexpected?" he repeated. "It is not new or unexpected to me. Do you remember that day last summer *at the bridge?* I had it all in my heart. then; indeed, it was on my tongue to utter, but I felt it was too soon. I have tried to be patient, to wait. It has helped me to wait to remember the touch of your arm round my neck that day. Tell me I need wait no more, for events hurry me a little. I have to start for Colorado to-morrow."

She was angry with herself for feeling on the verge of tears. It was the first time she had ever seen a man carried out of himself by feeling for her. He was pale, his eyes were shining, his whole face showed that he was in passionate suspense. She wished to say that there was no place in her life for love and marriage, but she could frame no words. He kept coming every moment nearer her, and she trembled.

"Amy," he said, "I can return in three months. Let me come back and marry you."

' "Oh, no, no, no!" she said, in absolute terror of him and the power he held over her. "I cannot marry you. I shall marry no one. I have other wishes, other thoughts."

Felix suddenly experienced a conviction that he must not press her too far. He went back to the window and leaned again.t the casement. "I wish you would tell me," he said in a soft, wheedling tone, "why you do not like me? I suppose it is because I seem a big reckless schoolboy to you."

"It is not that I dislike you, exactly," said Amy, tremulously. "It is that I do not intend to marry anybody. I insist on retaining my freedom, my independence."

"You have a theory that no woman needs a master."

"I shall never have a master," said Amy, rallying a little malice to her smile and looking at him half-mutinously.

"Every woman ought to have a master," Felix observed, "just as every man ought to have a mistress. I will not be a tyrant, Amy. Marry me, and you will say that you never before knew what freedom was, what it was to be throned. You shall govern me, heart and soul. You shall find me faithful, helpful. I can aid you, — I am taller, broader than you, stronger and more enduring. I can at least save you fatigue and vexation. You told me just now that you had developed. You don't know yet what possibilities are within you. We only advance as our hearts grow tenderer, our feelings warmer, our brains quicker, our knowledge broader. As a single woman you cannot be what you will become as my wife. Don't call me too bold, when I tell you your real career is to belong to me. The germ of complete sympathy is in both of us. I could not feel toward you as I do if you were indifferent. You may not know yet that you can love me, but give me a chance and you will."

"No, no, no!" said Amy, with a tone and look as if trying to free herself from shackles which hung a weight upon her heart and tongue.

He went up to her and took her hand. "I will not trouble you any more now," he said. "It is not quite a manly thing to make love to an unwilling woman. I ask one favor of you. Let yourself think of me a little. When you wake in the morning, for example, and lie looking at the curtains waving in the breeze; when you hear a thrush singing; when you are picking flowers, — you have to be thinking of something, — think of me."

"I have so many other things to think of, Mr. Goodeve," said Amy, with an irrepressible smile.

"Surely you need not be eternally thinking of whether those working girls prefer pink or blue chintz in their rooms," said Felix. "I have got a thousand things to think about, some of which bother me not a little. A new vein has been struck in an old mine which promises to be important; a rascal in Montana has set up a claim to some of my mother's land; one of our mills is burned down and must be rebuilt without loss of time. But I assure you you will not be crowded out of my mind. I shall not forget even that – little – white – ruffle – about your throat." His eyes softened dangerously.

"We must go home," Amy exclaimed abruptly. "It is of no use, Mr. Goodeve. I ought not to have let you say so much. I feel that you misunderstand —"

There was a half twinkle in his eye.

"I feel as if I understood perfectly," he said. "I think it is you who do not quite comprehend."

For half a moment she stood irresolute, as if summoning decision to answer him, then with a little petulant movement of her head said, — "We must go home. Come, Bessy. Please let her out, Mr. Good-eve."

"I had forgotten all about the child," said he. He unlocked the door, and was about to throw it open, when he discovered that it was bolted on the inside.

"Come, Bessy," said he, "I will let you out now."

"I don't want to be let out," answered Bessy.

"Oh, yes, come now. Why did you bolt the door? We are going home."

"I am going to stay here all by myself," said Bessy.

"I want you, Bessy," Amy struck in. "I'll kiss you three times if you will come out."

"No," Bessy returned cheerfully; "don't want to come out."

Felix and Amy looked at each other, repressing their laughter.

"I'll give you the little gold elephant on my watch-chain that you asked me for," said Amy.

"Sha'n't come out."

"I'll give you two little cakes with icing on top and seeds inside," pleaded Amy. "I saw Nora making some beauties."

"I've got some in my pocket," returned Bessy unexpectedly. "Nora gave me six to have a dog-party with."

Since the garrison was victualed, the matter began to look more serious.

"I'm going to New York," said Felix, "and I did think of buying Bessy a beautiful doll."

"How big?" asked Bessy, with a shade of interest in her voice.

"As big as Bessy is."

"Will she open and shut her eyes?"

"Yes."

"And will she cry?"

"A big, loud cry."

"What else?" demanded Bessy.

"What else do you want?" said Felix, at the end of his resources.

"She must have some clothes," said Bessy.

"Oh, yes, a sky-blue satin dress with spangles."

"What is spaggles?"

"Spaggles is stars like what you see up in the sky at night," explained Felix.

"Real live stars?"

"Yes, real live stars. Now come out."

The inner bolt was withdrawn. The last crumb of the last cake had been devoured, and Bessy emerged with the dogs, jubilant. Felix let the rest of the party go on while he stayed behind to lock the house. For five minutes he leaned against one of the pillars of the porch thinking over what had happened. He could see the slight, pretty figure of the girl in her gray gown show against the sky as she stood on the edge of the hill. Had she rejected him? Must he feel sore and grieved and cut off from all he wanted in life? With lightning-like rapidity his mind seized a dozen points in her words and manner which seemed favorable. She had trembled, smiled, sighed; as he held her hand, it had seemed to nestle in his. He had taken her by

surprise, but need a man grieve that he himself awakes
his Eve to the morning breath of passion? He determined to be happy. Why not? since not to be happy
was to be so miserable. When he overtook Amy he
was in the highest spirits. He rolled Bessy down the
steep grassy banks, he set the dogs chasing each other
in circles, he seemed, like them, to be working off a
superabundance of energy.

"You are evidently very happy," Amy said, letting
her eyes rest on him for a moment and smiling.

"Why should I not be happy?" he retorted. "I
am with you, and I hope. You have not told me I
must not hope, and I am certain you will not be so cruel.
Look at the clouds — how swiftly they come, like ships,
ay, 'like the winged ships.' Don't you long to float?
See that bird! How it whirls through the air! I feel
as if I too could dart into the blue."

"You are not a bird," said Amy dully; "don't try
to fly."

"Amy," he said passionately, "all the world is so
joyous, the season is so young, so smiling. In a
few days the trees will all be in bloom. See the tufts
of violets in the grass. How can you help longing to
be happy?"

She put her hand on his arm. His own instantly
closed over it. A deep flush suffused his face.

"I must tell you something," she said hurriedly, and
there was an expression of trouble, of compunction in
her face. "It was cowardly in me not to have told
you when you first spoke. The reason I withheld it
was that I feared you would attach importance to what
meant in fact nothing particular."

He looked at her intently, his mind evidently being

in conjecture as to what lay behind this preamble.
"Surely," he said incredulously, the flush fading from
his face, "you are not engaged to another man?"

"No, not engaged," she said. Her eyes fell, and a
crimson flush burned on her cheeks. "I have no intention of marrying any one," she went on. "I have
always disliked the idea of marriage. I — it is simply
this I wish to say: I have promised, in case I ever
change my mind, to — to — "

Let her struggle as she might, she could not command herself to finish the sentence. The color ebbed
from her face.

"You have promised to marry another man?" he
said, observing her quick breathing, her pallid features
full of an expression of suffering, although the eyes
were veiled by the lids.

"Yes," she said, in a voice he hardly recognized.

"How long has this been going on?" he inquired,
going by a swift jealous instinct of divination straight
to the truth, incredible although it appeared to him.

"Since last summer." She was evidently contending with some feeling which made the effort of confidence a penance. "I prefer to be perfectly frank with
you," she added, her voice sinking to a mere thread.
"It was to Mr. Henry Spencer I made the promise."

Felix did not speak, and the silence pressed heavily
upon her. He had lifted his hand from hers, but un-
consciously she still clasped his arm. "I felt that I
owed it to you to tell you," she said, in a voice she
could not command, "but at the same time it means
nothing, — nothing. I shall never marry."

"Do not say that," he answered. His tone made
her look up at him.

"Oh, you are very angry with me, Mr. Goodeve!"
she exclaimed mournfully.

" No, not angry."

Bessy came up at this instant. " It wains," she
cried, — " it wains. There came a big drop on my
hand. It wains, Aunt Amy."

And in fact, an April shower came pattering down
out of a cloud which had but just obscured the sun.
Behind loomed up darker and more threatening masses,
and the general aspect of things urged haste. Never
was call to action more willingly obeyed. Felix and
Amy each seized one of Bessy's eagerly outstretched
hands, and they scudded down the hill and along the
streets. By the time they reached the house the cloud
momentarily parted and a shaft of sunlight struck
through, lighting up the falling rain and the spar-
kling drops on the soft tender foliage into a lovely
iridescence, and the lawn and garden took on a look of
swift luxuriant growth, as if an enchanter's wand had
changed bud into leaf and blossom in the twinkling of
an eye.

Amy made some remark upon the sudden flash of
sunlight on the willows and a flicker on the ripples of
the little river, but all Felix said was : —

" I will then bid you good-by, Miss Standish.' I
start early to-morrow."

"Your mother invited me to her high tea to-night,"
returned Amy, embarrassed. "Perhaps it will be better if you take her my excuses."

" Surely not," said he. " I forgot the tea-party. My
mother will have no idea of what has happened. I beg
you to come."

" If you think best," said Amy, " I will go."

XV.

It was, in fact, the night of Mrs. Goodeve's annual Easter party, to which all Walford was invited. The festivities were to begin at half-past six, when about twenty people sat down to an ample "high tea," and at eight the evening company would assemble, all to be provided with a hearty supper at ten o'clock.

"I should have parties every month if it did not make your father unhappy," Mrs. Goodeve often said to Felix.

Mr. Goodeve was indeed wholly wretched at the thought of being interrupted in his favorite pursuits. It was an ordeal to put on his best coat at six o'clock, with nothing to do except to fidget about the parlor until the guests arrived, — guests whom it was necessary to talk to, listen to, seem to be interested in.

"I don't quite see, Laura," he now said, as he walked about pulling down his cuffs, "why this is necessary. Nobody else in Walford does it. It sets a bad example. Your mother," he added, turning to Felix, "is never happy unless she is upsetting the house. I hear her about in the morning and lie in my bed and groan. There is always something going on, — house-cleaning, entertaining, — something."

"It amuses her, father," said Felix, "so no matter if it is death to us. She will have her own way."

"I never had my own way in my life," said Mrs. Goodeve in high good humor. "There are a thousand things I long to do, Orrin; then I think of how you will groan over them, — and refrain. Felix, when I die, please tell your father all the things I have renounced on his account — parties, summer journeys, a trip to Europe, a constant succession of visitors."

"Better not," said Felix. "He may consider himself lucky to be delivered from such dangers, and will put *requiescat in pace* on your tombstone."

"Laura," said Mr. Goodeve in a hollow voice, "I will not have Mrs. Neal sit by me. I will try to bear anything else, but not that. The last time she was here she informed me that the story about the Charter Oak in Hartford was mere legend, mere myth."

"That was because you do not believe in her lost tribes," said Mrs. Goodeve. "Felix, you must take Mrs. Neal out, and be sure that you listen to everything she says. I will give Amy Standish to your father; that may make him forget how unhappy he is."

"Is Miss Standish sound on the Charter Oak question?" inquired Felix. "She has got subjects of her own. She might insist on his accepting her fetiches."

"One can at least always look at Miss Standish," said Mr. Goodeve, a trifle mollified. "So long as a woman is young one does not mind her hobby so much."

"One almost likes it, does n't one, Felix?" put in Mrs. Goodeve saucily.

Felix quoted : —

> "'One loves a baby face with violets there,
> Violets instead of laurels in the hair.'"

He was hard hit, but was anxious that his mother should gain no hint of his disappointment. His heart

had received a blow, and his pride was hurt as well.
To be balked in his passion was a bitter grief which
he had not begun to measure; what he felt to-night
was the rankling offense of having his enemy preferred
before him. Amy's statement that her relations to
Spencer amounted to "nothing in particular" was a
childishness to smile at. Nobody knew better than
Spencer how to insert a wedge into any place he found
it convenient to enter. While Felix had walked beside
Amy in the April shower, Bessy monopolizing the talk
with a long and incomprehensible narrative about "Sir
Waller" and Nix, the passion of his mood wrestled
itself out against his imperious self-control, and his first
rush of indignation soon gave way to a feeling of alarm.
He felt like vehemently imploring the girl to cut herself loose from a man who had more than once proved
tricky and self-seeking. But a complication of feelings
rendered such candor impossible. "She must have
loved him before she could have committed herself to
him in such a way," he said to himself; "and if she
loves him, — why, then — that settles the matter."

It was his last night in Walford for six months, at
least. Perhaps it might turn out that never again in
all his life should he see Amy Standish. He realized
now that he had thrown away his opportunity with her.
He had at first had a sense of rebuff, and he had held
aloof, or if thrown with her he had shown himself boyish, trivial, reckless. No doubt she had learned to hold
him cheap, for he had never tried to prove to her that
from the moment they met, beyond the admiration she
inspired, she had given him a living idea and hope.
Had he acted all this lost time on a sincere intention to show himself at his best, subordinated his

follies to the great task of winning her, might he not at least have had an equal chance with Spencer? What she had affirmed and reaffirmed about her disinclination to marry, he did not regard. Until he fell madly in love with her, he had had no wish to marry. He preferred she should have as little premeditation on such subjects as possible. Nobody who once met her eyes and smile could suspect her of being hopelessly cold.

Perhaps some lurking vanity, some youthful petulance, was at the root of Felix's desire to so appear before Amy this last evening that she should remember him. To begin with, he came down in evening dress, although evening dress was far from being rigorously compelled in Walford parties. His mother was glad of the attention. He was a handsome young fellow, and she laid it to his trim clothes that he looked paler, thinner, more eager, eyes, nostrils, and lips more resolute and alert, than usual. When his eye fell on Amy Standish she blushed vividly. Evelyn and Roger had stayed at home, and it had been no light ordeal for her to enter the room alone. Felix was talking to the Neals as she came in. Evelyn had chosen her gown, which was of soft, shining gray. There was a shimmer of coolness about her until she went out to the table, and taking up the branch of pink roses at her place put them in her bodice. It was at this moment that she met the eyes of Felix, who was in the centre of the table on the opposite side.

Mrs. Goodeve's hospitality was grandly open-handed. It was an experience to put guests into good humor simply to sit down at her board. She abhorred trivial economies when she spread her table and invited her neighbors to partake. Mr. Neal, the Episcopal clergy-

man, had come with his mother. Dr. Cutler, the Con-
gregational divine, and Mr. Robinson, the Baptist minister, had their wives with them. Mrs. Goodeve, though
a church-woman to the core, was not narrow. Dr.
Cowdry, the old-school physician, and Mrs. Cowdry
were there, also Dr. Knight, the homeopathist. There
were the two lawyers, and the Flaxmans and Joneses,
rival manufacturers. The hostess could look down her
long board and reflect that she had brought together
the wolf to dwell with the lamb, and the leopard to
lie down with the kid, and the calf with the lion, in a
millennium of good cheer. In spite, however, of such
generous breadth of intention, the practical effort was
narrowing as far as general conversation was concerned.
Each one of the three ministers had his own word to
say and his own blow to strike; each was so much in
the habit of making his ideas converge to one point,
exhorting and admonishing his followers to avoid the
heresies of the neighboring churches, it would have
seemed hardly consistent to exchange even obvious
remarks on the weather with men to agree with whom
might be a dangerous concession.

Dr. Cutler, being twice the age of the other clergy-
men, had been requested to ask a blessing on the feast,
and performed his part with such zeal and unction that
Mr. Neal, merely as a simple act of loyalty to his church,
felt impelled to remark impressively on top of his faint
" Amen," that after a long and rigorous Lent the late
Easter had ushered in a most beautiful Easter-tide.

" Easter-tide ? " repeated Mr. Robinson, with a swift
snort of astonishment, as if he found the phrase obnox-
ious. The Baptist minister had stubbly yellow hair,
which stood up aggressively, and an alert glance, which

seemed to offer battle to gentle, pensive Mr. Neal. Mrs. Neal, the mother, was of a different stamp from her son. She loved a fray. She was a large-boned woman, of strikingly intellectual appearance; her spectacles helped to give her a bland serenity of aspect from which nothing could move her. She now turned full upon her adversary, her glasses looming like two moons.

"Perhaps, Mr. Robinson," she remarked, with an air of benignant pity, "you are unacquainted with our church festivals. It seems strange to us that all the world should not know that our Lord is risen."

Felix instantly flung himself, as it were, between the two.

"I always thought I should like to spend Easter in Russia," he remarked, before the Baptist could take up this challenge. "There, you know, Mr. Robinson, you say to every one you come across, ' The Lord is risen,' and the reply comes, ' He is risen, indeed.' Then as you walk down the street you must kiss every woman you meet. Absolutely compelled to do it, you know."

"What law compels you?" asked Mr. Robinson seriously.

"I know what would compel me," retorted Felix: "the law of irresistible inclination."

"That is, you mean, if they were young and pretty," said Dr. Cutler leniently. "Now, the question is, whether there would not be a general turnout of the elderly and ugly ones on Easter mornings. I should like to see the experiment tried."

Mr. Neal was an ascetic besides being a celibate, and Mr. Robinson a bigot and zealot. Both regarded the plump, well-fed, self-satisfied doctor of divinity with a stony glare.

"As soon as Mr. Neal will introduce the custom,"
said Felix, in a mood to push the least joke to its limit,
"you and I, Dr. Cutler, will walk down Walford street
Easter morning arm in arm."

" Extremes meet," rejoined Dr. Cutler. "You shall
kiss the ugly old women, and I the pretty girls."

"Dr. Cutler !" said his wife, in a voice of admonition from far down the table.

"Oh, you will never fall to my lot, Mrs. Cutler," put
in Felix gayly. "The doctor has looked out for himself."

The note of warning had not, however, fallen on a
careless ear. Dr. Cutler knew that he was sometimes
carried away by high spirits, so he checked himself before he should give too much ground to his adversaries, and turned to his neighbor, who happened to
be Miss Standish, and began to inquire about her enterprises. Felix also saw rebuke in his mother's eye,
and realized that he was somehow failing in performance of his duty. He remembered that he had promised to devote himself to Mrs. Neal, who now sat silent,
chin in air, and with a clear intimation of displeasure
in her countenance. He felt that he had lost ground
with her by his flippancy; so he tried to rekindle her
respect by taking up some congenial theme. He inquired if she had written anything of late; he asked
what books she had been reading; he put on so re-
spectful and admiring a manner, he seemed so eager
for her answers, he led her so adroitly into congenial
paths, that she was presently in the highest good humor and ready to discourse. She had two favorite
topics, one of which was the Walford Book Club, and
the other the Ten Lost Tribes of Israel. Felix held

her as long as possible to the first theme, on which he betrayed a curiosity apparently insatiable. "What are the hundred favorite books?" he inquired. "What proportion of novels are taken out to solid works?" "Who is the favorite author?" Let him ring the changes on these valuable and interesting statistics as he might, the topic was finally exhausted, and she dismissed it summarily, justly considering that a young man so ardent in pursuit of knowledge ought to fasten upon some essential, vital facts on a subject of real importance. Accordingly, she began to talk about the lost tribes, solving the problem of their disappearance not only theoretically but practically, distributing them widely over the face of the earth. The tribe of Dan she was especially well acquainted with ; there could be no doubt that they had crossed Europe by land, having, indeed, marked every pause made on their route by a lasting monument.

"A monument?" repeated Felix, thinking of the crosses erected to mark the passing of Queen Eleanor.

"When I say a monument," observed Mrs. Neal, with awful majesty of glance, as if defying him to make light of her facts, "I mean something enduring, something more lasting than brass."

"More lasting than brass?" echoed Felix. "What is that?"

"I mean in a philological sense," said Mrs. Neal, "or perhaps I might use the word etymological. You can trace the course of the tribe of Dan simply by putting your finger on the map of Europe and following the names of rivers, towns, and cities."

"Is it possible?"

"It is," Mrs. Neal affirmed triumphantly. "After

leaving Asia, first they crossed the Don (that is, the Dan), next the Donetz (that is, the Danetz), then the Danieper, afterwards the Daniester; reaching the Danube they followed it up to its source, founded Denmark, of course originally Danmark, and finally Amsterdam (that is, Amsterdan)."

" You certainly make it as clear as light," said Felix. " Such facts are absolutely incontrovertible. Let me see : first the Dan, next the Danetz, the Danieper, the Daniester, the Danube, Danmark, Amsterdam. It is a liberal education." His eyes with a suggestion of laughter in them encountered those of Miss Standish, when she instantly turned hers away. " They showed capital judgment, to say nothing of a fine etymological sense, in dropping their names like milestones all along the route. I hate the mysterious ways of so many of those early peoples, leaving nothing but carvings on shin-bones and flint, and runic circles, and kitchen-middens for us to puzzle over."

" How interesting to pierce the very heart of the mystery of far-off ages by the ray of modern scientific interpretation ! " said Mrs. Neal.

" Oh, very, very much so, indeed," Felix murmured fervently. " By the by, Mrs. Neal, I once met an Indian chief, one of the Navajos, who told me his people were descended from one of the lost tribes of Israel."

" Is it possible ! " exclaimed Mrs. Neal, flushing with eagerness to find herself on the track of a new discovery. " That is profoundly interesting, not to say of the highest practical importance. It has been suggested that one of the tribes wandered over Asia and crossed Behring Straits, but I never before heard any precise facts on the subject. You don't mind my making use of this?"

" Oh, not in the least," said Felix.

"Had this Indian chief any — archæological proofs, any — any totems, for example," inquired Mrs. Neal, who liked to be scientifically accurate, "which put his statement beyond the possible cavil of skeptics?"

" He said a Presbyterian missionary told him he was descended from one of the lost tribes," said Felix, looking at Dr. Cutler.

Dr. Cutler's eyes did not twinkle in return. He was bristling with antagonism.

" Such speculations," he interposed in a portentous voice, "belong in general to the —"

" Doctor," interposed Felix, once more flinging himself, as it were, bodily between the two combatants, "what was the story about old Deacon Niles going to you and telling you he did not quite like two or three points of doctrine in your morning's discourse? 'Who cares?' you replied, turning around and buttoning up your coat. 'Who cares?'"

Everybody at the table laughed, and Felix, finding general conversation full of snares, monopolized it by telling old Walford stories. There had been another deacon, Deacon Walkley, who was in the habit of testing the orthodoxy of all he met by saying, "I hope, sir, you believe in everlasting damnation?" and Dr. Cutler's reply to him had been, "Oh, certainly; I hope *some* people will be everlastingly damned."

Dr. Cutler did not like these sayings of his repeated, particularly before his present wife, whom they antedated. But Felix went on, rasping and excoriating not only him but Dr. Cowdry, Mr. Robinson, and even

gentle Mr. Neal. The latter had once had to suffer ad-
monishment from his bishop and brethren on account
of extreme ritualistic tendencies. A committee of Low
Churchmen called to see him and were shown into his
vacant study, where, as it happened, a pair of dumb-
bells happened to be thrown down carelessly in full
sight in the shape of a Greek cross. One of the cler-
gymen, who did not happen to know the use of dumb-
bells, and who had an especial horror of Puseyite
practices, looked at this symbol in affright. "Do you
suppose," he gasped, "that *that* is *what he does it
with?*" Felix next proceeded to tell how in old days
Mr. Neal, when he preached a sermon, first summoned
all the evidence against his theory or dogma, and then
proceeded to topple it over by irrefutable arguments.
On one occasion, when discoursing at Christmas upon
the Nativity, he first adduced all the Arian and Socin-
ian objections to the divinity of the Saviour, with such
telling effect that old General Peabody and his wife
rose and stamped out of church, believing that Mr.
Neal had turned Unitarian, if not wholly infidel. This
story, which tickled Doctor Cutler, and even brought a
grim smile to Mr. Robinson's wooden face, Felix
capped by relating that General Peabody had been a
Scotch Presbyterian, but having married an ardent
Episcopalian for his fourth wife, attended church with
her for ten years after their marriage, then, waxing old,
declared it was time he took thought for his soul, so
used to hobble off alone to hear Doctor Cutler. "Only
just in time," Felix added gravely: "the general only
lived three months after he made the change."

By this time the meal was concluded, and Mrs. Goodeve led her guests into the parlors, where the evening
company soon began to assemble.

Henry Spencer was one of the first to come, and he
found his way at once to the side of Miss Standish.
It was a relief to Amy that Felix Goodeve was nowhere
to be seen.   For let her struggle as she might to summon all her power of self-command, she felt perplexed
and confused.   She had believed in her own dignity
and in her own prudence.   She suddenly found herself
in a position both inconsistent and absurd.   She wished
that she had not made that foolish confession to Felix
Goodeve; but how ridiculous that she should have
had a confession to offer!   Her cheeks burned as she
reflected on the impression it must have created in
his mind.   While she listened to him at table she had
understood his mood.   He had felt skeptical, defiant,
reckless, his will all astray, his mind delighting in anything which promised a moment's lightening of the
weight on his heart and brain.

She herself felt but one desire, which was to free herself from this present tangle.   Felix was going away;
that was well, and it must be easy to put herself upon a
safe footing with Spencer, who had, it is true, made
none of the passionate protestations of this other lover,
but whom she now began, after receiving this fuller
revelation of the possibilities of feeling, almost to dread.

Thus her glance fell somewhat coldly on the superintendent as he approached; but many a time before he
had disarmed her of her indifference, and he could, he
felt, soon interest her now.   He had been performing
certain commissions for her, and in a succinct easy
way gave the results of his efforts.   It was a relief to
Amy to have something definite to fix her thoughts
upon, for her own mind to-night seemed bare of con-
versational resources.   But all at once, while Spencer

was talking, she saw him look up with an air of surprise, while he flushed darkly. His thoughts wandered, he lost the thread of what he was narrating, and in another moment, murmuring something about a promise to Mrs. Goodeve to take a hand at whist, he rose and left her.

Amy, sitting in the bay-window, had scarcely noticed that the room had filled, but now as she turned she saw that all Walford was gathered. Her glance fell on a girl sitting at a little distance who was looking at her so intently that she believed they must somewhere have met, although she could not remember the face. She inclined her head slightly, at which overture the young lady bridled as if at a liberty. Amy turned to Mrs. Cowdry, who sat near, and inquired who the stranger was.

" Miss Leonora Sloper," said Mrs. Cowdry, with a half smile. " Did you never see her before ? "

" I do not remember her," said Amy. She rose as she spoke, glad to escape this sustained and apparently hostile scrutiny, and obeying Mrs. Goodeve's invitation went to the piano.

Poor little Leo had long been anxious to meet Miss Standish. Only recently had she heard that her old lover was apparently bound up in this stranger. Leo had known, it is true, that her own love-affair was not prospering. Spencer's tactics had been to let his connection with the Sloper family dwindle and die out. He had made no decided break, although he had for a long time been in a bad humor whenever he met Leo. Hers had indeed been the dreariest of dreary tasks, that of remembering days of joy when misery is at hand. Once he had admired everything she said, did, or wore ; had liked to be at her side adoring and con-

fiding. Leo was too sure of her own charms, too
wholly confirmed in feminine illusions, to be certain at
first what the change meant. He found fault with her
hats, with the buttons on her jackets, with the shrill
quality of her voice, with the over-vivid color of her new
dress. But his deepest displeasure was roused by her
father's imprudence and bad taste in blurting out the
news of their engagement at the club, — an engagement,
Spencer asserted, which only existed by reason of its
being unknown ; the moment it was talked about, it
could only do him harm. Leo, secure in her own at-
tractions, did not at first lose heart, and had considered
this waning and waxing necessary phases of courtship.
She accepted the necessity of silence and mystery in her
love-affair, and did her best to pacify her blustering
father, who "lacked advancement," and wanted the
family prosperity assured by his daughter's speedy
marriage. Alonzo was in fact only too ready to go about
breathing vengeance against Spencer unless he came
to the house frequently.

Leo was the last person in Walford to hear of her
lover's attentions to Miss Standish. Ever since this
news reached her she had wished to find out the truth
of it. When Mrs. Goodeve invited her to the Easter
party she realized that here was a unique opportunity
of which she must make the most. She intended
in the first place to outshine Miss Standish, next to
show all Walford that Spencer was her own possession.
But the triumphant flutter of the anxious little heart
changed to a throb of foreboding, when she saw his
look and manner as he sat beside the cold, quiet, distinguished looking girl. It is true that the moment he
caught sight of Leo he fled as before a spectre. But this

was by no means the effect Leo wished to produce. The party instead of offering the enchantment of triumph was flat and dull. Mr. Robinson, her pastor, said to her in surprise, ".What, you here, Leo ? That is very kind of Mrs. Goodeve." Mrs. Robinson found fault with her for not attending the sewing-society, and told her she was absurdly over-dressed. Not that Leo believed the truth of the latter statement : she was in pale blue and nothing could easily have shaken her clear consciousness of a becoming toilette.

The party progressed after the fashion of parties. Miss Standish had a sweet well-trained mezzo-soprano voice and sang every ballad that· she was asked for. The evening soon passed and was crowned by a supper. Miss Standish was taken out by Dr. Cowdry, one of the admiring group about her. Everything came easy to Miss Standish. By this time Leo was eagerly anxious to transfer her silent grievance to fighting-ground. Such haughty success ought to be made to endure its penalty. She studied how best to snatch the honors of victory from this over-victorious young lady. But everybody swept past Leo, leaving her stranded above high tide as it were, and she would not have been led in at all except for Felix Goodeve, who returned to the parlors, looked about, and catching sight of the girl, carried her to the supper-room with hearty good-will.

" Where shall I put you ? " he inquired.

" There is a place by Miss Standish," said Leo, resolute in seizing her advantage.

Felix, even if a little startled by the suggestion, saw no reason why he should not act upon it. The chair beside Amy happened to be empty at the moment, because half a dozen elderly men were playfully contending for.it. All drew back as soon as Leo claimed it with a toss of her pretty blonde head. Felix tried to divine her every possible requisition and then, sauntering out of the supper-room, first went to the front door and looked out at the moon toiling through billows of snowy clouds, then, coming back, entered his father's study. The room was not open to the company and was but dimly lighted. He sat down with a sigh of relief, glad to rest after playing a tiresome part. He could not get Amy out of his thoughts. She seemed tangibly, visibly, before him. When she put the roses on her breast he had felt their beauty and her beauty like flame ; it burned him. Yet it was not all pain. It was at least a pain worth all other joys simply to love her. He closed his eyes as if the more vividly to be dominated by the idea of her, and lost himself in a long reverie. He was roused by a whiff of rose-odor, and looking up saw the object of his thoughts within three feet of him. She had entered, followed by Miss Leo Sloper, who had closed the door behind her. Neither girl had seen Felix. Amy, looking back at her companion, said very gently, —

"I assure you I am most happy to listen to anything you have to say."

"Do you know who I am ? " Leo asked, holding her pretty auburn head high in air.

"I was told that you were Miss Sloper," Amy replied.

"Did you hear anything more about me?" demanded Leo.

" No."

" I am the betrothed of Harry Spencer," said Leo, firing her gun without useless preliminaries.

By this time Felix was on his feet.

"I beg pardon," he said. "I was sitting here when you came in. I will go away instantly." And giving no opportunity for a reply he left the room by an opposite door from that by which they had entered.

Leo was not ill-pleased to have had a spectator of her triumph, but, as if fearing that this interruption might have blunted the force of her announcement, she reiterated, —

"I am the betrothed of Harry Spencer."

Amy looked bewildered. "Do you mean Mr. Spencer, the superintendent of the Rexford Manufacturing Company?" she asked.

"I do," said Leo. "I mean the same Harry Spencer to whom you have been teaching French and German, whom you have kept dancing attendance on you, to whom you were talking when I came in to-night, and who ran away at sight of me. I thought," added Leo, with a tinkling little laugh, "you perhaps needed to be told that all Walford did not belong to you, and that other people had some rights."

It was in the tone and manner with which the words were spoken where lay their sting. There was saucy effrontery in the uplifted chin, in the insultingly artificial laugh. It seemed to Amy an impossible condescension to reply to accusations so belittling. She continued to stand in the same attitude of expectation, although what had at first been a languid acquiescence had become in reality an alarmed sense that a displeasing ordeal was to be endured.

"Perhaps," said Leo with another shrill laugh, "you don't believe me. See this ring on my finger; it is my engagement ring, it has his initials and mine inside.

This pin in my hair with the Rhine-stone was Harry's
last Christmas present, — these ear-rings he gave me a
year ago."

"I am quite willing to accept your word," said Amy
with the same exquisite politeness.   In spite of her
outward calmness her mind was busy on the probabilities of the affair.   She disliked Leo, yet was inclined to
exaggerate her prettiness.   It had probably been an
early mistake of Spencer's long since repented of, if
he had entangled himself with the girl.   She was inclined to pity him, perhaps to forgive him for retreating in time from a position so inconsistent with all his
ambitions, with all his better knowledge.   This pretty,
petty creature represented to Amy all that she wanted
her sex to rise above.   She belonged to the sort of women who cramp and thwart every generous aspiration
in men, and demand that their caprices shall be accepted
for laws, and their wishes for facts.

.   "Do you wish me to speak to Mr. Spencer?" asked
Amy.

"No, I do not," said Leo with decision. "If you tell
Harry what I have said I shall think that you are more
heartless, more unkind than I do now." Here her
voice failed her, and she was obliged to conquer some
emotion before she could resume. "He never thought
of any one except me before you came. He used to
say no girl in Walford could compare with me. But
you are richer than I am ; you have more to spend on
your clothes ; he looks up to you because you belong
to the Rexfords.   I suppose he thinks he may be a
partner at the Works if he marries you.   But I don't
think it is fair," she broke out with feverish eagerness.
"Suppose I were married to him, you would n't dare

have it said you were running after him, and where is
the real difference? Everybody speaks of your being
high-minded, of your doing so much good to the poor.
But I say to myself, 'She is n't high-minded, she only
wants to get herself talked about and have all the
beaux she wants.'"

Oppressed, suffocated by this torrent of accusations
which brought up all sorts of hopeless, confused, sickening convictions that she had been acting the one
part which she had believed impossible to her, Amy
stood looking at the girl, wondering what poisoned
arrow she would next let fly. Instinctively, as a simple relief from the heat of the blushes which had risen
to her face, she unfolded the fan of gray plumes which
she carried in her hand and began languidly to wave it.
Thus standing at gaze, she looked to Leo the image of
triumphant beauty.

What she experienced, however, was a timid distress,
a doubt.

"Is this all you have to say to me, Miss Sloper?"
she asked.

"I should like to ask one question," said Leo, with
a biting accent. "Do you promise to answer it?"

Amy suspended the waving of her fan a moment,
then said, "Ask any question you like."

"But I want you to promise to answer and to answer truly."

"I am not in the habit of answering questions
falsely."

"Have you promised to marry Harry Spencer?"
Leo demanded in a low, clear voice, bending forward
as if to read the face of her rival.

It was a moment of horrible humiliation to Amy.

She had been striving after what was noblest and best in a woman's career, and yet now found herself in the meshes which embarrass a vulgar coquette. To answer truly was to put herself in a hopelessly false position; to evade, equivocate, was actually less of a falsehood. But what an ignominy it was to say in a low voice, with an air of intense repugnance : —

"I intend never to marry, — not Mr. Spencer, or any other man."

"Then you ought to be all the more ashamed of yourself," said Leo. She instinctively divined the haughty reticence of the girl, and such proud reserve coming into contact with her own self-abasing revelations, gave her a fresh, vengeful desire to humiliate Amy and make her suffer some equal mortification. She did not believe the statement that Amy did not intend to marry; in fact, at the moment she found nothing tangible in life except the scorn of this elegant, handsome girl looking down upon her as she waved the gray ostrich plumes. She was furious with her mingled shame and resentment. She had a desire to scream out her rage, but her mood was too chaotic, too incoherent to find any single current of expression. Amy had abstained from giving a single peg to hang argument upon ; her attitude had been simply that of proud negation. But at this moment she stretched out her arm with a slight gesture as if about to speak. Leo parried it with a counter-movement of her hand ; then as if this act were too simple she struck at the fan and knocked it on the floor.

"You are a horrid, mean thing, and ought to be ashamed of yourself," she ejaculated.

Having thus freed herself by explicit action, Leo

darted away. Amy, left alone, stood feeling utter stupe-
faction at what had befallen her. She was only conscious of the sting of certain of her accuser's phrases
which bit themselves deeper and deeper into her perceptions. She felt a sudden dizzy need of something
to turn to which should sustain her. She tottered two
steps towards the easy chair and as she moved trod on
her fan. She lifted it, and seeing in its shattered
plumes the clear sign of the girl's violence, she began
to shiver and tremble.

"What has happened?" said an anxious voice near
her. Felix Goodeve had been lingering outside, and
when he saw Leo running away had again entered the
library. He had been sure that Amy was enduring a
very unpleasant quarter of an hour, but now he was
startled at her violent agitation. Her eyes were full of
tears, her lips were quivering; she looked up at him
like some lovely, hurt thing which runs to shelter.

"Oh, it is you," she said, with intense relief as if she
had dreaded some new enemy.

He flung his arm round her and she clung to him.
It was an experience hardly longer than a thought, but
one which answered at the instant her imperious need
of shelter and comfort.

"I am so foolish," she murmured with a sob. "But
no one was ever so insulting, so rough, to me before."

She withdrew from his arms and now stood three
steps away trembling. Felix brought a chair for her.

"Sit down," he said, and she obeyed him.

"I heard what Miss Sloper said," he observed in a
calm, deliberate voice. "I do not myself believe that
her statement was true. I once heard Spencer indignantly deny that he was engaged to her."

It was natural that his chief thought should concern
Amy's feelings on being told that her lover was bound
to another woman. Her ideas were colored by her own
impressions of Miss Sloper. She hardly thought of
Spencer at all.

"I did not believe it in the least," she said. "She
is so unlike all that he cares for. Oh, how terrible she
was! I long to go away from Walford and never see
the place again! I feel humiliated, — as if I must hide
myself."

He drew in his lips and forebore to reply for a moment. Her words seemed to make it unmistakable
that she held Spencer dear and found it impossible to
believe he could play an unworthy part. He had to
make a quick call upon his own forbearance to say
nothing at such a juncture to injure the chances of his
rival.

"Vanity has turned that little girl's head," he returned, bringing another chair and sitting down beside
her. "My mother invited her because she is always
kind to Leo, and feels sorry for her." He was looking
eagerly into Amy's face, perhaps trying to find there
something more of the weakness which had for that one
moment made her feel the need of him. Her eyelashes
were still wet with tears, and she looked up at him
mutely and wonderingly, as a frightened child might do.
He felt as if he ought to re-assure her. "My mother's
Easter party has not been a success," he went on; "I
tried to keep the conversation going while we sat at
table, but when I came out, my mother said to me, 'A
pretty figure you have cut, laughing at all my guests.'
Poor Mr. Neal had told her he was going home; his
feelings were so hurt at having been held up to ridicule

before the other parsons. I had to go down on my knees before Mr. Neal and swear by all I hold precious that I intended nothing derogatory. Intended anything? I should rather think not. I was simply eager to have it all over. Amy, — " his hand closed on hers, he leaned closer and looked into her face with passionate entreaty, — " I was so unhappy. I am so unhappy, unless — "

He experienced a flutter of hope for a moment ; the color rushed to her face and her eyes dropped. But if there were anything left of her momentary weakness it passed. She looked up and he saw that he was not to prevail. There was a new resolution in her look.

"Forgive me," she said, "you are going away tomorrow and you will have a chance to forget me too. I did wrong just now," she went on with a candid look, " it seems to me that I am always doing wrong, but I — "

"Do you mean when you showed for an instant that you trusted me ? " he asked again bending towards her.

She started away evidently with a heart - leap of terror.

"It was simply, — " she faltered, — "simply as if you were Evelyn, or your mother."

"Oh, Amy," he said, "oh, Amy ! That is just a little cruel. But understand that I am not your sister, Evelyn, nor am I even my mother. It was I you clung to, Amy, and it is I who will remember it. You say I shall have a chance to forget you. You don't know who or what I am when you say I shall forget you." His arm clasped her. "Amy," he whispered, " I must kiss you once before I go."

He did snatch two kisses ; that is, once his lips

grazed her cheek and the second time her hair.   She
had started up, eluding his embrace, and an indignant
remonstrance was just about to issue from her lips
when another voice broke the silence.

"This is the scene of my labors," said Mr. Goodeve,
throwing wide the portal of his sanctuary.   "That entire side of the room, Mr. Flaxman, is lined with volumes relating to the New England colonies, a history
of endurance, of lofty endeavor, of sustained high intention rarely equaled and never surpassed in human
history.   This book-case is filled with my authorities
establishing the facts of Sir Edmund Andros's tyranny,
a — oh, I beg pardon, — oh, — why, it is Miss Standish
and Felix!   Felix, what in the world are you doing
here!   I hope you have not meddled with any of my
manuscripts."

XVI

THE GIFT OF GOD.

It had been early in September when Bessy came back; late in the following May, Evelyn had a second child, a little son whom she called Theodore. She named the baby before its birth; it was to be Theodore or Theodora, *Gift of God*. In all her life Evelyn had never been so happy as in these three quarters of a year, and she tried to give expression to her sense of this new peace which passed all understanding. It is true that sometimes after the little girl came back Evelyn dreamed of the pain of the old wound, and waking with that spent anguish upon her, could only be soothed by clasping Bessy in her arms all the rest of the night. Mother and child were never far apart. Tricksy sprite as Bessy could be, full of droll naughtinesses, whims, and vagaries, when she was with Evelyn she seemed to need her mother as much as her mother needed her. It was indeed as if during that long absence, a whole river of love had been checked in both hearts, and now, released, it carried everything before it. Bessy was a beautiful, earnest-looking child; the little cherub face was set in a golden glory of hair; her eyes were a brilliant blue, her scarlet lips were at once mobile and decided; there was a charming curve to the upper one. She had a thousand pretty movements, a gift of eloquent expression, a touch of humor and a dramatic

instinct. She could be imperious, but when she turned
to Evelyn to offer some little show of love, the child
seemed to feel a surging of the heart, an inexpressible
yearning which nothing but a passionate enfolding of
her mother's arms could answer.

All this time Evelyn's partial loss of sight had had its
compensation in giving her the amplest leisure to devote to Bessy. It pleased her to pretend to be dependent upon her little daughter. There had been times
when, groping in darkness, she had been mocked by
the silence and emptiness. Now she could always clasp
this round tender form, be answered by these clinging
kisses. They had had a happy springtime, finding novelty and charm in exploring the lawns and gardens
about the Van Polanen place, — driving along quiet
country roads, and green cart-paths, and lanes full of
startled birds.

Then late in May little Theodore came.

Evelyn was lying placid and happy among the snow-
white draperies of her bed, when, after two days' exile,
Roger brought Bessy in, and lifted her that she might
kiss her mother's lips and eyes. Bessy's glance was
instantly riveted by the sleeping mite of a human being
lying in a crumple of lace on a pillow. "What is
that?" she inquired.

"Bessy, that is your dear little baby brother," said
Evelyn.

"What is a dear little baby brother?" demanded
Bessy aghast.

"Don't you see? He is a beautiful little boy."

"But what am I to do with him?"

"Only just love him, — love him with all your heart."

"He breathes," murmured Bessy more and more

startled. Theodore opened his eyes and uttered a soft wail. "Oh, I don't think I like baby brothers," she exclaimed retreating.

Nevertheless, the new-comer possessed some fascination, and she returned again and again to study him.

"He is so little, mamma," she would say tenderly, "littler than Felise." Felise was the huge doll which Felix Goodeve had sent her. "He has such beautiful little hands and he takes hold of my fingers."

"He knows that you are his sister," said Evelyn. "One of these days when he gets bigger you and he will have all sorts of good times playing together."

"Will baby brother grow bigger, mamma?"

"Oh dear, yes. He will grow every day. When next spring comes he will be running round on his feet just as you do."

Bessy found the thought of such development utterly incomprehensible.

"Why, Bessy," said Evelyn, "once you were just such an atom as he is, and lay on a pillow and sucked your thumb and slept from morning until night."

Bessy turned to her mother, all the brilliant color and roundness fading from her cheeks; a pathetic depth showed in her eyes and her lips quivered.

"Oh, mamma!" she cried as if in pain.

"What is it, dear?"

"Will he have to be carried off from you, mamma?"

"Oh, my darling, no."

"They carried me off," said Bessy shuddering and trembling, as if seeing threatening apparitions rise. "Oh, don't let them carry him off."

Her words and her tone shook Evelyn from head to foot.

"We will never let him go out of our sight," she said, with a spasm of the old terror.

"I'll take care of dear little baby brother," said Bessy, and from this time a new link of feeling bound her to the little insensible creature sleeping and feeding and wailing by turns.

"It is hard to tell," Evelyn said to her husband, as he was sitting with her one evening when the baby was about a month old, "how much of Bessy's idea of being away is memory and how much simply comes from the questions we have pressed upon her."

"She remembered a good deal at first," said Roger.

"If I could only know what happened from the very moment of our missing her," said Evelyn.

"Never satisfied with the enough," said Roger, taking up his wife's hand and kissing it. "Always demanding the too much. Now I feel comparatively indifferent about it all, I am so content to have her back, to have you better, to have my boy."

"A conviction comes over me at times," pursued Evelyn, "that she must have gone through some tremendous ordeal, something which developed a faculty not in her before. She is so intense, she has such a power of loving. And sometimes she says things I can hardly recognize as belonging to our old little Bessy's possibilities. She is immensely clever."

"Why should she not be?" said Roger. "You at least, are not an idiot, and positive genius has sometimes been developed in children of parents comparatively commonplace. You never seem to remember, Evelyn, that Bessy was growing, and learning, and developing, day by day all those twenty-two months. You apparently expected she was coming back to you precisely the same little thing of two years and three quarters who went away."

"She had not grown very much. I fancy she was not well fed. Oh, to think that she may even have been ill-used."

"Don't think of it. Let those two terrible years drop into the sea of oblivion," said Roger with feeling. "It is enough to know that she has come back. To both of us her return was the talisman of deliverance from every sort of torture. You never considered one aspect of the case, Evelyn," Roger went on, yielding to his glowing, expansive mood; "you never realized that Bessy's being lost or found meant for me either financial ruin, or ease and security. Of course such sordid practical considerations had only a feather's weight in the balance against real feeling. But all the same, every day and hour while Bessy was away, the sword hung over me, and I looked up and trembled."

Evelyn was lying on the lounge in her room, daintily arrayed in cambric and lace. The light was screened, but Roger's eyes used to the gloom could see how lovely, youthful, effulgent with happiness she was, and he also discovered that his words made her glance at him wonderingly. He reached out for her hand, wishing that he had not touched upon this theme, and clasping it he bent over her with a word of endearment. She smiled back at him, but it was evident that she was pondering his words, and that certain facts with which she was acquainted but had never looked at from this new point of view now for the first time gathered force and application.

"You mean that you were in danger of losing Madam Van's money," she said.

"Of course I mean that," said Roger lightly. "It makes some difference whether you are guardian of a property amounting to at least one hundred and fifty thousand dollars, or whether you have to hand it over to a lynx-eyed set of trustees."

"Do you mean that it made any difference in the business?" asked Evelyn uneasily.

"Now that the danger is past, I may as well tell you that if Bessy had not come back, I should have been routed, horse, foot and dragoons." He took an easy tone and laughed as he spoke, yet she was conscious of an excitement and exultation in him.

"I wish," she said with a thrill in her voice, "that we had not profited by Bessy's return. I wish it had been the other way, — that her being restored made us poor to the end of our days."

"That is very pretty for you to say," said Roger with a quick laugh. "Women, who sit at home and never know what's taxes, have leisure for fine sentiments. Why, dear Evelyn! Do you suppose I care about myself? What do I get out of Madam Van's money? Do I demand personal luxury and self-indulgence? All that I care for is peace of mind, the strength which enables me to look men in the face, feeling that I can meet my obligations, that I may do my duty by the workpeople. What I lived through, foreseeing calamity, yet feeling unable to avoid it, no woman can have any idea of. I suffered in meeting men in the street, I went out of my way to avoid the groups at the corner and the post-office. I was bereaved of my child, — that was part of it, but there was more behind, — the feeling that they would presently be criticizing and blaming me for mismanagement, for ruining what had been a great

business, for trailing the honest name of Rexford in the
mire. Don't you remember that I sometimes passed
whole days at the works, sending home for my luncheon?
Dearest, my comfort even in you was spoiled. I was
too harassed and irritable to meet you with the sympathy you needed. There was nothing in life for me
save a confused sense of trouble, suspense, danger,
failure. I went through mechanical operations and
took apathetic rest ; there was no help for me — none,
— tempted of the devil as I was. I felt like a whipped
dog, and it seemed to me I looked like one."

"Oh, Roger, I knew nothing of all this. I was self-
ishly engrossed in my own sorrow ! "

"Let it all go," said Roger with energy. "I wish
never again to think of that time. Now that I am
backed by Madam Van's money, I have no apprehensions. Besides, we are doing fairly well now; trade is
looking up."

"The money actually belongs to Bessy?" asked
Evelyn.

"When she marries or comes of age, yes. Both of
those are tolerably remote contingencies. Until then I
am executor and trustee."

"Suppose that Bessy were to die," said Evelyn.

"How can you speak of such a hideous possibility ! "
returned Roger with indignation.

"I want to understand. If Bessy were to die before
she comes of age the money would all go for the children's hospital ; you would simply have this place."

"Of course."

"I wish it were different," said Evelyn with energy.
"I hate to think we are using Bessy's money."

"*I* wish I had not broached the subject," retorted

Roger. "I wish I had held my tongue. Heaven knows I generally mean to bear my troubles in silence, and impose none of them upon you. I know that a woman is capable of nervous panic, particularly when no panic is called for. Now that I have a joyous sense of relief, feeling that my fight is ended and that I have won the battle, it seemed natural to turn to you for sympathy."

"But have you won it?" asked Evelyn. "As I understand it, instead of holding Bessy's money in trust for her, it is drawn upon for your business, subject to risks of all sorts. Suppose real disaster should after all overtake you. Where would the money be then?"

"Never marry a woman who understands arithmetic, or at least who thinks she does," said Roger, laughing and looking up to the ceiling as if addressing some invisible audience. "A little knowledge is a dangerous thing to your sex, Evelyn. You do not really grasp the meaning of what you are talking about."

"Felix Goodeve is your coexecutor, is he not?" she asked with peculiar eagerness.

"He is."

"Does he approve of your management?"

"Of course he approves," said Roger curtly.

"Don't be vexed with me for asking. All I want to be sure of is that Bessy's fortune is wisely guarded, put out of jeopardy. It seems as if it ought to be increasing every month and every year, so that by the time it comes to her it will be doubled or trebled."

"You are covetous as a miser for your daughter. I assure you that I intend her money shall be doubled and trebled, even quadrupled," said Roger. "Do you doubt my honesty or my capacity? There was a time when you used to look up to your husband and believe in him, Evelyn; I regret that you have apparently tried him in the balance and found him wanting."

She took his hand in hers, and kissed it passionately on the palm, then laid her cheek against it lovingly.

"I have not lost my faith," she said humbly, "I know that you are wise and strong, incapable of selfishness, incapable of even a thought that is not noble and brave. I suppose the truth is, I have been shut up so long, I have grown morbid. After all, if I am to accept anybody's generosity, why should it not be Bessy's? Only she gives me so much in other ways I should like to feel that in material things I could be bountiful to her."

"Don't be morbid," said Roger. "Get well, be sensible, be happy."

"I am getting well; I feel stronger every day. And, Roger, my eyes are better; I am not sure but that I shall see just as well as ever again. I feel no pain, now."

"All the doctors said that as soon as you were over this, you would be just as well as you ever were in your life," said Roger tranquilly. He gathered her to his arms, in a burst of passionate fondness for the pretty creature.

"As soon as I get well," Evelyn murmured, "you will see, Roger, that I have improved. I don't know exactly what I believe about special providences. It does not seem to me as if God could have robbed me of Bessy for a time, in order to strengthen and develop my character, but however it may be, I intend that my loss shall have strengthened and developed me. I am going to be a better woman, a better wife than I was before."

"Don't develop, don't strengthen, don't be better," said Roger. "You have always been divinely perfect. An abnormal development seems to signify to a woman that she shall think crudely and fanatically on subjects which do not concern her. My requirements of a wife are very simple. I like her to have beautiful clear eyes which look lovingly into mine, mirroring her whole spotless soul; arms to embrace me, and a kind tender breast to rest my head upon. You know I have always told you that a wife should be a pillow."

"But, Roger, it does seem to me that to be married means that husband and wife shall help one another, have joint aspirations, act together for the same ends. I don't think you quite do me justice. I am not clever like Amy — "

"I consider you far cleverer than Amy. In fact, you are the wise woman men have looked for since the beginning and only I have found. Now you have talked enough. There comes the nurse, and so, good-night."

" I was going to say," said Evelyn, "that although I am not clever, yet God has given me an atom of intuition which is part of me and nothing can rob me of. I want you to believe in* it, trust it, and help me to understand everything."

"I believe in it devoutly," said Roger, laughing. "Now, good-night."

XVII.

THE IMMORTALS NEVER DESCEND SINGLY.

ROGER acknowledged to himself that he had erred in judgment in taking his wife into his confidence concerning a dangerous crisis in his affairs, which, once bridged over, he himself longed to forget. He had spoken on a momentary impulse born of his joy in sitting beside Evelyn, feeling that she was rapidly regaining her old strength, that Bessy was asleep in the next room, and that his first-born son lay in the crib close at hand. This was reprieve after a long and torturing ordeal, and he exulted with the joy of a man who, after being galled by a weight, is free, and rushes towards his goal. He had dragged his chain a long time and had hated it. It had never suited his temper to be at the mercy of events; he longed to control them. He detested makeshifts, temporary expedients. Now, for the first time since his marriage, he could say to himself that he stood at the helm of his own affairs, accountable to no one. He intended at last to show the world what was in him. He abhorred regrets, useless repentances; his creed was, to seize present advantages and push them to success.

What a mistake, then, to have summoned up the ghost of his old troubles to vex Evelyn's joy! It had wounded him that her first thought had not been one of gratitude for his shielding her from his intense but

carefully hidden anxieties, but rather of apprehension
for the safety of Bessy's money. It was a thoroughly
womanish and illogical idea that there ought to be no
complications at all, — that instead of his trusteeship
offering him solid advantages, it ought to be his disinterested privilege to put the entire sum of the child's
inheritance into a safety fund where it should lie at
compound interest, enriching the directors, and the directors alone, until she should marry or come of age.

Still, Evelyn's unpractical nature was a part of her
charm for him. He liked her large interpretation of
the obligations of life. Utopian schemes yielding beautiful results, independent of processes, suited a woman
better than a clear knowledge of the evil in the world,
which cramps, thwarts, and makes impossible half the
good one would like to do if one could. He wished
he had not disturbed her, put nervous fancies into her
head and set her to thinking.

Walford people said to each other that Roger Rexford was a changed man since his little girl had come
back. Not one, except, possibly, Felix Goodeve, had
divined the enormous difference which lay between
having Bessy and losing her. Men had felt a strong
sympathy for Roger when they saw him ill at ease, resigning his old prominence in town affairs, avoiding
even the every-day salutations of life-long friends.
Now, when he seemed glad and proud to meet all Walford face to face, it was readily comprehended how the
loss of his child had for two years taken the heart out
of the man. Roger had always been one to whom all
sorts of public duties and honors came naturally. He
easily took command; he made himself felt; whenever
a leader was needed he was the one to turn to. He

had courage, and he had training, and could do with facility what was a task to different men.

In that dreary interval when the perplexities of his position had seemed so utterly maddening and hopeless, Roger had been so impatient of certain minor details in the business that he had thrust away all questions concerning them, willing to have Spencer choose, decide, and carry out whatever course seemed best. Nowadays, when Roger was again in command, it annoyed him to find that his subordinate was jealously guarding all these powers with which he had momentarily been entrusted, and showed the utmost reluctance to part with them. He seemed to have the idea that he had naturally succeeded to the management on account of his special and brilliant talents. His persistent conceit at first amused Roger, but soon irritated him.

"One would suppose you would be glad to have matters smoothed out," Roger had remarked on one occasion. "Hereafter I propose to take charge of everything that goes on inside the office, and you can confine yourself to your own department."

"The fact is," said Spencer, "I have kept all the wires in my own hands so long, I feel as if nobody else knew how to work them."

Roger lifted his eyebrows and shrugged his shoulders. He was habitually deliberate ; and for a time he made no reply. After a pause he said, —

"Certainly, your energy and zeal are worthy of all praise, but I was not aware that you had ever held all the wires in your own hands. You were of great help to me at a time when I was paralyzed by doubt, when I seemed to be simply living from day to day. I shall not forget how faithfully you stood by me."

Something in Spencer's look made Roger expect a rejoinder. He had flushed, and his lips worked. No words came, however. Hitherto, Roger's whole attention had been concentrated on the necessities of his own position, and Spencer had seemed to him a mere puppet carrying out his will. But from this time he became aware of a change in the superintendent, or at least of his own quickened consciousness regarding what might be going on in Spencer's brain, evidently busy with thoughts which he seldom uttered. He worked with a feverish energy; there seemed to be no bounds to his capacity for work. There was no call for such intense zeal, and it began to make Roger uncomfortable. Just at this time, as it happened, a chance remark of Evelyn's to her sister opened up a subject for conjecture.

"Amy, dear," she had said, "it is to be hoped that Mr. Spencer fully understands that your sole mission in the world is to regenerate society, and that you began with him simply because he was a corner which needed reforming. A man sometimes has the presumption to believe, you know, that a girl takes an interest in him as an individual."

Amy had given some light retort, but her cheeks had burned, and it was evident that Evelyn's speech rankled. The latter had confided to her husband her fears that Amy had roused expectations in Spencer she was far from being ready to fulfill. A few days later, Orrin Goodeve, junior, who was at the head of the Western branch of the Rexford Manufacturing Company, wrote to Roger, saying that he wished to take his wife to Europe for six months, and asking if one of the Walford men could not come out and fill his place temporarily.

This seemed to Roger a most favorable opportunity for disposing of Spencer. He confessed to himself that he was sick of the man and of his conceit, which obtruded itself in a hundred different ways. Roger had never liked partners. "He that hath partners hath masters," was a tenet in his business creed, and odd to say there was something masterful about Spencer. In short, he made Roger nervous ; he was in the way, and it would be a relief to get rid of him. Then, too, if there were any absurd complication between him and Amy Standish, absence would cut the knot.

It was on an afternoon early in July that Roger addressed Spencer on the subject of sending him to Chicago. It had been an oppressively hot morning, but early in the afternoon clouds had risen, a breath of cooler wind blew intermittently, and occasionally a rumble of low thunder sounded from behind the hills in the west. He had told Spencer he wanted to speak to him at four o'clock, and as he sat between the wide open windows in his office which commanded a full view to the north and west he felt an exhilaration from the rising storm.

Exactly at four o'clock the superintendent came in, looking, in spite of the heat of the morning and his own incessant occupation, neat and well dressed ; as Roger observed to himself, "as much of a dandy as a man could be in the dust and grime of a machine-shop." His eyes were intensely bright and his whole face showed animation. He evidently expected something. Roger began at once, " Spencer, here is a rare chance for you," and he read out a part of Orrin Goodeve's letter, then went on to explain the duties to be undertaken in Chicago. His salary would be increased, and the position, even if of more responsibility, would be one of more ease and consideration. Besides, every young man liked the West, Roger remarked; Walford was likely to seem a cramped place after he had had a little experience of a large city.

"I dare say," returned Spencer dryly, "but I prefer to stay in Walford."

"That seems to me a mistake," said Roger. "I think you had better reconsider."

"I know what I want," said Spencer quietly, "and going away from Walford is not what I want."

"What is it you want?" asked Roger, his voice just touched with acerbity.

"I want," answered Spencer abruptly, "to marry Miss Standish."

"Good heavens!" exclaimed Roger. He raised his head and stared at the superintendent as if incredulous. "That is quite a different matter."

"I know it is," said Spencer coolly. "When you told me to come in to-day at four o'clock, I was just about to ask you if I could speak to you."

"Very well, speak on. What else have you to say?"

"Only this: I wish to marry Miss Standish."

"Have you told her your wishes?"

"I told her more than a year ago."

"What answer did she make?"

"That she did not intend to marry."

"Well," said Roger, "I should suppose that ended the matter." His tone was light, and there was something almost quizzical in the way he elevated his eyebrows.

"Do you mean that you are against it?" asked Spencer, his eyes suddenly emitting a spark.

"Against it?   Against you marrying Miss Standish?
I never in my life supposed until this moment that
there was any idea of such a thing.   Miss Standish is
my wife's sister.   She is not a young girl, but a woman
of twenty-five or six, with mature views, and actuated
by some idea of making a career for herself.   If ever
a girl was capable of answering a man's proposal of
marriage it is she, and you tell me that she refused you."

"No, she did not refuse me," said Spencer doggedly.
" She gave me a sort of promise."

" A sort of promise to marry you?"

"She said she would marry nobody else, — that she
expected never to marry, but she finally yielded so far
as to say that if she ever did marry she would marry
me."

"But she intends never to marry.   Mrs. Rexford, who
ought to understand her own sister, says that she is
certain that Miss Standish will be Miss Standish to the
end."

"I do not feel sure of that," said Spencer.

"It is impossible to predict what will happen," observed Roger; "but I should say it looked rather hopeless for you."   He bent a straight, square glance upon
the other.   "Spencer," said he, "I do not often listen
to gossip, but I have been told you were engaged to
Sloper's daughter."

"That's a Walford lie," said Spencer angrily.   "I
am not engaged to her.   It may be that rumor which
is influencing Miss Standish.   She wishes to take back
her promise to marry me."

"I do not see that she ever promised to marry you."

"She said if she ever did marry, she would marry
me."

"What sort of a promise is that? It is better not only for herself but for you to end such an absurdity."

"I decline to have it ended. Such a promise was trying and unsatisfactory to me, but it was better than nothing. Much as I wish her to marry me, I am not insisting upon it. All I insist on is, that she shall marry no one else."

"She is not thinking of marrying anybody else."

"I hope not, — I hope not," said Spencer. Something in his look and tone gave Roger a desire to order him out of the room. He did not, however, act on his impulse, and Spencer went on impressively, "I wish, Mr. Rexford, you would speak a good word for me to Miss Standish. I expect you to give me a chance with her."

Roger could hardly understand how he accepted the embassy. There was nothing to captivate him in the idea of having Spencer for a brother-in-law. It seemed to him, indeed, arrant presumption for the superintendent, — who had risen by gradual steps from the most inferior position, — to think of gaining Amy. But he had always, like Faulconbridge, shown "a mounting spirit," and had hitherto succeeded so well in all he undertook that his vanity misled him.

Roger had felt all through their interview that what was required was that he should give Spencer a hint that he was overstepping bounds ; that his love affairs in no wise concerned the Rexford Manufacturing Company and had better be kept distinct. Why had he not set the conceited puppy right? Roger asked himself when left alone. What mean desire to propitiate the man had compelled him to assent to his request that he should speak to Amy?

The fact was, Roger dejectedly confessed to his own heart, he somehow had been afraid to refuse. After a man has once trembled, the old dread continues to vibrate to the end. When Spencer looked at him Roger was conscious of a strong, cold will behind the superintendent's words. Spencer was not talking idly; he had something with which to substantiate the justice of his demand. Evidently he had got hold of some little coign of vantage. Roger recalled certain indications he had once given of knowledge that Madam Van Polanen's money was involved in the concern. Even if that was the case such suspicions could amount to nothing. Since Roger was full trustee any little irregularities in his management of the property, past, present, and future, were his own affair. No, Roger said to himself, he had been trembling at a fiction of his own imagining. It was a mere survival of the old terror, — he had so long felt that he must run away from something that he still had the instinct to dread and flee. He was anxious to end the suspense, and although he had told Spencer he would speak to Amy sometime within a fortnight, it was in fact only three days after the interview we have described that he looked up from his desk late one afternoon, as Spencer came in with a memorandum, and said : — " Just shut the door. I may as well tell you that I spoke to Miss Standish as you wished, and she has put the whole matter beyond doubt. She will never marry you."

Spencer's face grew black.

" Look here, Spencer," said Roger, "you must make up your mind not only that she is out of the question, but that what you call her promise to you was a mere polite concession to your importunities. She says you urged her so strongly that she felt worn out, that nothing seemed to matter ; accordingly she accepted the formula of words you offered, which she considered of little or no meaning, never intending that they should arouse any definite hope of yours. She regrets having been so inconsiderate, but she insists upon having her freedom."

" She wants to marry Felix Goodeve," said Spencer between his closed teeth.

" Nonsense."

" Look here, Mr. Rexford," said Spencer, with energy, "*you* must be on my side."

" On your side ? "

" Did you advise her to marry me ? "

" I gave no advice whatever."

" Should you be perfectly willing to have her marry me ? "

" I should never think of opposing it. She is a free agent."

" But you don't advise it," said Spencer.

" I hardly understand your right to cross-examine me. I may say this. Miss Standish has enjoyed every advantage of education, has lived everywhere, has studied as few girls have studied. She was adopted by her paternal grandfather, who left her all his money. She can live anywhere and do anything she chooses to undertake. She has the best connections, and with her beauty could make a brilliant marriage if she had not chosen to take up these humanitarian fads. Her coming here was, you might say, an accident ; she answered her sister's dire need. Thus Walford is a mere episode in her career. My wife will soon be well, and her sister is likely to go away at any time. However, she is one of the new-fashioned sort of women of whom I do not like to predict anything. They want to make over the world, and would do it without loss of time if they could only make the sun rise in the west and set in the east and the seasons go backward."

"She probably considers," said Spencer, with new determination in his look, "that I shall limit her career. She sees that I am a mere subordinate, that I have no capital. I live on a small salary, I am tied to a post. But, Mr. Rexford, you may tell her that although I am not a rich man to-day, nor shall be to-morrow, yet the time will come when I shall be a rich man."

"That does not touch the root of the matter," said Roger.

Spencer's face showed at first a slight quiver of the lips, betraying an internal spasm of excitement held well under control. Now all at once he seemed to throw aside a veil. The color rushed to his temples and his eyes blazed.

"Mr. Rexford," said he, "when are you going to take me into partnership?'"

"Oh, that is what you have got into your head," exclaimed Roger.

"Well, why not?" said Spencer doggedly. "I have been tried and tested. I have never failed. You are under some obligations to me — "

"I confess all that, but if you look back at your own rapid advancement — "

"I want that to be a stepping-stone to a real position."

"Rome was not built in a day," said Roger. "Better be slow and sure."

"I might ask," retorted Spencer, "where you would

be now, if everybody had taken 'slow and sure' for a motto."

" I don't know what you allude to," said Roger, with the old cold clutch at his consciousness that some threat was behind Spencer's pertinacity.

" Who always told you that the little girl would be found?" said Spencer. " Who insisted that she *must* be found, so that you need not have to give up Madam Van's money?"

" I remember you were always harping on what was to me a most painful subject."

" A painful subject? I should think so. Where would the Rexford Manufacturing Company be to-day, or at any rate where would you be, Mr. Rexford, if all that estate had to be passed over to a different set of trustees?"

Roger held an impassive face, never flinching, but made no reply.

" Do you suppose I did not know just how you stood?" said Spencer. " Did you think I was blind to all that had gone on?"

" What insolent accusations are you bringing up against me?" said Roger, with a glance which was not tender. " I am strangely patient not to throw you out of the window."

" You are strangely patient because you are well aware that you are under strange obligations to me," persisted Spencer, flushed and excited.

" Once for all: what obligations do you mean?"

" You have got your little girl back, and you are in possession of all that old woman's money."

" I was not aware that you restored my child to me. What had you to do with it?"

" Not quite so much as one or two other people, it is true," replied Spencer. He seemed irresolute whether to go on or stop short. Roger waited a moment, then said : —

"Orrin Goodeve, junior, wrote to me from Chicago. I did not even show you his letter ; as it chanced there was no time. You knew nothing of what had taken place, until I myself told you I had found Bessy and brought her home. I recall your expression, your very words of joyful surprise."

" It had been I, and I alone, who insisted that the child must be found, who told you that you could not afford to give her up as irrevocably lost," said Spencer significantly.

" Why do you keep harping on that ? "

" Now, Mr. Rexford, do you mean to say," said Spencer, with quiet deliberation, "that you did not understand it was all a put-up job ? "

All the color faded out of Roger's face, leaving him gray and lifeless. " What craze have you got into your head ? " he gasped.

" Do you actually suppose that little girl at your house is your own child ? "

" My child ? Of course she is my child. What earthly doubt could there be ? She answered every sort of test. From the moment I took her in my arms she felt that she knew me. She said 'mamma' when her eyes first fell on her mother. But that was little or nothing. She had a thousand little tricks, sayings, habits, which had always been our Bessy's instinctive and individual traits. She had little phrases which she uttered in her mother's very tones. There were some very curious and striking coincidences which not only satisfied ourselves but the Goodeves, my cousin Rexford Long, all who saw Bessy.   No one has ever thought for a moment that there could be any doubt, and beyond all other doubts there was the most jealous and suspicious of all, — the mother's.   She recognized Bessy as her own child."

"Oh, I know," said Spencer.   He smiled.   " It was a cleverly executed trick and took everyone in, but I never exactly believed, Mr. Rexford, that *you* were taken in."

" What trick was possible ? " said Roger indignantly.

" Don't you see it was that Italian fellow, Nino, who was behind it all ? "

Roger's hand went up to his head as if he were dizzy.

" Nino ? " he repeated dully, — " Giovanni Reni ? "

" He was here, you remember, Mr. Rexford.   Well, three months or so afterwards he wrote to me, asking for pictures of yourself and Mrs. Rexford.   I did not mention the matter, but sent them.   After that I felt sure something was going on and was likely to happen. I did not know from which corner of the horizon the lightning would come, but was sure it would come sooner or later."   The haggard gleam of Roger's eyes startled Spencer.   " Of course," he went on, " I don't know absolutely about all this.   I have not seen Nino since he was here.   Then we had a little talk, and he said it seemed as if the child could be found, and she ought to be found.   I agreed with him.   I should be willing to wager a good deal that he and the nurse-girl, Jenny, looked up a little girl resembling your lost Bessy and trained her."

" Trained her ? " muttered Roger, in a husky voice.

He started up as if under the impulse of an electric shock. "Trained her?" he repeated again, and put up his hand as if to ward off some danger. Everything in the office seemed to be circling round him. If Spencer had not caught hold of him and supported him to the seat he had left, he must have fallen heavily to the floor. He lay huddled together in the chair, his jaw dropped, his face like that of a corpse. Spencer, who had not foreseen the effect of his words, was absolutely frightened. For a few moments it seemed to him that he had killed the man. He dashed into the outside office for help, forgetting that the six o'clock whistle had sounded ten minutes before, and that the place was emptied for the night except for the watchman. He called loudly, but no one answered. Returning, he sprinkled water frantically into the face of the fainting man.

Roger had not, however, fully lost consciousness. Presently he moaned, lifted his hand and shook off Spencer's eager clasp. Then with a blind movement he rose and tried to cross the room, but his gait was like that of a drunken man. He grasped at the table and fell across it with another deep groan.

"Oh, sir, I am sorry, I am ashamed," Spencer faltered. "I did not intend to hurt you like this. I had taken it for granted you entertained some suspicions. The points of difference between the two children were to my eyes more striking than the similarity. This one is slighter than Bessy, and fairer. It was to me the most natural thing in the world that you should have been willing to take another child. It did no one any harm; and it accomplished a world of good. I said to myself that Roger Rexford was a wise man and would alter events to please himself."

But he could not tell whether he was speaking to ears
that took in his words.　Roger lay across the table and
did not move.　Spencer was at his wits' end.　The idea
suddenly crossed his mind that possibly the stricken
man had risen to go to the closet by the fire-place, and
that he probably kept stimulants there.　He opened the
little door, reached the shelves and found several bottles,
one of which contained brandy.　He forced a small
glassful upon Roger, who after the first swallow raised
his head and drank off the whole.　Spencer watched
him with a mute eagerness to offer some further help,
but Roger would accept no more.　After a time, he
staggered back to his chair and sat there stony and
rigid, like a corpse galvanized to life.　Although he had
almost fainted, thought had not been suspended, and his
mind had fastened with an obstinate clutch on certain
doubts of his own which had kept him in suspense
until the ordeal was over and Evelyn had declared that
Bessy was her own child.　There had been certain dis-
crepancies in Mrs. Lorenz' story ; the hiatus between
Bessy's disappearance from Walford and her appearance in Chicago had never been filled up.　No adequate cause for stealing the child had been supplied ;
it could only be supposed that Bertha Lorenz had
already been insane when she committed the act.　Of
the child's likeness to Bessy there could be no doubt,
but it was a flattered likeness.　What had after all
puzzled him most had always been that she could have
remembered so clearly, so accurately ; could have re-
produced so unerringly little phrases familiar to them
all, when she had, for almost two years, been not only
among strangers, but among people of a different class.
Evelyn had more than once triumphantly adduced

some little confirmatory instance of Bessy's clear remembrance of her teachings of table manners. It had seemed to him a singular fact that these trifling niceties should have been retained among surroundings where fastidious requirements could not easily be met. Still, it is impossible to be certain just how much any child knows and remembers and how long it remembers, and it was unprofitable to study Bessy's freaks of memory. Thus he had not allowed himself to think about these phenomena nor encouraged Evelyn to talk them over. All the doubts which had ever drifted across his mind had now returned with obstinate reality.

"Spencer," he exclaimed, after a long silence, "can you swear to the truth of what you have said?"

"No, I cannot."

"Then you are the devil, — the very devil, — to have spoiled all our happiness with this horrible doubt."

Spencer's self-command had vanished; he spoke with agitation.

"Mr. Rexford," he said, "I wish to heaven I had not spoken. On my word and honor, had I supposed you did not see into the trick I should have held my tongue. I am sure I should, although I spoke in a passion. I took it for granted you looked the facts in the face, examined them and made the best of them as a man should. The loss of the little girl was killing Mrs. Rexford. Everybody said she was dying. Dr. Cowdry declared, in spite of all the New York oculists said about her eyes, that what ailed them was her anæmic condition, that her heart had no proper action, that a breath would carry her off. Some miracle had to be performed for your wife's sake. The very finger of God's providence seemed to be in it that she was half blind when the child came."

Roger made a gesture as if to repel a hideous suggestion, but Spencer, driven on by a wish to justify himself,
continued : —

"To Rexford & Company, it was salvation to get the
child back. Great interests were at stake. Besides, it
would have been a cruel wrong to have John Rexford's
money alienated from Walford and from the works
where it was made. The whole thing was an unmixed
good."

"If you knew how your accursed sophistical arguments sounded in my ears you would —"

"But, Mr. Rexford, I want you to feel that no harm
has been done, — quite the reverse."

"Then — my God ! — let the subject rest."

"It shall," said Spencer, awed by the expression in
the other's face.

The silence which ensued was hard to bear, for every
moment it pressed upon Spencer that he had wrought
irretrievable mischief. He wished with all his heart he
could put back the clock of time an hour, leave the words
which had for weeks been burning in his heart still
unuttered, and allow Roger Rexford to drift on blind
and secure in his haughty self-belief. The effect of this
disclosure seemed so wholly incommensurable with his
motive in making it that Spencer could not recover from
a sort of fright, as if he had started an engine of destruction by simply putting his finger on some unimportant screw.

After a time Roger said in a deep, stern voice :
"How many people know of this? How many besides
you and Nino and Jenny and that Mrs. Lorenz? How
many in Walford ?"

"Not one, — I feel sure of that. I have been almost

surprised that so far as I know there has never been a doubt expressed," replied Spencer eagerly.

Roger felt himself thrown back into the old fluctuations of feeling, at once perturbing and hopeless.

" If this is not my child, what became of Bessy ? " he asked, his mind feeling out the old tracks of thought he had supposed closed up by certainty. " Do you know what became of Bessy? You seem to be omniscient."

" I know nothing about it, nothing," faltered Spencer.

"Nor do you know anything about any of the accursed business. You have simply gone to work with devilish craft to make mischief. I would rather have died, — I would rather have died a hundred times over than have heard this thing," said Roger with a look and tone which again moved Spencer to the very soul.

" Oh, sir, I am sorry," he faltered with genuine humility.

" Don't be sorry," retorted Roger with irony. " You wanted to get me into your power. I have seen for some time that you were holding a dagger in reserve ; it was this. Go on, make everything perfectly clear. What is your price? What do you expect to make out of your suspicions ? "

" I see what you are thinking," said Spencer, with a momentary genuine self-abasement. " You believe me to be a villain. I confess I was angry ; it seemed to me you took a tone as if — Then, besides, I have always hoped to be your partner."

" You evidently intend to take any position you choose," said Roger, still with biting irony. " If what you say is true, I am completely in the meshes. I don't know exactly what sort of a criminal I am, but there has been a crime committed and I am the gainer by it."

" You are not a criminal, you are not in any meshes," said Spencer, laying his hand on Roger's, with an imploring look. It cut him grievously to be accused of intentions he hardly knew how to repudiate. " No wrong has been done, but if some splitter of straws could call it a sort of crime, it was not you who had anything to do with it. I ask for nothing which does not belong to the natural process of my advancement. I want to be a partner. I always hoped to be one of Rexford & Company. I want to marry Miss Standish. I —"

Roger started and flung off Spencer's hand as if stung.

" I am not a villain and I am not a schemer," said Spencer reddening. " I will never allude to the subject again. I am not so little of a man that I cannot understand how it touches you at every point. I wish I had not spoken. I may be wrong ; the child may be Bessy after all. I confess the idea was in my mind, from the moment I heard about Madam Van's will, that she held out a damnable temptation to Nino. Not a penny unless the child was found, and then, fifteen thousand dollars. I said to myself then, if I were that Italian fellow I 'd find the child, or some child. In a world swarming with children there must be somewhere a child like Bessy."

Roger's face showed that Spencer's words carried weight in some direction. " It was a big bait," he said. " I had other anxieties at the time and thought little about it. When I was sending the money to him last autumn, it crossed my mind that it was a singular circumstance that events in which he had no practical concern should yet have done so much for him."

" You heard from him after you sent the money ? "

" Yes ; the legacy was paid over by our consul at

Naples. I had the official receipt, and besides that, I received a few lines from Nino himself expressing his gratitude for the money and his pleasure that my daughter was restored." Roger mused a moment. " I suppose the best way will be to go over there and look him up."

"What good would that do ? "

" It would settle the matter. I can't live in this state of mind."

" I don't believe you could find the man if you searched Italy over," said Spencer, with decision. " He would suppose you were after his money and would hide himself. Surely you would not spoil your wife's peace of mind again. Everything is going on as well as it need be. Simply put this suspicion out of your thoughts and let it all be as if I had never spoken."

"Easily said."

"It was a mistake of judgment on my part."

"You were sure to have done it sooner or later," said Roger dryly. " It was the sword of Damocles over me, and you meant it should fall."

"Our success or failure is identical," said Spencer. "What you gain I gain, what you lose I lose. After all, since we have to work shoulder to shoulder, is it not better that each of us should have a clear mutual comprehension of facts than to be watching, measuring, and studying what is in each other's mind ? "

" You see into things, Spencer," said Roger, wearily. "You have eaten of the fruit of knowledge of good and evil. I feel beaten. I think this has killed me. I see nothing, I understand nothing. I have no grasp."

Spencer was stung by what he considered to be irony. His idea of Roger Rexford had shifted many times during this interview. Of old he had credited him with

boldness and sagacity, a determination to protect his
own interests at all hazards, no matter how dangerous
a game he played.   He could do wrong, not drifting
weakly into a false position, but knowing that he was
doing wrong, looking at facts squarely, nothing daunted
by the worst of them.   Seen in these new lights, Roger
Rexford had many a weakness.   He had accepted the
little girl as if miracles happened every day.   Spencer,
himself, skeptical and incredulous of anything out of
the usual, with a vulpine instinct for fastening instantly
on a limping argument, could not comprehend that
Roger had rested for a moment with certainty on the
belief that Bessy was his child.   The cool looker-on
had failed to realize how great the bribe had been, and
how magically it had silenced all doubt.   He had made
a mistake, — possibly a mistake which would affect his
own chances.   He could not yet predict what would
happen.   It was evident that Roger was at present in a
mood of deep, dreary self-abasement, for which Spencer
could see no adequate cause.

"How do you suppose," Roger said, rising, "that I
am to go home and face my family, seeing everything I
love tainted by this lie?"

"Don't talk so," said Spencer, disturbed.   "Kicking
against the pricks is unremunerative.   I'd be hopeful.
Nothing I have said alters the real outside facts of
your life."

What Spencer could not quite grasp in the other's
character was the fact that Roger had always had an ideal
aim, — that of being a good man, sound and sweet all
through.   The tragedy of his career so far had consisted
in the perpetual opposition between his real ambitions
and his performances, his expectations and his results,
his outside pretensions and his intrinsic failure.

XVIII

THE DIVINE FEMININE.

SOME writer, in discussing social evolution, argues that the worst enemy women will have to contend with, in their struggle towards a life of higher and more altruistic aims than those which have in general governed their sex, is likely to be that " Divine Feminine " in themselves, which must remain a force not calculable in its influence nor in the machinery it sets in motion.

Amy Standish, however, in spite of her unusual mental equipment, perhaps for the very reason that she had had a tolerably thorough scientific education, and could, at a glance, class various human instincts as vestiges of early savage life, survivals of animism and the like, had not paid a great deal of attention to what is elementary and indestructible in human beings. When Spencer had made love to her, he had done it in a roundabout fashion, putting the feasibility of their marriage on a practical basis. He had not made her feel that the acceptance of his suit made a turning point in her life, but simply that he was indispensable to her in carrying out the details of her various schemes, and that she could not afford to lose his practical help.

Such a marriage, even to a woman of the most advanced ideas, ought to seem a fact in the line of progress, not of decline. Felix Goodeve had taken a very different tone. " Your destiny is to belong to me," he

had affirmed, and he had seemed to be urged by an intense, a vital need of her, herself. And as he uttered
these words his tone and look had shaken her as she
had never before in her life been shaken ; they had
been over-masterful, but their meaning had penetrated
her heart and intellect alike with the life, the light,
the stir of fresh sensations and new powers. She had
had her own pleasure in this experience ; when her
mind lingered over some of his words and looks and
phrases, she understood better than before how a woman's intellect is subtly colored by the generations who
have preceded her and have been subservient to men.
This was a clear gain, for half the meaning of human
history escapes our grasp, without our clear recognition
of the fact that men have exerted an irresistible influence upon women, an influence, indeed, almost hypnotic.
Mr. Casaubon, it may be remembered, when he found
himself hopelessly wooden and without a thrill in the
presence of his lovely Dorothea, concluded that the
poets had enormously exaggerated the force of masculine passion. Amy, on the other hand, suddenly awakened to the truth of the story the poets had been telling ever since the beginning of the world. It was quite
within the domain of clearly proved phenomena that
Eve should say to Adam, "God is thy law, thou mine,"
and Miranda to Ferdinand, "To be your fellow you may
deny me ; but I 'll be your servant whether you will or
no."

Felix Goodeve had left Walford the morning after his
mother's Easter party. Then followed several weeks
in which Amy's anxiety concerning Evelyn again rose
to fever-pitch, and indeed, it was June before she was
free to go about the place in her usual way. All this

time she had endeavored to put away from her mind the disagreeable thought of Miss Sloper. It had been easy to say that the girl was tasteless and indiscreet, that she had shown herself vulgar and impertinent. It would have been no difficult matter to despise her, but hitherto Amy had not expected that humanity should attain an ideal standard before she accepted it, loved it, and offered herself to it. Indeed, humanitarians who insist that ugly, stupid, lazy, and wrongheaded people shall rectify their intellects and their dispositions before they receive sympathy and tolerance will be likely to find few objects for their efforts to be expended upon. Had Miss Sloper been a shopgirl, a seamstress, or a hard-worked young mother, her saucy manner would not have repelled Amy, who would have looked through mere outside foibles to grasp the needs of a living, breathing fellow-creature. What made this experience irritating was that she felt humiliated at having been obliged to evade and equivocate, and even then not to be able to free herself from the hopeless tangle. For a time it was pleasanter to put away the thought of Miss Sloper, and postpone decision as to her possible duty in the matter. Her old theories did not seem to cover present exigencies. Amy had to confess that she had acted thoughtlessly. Evelyn had once said to her, " Amy, dear, it might be safer if your missionary zeal should take the form of interest in married men and their wives, particularly their wives." Somehow Evelyn always had happy intuitions, an easy insight into natural processes. Amy had enjoyed helping Spencer, who was so eager to improve. Now and then it had occurred to her that the emphasis of his appreciation of her services seemed to

fall in the wrong place, alighting on what was trivial
and unimportant, — for example, when he had in a glow
of gratitude asked her to marry him. Such a request
came from old-fashioned habits of erroneous thinking.
When she tried to make his mistake clear to him, he
proved so logically that his sole object was to keep
near her, to be of use to her, he was so patient, so
meek, so discreet in avoiding any disturbing phrase, he
insisted so eloquently that it would do no harm if she
would show her friendship for him by promising to
marry him if she ever made up her mind to marry, that
she had yielded finally on a sudden impulse not to be
outdone in magnanimity. This had happened shortly
after Felix Goodeve's advent in Walford.

It was, of course, a foolish, inconsequent admission.
"I have no intention of marrying," she had wished to
declare. "I particularly wish never to marry. Thus
it makes no difference when I promise to marry you if
I should ever change my mind, for under no possible
conjunction of circumstances shall I ever marry." It
was an act not unlike a man's putting his name to his
friend's note. The signature is a mere matter of form;
still, many an indorser has had his night's sleep spoiled
by the thought that he has possibly laid up trouble for
himself.

Amy had more than once felt uneasy when Spencer's
manner reminded her that he had wishes which concerned her intimately. Not that he ever ventured far
enough to deserve rebuff. He had appointed a rôle
for himself, — to give all and claim nothing; but in
resigning small claims he made it clear that he longed
to demand much. In taking his leave of her he would
sometimes stand for a moment letting his eyes devour

her; if she gave him her hand he relinquished it grudgingly. Finally, she flamed out in open rebellion, and, as Spencer had told Roger Rexford, demanded that he should let her take back her illogical promise. He declined to give up his vantage ground, and, as we have seen, endeavored to gain a powerful auxiliary to his cause by sending her brother-in-law to her.

One day, shortly after the conversation in the preceding chapter, Spencer was electrified by Roger Rexford's bringing him a message from Miss Standish, asking him to call at the house that evening. Roger made no comment and gave not even a glance; he vouchsafed few words and few looks in these days. He was in a bitter mood, rehearsing to himself his endless grievances, that he had always to submit to events brought about by some malign power he could not control, that he was never able without risk of perdition to give a turn to the wheel and arrest it, — all he had to do was to lie down and be ground beneath it.

Spencer had recovered his buoyancy by this time, and, realizing that Roger Rexford's gloom was something time would dispel, was busy with his own plans. He was stirred by an irrational hope that Amy had been brought over to his views; at least, some advantage must come from this chance of meeting her. He reached the house just before sunset, and being told that Miss Standish was walking somewhere about the grounds he volunteered to go out and find her. He thought he saw a gleam of her white gown near the river, so descended the lawn. It was only a reflection in the water. The little stream had taken on color from the clouds, and rippled on, a sinuous fluctuating track of rose and flame. Amy was not there. He stood for a moment looking up and down the banks, noting the swaying of the branches of the willows dipping into the water, and rising and falling with its motion. She was likely to be in the garden, he said to himself ; so, ascending the slope and skirting the shrubberies, he went round the house.

Here he came upon her. She was looking at the primroses. They were banked against a hedge of laurels and rhododendrons, and for the past hour had been getting ready to open. She was gazing so intently that she did not observe Spencer's approach. A beam from the sinking sun touched her face and set off its contour with the gem-like color with which Millet invested the outlines of his peasant-girl in the Angelus. The sun dropped and left her pale. At the same moment a visible tremor shook the buds of the primroses ; the outer petals unfolded, the calyx in another instant burst its sheath and the full blossom expanded its lovely yellow corolla. Not one, but a hundred flowers had come out as by the stroke of a magician's wand.

What Spencer saw, however, was the smile which illumined the girl's face. She turned as if eager to share the charm of the moment with some one, and when her eye fell on him she exclaimed : —

" Did you see them open ? "

"I only saw you."

" But watch," she said, "the others will come out in another instant. Look ! Is it not exquisite ? Is it not a miracle ? You can actually hear the petals part ! And is not the fragrance delicious ? Almost like jessamine. To-morrow night I must beg my sister to let me keep Bessy up to see them. She delights in flowers, and I wonder why it is that night blossoms are always so beautiful. Did you ever see the cereus unclose? It begins to palpitate in the afternoon, but the great white and golden heart of the blossom is not all out until towards midnight. Oh, they are so superb! Nature is so various and so beautiful. She can give us such loveliness, such happiness, and yet human life remains so ugly and so unhappy."

These words had burst out as if she spoke not to Spencer, but in excited revery. "Why is it," she went on, "that nature does not lift people out of their indifference and stolidity? I want people to be just as happy and perfect as these flowers."

"*You* are," said Spencer. At the same moment he picked half a dozen of the lovely pale yellow blossoms and laid them against her braids.

She gave a little cry.

"Oh," she exclaimed, "how heartless to pick them!" She retreated a step or two and the spray fell to the ground. She experienced not a little indignation, but what she chiefly showed was a richer glow, a more brilliant glance and an attitude more full of life.

"Will you not accept my poor flowers?" he asked.

"I never wear flowers," she said.

"They would become you. I wanted to see the primroses against your hair, then I could have looked at them."

"There come the moths," she said, kindling anew. "They are the great humming-bird moths. See how they poise, with just the flutter of the humming-birds' wings."

"I too am a moth, drawn by the sweetness and richness of a marvelous flower," Spencer remarked fervently.

"If you knew, Mr. Spencer," said Amy, "how uncalled for I find that tone of yours, — how offensive in the light of what happened yesterday."

"What has happened?" said Spencer, startled.

"I asked my brother to tell you I wanted to see you," said Amy. "It seemed to me best to be entirely frank with you."

He looked up at her with a burning anxiety.

"Let us walk down the garden path," she said; "or should you prefer to go inside?"

"Let us walk down the path," he replied. "The night is beautiful, although I confess the beauty of the world has lately meant nothing except to remind me that you were once more kind than you are now."

Her eyes looked as if she were ready to flash forth some rejoinder, but after a minute's pause she said, —

"I had a visitor yesterday, Mr. Spencer; can you guess who it was?"

The blood rushed to his face. "No," he replied, but he was thinking of Leo.

"It was Mr. Alonzo Sloper," said Amy, with a demure glance at Spencer, which brought a deeper flush to his cheek.

"Mr. Alonzo Sloper," he repeated, as if the name was indifferent to him. "He is one of the old Walford characters. Did he amuse you?"

"A little, by his ponderous politeness and his solemnities of self-importance," said Amy. "But he came not in peace but in war." They had been moving along the broad graveled path bordered with closely clipped miniature hedges of box, and had now reached a bed of foxgloves, when Amy stopped short and stood still, looking down. "He came," she went on hurriedly, for she knew that she was imposing a painful ordeal upon her companion, "to tell me that you had long been engaged to his daughter. He believed that I was exerting some influence which made you unfaithful to her. He had heard that I was to marry you, Mr. Spencer. I could only assure him that it was not the case; that I was not engaged to marry you; that I intended never to marry at all; that I had heard nothing about the engagement he alluded to, but that I felt certain, having seen you and known you ever since I had been in Walford, that you would always fulfill your duty to the uttermost."

Spencer was shaken by an anger which hardly permitted him to speak coherently.

"It is a — lie," he exclaimed. "It is a conspiracy, it is blackmail. I am not engaged to her — I — "

Amy was startled by the black wrath visible in his face. She had always seen him so cool, so smooth, so wholly the master of himself; this did not seem like the same man.

"Do not be angry," she interposed softly. "There is evidently some mistake, for — for — I saw the daughter herself to-day."

He made a gesture as if he had lost all power of self-command; he was about to speak, then stamped his heel into the gravel, and, dropping his eyes to the ground, stood like a man who held a guard upon himself, not daring to move hand or foot.

"I have been to see her," said Amy in a quiet, even voice. "I had met her once before, and as our interview then was unsatisfactory, I had often had it in my mind to call upon her. I went to-day. I intend to see her very often. Perhaps I may help her. She is an

ardent little creature, eager for life. She has had little
chance so far ; but, Mr. Spencer, I do think she is very
interesting in her way."

Spencer had been wholly taken by surprise. He had
rehearsed many possible parts which might be offered
him in the coming interview, but this especial rôle had
not been one of them. All this past year he had been
piling up wrath against Mr. Alonzo Sloper, whom he had
begun to look upon as his evil genius. Being a man
of generous leisure Mr. Sloper had grown ubiquitous.
He had a habit of looking in at the works with a bunch
of flowers, which he would intrust to one of the clerks
in the down-stairs office "for Mr. Spencer, with Miss
Leo Sloper's compliments ; and would he be sure to
come to tea that evening at half past six .o'clock ? "
Now and then Alonzo would sit down, and, while he
waited for Spencer to appear, would converse affably
with anyone who would listen on the subject of the
young man's engagement to his daughter. In fact,
Spencer had of late been obliged to brace himself
against a possible encounter, in any and every place,
with the red-nosed, purple-cheeked toper, who greeted
him with maudlin reminders that his dear Leo was sitting at home playing the part of Mariana with a perpetual refrain of " He cometh not." Spencer had
learned to parry these thrusts with apparent good-
nature, but the effrontery of .Mr. Sloper in intruding
upon Miss Standish passed the limits not only of experience but of imagination. This was too much. He
said to himself that his patience with the Slopers was
at an end ; his account with them must be settled.
His present task, however, was to make it clear to
Amy that he had been slandered.

He had regained his hold upon himself. " I wish," he said in a quick, earnest way, " you would forgive my outburst. If you knew just how exasperating it was to me to think of that tipsy wretch troubling you with his drunken nonsense, you whom I wish to throne high out of reach of all annoyance, you would overlook my violence. I have never been engaged to Leo Sloper. I swear before heaven I have never for one moment been engaged to her."

" Like Ophelia, then," said Amy, "she was the more deceived, for evidently you made her believe you loved her."

" I am very sorry," said Spencer in a tone of genuine feeling. " I am the last person in the world to go forward and back, but something must be allowed a man in the way of selection and choice ; he must have some opportunity to apply a test. When I first met Leo she attracted me. I was lonely. I was young, — after my hard, sordid laboring days, I needed some relief. I hoped I should find in her something congenial. I was soon undeceived. However, it is an ungracious statement for a man to make, that he discovers blemishes and imperfections in a girl. My acquaintance had been purely experimental ; if it was misunderstood I cannot blame myself for her mistake. Leo naturally wishes to marry and escape from such a home. But, Miss Standish, I never promised to marry her."

By this time the golden and rosy light in the sky had changed to violet, and that in its turn had faded into gray. It was now late dusk; still, looking in his face she could clearly see that his expression was full of candor, just dashed with scorn. She could readily believe him, for well she knew from her experience among girls that half their waking thoughts are taken up with groundless hopes about some possible lover, ecstasies of sweet imaginings over the recollection of a kindly glance or a lingering pressure of the hand, with infinite capacity of flattering interpretation. Very likely Leo had allowed her imagination to run away with her judgment, and had let her heart instead of her ears listen when he spoke. After a moment's pause he proceeded.

"All the effect she had upon my heart, Miss Standish, was to teach it what it demanded; it asked for a nobler woman."

"I think Leo could easily develop into all you wish," Amy made haste to say. "She has so far had the scantiest opportunities. I am going to teach her all sorts of things, Mr. Spencer. She is to come to me every day for two or three hours. She has a sweet little voice and I shall try to train it; and she is wonderfully clever with her hands. I fancy she can both design and color creditably after a little instruction. She has had to depend upon herself, and her manner has grown perhaps a trifle aggressive; but all these trifling faults will easily correct themselves. She touched me very much. At first she was proud and reluctant, but when she realized that I was actually her friend, not a rival, but a sister, a helper, she turned to me in a way which went to my very heart. I can do a great deal for her. I am going to do all I can, and for her mother too. I saw Mrs. Sloper, and talked with her. She had run away from the house, but Bessy was with me, and she went after the poor timid woman and made her acquaintance. Bessy seems to win her heart. She showed us her flowers; she is fond of flowers, and that was a link of sympathy. It is one of those cases when a little outside help can do a great deal of good. I am only sorry I have lost so much time. But I mean to accomplish miracles." She had spoken very softly, in a quick, ardent way, looking all the time into the face of her companion, who had shown that he was not a little restless, had bitten his lips and averted his eyes. She now gathered herself up for a final appeal. "Mr. Spencer," she said in a tone of caressing sweetness, "you said that Leo at first attracted you. I am sure that she will deepen and fix the impression she made first. It is a great deal for a man to have taken possession of a girl's whole soul and heart as you have taken possession of hers. Her feeling for you is an · immense stimulus, a mainspring of — "

Spencer started as if struck a blow. "Do you mean," he said in a voice choked with some emotion, "that you are kindly undertaking to develop Miss Leo Spencer's artistic capabilities on my account? Perhaps you have promised me to her as a sort of medal, Miss Standish. I assure you, you are altogether mistaken if you suppose that it would ever make the slightest difference to me whether she paints, sings, or speaks all the languages." His voice had cleared and he spoke with strong sarcastic emphasis. "I admire your generous impulse," he went on, "your disinterestedness and magnanimity are of the loftiest description. I only regret that they are to be wasted on Alonzo Sloper's daughter."

"I don't think it is fair to judge Leo by her father, Mr. Spencer," said Amy. "She is a sweet, bright, innocent young girl; she would make you a — "

"Heavens and earth!" cried Spencer, flinging up both

arms as if in a frenzy, "you are talking to a man with aspirations far above Miss Leo Sloper. She is nothing to me. She never can be anything to me. It seems to me the very extremity of cruelty, Miss Standish, for you, who know perfectly well how every thought of mine has been given to a far different object, to suggest the idea of my caring for that girl. Asking for bread and getting a stone in its place is nothing to it; it is invoking an angel and having the foul fiend rise in its place."

Amy stood aghast at the havoc she had created. She began to fear that she had meddled mischievously. It would have given her such complete satisfaction to have arranged Spencer's future life for him; but instead she had hurt his pride; worse than that she had given his vanity a cruel stab. His violence frightened her; and in miserable doubt what to say or do next, she moved on and sat down on the steps of the arbor.

He followed her.

"You hate me, you despise me," he said with emotion.

"I do not hate you, I do not despise you," she said, gently.

"You know that I worship you, that I wish to marry you, that I have had no other thought since the first moment I saw you, yet you count my feelings as nothing. You dismiss me as a presumptuous fool who asks too much, and must be satisfied with what he can get, that is, with a Leo Sloper —"

She shuddered and turned away with a gesture which seemed like an entreaty that he should not continue the subject.

"Please answer one question," he said pleadingly.

"Do you want to get me out of the way because you have different plans for yourself?"

"I do not understand you," she said coldly.

"Unless you are engaged to another man," he persisted, "why may I not remain your friend? If I could be absolutely sure that you are not thinking of marrying—"

"If you knew how I hate the idea of what you suggest," Amy burst out petulantly, "you would not offend me in that way."

"I will offend you no more," cried Spencer, with a great effort of magnanimity. "If I have stepped over the bounds you appointed, it was only that I was tortured, jealous,—that I dreaded lest the sweetness you withheld from me was given to—"

She had risen.

"I warned you not to offend me in that way," she said almost fiercely. "I am cold," she added, shivering. "I must go in. I bid you good night."

She swept past him. He did not attempt to follow her, but sat watching the tall, slim figure swiftly ascend the garden walk. It paused one moment before the primroses, then faded into the surrounding darkness. His mind was busy thinking over what had been said and not said between them. He felt as if he had at least partly succeeded in reëstablishing himself with her, and he continued to sit looking up at the blinking, mocking stars and devising the best means of keeping some hold upon her.

Amy herself was experiencing a sensation of defeat. She had acted injudiciously: she was always acting injudiciously. She could not understand how she had allowed her interview with Mr. Spencer to take such an

absurd course when she had a hundred specific things
to say, not one of which she had fairly uttered. She
looked up at the stars ; and as she looked she seemed
suddenly to have an instinct that she need not always
feel the impatience, the uneasiness, the disappointment
she had experienced of late. A longing for happiness
assailed her. She did not put into words what happiness might be, although she had often defined the conditions. This sudden effervescence of the soul, this
desire to love and to understand and to be loved and
to be understood, was new.

XIX.

DOUBTS.

ONE Sunday afternoon Evelyn lay on the lounge in her room resting. She had dozed a little, but had not actually slept. It was one of those midsummer days when the jubilant robins sing from dawn till past sunset, and the moment she lost consciousness a fresh carol from out-of-doors gurgling forth from some swelling little throat was certain to rouse her. She did not begrudge the birds their burst of rapture. She lay, her eyes closed, feeling blessed and happy ; and they voiced her own mood. She had not been asleep, she was certain she had not been asleep, when a slight sound in the room startled her. Glancing towards the open windows, she saw that her husband had come in and was sitting there with Bessy standing between his knees. He held the little face between his two hands and was looking into her eyes intently with a peculiar moody expression. Then all at once he pushed the child away, started to his feet, and at the same time flung up his hand as though in extremity of physical or mental pain, then brought it down, striking his forehead with a gesture which suggested impotent despair.

Evelyn had raised herself on the lounge.

"What is it?" she faltered, hardly sure whether she was awake or dreaming.

"What is what?" returned Roger in his usual voice.

He came to the lounge and sat down in a chair beside her. "You have had a long nap," he said. .

"I don't think I have been asleep," returned Evelyn, gazing at him in astonishment. "What was it you were doing to Bessy?"

"Doing to Bessy? What should I do to Bessy?" said Roger lightly. "She wanted to give you some roses and I was afraid she might disturb you."

Evelyn held out her arms to the little girl, who ran into them. "I brought you nine roses, mamma," she exclaimed, — "nine red roses, and I brought you a hundred million kisses."

Evelyn had been sharply startled and could not recover from her impression that her husband had been rough to Bessy, but did not like to utter the accusation. She continued to gaze from one to the other questioningly.

"You have evidently been dreaming," said Roger soothingly.

"No, I was not dreaming," said Evelyn. "I opened my eyes and I saw you staring into Bessy's face, then you jumped up and made a gesture as if you were appealing to heaven."

"Oh, good gracious !" said Roger. "What a thing it is to have an imagination."

"It was not my imagination !"

"Don't have nerves ; don't have fancies," he said uneasily. Evelyn, when her first impression of the incident died away, began to tell herself it was possible she had been dreaming. Or if she had not been dreaming she could account for it in some other way. Roger had not been in his usual spirits of late ; he had not slept well, and explained that he was thinking about business matters, — that he should probably find it necessary, since Orrin Goodeve was to spend six months abroad, to go to Chicago himself. Evelyn's conjectures might thus be plausibly answered, and she could account for his moodiness and lack of spirit by his sorrow at leaving home. Still, in spite of all these reasonable hypotheses, she could not forget the expression he had worn as he stared haggardly at Bessy's face. What did it mean, what could it mean, except that he wished to find something there to answer his need? Why should he repulse her with anger? Evelyn was by this time almost her old self. Bessy was perpetually beside her as she went about full of interests and energies, and the child's endless pretty ways, her incessant chatter about every thought which passed through her active little brain brightened the whole household.

It gave Evelyn pain to observe that Roger was not happy with them. It seemed as if, instead, he wandered joyless, having no solaces, no consolations; even preferring a chilling solitude to their companionship.

"Roger, you are not well," Evelyn would say, clinging to him.

"I am perfectly well," he answered.

"Are you happy?"

"Who is happy in this world?" he would reply. "That is, except you and Bessy."

Then Evelyn said to him, startled, "Roger, how gray your hair has grown! It has changed in a fortnight."

"You are getting back your eyes," he replied, "and are beginning to find out what an old fellow I am. For two years you have seen nothing to speak of; your fancy has made me out young, blithe, and good-looking."

"It was losing Bessy that made you grow old," said Evelyn, with a sharp pang of conviction that it had been Roger and not herself who had tasted the misery of the cruel experience, and felt not in imagination but in fact the sharp thorn of care.

"Yes, that cut deep," said Roger. "After a man is thirty he does not get over an experience in a day."

And yet, Evelyn said to herself, she had recovered from it. Only by the strongest effort of mind could she now realize that she had once been ready to accept the fact that Bessy was dead. All these thoughts had passed over her and were gone, utterly swept away by the demands of the new life. If Roger too could only begin again afresh, — put away that sadness of remembrance, that unquenchable regret, and partake of this actual, satisfying happiness. Why could he not? Had he any doubt? The intellect, subtle although it is, must have something tangible to work on.

One rainy day, when Roger came in, he found that Evelyn had been occupying herself by collecting all the pictures that had ever been taken of Bessy from the time she was born and had ranged them together with a view to comparison. There were several showing her as a mere baby, then a beautiful colored life-size portrait made when she was two years old, a *carte de visite* finished only a month before she was lost, and several which had been taken since her return.

"What are you doing?" Roger asked sharply.

Evelyn looked up with an excited face.

"I was comparing the late and early pictures of Bessy," she replied. "See how unlike they are."

"They are no more unlike than two pictures of yourself taken within one year might be," said Roger with strange vehemence. "It is the most unusual thing in the world for one photograph to look like another. Photography more often caricatures than gives a real impression of a face."

His tone was rough and his face showed agitation; Evelyn looked at him with curiosity.

"That picture taken when she was two years old is exactly what she is to-day," Roger pursued, pointing to it and then to the child.

"Yes," said Evelyn, "I was thinking it is more like her than the photographs which have just come home."

Roger sank down with the look of a man who experiences unexpected relief, yet whose nerves are still quivering from the ordeal he has passed through.

"You are never satisfied, it seems to me," he said in a tone of suppressed irritation. "You always want too much; you never have enough."

Evelyn bundled all the smaller photographs together, and put them in the drawer, and restored the large one to its nail on the wall.

"Having you and Bessy and Theodore, I have enough," she said archly; and she began to tell stories about Bessy, whom some neighbor had tried to lure into her house on promise of showing her their baby.

"I 've got a baby myself," Bessy had returned with some haughtiness. Roger listened ungladdened. Indeed, his feeling nowadays was that he could never know pleasure again. He had for one moment dreaded lest Evelyn should be prying into the secret; lest she too had begun to mistrust that after all this Bessy was not her Bessy. Then his sickening fear had passed, and he had wondered he could even momen-

tarily have entertained it.   He was growing eager to
leave Walford, feeling that life among familiar scenes
and people had become only an experience of ingenious
lying.   Away from this daily, hourly call upon his self-
command he hoped that he might re-gather his forces
and be able to look upon his position coolly.   He was
yet to find out that the moment he was at a distance, he
would be haunted by a fear lest something should be
taking place in his absence; that some horrible suspicion begotten and nourished in silence and conceal-
ment might suddenly leap forth and disclose the real
facts.   There had been one resource open to Roger Rexford after Spencer's communication.   He might have
thrown up the game. declaring he would be no party to
a fraud ; he might have challenged the opinion of all
the world as to Bessy's identity.   Fvidence could
somehow, somewhere, have been found which would .
have made the matter clear.   At times, in half delirious
visions, as he lay sleepless at night on his pillow, he had
been urged to this disclosure.   It seemed the easiest way
out of the trouble ; it would divide the misery among
others, he would not have to bear everything alone as he
had borne it so long.   Evelyn was stronger now, and
she could accept her share.   More than once he had
risen in the morning with a resolution to take direct
measures for bringing the whole story to light.   But by
the time he had dressed, eaten breakfast, met his family and set out for his office, the spectre which had
pursued him had become a feverish fancy of the night.
    He saw too clearly the fatal consequences of disclo-
sures.   The present situation held definite advantages,
and it would be mere selfish cowardice to throw up the
game.   If there were strength, safety or comfort in

truth he might have been glad enough to establish the truth. But the only hope for himself, for Evelyn, for Bessy, lay in this falsehood, which after all might be no falsehood at all. He was at times conscious of a sombre heroism in accepting his position and making the best of things.

He had at first recoiled from Spencer, ready to loathe the idea that they were actually confederates in a crime. But that feeling soon died away; the gap and chasm closed, and Roger found a certain comfort in their intercourse. It is always a relief when one is suffering to have one's sufferings understood. Evelyn might put her cheek against her husband's, look into his eyes and plead with him to dismiss his regrets and be happy, but such consolations only intensified his sense of isolation. Anxiety and alarm had sucked all the sweetness out of her caresses and had put a sting in their place. He was always afraid that her quick brain was busy constructing reasons for his apathy and gloom. In Spencer's society there was a sure relief. Spencer knew that he was wretched, understood just why he was wretched, and had respect for the stupefied bewilderment which comes upon all of us mortals when we see the catastrophe which might quite logically have overtaken some less worthy person by some inexplicable perversity of fortune fasten its deadly fang upon our own lives. Half of Roger's present misery came from the conviction that it was cruelly unjust that *he* should be thus smitten, that *he* should suffer pain.

Spencer made no more false moves; he was adroit and full of tact. He had wished as delicately as possible to rouse Roger Rexford to a sense of obligation, and so far his course had been as effective as he himself could desire. His salary had been doubled; he had been made manager of the works with full powers in the absence of Roger Rexford, who would spend the greater part of the next few months in Chicago. He was not yet a partner; still, even that ambition might be gratified when the present agreement expired.

But his love-affair was not advancing so fortunately. Miss Standish had given his vanity a cruel blow. It was a relief to his feelings for a few days to call the Slopers individually and collectively by every unflattering epithet he could devise. His sentiments towards Leo and her father had acquired a keen edge. He had never supposed that old Sloper possessed the requisite wit to mature a plan for turning the situation and making Miss Standish herself his auxiliary, and to discover craft in an adversary he had hitherto despised as an inert lump of clay did not make Spencer more charitable. It was time that Alonzo Sloper should be taught a lesson, and Spencer laid his plans and arranged his moves with deliberate malice. He held a mortgage on the Sloper place. It had been running for many years, and had come into his hands at a time when the original holder was about to foreclose. Spencer had settled all claims, and the deed had been made over to himself. He had done this to avert catastrophe from Leo, who was at that time dear to him. Still, the mortgage was well covered by the property and was a fairly good investment, so he argued, making light of his generosity. Certainly the fact of his holding this lien ought to give him the whip-hand on Sloper, and Spencer now set to work to prove that he was master of the situation.

It was characteristic of him that being able to

expend his wrath upon the Slopers enabled him to see
Amy's conduct in a better light. He realized her fever
of compassion for anyone in suffering. It was like her
to show the loftiest magnanimity for a weaker rival.
He was soon ready to believe that her coldness proceeded from her belief that he was in honor bound to
Leo Sloper. When his vanity ceased to tingle, he
owned a tantalizing charm in the attitude she had assumed. Her belief in his docility was so naïve as to be
amusing. He had always piqued himself on the ease
with which he had established an intimacy with the
proud, reserved girl, and he now reinstated his self-belief by recalling clear signs of her preference. She had
always been somewhat of an enigma to him, and this
touch of purely feminine jealousy gave him the key to
a thousand little haughtinesses, caprices and touches of
charming disdain. In what an entrancing light it disclosed her feelings for him when she pretended to step
back and put Leo in her place! "No, indeed, my
beauty, not yet. I know a trick worth two of that."
So ran Spencer's thoughts when he revolved Amy's
compassionate effort to sacrifice herself.

He was, however, too busy a man in these days to
give himself up to making love. Pleasanter matters
would settle themselves; meanwhile he was getting
ready to inflict some form of punishment on Alonzo
Sloper.

There was an infinity of legitimate business to be
transacted for Roger Rexford as he came and went.
Spencer was pushing on certain schemes which were to
result to everyone's advantage. He had for years been
studying the practical workings of the Rexford Manufacturing Company and had views to offer. In old

days it had been simply a matter of course to make
a steady ten per cent, year in and year out, which in
prosperous times was doubled and sometimes trebled.
The business had then been carefully managed, and
they surpassed all competing manufacturers in equipment. In spite of Roger Rexford's expensive outlay
in machinery a few years before, there was still much
that remained to be done. Spencer had knowledge of
a new invention which could be secured and would be
of the utmost advantage. He had a sure instinct in
winding his way into the citadel, and he soon brought
over all opposition, — at least, bore it down with a high
hand.

Such success restored his glow of self-approval. A
man with a strong grip upon his business was sure to
have his way. He was certainly justified in believing
that he must by this time seem to Roger Rexford a
most desirable brother-in-law. He confided to him the
whole story of his love-affairs, with such reservations as
seemed most consistent.

Roger Rexford listened, saying little in return, generally sitting motionless, with eyes fixed on the ceiling.
When Spencer resolved to show that Amy had been
kind to him, and went on telling over one little sign of
preference after another, Roger might change his position slightly, but never expressed incredulity. Once
when Spencer made definite demands upon his fraternal
co-operation, insisting that he should talk over the
matter again with Amy and this time urge her consent
to Spencer's proposals, Roger at first stared with eyes
which seemed ready to express some strong feeling.
Then he shrugged his shoulders and consented. He
was ready to assent to anything in these days, not from

love of action but from abhorrence of making an effort to think. His chief consciousness was a vague desire that time should pass. The world seemed phantasmal and unsubstantial ; he had no real impulses, no vital wishes ; all he wanted was to have the suspense over.

XX

EVELYN AND REXFORD LONG.

REXFORD LONG usually spent part of August and September in Walford at the Goodeves', varying his long stay there by short visits to the Rexfords. This year he had especially looked forward to seeing Roger's wife, once more happy with her two children.

He seemed to find a new Evelyn; an Evelyn who had suddenly become a woman. She had grown handsome; her manner had attained an equipoise it had never before shown. She had lost her old impatience, her once impetuous haste, her self-assertive willfulness. She was in good health; the alarming weakness in her eyes had been gradually overcome. Everything in her condition was at last normal. Long admired her development, physical and mental, and said to himself she was turning out just the woman her well-wishers might have hoped for. In his own heart he sighed a little for the girl; not only the girl he had known before Roger Rexford knew her, but the girl who had for four years remained unspoiled by marriage, with charming prettiness, sudden hauteurs, frowns and blushes, wishes unreasonable and infinite, each of which must be granted on the instant; at one time easily led, at another rebellious and headstrong, but always beautiful, always lovable, always bewitching.

"Evelyn has improved," Mrs. Goodeve confided to

Long one day, "but sometimes I long for my old Evelyn."

"Is it Amy who has influenced her?" he inquired.

"Perhaps, a little. But you could hardly expect that after that long struggle Evelyn would come out just as young as she went in."

Long found many things in Walford changed, — his cousin Roger, like everything else. Roger came and went; sometimes staying at home three days and then going away for a week, again in Walford but a day and a night. He was no doubt absorbed in his business; important changes were in progress. Long told himself that perhaps the trouble was that he liked to come back to the place and find events standing still. In old times the summer holidays had been full of picnics and excursions. Nobody seemed to have anything to do except to take long drives to all the mountains and lakes within reach, eat salads, patties and cakes, and return by moonlight. Of course, for two years the joy of existence had been at a low ebb, but he had expected that the old pleasures would now renew themselves, and he was inclined to attribute the change to Amy's intense and diversified energies. Mrs. Goodeve still had picnics, it is true, but now they were for the working-girls; and much against his inclination Long was obliged to give a lecture on botany after the refection was over. No more sitting on rocks in idle talk, bringing up old reminiscences, talking of new books and old, making jokes, seizing the spirit of the hour. They took their pleasure sadly nowadays; there was a strain on energies which of old it would have been a relief to let lie dormant. There was always some scheme for amusing the working-girls. Once it was kings who had to be amused by their subjects, but the world is turned upside down. Amy had a stereopticon, and Long was called upon to lecture on the English Lakes, Paris and Switzerland, in order to describe the set of plates in which the young philanthropist had invested for the benefit of the factory operatives and seamstresses. Long, never in love with the sound of his own voice, found it difficult to keep his courage up to the point of taking the platform. Then the instrument thwarted and depressed him at every turn, refusing obstinately to work at the right moment, always coming up limping with a view of what he had been blandly describing a quarter of an hour before.

However, the weeks passed, and mid-September came all too soon for Long. The month had come in cold and rainy, and pleasant weather had seemed to be over ; then the storms cleared and there ensued a stretch of perfectly beautiful days. Flowers budded again and blossomed in a riotous late summer luxuriance ; there was a sweet disorder about the gardens and hedges ; a scent of fruit was in the air ; the horizons showed an indescribable richness of atmosphere.

One morning Long was at the Rexfords', and he and Amy and Bessy were wandering about the place looking at the ripening fruit. As they walked under the trellises it was pleasant to look up and see the grapes hanging between the great transparent leaves. One vine held up half a dozen bunches fully ripe, which showed almost black against the blue sky. Bessy longed for them and she and Amy went off to find the gardener and bid him bring a ladder. Meanwhile Evelyn sat down on a bench and Long took a place beside her. A bee buzzed by them and a bird flew past and looked at them both.

"It is pleasant," said Long; "but I have to go away."

"When?" asked Evelyn as if startled.

"I must be in New York next Monday; perhaps I can stay until Sunday night."

"Every day," murmured Evelyn, with a sudden change of features, "I have said to myself, 'To-morrow I must have a talk with Rex.' Now it must really be to-morrow."

Long had a sudden vivid impression that there had been a veil between them all these weeks, and that at last it was down. He seemed to see her for the first time face to face.

"Can you not speak now?" he asked, feeling as if he could not endure any suspense. This was his old Evelyn, with supplication in her face.

"No; not now, not here," she said with decision. "I want to be certain that no one will interrupt or overhear us. To-morrow morning I will take the children up to Wolf Hill. You will find me by the brook under the hickory trees."

"I will be there."

"Rex," she murmured with a quivering lip, "I suppose one goes on trusting what one trusted in first. You have never disappointed me. There is no one like you, — no one. I have been afraid of making a mistake in speaking to you, but I might make worse mistakes if I kept silent."

His sudden impatience had passed. He suffered instead a curious shrinking from the ordeal she was to impose.

Birdsey brought the ladder and put it against the side of the arbor, remarking doubtfully that his weight was

too much for the trellis. He looked at Long as if pro-
posing that he should go up and pick the grapes, and
the latter mounted with alacrity, glad to escape from
the necessity of finding words to say to Evelyn and
Amy. The latter had given him a basket, a cord and a
knife, and after he had cut the ripest bunches, he carefully lowered the precious basket to the ground lest
the grapes should be crushed. He heard voices and
laughter beneath him, but did not listen ; he wondered
that Evelyn could seem to be making merry. He forgot that he had to descend, and sat staring blankly at
the sky, feeling as if human misery reached out to its
illimitable span. He had been happy until Evelyn had
spoken, but it was a meaningless happiness ; a breath
had killed it.

"Come down, Uncle Rex," cried Bessy. "Come
down and eat the grapes."

Then there was a fresh burst of laughter. They had
been playing him a trick. All three, Evelyn, Amy and
Bessy, had dragged the ladder away. "The grapes are
delicious," they called to him. "Unless you come they
will all be eaten up."

Their mirth seemed so far off it could not reach him
nor gladden him ; their little joys made the depths of
his trouble apparent to him. However, he defeated
their merry malice by sliding down the pillar, and
claimed his share of the grapes.

He found the day endless. Let him try as he might
to master, at least suspend, his curiosity, it was impossible to exclude the rushing train of conjectures which
followed Evelyn's words. All the probabilities pointed to
Roger as the source of trouble. Rex now confessed to
himself that his mind had been more or less busy about

his cousin all through this visit. "There is something wrong about Roger," he had said to himself more than once. Now that he tried to define what he had seen he found that there was a jarring pain in giving clear shape to what he had all the time dreaded. He had observed a change in Roger's manner; he was impatient of small talk, his eye wavered, he had grown indifferent to trifling niceties of behavior regarding which he had formerly been punctilious. These were mere unimportant details, but twice Long had gone to the office and found Roger in a condition which showed plainly that he had been drinking. Once, it is true, he had explained the presence of a bottle on the table by saying that he was trying to deaden a neuralgic pain in his jaw.

Then Long had been startled to see Spencer's supremacy at the works. He had besides heard not a little talk of the young fellow among Walford people, who enjoyed calling him a "beggar on horseback," and leaving his end to be inferred.

It seemed to Long that if Evelyn's revelation were to hinge on the fact of her husband's deterioration and his subserviency to this ambitious young fellow who was perhaps playing on Roger's weaknesses, he must be ready with arguments to convince her she misjudged, saw things in a false light. Long felt that he had borne much; he could not bear to hear that Evelyn was not perfectly contented with her husband.

He had always looked up to Roger, who was four years older than himself, and who at school and college had dazzled him with a trick of easy superiority. Long had had a lonely boyhood, and it had been delightful to be admitted into the luxurious Rexford household where Roger had been the petted and only child. Long recognized in himself a capacity for steady, faithful work, but mistrusted his faculty for getting what he wanted out of life. Roger had always been able to allow himself all the advantages of deliberate selection and fastidious choice. When he had said, "I am going to marry Evelyn Standish," Long had faced the ordeal and felt that he ought to have expected it. Roger had trusted Long incredibly since his marriage; trusted him with the blind, implicit belief which has made hounds of some men and heroes of others. Long had sometimes bitten his lip in a half rage to see how he was trusted. He did not call himself fine names. He hoped and prayed that Evelyn would never tell him Roger was not a good husband to her. He had never tried to love Evelyn less; life contained nothing for him unless he loved her.

He slept at Mrs. Goodeve's that night, told her he wanted to take a long tramp across country to Wolcott, and set off next morning while the sun was still low. He had always liked long walks to the hills, and Mrs. Goodeve gave him an early breakfast, talking vigorously about her son all the while. She had always wanted Felix to marry, she declared; she had almost made up her mind at one time that he had fallen in love with Amy Standish, but here he was writing her descriptions of every woman he met in Montana, sometimes even inclosing photographs, and putting the question beneath, "How would *she* do as a daughter-in-law, eh?" Mrs. Goodeve's apprehension lest her son should not marry seemed rapidly to be turning into a lively dread lest he should. But she was not so blind that she did not see the reflection of trouble in her nephew's face. He looked as if he had not slept,

and after he had set out she said to herself that perhaps she had bungled, and perhaps he was himself in
love with Amy Standish.

Meanwhile Long was walking toward the west with
great strides. He had little joy that day in the opal
morning lights with refractions of loveliest color from
every drop of dew, every tint of a flower, every wing of a
bird that flew. Yet he was glad that the sun shone ;
when he crossed the little river he thought within himself
that Evelyn would follow his steps later, and he hoped
she would have time and heart to watch the stream
twisting and twirling through the green meadows, the lily
leaves and rushes swaying with its ripples.   For himself, an odd jumble of past, present and future was
running through his mind. He expected nothing for
himself, he hoped nothing for himself. He had learned
the negations of a reasonable despair. What interested him in life was thinking about Evelyn. Thus the
pretty pastoral sights, the cows standing knee-deep in
the water switching their tails, or gathering in the
shady corner of the pasture, the shadows trembling and
quivering, the young birds fluttering from bough to
ground and from ground to bough, the luxuriant tangle
of golden-rod and aster, butterfly-weed and cardinal
flowers were simply sights which Evelyn would be sure
to like. He wanted the pleasant show of things for
her. Nature had intended her for feeling and diffusing joy. She ought to have a life in which what was
deepest and sweetest went on forever, shifting into
combinations lovely and always more lovely.

He walked towards the west until it was ten o'clock,
then, as if mechanically, turned and walked due east.
He knew his bearings, and at a quarter before eleven

emerged from the woods and struck into a cart-path which traversed a stretch of rough uncultivated land cleared years before, then given over to blueberries and hazels. As soon as he was outside the woods he discovered that it was a day of intense heat and of blinding light. The sky was less blue than opal, and in lieu of ordinary yellow sunlight the eye was conscious of iridescent scintillations ; the whole atmosphere seemed to give out radiance and invested all the distances with a gem-like quality of color.

"It is so warm, she has probably decided not to come," Long said to himself, hardly knowing whether the absence would give him most disappointment or relief.

But Evelyn was waiting for him at the rendezvous. He saw her in another moment waving her parasol. In spite of the distance he could see her clearly, for to-day not only colors but contours were sharply and luminously defined. She was sitting on the rocks under the clump of hickory trees, and made the riveting point of a picture limned with the delicate and vivid touches a Madrazo might have given it. Long could hardly have explained why instead of striding forward he suddenly loitered, raising his eyes persistently to the skies, as if scanning the signs of the weather, stopping even to note a bunch of blue gentians behind a rock, its fringes just beginning to show. Was it that his dread of Evelyn's possible revelations had returned ?

Bessy had been sitting beside her mother, but now ran forward with rapturous greeting, took his hand and pulled him rapidly towards the group under the trees.

"Have you got lunch enough for Uncle Rex, mamma ?" she asked.

Evelyn smiled and nodded as they approached. She had brought both children, and the little Theodore lay fast asleep in his carriage, which was drawn up close beside her. She wore a wide-brimmed hat, a white cambric dress made like a child's frock and belted by a blue ribbon. She had thrown herself down, half reclining against a higher rock behind. Both her trim feet were visible, planted on a sort of footstool below her. She reminded Long of the time when she was a schoolgirl. The heat had flushed her and her eyes seemed half asleep. She looked very youthful, and a child's seriousness of aspect was apparent in her eyes and lips. She made no salutation, only looked at him steadily; but as he came nearer her face suddenly broke into a smile.

"Rex," she said, "how slow you are! I should know you were not in love with me by the way you approach. What Frenchwoman was it who lived at the corner of an open square and had a lover who used to go and see her every day? She observed that while his feeling was fresh he used to cross the square diagonally, but after a time he used to walk around the full distance. 'Ah,' she said, 'I see it is all over.'"

Long sat down on the rock at her feet.

"Don't talk about Frenchwomen and their lovers, Evelyn," said he.

"I beg pardon," she returned with a slight shrug. "Roger has always told me I made the most dreadful speeches. Once he flung down a dish-cover out of our best dinner-service to hide one of my enormities."

Rex had been oppressed as by a nightmare, but sud-denly seemed to wake up and find out that he was dreaming. This little note of petulance in her voice was so natural, so characteristic, he laughed. "You ought to provide him with inexpensive china to smash," said he. "I like your *enfant terrible* speeches. I prefer to feel that you have not the least idea that there is anything evil in the world."

She straightened herself up. "I wish I had not," she said, in a weary voice. "I hate evil. I like to feel happy. I want to wake up in the morning and say to myself, 'Oh, another day!' and feel as if I had wings to soar into the blue. This morning as I lay in my bed there was a flutter of the curtain; the leaves played across the patches of sunlight and made beautiful arabesques of shadow. It was one of those mornings when everything is alive; Sidney Lanier expressed it when he wrote, 'The little green leaves would not leave me alone in my sleep.' Such mornings used to be an invitation to jump up and run out-of-doors into the garden to see what flowers had come out, — in fact I used to feel myself open like a flower expanding petal by petal. This morning I just covered up my head and tried to shut it all out."

She became conscious that Bessy was standing before her.

"Mamma," she said, "please tell me how Princess Margaretta got off that tree!"

"What tree, darling?"

"Don't you remember?" said Bessy with indignation. "She had gone up the tree because the squirrel told her she might, but when she got up the squirrel jumped on the next tree and laughed at her, and then the Princess saw that there was a pelican sitting on one of the branches making a bed for its young, and it asked the Princess —"

"Oh, I remember," said Evelyn, going back to the story she was telling to while away the time until Rex should come. "The pelican asked the princess for the feathers on her hat, and she gave the feathers on her hat, and then for her silk fichu and then she gave up her silk fichu, — but then the pelican demanded her China silk gown, and the princess said, 'No, one must draw a line somewhere!' The pelican thought so too, and was about to give the Princess a scratch with its bill, but Margaretta was too quick. She ran out to the end of the bough, which broke down with her weight and touched a lily leaf, and the princess jumped upon this lily leaf and it floated down stream. That is all. Now go and play with the dogs, — make them walk through the water and cool their feet."

Bessy ran to the little stream, a mere rivulet now, but which, as might be seen from the rocks and boulders along its course, had gathered volume in many a freshet. Rex took a few steps down the bank with the child, then went back to Evelyn. He could not tell how serious her trouble was. There was a soft childishness about her which made him hope that she had been merely fanciful the day before.

" Rex, I do feel so unhappy nowadays when I wake up," she said with a trembling lip.

" I think Roger ought to have sent Spencer out West, and himself have stayed in Walford," said Rex.

"I am happier when Roger is away than when he is here," Evelyn said in a clear, low voice. "Is it not dreadful? It is a relief nowadays when I feel that I am not to see him."

Rex had sat down, but at this he started up. " Evelyn," he said in a tone of horror, " don't say it ! Don't think it, but above all do not utter it. Our spoken words make a bond for us ; we try to keep to them. Roger is your husband. Whatever trouble has come between you, you love him and he worships you."

" I used to love him and he used to love me. But nowadays I am as certain as if I could read every feeling of his heart that he is just as glad to escape from me as I am to escape from him."

" Mamma," cried Bessy gleefully, " hear the water in my shoes. It goes glump, glump, glump."

Evelyn's words had not come easily but rather as if they grated and wounded her ; she had looked round fearfully as she uttered them and Bessy's voice startled her.

The child had at first ordered the dogs through the brook ; then, when they did not obey her, she set them an heroic example and herself walked through the three inches of water, followed by them, and thus backwards and forwards until she was conscious of carrying a heavy weight on her feet.

" They go glump, glump, glump!" said Bessy, and it was not hard to distinguish the sound of the water in the low shoes.

" Bessy, why did you go into the water ? " said Evelyn.

" You said I can put Sir Waller and Nix in the waters, to cool their feet, and they did not know how to go in unless I showed them the way. My feet was hot too ; now my feet is cool, Sir Waller's feet is cool, and Nix' feet is cool. They is muddy too."

" Take off your shoes and stockings, Bessy," said Evelyn, "and lay them in the sun to dry. Come here and I will do it for you."

Bessy approached with large, serious eyes.

" Is I naughty ? " she asked.   " Is I velly naughty ? "

" I hope you did not mean to be naughty," said Evelyn.   " Next time ask me just what you are to do."

She pulled the soaked shoes and stockings off the chubby feet and legs, at which Bessy looked with intense satisfaction.

" Now I can go walk through the brook, mamma," she said.

" Don't you want to eat your lunch ? "

" I wish I can have my lunch.   I 'm velly hungry."

" Take it across the brook and sit down in the shade and eat it."

" All by myself ? "

" Take the dogs with you."

" May I give some to Nix and Sir Waller ? '

" If you have more than you want."

" Am I to walk through the brook, mamma ? "

" If you like.   Or Uncle Rex will jump you over the brook.   There are two oak trees, and you will find acorns on the ground.   They say fairies use the acorn-cups for plates and saucers."

" I wish I can have a fairy, a live fairy to play with, mamma."

" Set a table for the fairies, and perhaps they will come."

Rex took the child across the brook and established her with her lunch basket beneath the trees.   A dog crouched with bright expectant eyes on each side of her, maintaining an air of rigid attention which Bessy could but feel was not wholly disinterested.   She began to lecture them on their manners.   Evelyn rose, lifted the veil for a moment from the sleeping boy, then went

back to her seat just as Rex returned. They could
hear Bessy gurgling with laughter as the dogs en-
croached more and more upon her, Sir Waller putting
an imploring paw on her arm and Nix jumping up and
licking her face.

"Mamma," cried the child, "I wish Uncle Rèx can
keep the dogs while I eat my lunch. I am afraid to
open the basket."

"Take out a little bit of bread and butter for each
and throw it very far off for them," said Evelyn.

Rex sat down, his look fixed on Evelyn ; he had a
dread of words, he was afraid to define the impression
she had given him.

"Something has come between you and Roger,"
he said, after a little time, — "some trifling misunder-
standing which a candid explanation will remove. Can
it be that he is jealous of your love for Bessy ?"

"Rex," said Evelyn with a quick sigh, "I had wondered if you suspected anything about her."

"About his jealousy of her ?"

She put her hand on his arm. "Do you still believe
that she is my own child ?" she asked in a whisper.

"Why, of course."

"She is not," said Evelyn. "She is not my child at
all."

Rex felt as if overpowered by a stupor.

"You know this, and do not dare tell Roger ?" he
said, gazing at her with a feeling of hopeless despair.

"He knows it. He hates the sight of the child. It
was the knowledge of that which made all my suspicions come back."

A sharp spasm of pain had darted through Long
as he listened. He had thought of everything since

yesterday which would come between Roger and his wife, but he had not thought of this. In the surprise of the moment all he could do was to thrust away the horror, — to deny it.

"Evelyn," he said, as if with resentment, "are you speaking from clear knowledge, or from some ghastly morbid doubt which you ought to dismiss? I had believed you were so happy in Bessy, —" his voice, in spite of its stern note, broke, — "the sweetest, brightest little girl that was ever born. It cuts me very deep to think of your shutting her away from your heart."

"I am not shutting her out of my heart," said Evelyn with quivering lips, while a great tear rolled from under her lowered eyelids. "If she were my own Bessy, I could not love her better than I love her. I should have died if she had not come. If I gave life to my own Bessy, this Bessy gave me back my life. Oh, I love her, you need not doubt that. Still, if I had died it would have been better."

"Evelyn," said Long, his whole being shaken with passionate repugnance at the idea, "you are wrong; I am certain you are laboring under a mistake. You have got hold of some theory which is mere smoke, vapor, illusion."

"I forgot that you did not understand. I always feel as if I were made of glass and you could see through me," said Evelyn. "Rex, when Bessy came, you know I was half blind; there had been such pain in my eyes that for months I had had atropia put in every day. I could not see her quite plainly. There she was, a lovely little fair creature with golden hair, a white skin, blue eyes and a sweet little mouth, just like Bessy, and yet, when I first heard her voice, it was not Bessy. But she was so beautiful, so sweet, so winning, she kissed me so hungrily, she clung to me so longingly, I turned to her with a sighing sense of rest, — I forgot my doubts. It was like being held up by the everlasting arms. It was easy to explain any little difference. Every one was certain it was Bessy; and oh, Rex, the peace, the blessed comfort of it ; the fun, the little gushes of laughter, the bubbling talk, the play, the caresses, the kisses, the something to love, to live for, to hang over, to wake up in the morning for ! It was, — I felt it in every fibre of my being, — it was a gift from God. I asked no more. I was happy. I was happy all the fall, all the winter, all the spring ; indeed, I could be happy now, if —"

"Evelyn, when did your mind first begin to rest on the possibility that she was not Bessy ?" asked Long, interrupting, for he was harrowed to the soul by these tormenting suggestions. He wanted facts.

"After Theodore was born," said Evelyn, "my eyes were clear, although for a time I could not bear much light. But Roger had got used to my being blind, and he did not realize that I was so used to the dark room I could see as well as if it were bright. One day I saw him looking into Bessy's face ; when he turned away his expression startled me very much. Then I noticed that he avoided her, would not kiss her if he could help it, and if he had to speak to her, something came into his voice I had only heard before when he was displeased. By this time I was well. I could use my eyes like other people, and I could see that the darling was not my Bessy, not my Bessy at all." Her voice was choked as she uttered these words. She looked at Long with beseeching earnestness. He did not speak, only gazed back at her intently.

"Children, — that is, fair-haired, blue-eyed, round-cheeked children, — look a good deal alike," she went on. "My Bessy had a bright little head; this Bessy has a bright little head, with a golden glory round it. But underneath my Bessy's hair was a paler brown tint, and I had always known that it would all grow dark; her eyebrows and eyelashes were darker than this Bessy's. This Bessy's hair is deep gold all through, and her eyelashes and eyebrows are the same color. My Bessy's eyes were a grayish blue at times; this Bessy's eyes are always blue, there is never a glint of gray in them. Then this Bessy is just a wee bit fairer than my Bessy; in fact, she is a more beautiful child. She is the very perfection of the same type."

There was a slight pause.

"You don't seem to reflect that she had two years to develop in," Long said, then. He was undergoing a contest of feeling, and spoke with a strong assertion of conviction, not only against her arguments, but against shadowy doubts which had come up only to be banished from his own mind, but which now reasserted themselves.

"I have reflected," said Evelyn quietly.

"How could you explain the fact that she remembered you? There were all sorts of coincidences —"

"I know," said Evelyn, significantly.

Rex uttered a groan.

"Why not be content, Evelyn?" he said aloud, with a feeling of desperation. "Grant that it is all as you say, — that a mother has instincts beyond knowledge; accept the idea that she is not your own child, — yet the fact remains that she is a gift from God sent in the place of your child. You must not forget that these doubts and hesitations may cost many people their whole life's happiness."

"I grant it all," said Evelyn in a low voice. "I have told you I love her. She has filled up the void. I can say, 'If I am bereaved of my own child, I am bereaved.' The sting of it is gone. I could be happy with this Bessy, perfectly happy if only —"

She looked into his face, and he was startled by the intensity of her glance and the expression of painful resolution about her lips. It was evident that she suffered in speaking. Her words came as if forced from her.

"If only," she went on, "I need not fear that Roger planned it all to get back Bessy that he might keep Madam Van's money."

"Evelyn !" cried Long, starting as if he had been pierced by a sharp weapon.

"He told me," murmured Evelyn in a dull, hopeless voice, "that unless he could have kept Madam Van's money he must have been ruined. He said he had been bound hand and foot ; nothing else could have extricated him. He said he had been tempted of the devil, — that was his very phrase."

Long had started up. "Great God !" he burst out. "What you say is abominable ! A woman thinks it nothing to strike a blow at a man's honor."

An indignant cry came from the other side of the brook.

"Mamma, Sir Waller has eaten my cake ! He snatched it out of my hand and gobbled it up."

"Ah, poor Bessy ! Never mind ! Take another cake !"

"Mamma," in still intense wrath, "Nix has stealed two cakes out of my basket."

"Naughty Nix! What bad, bad dogs!"

"What shall I do to them, mamma?"

"Make them sit down, and talk to them and tell them how greedy they are."

Bessy had laid hold of her basket, and for security was holding it high above her head.

"Sit down, Sir Waller," said she. "Sit down, — sit down, I say! I won't have any more disobelience. Sit down, I say; you is a bad wicked dog, Sir Waller, and Nix is badder and wickeder. It is velly bad manners to snatch cakes out of people's hands, but to go to a basket and steal, that is a thief, a velly mean thief. It was my lunch, my lunch to eat all myself. It was not too much for me, but I would have given you a little bit."

Rex was pacing the turf. He was full of intense resentment towards Evelyn, resentment of a truly masculine sort; she had offended that sense of loyalty to the ties of blood which has often made a man more willing to doubt his wife's honor than the word of his mother and sisters. In part, too, it was a feeling that it was the old story of Psyche sacrificing everything in life to gratify her curiosity.

The pity of it! The blind folly of it! Evelyn knew not what she was doing. She had dashed down a beautiful crystal vase, the only one for her in all the earth; it could never be replaced, never be repaired. It held, too, her elixir of life.

She could read his thoughts.

"You are angry with me, Rex," she said.

"What you have said strikes at the root of everything."

"Do you suppose I do not know that? Am I

happy in believing it, in telling you of it? Do you
suppose I am eager to believe that Roger can do
wrong? What have I left if I have no faith in Roger?
One might say I had the children, but not even children are enough when — Why, Rex, it was only a little
while ago that if Roger opened his arms to me it
seemed as if heaven came down. Trouble ended, love
was enough. I am not like Amy; Amy says a woman
need not be dependent, but I am dependent. I need
to be loved; I like to feel a warm glowing sense that I
am beloved. I see nothing in life worth having except
giving one's self wholly, — I like to spend myself and
be spent in the service of those I love. When I love
everybody and everything it fills my heart and over-
flows my eyes and lips. I don't know how to be cold
and guarded."

They looked at each other in silence. Rex dared
not speak. He had never known trouble until now.

"When I married Roger," Evelyn went on, "I loved
him so well that I do believe if he had come to me and
proposed something wicked, — told me his welfare was
at stake unless he committed a crime, — I should have
stood by him and said, 'Whatever you ask is right. I
love you through everything. Lead me to heaven and
I will love you there, lead me to hell and I will love you
there as well!' It used to seem to me that that alone
was love. I hate half gifts which one takes back, — I
hate half surrender. I like to feel myself in the hollow
of his hand."

Another scream from across the brook.

"Mamma, Sir Waller has got my last cake."

"Never mind, dear. He enjoyed it more than you
could."

" But what am *I* to eat, mamma ? "

" We shall be going home to dinner presently."

"But I 's so hungry, mamma, I 's velly hungry indeed."

Rex suddenly thrust his hands into the pocket of his jacket, and drew forth a paper full of sandwiches which Mrs. Goodeve had given him when he set out.

" May Bessy have these ? " he asked Evelyn.

" Oh, yes."

He leaped across the brook, and lifted the child to the broad low branch of the oak.

" Now," said he, " eat those, Bessy, and make the dogs as miserable as you like. You can say, ' Sir Waller, do you love sandwiches ? Then see me eat them.' "

He went slowly back to Evelyn. He felt under the baleful coercion of something not destiny, but which might easily assume the power of destiny. He was thinking of Roger's confession to his wife that Madame Van's money had been essential to him. What could he have meant by making such a fatal admission ?

" Evelyn," said Rex the moment he was within hearing, " I cannot help feeling that you misunderstood Roger. It is not easy for a woman to grasp business secrets. But say he did tell you that unless he could have kept Aunt Lizzy's money he would have been ruined, — be careful how you judge him. You don't realize his responsibilities. He has had a hard time for years ; on all sides there have been hidden threats and masked vexations which he has had to be prepared for. What he meant was doubtless that he had hypothecated some of Aunt Lizzy's money, that is, temporarily pledged it to maintain his credit. I cannot quite understand the necessity for such a sacrifice, for the

Goodeves are rich enough to bolster up forty com-
panies. But then there are complications in business
which no outsider can grasp the meaning of."

"Don't you see a change in Roger?" demanded
Evelyn.

" He has been absorbed in his business, he has had
to look after the Western branch — "

"Do you see no other change in him?"

"Don't ask me," said Long. "I believe in Roger;
I must believe in him. I know no man who has had so
serious and noble a purpose in life, and it has been
galling to him to fall below his ambitions. His position has been a trying one, — neither you nor I can
know how trying."

"He has always shut me out from his business perplexities," said Evelyn. "The moment he has trouble
he separates himself from me."

"Have you told him your suspicions?"

"Not in words. I do not think I need to tell him."

"You have shown him that you are not happy?"

A little sob burst from her breast, the first sign of
uncontrollable emotion she had shown.

"Once," she faltered, "I fell a-crying. He did not
ask me what was the matter, he only patted my head
and went out of the room. I believe that he realizes
that I have discovered the whole story. That is what
makes it so horrible for me to see that he loves better
to be away than at home. I feel as if perhaps I ought
to take the children and go somewhere out of his sight.
He will be at home to-morrow, and when I think of it,
I wish, — I wish that he need not find me here."

As she spoke with passionate abandon she encountered Long's gaze. Involuntarily she uttered a little

cry and stretched out her hand to touch his. " Rex,"
she said in a despairing tone, " I have made you unhappy."

" Yes," he said, " you have made me terribly unhappy."

He had been standing before her and looking down
at her ; now he turned away with a dizzy gesture.

" You always helped me, Rex," she said tremulously.
" Help me now ; I wanted to tell you everything. As I
said yesterday, you are like nobody else."

Her words calmed him. He hardly understood the
whirlwind of feeling which had swept over him. It had
its root in pity for her, perhaps, but it was a sort of
angry horror he had felt. But her simple and confid-
ing manner brought back his senses.

" You wish me to tell you exactly what I think ? " he
asked.

" Exactly," she answered.

" It seems to me you are in great danger," he said
quietly. " I had hoped you were safe from such dangers, Evelyn. But perhaps every soul has once to take
its choice. Look forward and see which way is success
for you and which is failure, which is safety and which
is perdition."

" That is just what I have not seemed able to see."

" When you come to die," Long went on gently,
" suppose you have it to remember that at a trying
time in your husband's life you withdrew your love,
your belief, your companionship from him, that you
condemned him on suspicion, became his accuser, —
would that thought bring you comfort ? "

" No."

" When you come to die suppose you can say to

yourself, 'I did all I could. For a time it seemed doubtful whether I could ever be happy again, but I waited, I neglected no duty of my own.'"

She looked up at him with a strange wistful expression.

"You consider I have nothing to do except to go on," she said, "silencing my doubts and waiting for Roger to come back to his old self?"

"I want you to remember that he is your husband, Evelyn. He is your husband, bound to you indis. solubly. Neither of you could live apart from the other." He paused a moment, then went on: "Acting promptly is so very easy. Thinking and judging wisely are so very difficult. You may destroy in a minute what a whole life-time cannot reconstruct."

"But, — but the money, is it not wrong to — " Evelyn faltered out so much, then was silent.

"There are all kinds of evil in the world," said Long; "what I want is to feel sure that you commit none." He spoke almost with sternness, and she looked at him in sorrowful surprise, feeling as if, since Rex blamed her, all things were slipping from her.

"You evidently have a bad opinion of me," she said timidly.

"Oh, Evelyn, dear child," he said. The cold, far-away look he had summoned left his face; the color flashed back. She was breathing quickly and biting her lower lip; there was a pleading look in her eyes. "Dear child," he said again, "I don't dare tell you just what I feel. Trust me. I cannot decide on anything, cannot make up my mind about anything to-day. Don't speak of this again, don't think of it again, unless you tell Roger. There ought to be no silences, no secrets, between husband and wife."

"I want to be sure of one thing, Rex," said Evelyn, with emotion; "that is, that you don't like me less for telling you all this."

"I've got a trick of liking you, Evelyn. I could not get over it easily. But you have startled me. You have not at all convinced me. I want you to forget all your hallucinations. A fixed idea may become a fate by being brooded over. As to Bessy, I constantly seem to see you yourself looking out of her eyes, laughing in her laughs and speaking in her voice."

"Where is the child?" said Evelyn.

There had indeed been a long silence on the other side of the brook, and one might have wondered what it portended had not the eager gaze of the two dogs, as they sat on their haunches looking up into the branches, shown that their little mistress was there. She was no longer in sight, however, but little by little had crept up into the body of the oak tree.

"Bessy, Bessy," called Evelyn. No answer came. "Speak to me this minute, Bessy."

"I am a squirrel, mamma; squirrels can't talk."

"Come down this instant."

"I'm a squirrel and am going to live here all by myself."

"We shall go home to dinner then. You can live on acorns."

"What is to be for dinner, mamma?"

"Soup and lamb chops."

"What else?"

"Corn and beans and cauliflower."

"What else, mamma?"

"Strawberry marmalade."

"On bread and butter?"

"An inch thick; and a peach."

"A peach all by myself?"

"Two peaches all to yourself."

"I'll come down," said Bessy; but in spite of the easy promise, descending safely was too hard a task, and Long had to help her.

XXI.

REXFORD LONG stood not upon the order of his going away from Walford, but went at once, saying both to Mrs. Goodeve and to Evelyn Rexford that he hoped soon to return. He did not wish to meet his cousin Roger, at least until he himself was more calm, until he had thought over Evelyn's revelations dispassionately; that is, if he ever could regard anything which concerned Evelyn dispassionately. What she had said about Bessy's identity had after all made a very slight impression. It was an hallucination of Evelyn's. She had lived on retrospects and fears so long that her love for the child was all the time quivering into alarm and doubt.

Something was wrong about Roger, no doubt of that. What was it? Could it be that the Rexford Manufacturing Company was coming to grief? Roger did not stand alone; the riches were not merely his. All the Goodeves were involved with him in the fortunes of the concern, and the Goodeves were prospering in every kind of way. No, it seemed to Long impossible that money troubles should be behind Roger's moodiness, his restlessness, his avoidance of his family. When Evelyn had said that her husband seemed always eager to get away, Long himself recalled Roger's manner as he came and went. When he had returned

after a brief absence he was in an eager mood, sometimes showing even high spirits, — then they ebbed,
leaving him heavy and lifeless, and he was only anxious
to start off again, displaying a feverish desire to be on
the move.

His symptoms were those of a man who is unable to
maintain his recognized supremacy among familiar
friends, and longs to be where no demands are made
upon him.   His eyes showed that he brooded over
thoughts of which he never spoke.   He had seemed
not to care to talk; had no interest in politics or in
any question of the hour.   Seeing him absent-minded
Long had taken it for granted that he was thinking
about some problem connected with the new machinery, so after a few attempts to bring him into the cir-
cle of talk had left him alone.   In the light of Evelyn's
words, how wide the distance loomed between Roger
and his nearest and dearest!   Long's thoughts going
forward and back took on a singular vividness.   He now
believed that even before Evelyn's confession of what
was wrong between her and her husband, he himself
had experienced an indefinable sense of distance, an
ominous hint of a deep gulf fixed between his cousin
and the world about him.

What did the difference in Roger point to except to
some secret hidden sin?   Had Roger become a drunk-
ard?   It seemed to Long incredible that the strong,
healthy man could succumb to any vice.   Yet he knew
that men as strong physically and mentally had become
victims not only to the alcohol, but the chloral and
morphine habit.   Long brought himself with a shudder
and a tingling sense of shame to study up the scientific diagnosis of such cases.   The more he studied

and the more he recalled trifling incidents of his intercourse with his cousin, the more he was convinced
that some detestable habit of self-indulgence was behind the change in him.

It was the harder for Long because his old pain had
returned. It smarted like an old reopened wound. It
was not only Roger, his cousin, whom he was suspecting and prying out, — it was Evelyn's husband, — the
man to whom he had resigned the girl he loved, whom
he had himself wanted to make happy. She had not
needed to tell Long that she had once worshiped her
husband. He had known it as we only know what we
are obliged to measure by the contrast between the
emptiness which is the sole answer to our great craving
need and the full boon freely granted to another. He
had experienced something almost like anger while
Evelyn was telling him how lonely, how hopeless she
was. Afterwards reflecting more calmly on the matter,
thinking of her treasures of love ready to be spent yet
left unopened, the fountain of feeling lost in a desert,
Long had a painful and intolerable sense of the irony
of life.

He could recall his first visit to the Rexfords' after
their marriage. Bessy was a cooing, laughing baby of
five months old. The season was early summer. Evelyn used to come down to breakfast in white embroidered gowns, her chestnut hair falling over her shoulders
in a great braid tied with a blue ribbon, her face fresh
as a newly-opened rose. She was sure to be bubbling
over with talk, every word, glance, and smile aimed at
her husband, each suggestive of a thousand intimate
sacred happinesses, associations, and hopes. Before
this spectacle of married joy Long's trouble died a

natural death. In this clear reality that Evelyn was contented lay not only the sanction of heaven upon her marriage, but an imperative behest to himself. He experienced no shrinking, no jealous irritation. Evidently Evelyn had been made for Roger and Roger for Evelyn.

"And besides," he added whimsically in mental argument, "I never could have stood it to be married to Evelyn. I should have gone stark, staring mad with joy."

Roger took his bliss more easily. He was fond of the pretty creature. It was natural for him always to claim the first place and let others fall into subservience. It is for bachelors to find a profound and mystical beauty in a relation which soon becomes a simple, everyday affair to the married man. Long had sometimes been ready to resent a certain matter-of-factness in Evelyn's husband. The idea of the girl he had loved, dreamed of, longed for, never possessed, was as fresh to Long as it had been years before. And to be compelled to reflect that she was not as happy as be had believed, that she had found only the mirage of a joy which had left her more thirsty and craving than before, was not only a sorrow, but a sorrow which contained an arrow with a poisoned sting.

Brooding on these ideas and memories, with some different intentions each day, starting to and fro between the detached and formless results of his perpetual thinking, Long passed three weeks in town without making up his mind on any point. He had a half expectation that nothing would happen to make the whole situation clearer, and at the same time a shuddering dread of anything new happening. Events seemed hurrying towards him, and he felt the need of being prepared. But who could tell how to be ready for accidents as incalculable as the settling of thistle-down?

Long's premonition that something would occur to make his way clearer was answered, but in a way wholly unlooked for. He had been out on a business errand one day, and coming back, heard that a foreign-looking man had called to see him, and finding him absent had inquired his place of residence.

"A foreign-looking man," said Long, half-puzzled, but his thoughts reverting to certain Germans who had at odd times made translations or executed other stray literary jobs for the Synnots. "Why should he want to go to my rooms?"

He thought no more about the matter, dined at a restaurant, and did not go to Sidney Place, where he lived, until nine o'clock. Entering the house, then, he was met by the announcement that a visitor had been for three hours awaiting his return. He was now sitting in a small reception room, and Long turned into it.

The light was not bright, and when a tall, slim man of dark complexion rose and bowed, there was nothing distinguishable about his appearance.

"You do not remember me, Mr. Long," he said, in a peculiar melancholy voice which struck Rex as familiar. There was little or no foreign accent, but the intonation suggested a habit of other languages.

"Have I ever met you?" Long asked.

"I was in the service of your aunt, Madam Van Polanen."

"Oh, the courier — Giovanni Reni," said Long, sharply startled. "Of course, I remember you perfectly."

Nino made a gesture with both hands and bowed.

"Mr. Rexford told me you were living in Italy," said Long.

Nino assented with a brief shrug. "You have an apartment here?" he asked, and Long was conscious of his awkwardness in keeping the man talking here within reach of all the ears in the house. He led the way up-stairs, followed by Nino, ushered him in, turned up the lights, poked the fire and drew chairs; at first without anything more definite in his mind than a feeling of blank surprise. Then he began to have a presentiment of something disagreeable, but his mental processes were like the vague fluctuations of a dream.

"I remember hearing of you at the time you received Madam Van Polanen's legacy," he finally observed in order to break the silence, and the words brought a sudden pressure of dread. Nino did not answer except by gesture, and Long added, as if to gain confirmation of some doubtful facts, — "Of course you are in full possession of the money."

"I have the money," said Nino in a plaintive voice. Long had told him to sit down, but he stood leaning against a high secretary, which was at the left of the fireplace.

"Have you any family?" inquired Long, himself sitting down.

"I have a wife," the man replied in his drawling, monotonous voice; "I have a little son; besides, my father still lives."

"And now you have come back to America," said Long, looking at the Italian, with a quick mental observation that he had grown ten years older in looks since they met last. The black hair was streaked with white, and there were deep lines on the face.

"When one has lived in a country, and when one has known people in a country," said Nino, "a part of one's life is there. I was not happy in America. I was glad to get away from America, but all the same the old thoughts follow; the old recollections, they drag like chains."

There was something singularly impressive in the man's intonation and emphasis to Long, who had been for weeks in a state of keen sensitiveness and nervous apprehension.

"Mr. Long," Nino went on, fixing his dark, melancholy eyes on the other's face, "have you been to Walford since — since the child was found?"

There was a flash of emotion across his features which was answered by a gleam in the other face. Then both men suddenly grew pale.

"Yes," Long answered by an effort.

"They are happy?" Nino asked. "Mrs. Rexford is glad to have the little girl again?"

"Mrs. Rexford is very well now and happy," said Long. "Bessy is as she always was, a beautiful, bright little creature. There is also a son now, a fine fellow of four months old or more. Quite a little family."

"Ah," said Nino, with his gesture. He was silent a moment, then resumed, — "I too am a parent. There is nothing in the world that speaks to the heart of a man like his own child." He took a step towards Long. "I have come all the way from Italy," he said, "to tell you something."

It was some momentous revelation, — Rex felt certain of that; but his dread could take no shape; he still sat as if in a stupor.

"You are a friend of the family," Nino went on.

"You are a silent man, a just man, a wise man. I have come to end a long deception. I want peace of mind."

Rex had a dream-like sense that he had known before that all this was to happen, that he was to receive some revelation which would verify any wild conjecture of Evelyn's. He tried to assert himself against the conviction, but the man fascinated him; his eyes burned with a melancholy fire, and although there was something theatrical about his deliberation, his emphasis, as if he had carefully rehearsed his words, it would not have been easy to believe that he was not now speaking out of an overcharged heart.

"I wanted my legacy, and I have my legacy; but money is not everything," said Nino, with a gesture which seemed to pile wrath and scorn on his riches. "It gives a man indeed more leisure to remember, it gives him more to dread. It may furnish him food to eat, but it cannot bring appetite; it may provide a bed, but it cannot make him sleep at night; it cannot make his heart leap up in pure joy at the voice of his child."

An idea returned to Long's mind with such force that he felt it like an electric shock. He remembered the vague suspicion which had rested on the Italian at the time of Bessy's disappearance.

"No," he said with a marked change of tone, "not if he has a bad conscience, not if he has committed a crime in order to get hold of the money."

"I have committed no crime," said Nino significantly. "I have done no wrong to any man. I have prevented a wrong. I have made many people happy."

"You said you had come to tell me something,"

said Long, suspicion and repugnance rising strongly within him. "Let me hear it at once. I begin to guess what it is disturbs you. Out with it. It concerns —" but it was hard to frame his conviction in words.

Nino also shrank, — there was a visible tremulousness about his whole figure.

"It concerns Bessy Rexford," said Long in a deep voice. "I mean the child who was carried off."

"She was not carried off," said Nino; his face was ghastly.

"What happened to her?"

"You must promise to do me no harm if I tell you," faltered Nino in an agony of terror. His whole aspect was changed; he had been plucking at his hair and it now hung in disordered locks about his gaunt, yellow face, and he shook as if in an ague.

"Surely," said Long in a strange voice, "you did not murder her."

"I did not hurt a hair of her head," muttered Nino. "I would not have done it. I could not have done it. I did, — I did a strange thing because I was mortally afraid of madam's saying it was my fault, but do not suspect —"

"I suspect nothing," said Long. "Speak out. You are driving me mad."

"Will you promise that when I have told you my story I may go away safe and unharmed?"

"I promise sacredly; but tell me this instant, tell me the exact truth, what happened to Bessy?"

"She was drowned."

"Drowned? Where was she drowned?"

"In the river."

"She fell in ?"

"I will tell you all I know," said Nino. "I was on the bridge with Jenny. We were talking. I was angry. I was carried out of myself. She forgot Bessy. Then all at once it grew darker! Where was the child? She was not to be found."

"And where was she?"

"I know no more than you. She had been close beside us flinging stones into the water; then a carriage passed and she was not there. She could not have fallen off the bridge. There was no place up or down the slope of ground to the bridge where she could get at the water. I told Jenny she had gone home. I tried to believe it, but I was trembling all over. I thought to myself, If madam asks, 'Where is the little girl?' what am I to say? I thought perhaps she had gone back to the house. I tried both gates, and both were shut. She could not have got in, I said to myself. Yet I ran everywhere, — down to the river, — I looked into the shrubberies. I called her name softly all over. Then, saying to myself, 'Of course, she is at home; Jenny has found her by this time;' I tried to be calm. I went back to the house. But my heart was bursting. Every minute was like an hour. If anything had happened I knew that madam would blame me. She had said to me once, 'You are jealous of that child, and you Italians are so revengeful that I sometimes feel as if it were not safe to let you stay here. You look at Bessy sometimes as if you wanted to do her a mischief.' Madam had an eye like a lash, a tongue like a stiletto. She made a coward of me. So when the news came in that the child was lost I was like a man under sentence of death. My knees were like water; I fell on the floor, I groaned, I cried, I was like one bereft of his senses. Madam ordered me to get up and go find the child. I went out. Everybody questioned me as if I were a criminal. Men were going up and down with lanterns and searching the river in a boat. I started to go with them. Then the constables came and said that Jenny had talked about a carriage; had said that the people in the carriage had carried a child off. When that came back to my mind, I answered, ' Yes, that is it; brigands must have carried off the little girl that they might get a reward.' When I said this the constables arrested me, took me to the town hall and locked me up until midnight. Then I was let to go. Mr. Rexford and you yourself, Mr. Long, gave me a good character. Everybody could see it was all a stupid mistake. I have a soft heart, I could do no one any harm. I had been frantic with my fear, that is all. My mind went forward and back. I said first one thing and then another. I was out of my head; but it was cruel, it was unjust, to suspicion me, — to — "

" For God's sake, go on," said Long. " Never mind anything except the story you have got to tell."

Nino pushed back his hair from his wet forehead. "Yes, I have got a story to tell," he said under his breath.

"Go on."

" I came back to the house at midnight. Everything was quiet. I did not try the door. There was a way of getting in from the side porch. I climbed up, entered, went to bed. My room was in the west gable, looking over the river. All the others slept on the east side of the house. The wind had come up and roared in the

trees and made strange noises which did not let me
rest.   After a time it seemed to me I heard something
besides the wind; a little cry, not exactly a child's cry,
but with all those fancies in my mind, I could think
of nothing but a child.   It frightened me.   At first I
got up and looked out, but all was still.   I went back
and covered up my head; I tried not to hear it, but the
more I tried not to hear it, the more it seemed to cut
into my very heart and soul.   My hair stood on end,
my tongue clove to the roof of my mouth.   It seemed
to me something was in the room with me.   I could
not stay there.   I rose and dressed myself.   I went
down the top stairs to the window in the hall; I got out
and slid down the pillar that I had climbed up.   I was
on the lawn, — the lawn towards the river.   The
moonlight was very bright.   Though the storm of wind
shook the trees, there were only a few clouds, and they
shone too, and helped to make it as light as day.   At
first I thought the sound was not there, — then all at
once it came again; it rose from the river.   I tried to
get up my courage, but that voice froze my blood.   I
wanted to go and see what it was, but my legs bent
under me.   I could only get down and crawl on my
hands and knees.   As I got near the water, Fido came
running up to me."

"The Rexfords' old dog, Fido?"

"Yes.   He was wet, — he had been in the water.
He was panting, he was worn out, he looked up in my
face and made that same cry.   Then he ran back towards the river and stopped, then looked at me, wagging his tail, and cried again.   I knew at last what it
was."

"Bessy was in the water!"

" She was in the water. It was just where the great roots of the willows bend over and the water runs far under the bank. She was caught there. Fido was trying to get her out, but he could not. It was I who drew her out and laid her on the grass."

Long had started up with an attitude, as if trying to ward off something threatening.

" She was dead ? " he said.

" Oh yes, sir, she was dead."

" Drowned ? "

" Drowned."

" Oh, my God ! " said Long, pierced to the heart. He flung up both arms as if to stay the descending rod. " Oh, merciful God ! " he muttered, " must this be borne ? " The old pang bit him afresh. He saw that little dear face, the yellow hair, the tireless little frame. " It seems to me," he said under his breath, " this will kill me." He walked to and fro, striking his clenched fists against his temples. Suddenly he turned. " What did you do with her ? " he asked in a tone of awe.

" She lay there," said Nino, the tears running down his face, " and the moon shone on her. Everything was dripping wet, — the little seal-skin coat madam had put on her, the little hood, — but nothing out of order except half the lace scarf ; the end of that was in her teeth. I drew it out. I somehow put it in my pocket. While I sat there looking at her, I heard the town clock strike four. It would soon be light, I said to myself, and I trembled more and more. Mr. Long, you cannot think how I suffered. I am not a brave man. I whispered to myself they would say I had done it, and it seemed to me, driven wild by fear, that

I had done it. I knew that I had not hurt a hair of her head, yet I understood how a murderer feels, seeing his innocent victim." He paused and looked at Long, who gazed back at him dumb, then asked again : —

"What did you do with her?"

"I buried her."

"Why did you not give the alarm? Why did you not let us all know?"

Nino made a despairing gesture. "Why did I not? A day later I would have done anything to have acted differently. At the time I was afraid. I was in the clutches of a terror."

"Where did you bury her?" asked Long dully.

"Among the rhododendrons close by the river. The gardener had been setting out shrubs that day. The ground was not hard to work. I had my own tools, for I sometimes took care of the vines. I dug deep — as deep as I had strength for — and laid her down. By the time I had covered her up, the sky was half rosy, half yellow. When I saw the new day I sat down and covered my face."

"Is this story true?"

"As true as the wounds of Christ."

"The gardener must have seen the traces of your work?"

"The wind brought down the leaves, the whole ground was covered, and soon the rain came."

Long's mind fastened on all his recollections of that fateful night, which had always remained clear as fireworks in the darkness.

"The gate must have been opened; she must have wandered back and got into the grounds before Birdsey shut it," he said.

Nino shook his head and shrugged his shoulders.

"I know nothing," he said.

Little disjointed incidents which had never been quite explained came up to be fitted into this outline of bare inexorable facts.

"What happened to Fido?" he asked. "Did you kill him?"

"No. I would not have killed him. I kill no living thing," said Nino. "When I had pulled the child out of the water he was frantic with joy; he jumped up and licked my face, then lay down and I saw him wag his tail as if he were glad. Then I thought of him no more for a time. When my work was done and I looked about to see that I had left nothing, I found that he lay stretched out in the same way, but dead. I carried him round the house and put him on the east porch."

Everything had happened by chance, Long said to himself; no prudence, no wisdom, no foresight had been of any use. The little maid had wandered back; she had taken a misstep on the river's brim and that was the end of it all.

"How about the half of the lace scarf?" he asked. "Did you throw it among the leaves over by Chauncey station?"

"I must do something with it," said Nino deprecatingly.

"You coward, you black miserable coward!" said Long, a storm of anger and disgust and grief shaking him from head to foot, as all the complications, all the far-reaching consequences not yet ended, forced themselves upon his mind. "If you could only have told the truth, it might have been borne. The truth can always be borne."

"You can say nothing to me I have not many times said to myself," said Nino plaintively. "When I found the dog running backwards and forwards between me and the water, why did I not shriek out and bring the whole household? It was because my nerves were upset. I felt that madam would have me punished. She would say I had thrown the child into the water. I have always been timid. My heart goes down if I see an angry glance. Then besides, I was afraid of going to prison. Once I was in prison for three months; it was for nothing. I was not at fault, — a little quarrel about a girl. But it robbed me of courage — "

Long was not listening. He had thrown himself into his chair again and sat bending forward, his elbows on his knees, his chin in his hands. Now that he knew what had happened in the past, the facts of the present asserted themselves.

"This was the Bessy who was lost," he said, after a time. "Do you know anything about the Bessy who was found?"

He lifted his head and looked at Nino. The probability seemed to him slight that Nino knew anything about the substitution of one child for the other, but the essential motive was there. It was in favor of the Italian's own ends that the Rexfords' little girl should come back.

Nino looked back at him with his little gesture.

"You have guessed it," he said.

"Guessed it!" said Long bitterly. "I might easily guess that you were at the root of all mischief. The child we believed to have been carried off was lying in her little grave almost under our feet. You could not have the legacy unless she came back. I see it all."

"It was the best thing for the mother," said Nino eagerly, "to have something in place of her child. It was not alone the money; Jenny felt always that she had been forgetful, that she was at fault."

"Jenny!"

"Jenny has been my wife for two years and more," said Nino quietly. He was beginning to recover from the horror of his own recital. He pushed back his hair from his forehead and looked less than before like a lost spirit wandering unconsoled.

"Whose child is it?" said Long hopelessly.

Nino shrugged his shoulders. "She was with the holy sisters in Montreal. She is an orphan. We adopted her. It was not easy to find a child like Bessy."

"You went about looking for a child resembling Bessy?" said Long, under the pressure of an impotent rage and exasperation which made it almost impossible for him to speak.

"It was not only the face and the hair," said Nino, "but she must be a little princess. She was smaller, she was younger than Bessy; but we fed her well and she grew. She was a very fine child; she was more beautiful than the other Bessy, she had more wit," Nino went on, expanding with his subject and evidently feeling a pride in his protégée. "She was quick to learn. Jenny remembered all Mrs. Rexford's ways."

Long could fill up any gap the words left. He remembered the quick-witted English nurse. She had taught the child phrases, intonations, even tricks of tenderness and fashions of caresses such as had been common between Evelyn and her first-born. The twig had been flexible to the resolute touch; no lopping, no pruning had been necessary. A little heart longing

for love and a little brain stuffed full of images of a
mother; then an eager gush of feeling as she clasped
somebody who seemed to be all she had remembered
and hoped for.

"Tell me one thing, Nino," said Long gently. "Tell
me the absolute truth. Did Roger Rexford know anything about this conspiracy?"

"I do not believe it," said Nino. "Mr. Spencer —
Mr. Spencer knew."

"Mr. Spencer?"

"He must have known," Nino went on. "It was he
who said to me, 'That child ought to be found. I
know if I had a handsome legacy depending upon it, I
would find the child.'"

"Spencer!" repeated Long in dismay. He had tried
to keep his grasp on the hope that Roger knew nothing
about the matter; but Spencer's name troubled him;
he felt a new involvement, a new complication.

"It was Mr. Spencer who sent me Mrs. Rexford's
picture," said Nino.

Long drew out his watch. It was midnight.

"I want to think everything over," he said with
decision. "Come to me to-morrow morning at eight
o'clock. I can stand no more now. Tell me just one
thing, that I may see it more clearly. Who was the
Mrs. Lorenz who had the child in Chicago?"

"She is a cousin of Jenny's," said Nino. "All that
she told was true, that is, it was in a way true. Her
husband had died and her husband's sister had died."

Their eyes met. "Now," said Nino, "I have told
you my story, Mr. Long."

"There are many questions I have yet to ask," said
Long.

"To-morrow," said Nino. He made a low bow, almost a salaam, and went out at once.

Long, left alone, paced the floor for hours. Mentally surrounded by the past again, he tried to reconstruct events by the light of these abhorrent discoveries he had at first longed to conjure back into the darkness. There were still many doubtful points which he longed to clear up, and he felt too impatient for his next interview with Nino to be able to sleep.

At breakfast, the following morning, however, this note was handed him.

"When you receive this, Mr. Long, I shall be far out at sea. I am to sail at daybreak. GIOVANNI RENI."

XXII.

ALONZO SLOPER'S LOST ILLUSIONS.

MR. ALONZO SLOPER had found some mild excitement all this past year in trying to worry out Spencer's
patience, arguing that when the young man could no
longer bear the incessant mortification, he was sure to
come back to Leo and marry her out of hand. It gave
Mr. Sloper occupation; his life had long been aimless,
and it was something to have a daily errand to take him
out in search of his daughter's lover, also a topic of
conversation which never failed to interest him as he sat
fuddling himself at Barker's. This latter process was
habitual with him, and had been for at least ten years.
Drinking five or six times a day is not a good preparation for clear thinking, and Mr. Sloper's thoughts were
seldom or never entirely clear. They were, however,
persistent. Day after day, for months, he had spent
afternoons and evenings in telling his convives at Barker's that his daughter, by all odds the prettiest girl in
Walford, was engaged to Harry Spencer, who was on
the very top of the climbing wave in the Rexford Manufacturing Company, and was certain before long to be
an important member of the concern. Mr. Sloper was
dimly aware of the fact that his unsupported words did
not carry weight ; accordingly he would substantiate his
statement by giving all sorts of details. He reported
imaginary conversations between Spencer and himself

in which his son-in-law elect was urging the bride to fix the day, which he, like the wise and prudent parent that he was, insisted should be postponed. He described the presents the ardent young fellow brought to Leo. Mr. Sloper was, in fact, a man of imagination, and it had been his unique consolation to press his fancy into active service and compel it to lighten the heavy facts of his life. He felt the need of some horizon. His way was to go to Barker's, order his favorite beverage, drain it off, settle himself squarely, puff himself up, pass his hand through his hair, and begin to tell about what he should do when his daughter was married to Spencer. " Silver and gold have I none," he remarked that he had said to his son-in-law, " but such as I have give I thee," and that Spencer had replied that he would rather have Leo without a dower than a queen on her throne with a whole treasury of gold and silver.

Mr. Sloper had, to sustain him in the delivery of these pathetic confidences, which sometimes roused derision in his hearers, the heroic feeling that he was performing his duty. If the conversation he reported had not taken place, it ought to have taken place. Nothing is accomplished in the world without some effort, he said to himself, and it was under the stimulus of this conviction that he had gone to see Miss Standish.

He was immensely pleased at first with the results of this effort. Miss Standish came to his house and at once made, as Mr. Sloper touchingly remarked to his cronies, "a bosom-friend of Leo." Leo was to learn everything, preparatory of course to her marriage with Spencer. For all the talk in Walford about Spencer's attentions to Miss Standish was mere gossip.

However, Mr. Sloper's Alnaschar-visions could not continue. He was soon to discover that he had made a false move.

The next time he went to the works to take a message to Spencer from his daughter, he was invited to go into the new manager's private room. He entered with his head up, his mien proud, as a man should who is the prospective father-in-law of a very magnificent three-tailed bashaw.

He emerged half an hour later, quite chop-fallen. He had tasted in that interview more unalloyed misery than had ever come to him in all his life before. Spencer knew the man he was addressing, realized that his intellect could only be reached by words which cleaved through the layers of vanity, arrogance, and folly. Mr. Sloper was the dupe of his own exaggerations ; his dreams mounted to his head, and he had passed the chief part of his life in a state of double intoxication.

Spencer intended to make his meaning clear, and he succeeded. Every word he had uttered cut like a lash. He would not allow his visitor to enjoy a single advantage to be gained from the situation. Some people take the platform easily, and Mr. Sloper was one of them. Had Spencer permitted him to voice his own despair and weep over his own pathos it might have been safer. As it was, he was not allowed to utter a syllable. After Spencer had poured out his wrath and scorn, and had disowned utterly his engagement to Leo, he drew from his desk the mortgage he held against the Sloper estate, and reminded his debtor that he was heavily in arrears for interest, and that if he ever again uttered a syllable in Walford concerning any fancied obligation of his towards Leo, the mortgage should be foreclosed by the swiftest processes of the law. After thus defining his position and his intentions, he ordered his visitor out as he would a dog.

It was a most unpleasant experience for Mr. Sloper. He had gone in in a beautiful and trustful spirit; he came out with all his buoyancy of feeling crushed out of him. As a rule, when facts had been unpleasant he had accepted them only conditionally, reserving to himself the privilege of altering them a little when he should talk them over. Now he seemed to have no power to change anything. Every word Spenser had uttered pressed upon him hard and relentless, enforced by a glance of the eye and a stiffening of the lips which had an unmistakable meaning. Mr. Sloper left the works with his head between his shoulders as if he were breasting a storm. He was utterly miserable and cast down. It was a melancholy sight to see him sitting at Barker's crushed, hopeless, beaten, afraid of the sound of his own voice. If he uttered a word aloud the threatening apparition of Spencer seemed to rise and freeze him into silence.

Nevertheless, in a month's time, finding himself still alive and his house still over his head, Mr. Sloper began to rally. His daughter had taken up her new occupations with eagerness, and her good spirits diffused pleasantness into her home relations. Mr. Sloper felt that he had been too much depressed. His fault always was that he was too sensitive ; it was clearly his duty to take a more hopeful view. What had cut him deepest in Spencer's tirade was the young man's unstinted expression of scorn of himself; the declaration that he would not marry an angel out of heaven who happened to be old Sloper's daughter. After having so long paraded Spencer's attachment to himself, and given instances of the tribute of complete deference the lover of Leo paid to his future father-in-law, it was bitter to be undeceived. Alonzo for a time almost had a suspicion that he actually was a discreditable old toper.

However, such lack of self-belief showed an abnormal, unhealthy condition in Mr. Sloper. Truth and an india rubber ball when crushed to earth will rise again, and Mr. Sloper rebounded against humiliation. Six weeks after Spencer had ordered him out of his office, he had begun to forget the lesson he had learned when quailing before the young man's cold, resolute bearing. He had resumed all his old habits and was bragging away, as before, about his daughter and Spencer, embroidering his canvas a little by an account of the splendid quarters the new manager had shown him at the works.

Perhaps he believed that Spencer would know nothing of what went on at Barker's; but Spencer had begun to feel eager to get rid of the Slopers. It annoyed him to hear of Leo's being taken under Miss Standish's patronage; more than once of late he had encountered the young girl, who had treated him with a light, airy disdain which, laughable although it was, yet stung. Spencer, in fact, nowhere found the satisfaction which ought to belong to his improved fortunes. He had received more ironical congratulations on his ascendency at the works than sincere expressions of pleasure in his success. Miss Standish was in a measure alienated. There was rumored talk of a general strike among Walford machinists for fewer hours and higher wages, and altogether Spencer's was no bed of roses.

He began to attribute everything he found not to his mind to the influence of the Slopers. He was surprised at himself for having been indifferent to the absurd rumors they had set afloat. These new susceptibilities gave him uneasy presentiments, and he chafed over the least sign that he had in any way lost his old supremacy among the men at the works or among his friends in Walford.

Thus, when he heard, as he was certain to hear, that Mr. Sloper was again talking about his daughter's love affair, Spencer felt ready for cool and calculating action. A notice was served upon Sloper next day that he must at once pay up the overdue interest on his mortgage, or foreclosure would ensue. The creditor took no pains to repeat his former incisive statement that he would have no damaging talk go on about himself. It was by process of law that Mr. Sloper was this time to be penetrated by the realities of the case. He could only feel again that he had made a terribly false move and done worlds of harm. Before, he had been stunned by a terror of Spencer, and had deprecated his anger. But now he had a fit of blind rage against the man who was putting the screws on him. He was in a way afraid of Spencer still; but brooding over his wrongs, real and imaginary, his temper grew fierce, and he began to think of some sort of safe revenge he could take upon the upstart who was having it all his own way in Walford.

He sat moody and dull nowadays over his cups, and his thoughts, instead of expanding in loose talk, narrowed down to an endless iteration of a wish to do something to spite Spencer. He wanted to disgrace him, to ruin him, but did not know how, and the mad-

dening impotence of his unsatisfied rage against the
man he had once loved, warmed in his bosom, and
fed from his cup, made him very dangerous. If he
could have convicted Spencer of stealing, of defalcation,
of some crime, that would at first have contented him·
Having no means in his power of fastening such accusations upon him, he thought of some way of taking
revenge upon him by beating him, even killing him.
He felt that it might be enjoyable to hold Spencer's
life in his hand, as it were, — perhaps see him on his
knees begging for mercy. These dreams were not
without charm, but they made him quake and tremble,
and he would reach out for another glass of whiskey.
But not even that could make him feel fully equal to
getting the upper hand of Spencer physically. Mr.
Sloper confessed to himself that his nerves were worn
to fiddle-strings by struggle of thought and perturbation of mind.

As he thought of Spencer standing in his room at
the works feeling himself every inch master of the
whole place, Sloper said to himself it might be a pleasing climax of such puffed-up pride and consequence if
he were to be trapped in his own office, burned up or
blown up. It was not easy for Sloper to get hold of a
clear sequence of ideas, but all the processes necessary
to this result seemed simple. Spencer was frequently
in his office until eleven o'clock at night. His light
could be seen, and he himself could be recognized
coming out and going home towards midnight.

XXIII.

A MAN must live, and if he has to bear a burden, he can fit his neck to the yoke, or the yoke to his neck, and so go on his way. Thus Roger Rexford began after a time to feel that he might somehow rearrange his life. One's ambitions alter or are at least modified by circumstances. One may begin by wishing to be brave, honest, upright, true to the core, with perfection in the inward parts, and may finally settle down into the belief that after all it does very well if one keeps a brave front to the world, and plays the cards that are dealt out as skillfully as one may. " The good and the evil lie down together, the earth covers them and there is no difference," Roger often said to himself.

As weeks and months went on, he no longer looked to the horizon for the coming storm. For a while after Spencer's disclosures, he had lived only in his fears. The lie imposed upon Evelyn, upon all the world, seemed to him so palpable that he expected the very stones must cry out. All summer, as he came and went, he watched for some sign that the imposition was discovered ; then, finding none, his dread died away. There had been moments when it had seemed just possible that Evelyn shared his doubts concerning Bessy, but as autumn advanced this apprehension died a natural death. Evelyn was as transparent as crystal, and it was clearly impossible that she could have kept such a secret to herself. Her actions were invariably the product not of logical reflection, but of intuition and impulse. She had never had a definite intention without betraying it. The secret of her charm for him had always been largely in her simplicity and directness. No bribe could have kept her silent, he believed, if she ever mistrusted Bessy's identity. When, then, he saw the two together, linked by the closest tenderness, talk bubbling, laughter gushing forth, caresses intertwining, he gave up that haunting apprehension, feeling certain that if Evelyn had the faintest mistrust no glamour could make Bessy's beautiful little face lovely to her.

If, for a time, he had seen a change in his wife, had been conscious of a question in her glances which probed heart and conscience, he now attributed it to a fault in himself of which he was but too conscious. Suspense, frustrated hope, the mean degradations which had been forced upon him, had had their effect. If he had drugged himself, it had been from no weak yielding to any cravings of appetite. But a woman could little understand the depressing struggle he had gone through. He had been worn out, and knew of but one way to secure relief. Now that his nerves were calmer he hoped to be able to regain his self-command.

Spencer's improvements had by this time been practically tested in the works. He had planned largely, and so far, it seemed as if he had planned wisely. But a man spurred by a sharp personal ambition to make himself rich is an object for general criticism, envy and detraction. Walford people found something questionable in his fitness for a place which had been held by Rexfords and Goodeves. Then, too, there were evil predictions for an upstart who, not content with business methods by which better men than himself had contentedly made hundreds and thousands, set out in larger operations, bid for wider fields and planned to realize tens of thousands. Spencer was conscious that he was not popular in Walford just now, but he maintained an even course, kept himself well in hand, betrayed no sense of having risen in the world, was punctual, zealous, absorbed, and showed no change of tone either to his equals or his inferiors. He still knew more about every department in the works than the head of it, and the web of tangled details had no perplexity for him. There were apprehensions of a strike, but there was likely to be no trouble between master and men.

"I think of taking a little holiday. You can get along without me," Roger said to Spencer in October, and Spencer assented, saying that it might be better not to go to any great distance until they knew better if a strike were coming.

Roger wanted to take his wife away from Walford for a time. He himself required a change, and Evelyn was certain to be grateful for a little experience elsewhere. Settled in New York for a few months, with common occupations and interests, he could summon back the old lover-like habits which he was but too conscious he had lost. Evelyn had of late found him careless, and had brought herself to accept a sort of coldness and dullness between them which was very far from being her ideal of married life.

He told her one evening when they were alone together that they might as well go to New York to spend the winter. He expected to see a bright answering glance. To his surprise she did not look up, but dropping the work she held she clasped her hands in her lap.

"Don't you want to go?" he asked.

She murmured something inaudible about liking Walford best. "Besides," she added with sudden eagerness, as if grasping at a substantial reason, "Amy is here."

"Amy can stay and keep the house if she likes," said Roger, "or she can go with us."

Evelyn looked disturbed; she bit her lip; she began phrase after phrase, but could not finish any of them.

"Don't you want to go away with your husband?" demanded Roger, trying to read these signs but gaining no clear impression. "You used always to be begging me to take you away."

"I have grown older, more settled," Evelyn faltered.

"I could not command the money or the time then," said Roger, with an effort at lightness. "Now, everything is more easy."

She said nothing, but although she sat apparently passive he saw signs of rebellion in her.

"I do not understand you at all," he broke out. "It is as if you no longer loved me."

"No longer loved you!" she stammered. She turned and their eyes met. She looked as if convicted, caught in the act.

"You loved me once," said he. "You promised to love me always. You took me for better, for worse, for richer, for poorer."

She laughed slightly; she flung up her head in a way she meant to be arch.

"Tell me in what wifely duties I fail," she said. "I like to know my faults."

"You fail in no duty," said Roger, fixing a deep glance upon her. "You are like the good wife in scripture."

He spoke in a melancholy tone, rose and paced the room for a few minutes, then returned to his chair.

"Evelyn," he said gently, "come here."

She looked at him in surprise, then, meeting his compelling gaze, she rose and went towards him as if coerced beyond her will. He smiled at her as at a lovely child as she approached him, and when she was within reach he caught her hand, drew her to his knee and put his arm about her.

Her color came and went. She was like a girl of sixteen with a bridegroom she had never seen.

He held her close a moment, her face turned towards him, bending all the time that straight persistent gaze into her eyes. Every moment she grew more shy; her breath shortened; her color ebbed and did not return; she seemed on the verge of tears. He released her, leaned back in his chair, dropped his chin on his breast and covered his eyes with his hands.

"You do not love me," he said in a low voice. "I am not sure that that is all. I believe you hate me."

Although she felt herself dismissed, she continued timidly to perch on his knee in heavy-hearted silence. Then, when he seemed to shrink back from her, she hesitatingly crept to a little distance and sat down.

He raised his head. "Evelyn," he said sternly, "what has come between us?"

She shivered and turned her face wearily away.

"Is it another man? Do you love somebody else?"

"No," she said petulantly.

"It is not so very long ago," he said in a deep,

strange voice, — "when if I opened my arms you ran into them gladly. You were always asking me if I loved you. Love me, love me, love me! was your incessant demand."

She gave a little cry as if pierced.

" Do you taunt me with it ? " she exclaimed.

"'Taunt you with loving me ? For being hungry for my love ? It was my right. It is my right, and a man may claim his right. You are my wife. Why are you cold to me ? "

His persistence began to tell on Evelyn. Instead of a danger to be avoided, full confession began to seem a temptation. The habit of loving, joyful obedience was strong in her ; no self-questioning could make it right to withhold her thoughts from her husband. Then it was possible, it was just possible, as Rex had told her, that she was laboring under a mistake.

She sprang up again, and slowly, inch by inch, went nearer to him. He could read a new impulse in the vividness of her glance, but this time he did not put out his hand to draw her towards him.

"I used to love you, Roger," she began in a soft, clear voice. " I am not ashamed to confess that I loved you with all my heart. From the first moment I saw you, you seemed to me stronger than other men. You domineered a little. You asked more of me than anybody had ever asked of me, and I loved to feel your strong will over me. I liked to be under your foot, for I said to myself that you were not alone stronger, but you were wiser, better than I was. I trusted absolutely that you knew what was best for me. I do believe, Roger, if you had pushed me over a precipice, I should have said that I ought to go over the precipice."

But even while she poured forth this revelation of passionate feeling, he did not venture on a look or a caress, although she was standing close beside him.

"But you no longer love me," he said coldly.

" I want to love you."

" But you do not.   There is the pith of the matter. You hate me instead.   What have I done ? "

" Do you guess nothing, Roger ?   Do your thoughts give you no name for symptoms of change in me ? "

"I want your accusations.   What have I done ? "

She looked at him, her face blanching.

" Tell me," he said imperiously.   " I want a definite charge."

She made a convulsive effort to speak, but no voice came ; another struggle, and she faltered in a stifled voice, —

" You wanted Madam Van's money."

" Evelyn ! "   He stared at her in blank surprise.

" You — you — " she began, but the words froze on her lips.

" Go on," he said in a strange voice and with a strange glance.

" The child," she whispered ; "you got another child to put in Bessy's place."

He cowered as if under a physical blow ; he pressed his hands against his eyes as if to ward off the sight of some stark, staring horror.

" You do not deny it," she said, in a spent, stifled voice.   " You wanted Madam Van's money.   You knew that Bessy was not our child, but as I was half blind, —" she broke off.

Then followed a long silence.   He sat huddled together like a man in some deadly extremity of bodily pain. A strange awe and terror came over Evelyn. He seemed to be saying something; she could detect an indistinguishable thread of whisper, and leaning close she heard him mutter, —

. "This is my wife. God pity me! This is my wife!"

Had he shrieked out his denunciation it could not so have jarred and distressed her. This voice of woe wrung from some deep-seated source of anguish pierced all her sensibilities. A moment before she had had a terribly distinct vision of her own grievance. Now, she saw nothing, except the clear fact of her own disloyalty. Having spoken out, no longer being under compulsion to speak, to end the suspense, she saw herself in a new light. Scruples long dominated by her own ever-recurring dread asserted themselves. Rexford Long had warned her to beware of a fixed idea which would become a fate by being brooded over. He might well have warned her. With what true and loyal feeling Rex had combated her treason! She felt, as she had never felt before, the hideousness of her having pained him with the story. But all that was nothing compared with this horrible deed. She saw the strong man suffer before her eyes and felt as if she had killed him.

She threw herself on her knees beside him.

"Roger," she said, "tell me it is not true, and I will never have a doubt again."

He answered nothing.

"If I have done you wrong I will expiate it in any way you appoint," she gasped between her sobs. "I will go away. I will die. I feel indeed that I ought not to live —"

He did not seem to hear her.

She twined her arms about him, with all her strength drew his face down to hers, caressing and fondling him. But let her lay his cheek against hers as she might, let her even meet his eyes, she did not seem to reach him. Something separated them more hopeless than any distance. She tried to explain, to argue, to justify herself, but it was like trying to drive a nail of wax.

Amy had been out, but returned, bringing with her a breath of the frosty air outside. As she entered, Roger rose without a word and went into his library. Evelyn met her sister with what serenity she could command. She saw her husband no more that night, and for many days afterwards he came and went without a word, almost without a glance towards her. The silence chilled Evelyn; his self-command smote her mercilessly. He sat at table talking on indifferent subjects; he sat between his wife and her sister, sometimes reading aloud. How strong he was, how sure of himself, how indestructible his poise, his proud reserve! How weak a woman was in comparison! At how few points she is actually in touch with a man! She has her little vantage-ground; she moves his heart, rouses his tenderness, but let her step one foot over her appointed boundary and she is in a hostile territory; his pride, his intellect, his will are all in arms and warn her off the yet unconquered province.

Thus ran Evelyn's thoughts in these days, with shame and regret and yearning, dimly descrying how presumptuous she had been and how utterly she had failed. She understood now what Rexford Long had meant in saying, "Remember, Evelyn, he is your husband — *your husband.* Don't let yourself think evil of any one

so near to you. You have got to stand at his side always, not apart from him, choosing your own way, but
at his side."

If she opened a book the same lesson spoke from
the printed page. Odd, detached sentences conned
from great writers years before asserted themselves in
her memory. One was

> "Think much
> Before this sin be sinned, before thy dearest
> Thou turn to deadliest foe."

Had she made an implacable enemy of her husband ?
she asked herself with fantastic repentance, with gro-
tesque and horrible misgivings of conscience. It is
not the wrong done us, but the wrong we do, which
haunts us and makes our days and nights hopelessly
miserable. Through Roger's apparent calmness she
saw, as through a veil, the bitterness of his disappointed, disenchanted soul.

She had heard the question discussed as to whether
a woman owes a higher allegiance to her husband or to
her children. Now that she herself had been so per-
fidious, she could reflect that her first duty was to her
husband. Nobody can help loving a child ; that is
pure instinct. The little creature reaches towards its
mother so helplessly, so imploringly, she must give
herself wholly in return ; that is sheer happiness, no
duty at all. But a husband ! there is a bond, a sacred
obligation ; she has promised to endure the stress of
life with him. What falsity, what ingratitude she had
shown ! Her memories of what Roger had been to
her in old happy days, her swift conviction that what
had lately distressed her had been her own fault, all
combined to give her an intense horror of this alienation.

One day when he entered the house she waylaid him, took his arm and went with him into the library.

"I can't live this way any longer," she said to him.

He looked at her with the same cold composure he had worn of late, but answered nothing.

. "I wish you would listen to me, Roger," she went on. "I do not ask you to forgive me. I have offended too deeply for that. I ought never to be forgiven. Still you must forgive me enough to let me say one thing to you."

"I am ready to hear anything you wish to say," he replied calmly. "Say on."

She looked up at him with a swelling heart out of which came a sob. "I cannot say anything when you look at me like that, as if you were made of marble. I may not deserve forgiveness, but, nevertheless, I can't go on living unless you do forgive me. You must forgive me. That is all I wanted to say. I thought I had something to explain, but let it all pass, let it all go. Forget that I did not believe in you, Roger; I do believe in you. Take me back. It kills me to have you so cold. Show me you have forgotten and forgiven. Set me a hard task, something difficult, something that needs all my strength, only —"

He took her in his arms and caressed her.

"Oh, I forgive you, Evelyn," said he. "Poor child, you have had a hard time. God knows when I married you, I meant to make you a proud and happy woman, but fate has been against me. I wish I could die and set you free of me."

"How horrible of you to say that!" cried Evelyn clinging to him. "You do not forgive me, or you would not have such a thought. You are remembering how cruel I was, how selfish, how ungrateful! You are treating me, not as if I were your wife, but somebody accidentally in your way, that you can take or leave as you choose. I know it is all my fault, I know that I have not been a good wife of late, but that does not after all make me less your own wife."

He looked down at her and pushed the little curls off her forehead.

"Yes, you are my wife, Evelyn," he said, "we cannot get over that. I may not be worthy of you; that is your misfortune and my fault, but it does not alter facts. So long as I live no other man can kiss your lips or look into your eyes like this."

She smiled back at him, her whole face illuminated with sudden gladness.

"But if a man may not surrender himself to his wife and rely on her comprehension and mercy as on his God's, she is not his true wife," he went on, and his tone and look made her tremble.

"Oh, Roger," she exclaimed, "trust me. Tell me everything. That is, if you choose, tell me everything. If you like best to be silent, then say not a word. Only believe that henceforth always, through everything, I am here, ready, waiting, believing, knowing with all my heart and soul that you are strong and brave and good. I never will doubt you again."

He was moved.

"Look here, Evelyn," he said with a husky voice, "I have no strength to say more than this now; besides, I am not a man who indulges in confession and repentance. I only want to justify your faith in me to a certain degree. If wrong has been done, it was not of my contriving; if there is anything false in the situation, it was forced upon me. I have been at the mercy of circumstances which held me in their meshes; and let no one who has not known how I have struggled, and who has not himself struggled in the same way, judge me."

"That was what Rex said," murmured Evelyn.

"Rex?" Roger exclaimed in a different tone. "What did Rex say?"

"He said you had had heavy responsibilities, cares, anxieties, that what seemed inconsistent in your—"

"Do you mean to say that you told Rexford Long your infernal suspicions of me?"

He pushed her off and held her at arm's length, looking at her while his face flushed and darkened.

"Yes," said Evelyn, growing white to the lips.

"Told him you believed I had substituted a child for Bessy in order to get hold of Aunt Lizzy's money?" He shook her as he spoke.

"Yes." She looked at him imploringly. "I always did tell Rex everything, you know," she said in a pitiful voice. "And I was very lonely, very unhappy. You were away, and—"

"Rex was here. I see." He spoke with sharp, bitter irony. "What did he say to your story?"

"He did not believe it; he told me I was under some hallucination."

"What else did he say?"

"That he was certain you were incapable of doing wrong."

"Noble, magnanimous Rex! What else?"

"I do not remember," she faltered, feeling as if some threat, some accusation lay behind her husband's ironical smile.

"I congratulate you on your bad memory," said Roger. "It might be inconvenient to tell me all he said to comfort you."

"He did not comfort me! He was angry, horrified at me!" she cried out sharply.

"Not comfort you?" said Roger, with a short, bitter laugh. "How disappointed you must have been! That was remiss of Rex. He did not play up to the part you had assigned him. I always knew he was poor-spirited, hesitated to call his soul his own, but I should have supposed the tamest man in the world could rise to the occasion when a wife complains to him of her husband."

She gazed at him with startled, dilated eyes.

"I don't know what you mean," she said uneasily. "But if you intend to impute anything evil to Rex, you are wrong. He was true to you that day, true as steel."

"Little you know just what his feeling is about me. He is eaten up by jealousy. He has been head over ears in love with you for years. When I told him I was going to marry you he sat all night in his room, staring at the wall. I looked in twice, but he was like a man in a trance and saw and heard nothing. He has never got over it. He has felt robbed and despoiled ever since."

She uttered an exclamation, perhaps to arrest further speech, but he went on. "'Beware of long absences and long silences,' they say," Roger pursued in a low, even voice, but with his face showing a white heat of anger, "but I did suppose my wife was a woman I could trust."

She looked back at him hopelessly, but said nothing.

" I might have known — I ought to have known," he
went on. " I remember how you kissed him the night
Bessy came home."

She gazed at him, her thin nostril swelling, her lips
just curled, a look in her eyes ‹as if she were about to
retort, but she did not at first move or speak. After
a little silence she said, with perfect self-control, —
" You did not mean that, Roger. I don't think you
have meant any of this. You do not distrust me. You
do not distrust Rex, it is only — "

" It is only that I forbid your speaking to Rex henceforth except in my presence," said Roger firmly. " I 'm
sick of having him put before me ; I 'll not have it."

He flung himself into his chair before his desk,
leaned forward and buried his head in his arms. A
miserable silence ensued. Evelyn had not let herself
take in the outrage his words had implied. She felt
only for Roger : his attitude, his averted face, his whole
expression of suffering tormented her. She knelt down
before him and clasped her hands on his knees. After
a time her presence, her touch, her unspoken entreaty
all made themselves felt. He raised his head and
looked down at her. Their eyes met.

" Poor little Evelyn ! " he said gently. " I 'm sorry
for you. It is all a tangle. I don't see my way out."

He leaned down and kissed the parted lips, then
resolutely rose, as if putting the whole subject away,
and resumed his usual demeanor.

XXIV

REX GOES TO WALFORD.

ALL these weeks Rexford Long had been irresolute as to which way lay his duty. The question of absolute right or wrong in the matter about Bessy, he had not attempted to grapple with. He wished only to avert suffering.

He at last decided to go to Walford; once on the scene he might better be able to judge about the course he ought to pursue. He reached Mrs. Goodeve's late one evening, and next morning at ten o'clock went to see Evelyn. He intended to have a talk with Roger, but first he wished to feel the pulse of events and know what had been happening. He came upon her and the two children as soon as he turned into the grounds. She was carrying Theodore in her arms; and Bessy in a scarlet fez and red dress, with her hair in a golden glory about her head, had a rake in her hands and was gathering the dead leaves into heaps. The dogs considered her occupation an effort for their own amusement and dashed about her with a glad exuberance of life. The sight smote Long with a vivid suggestion of what Nino had described as happening on this very spot. He had visions of a still little figure lying on the bank, and his eyes sought the spot shudderingly. He was indeed so strongly dominated by what was going on in his own mind that he was comparatively unobservant of Evelyn. He did not see that she gave a start as she recognized him, flushed painfully and for a moment seemed reluctant to advance.

"Here I am," he said, holding out his hand. "I told you I should come back."

She uttered some form of greeting, held up Theodore for his admiration, and called Bessy. He took the little girl in his arms and kissed her, then turned back to Evelyn and looked closely into her face.

"You are not well?" he exclaimed.

"Oh yes, I am well."

"Is anything wrong?"

"Oh no, oh no."

"How is Roger? Is he at home?"

"He is at the works. Go and see him," said Evelyn, and as she spoke a little spot of red came into each cheek. "Go and see him, and perhaps he will ask you to come back and lunch with us."

"You will not ask me to stay, then," said Long with a half laugh.

"No," she said with a slight trembling of the lower lip, "I shall not ask you to stay."

"Have I offended you, Evelyn?"

"No! Oh no!" she said, with a glance upwards and a half smile.

"Roger is angry."

She nodded.

"You have told him what you told me in the summer," he said, with swift divination.

She nodded again.

"He knows too that you told me."

"Yes," she murmured.

"It is reasonable for him to be angry," said Long.

"You mean that I ought not to have told you," faltered Evelyn. "I see now how wrong it was, but then I felt that it was perfectly natural, inevitable that I should tell you. I could not have told Amy, I could not have told Mrs. Goodeve, but I turned to you, — you have always been like my brother."

"I know, I know," said Long hurriedly. He had dropped his glance to the ground. "I will go and see Roger," he said. "Probably I shall come back later."

As he turned, Bessy came up and begged him to stay, and when he said he was in a hurry, she fell to prolonged weeping.

"Don't cry, Bessy," said Rex.

"I must cry, — I like to cry," she returned with a loud wail.

"What are you crying about?"

"Oh, lots of things, whole heaps of things."

"What is one?"

"First, the wind blows the leaves up and down and all over," said Bessy indignantly. "It is just as if they were alive, — they will not keep still a minute. Then if I get a pile of them and try to bury Sir Waller and Nix like the Babes in the Wood, they won't be dead, — they jump up and scatter them all about. And then — then — you go away."

"That is not worth crying about. Don't cry. Happy little girls shouldn't cry."

"Who ought to cry then?" said Bessy, with remorseless logic. "Dogs don't cry, and you don't cry, and mamma don't cry."

"Theodore cries sometimes," suggested Evelyn.

"He cries because he don't know any better," said Bessy with disdain. "I cry because I like to cry. I am going to cry velly hard indeed."

But by the time Rex reached the gate and looked back, Bessy was laughing more loudly than she had cried, and had evidently prevailed upon her mother and Theodore to play the part of Babes in the Wood. Rex went rapidly on to the works, but although his thoughts might well have turned with some apprehension to his coming interview with Roger, they lingered persistently upon this encounter with Evelyn. She had been dressed in dark tweeds, and the contrast of the heavy rough material had given added delicacy and even fragility to her face. She had never in his remembrance looked younger. He counted her age on his fingers ; she was fifteen when he first knew her, accordingly was not yet quite twenty-five. Something pathetic in the expression of her eyes and lips cut him to the heart. She was patient, and he remembered her so impetuous ; she seemed to him half hopeless, and it was impossible to conceive of Evelyn as anything but hopeful : to think of that bright young creature at the end of her joys darkened the universe for him.

Thus busy in conjectures he was in Roger Rexford's presence before he had thought of what he wished to say to him. Roger happened to be for a moment in the counting-room speaking to Spencer, and the two cousins shook hands with a sufficient show of cordiality before the new manager and the half-dozen men at the desks.

" Did you wish to see me ? " Roger inquired.

" If you are at leisure."

" Come into my office," the other returned, and led the way in and shut the door.

The moment the two were alone, the smiling mask dropped from Roger's face.

"I did not know you were in Walford," said he. "How long have you been here?"

"I came last night."

"You evidently are a man of leisure," said Roger offensively.

"Evidently you are not," observed Long. "I can go away."

"Have you been at my house?" demanded Roger.

"I have."

"You saw my wife?"

"For a few moments."

"Please to absent yourself from my house in future," said Roger. "If time hangs heavily on your hands waste it elsewhere than beneath my roof. There is a fatal facility about men like you, — you creep in insidiously."

"You evidently wish to insult me, Roger," said Long. "So be it. I have, in my time, borne some things for old affection and old habit, but there is a limit. I have had a long patience with you. You are angry now and not quite yourself, — but before I go I will say simply that you have no cause to be angry with me."

Roger's face had darkened, the veins on his forehead stood out, his lips were set. He spoke thickly.

"It is hardly worth while for you to come and tell me I need not be angry with you, as if I should take the trouble to be jealous. As for your long patience with me, I should say it was the other way. You may imagine that I have not known all the time exactly how you regard my wife."

"As a saint; as the purest and loveliest woman on earth," said Long, his eyes fixed on his cousin as if his condition were something to study curiously.

"No thanks to you if she is a saint," said Roger. "Her indifference is a sure safeguard. She never cared for you. Of course, the moment I first saw you with her I knew that you were in love with her, — but she had never thought of you."

"I am well aware of that."

"If she has turned to you, if she has seemed to depend on you," Roger pursued with a look and tone of bitter scorn, "it is with the same feeling with which she would call a tame spaniel. She has never regarded you otherwise."

"I expect nothing else. I wish nothing else," said Long.

"Yet you talk of a long patience with me, when I have been such an easy-going husband as to allow you to sit and walk and ride with her; to spin fine-drawn prettinesses of talk; to discuss books, music. It saved me trouble. That sort of lap-dog trick belongs to men like you. A different sort of man feels that a woman is a pretty thing to humor when it suits his convenience, but to whom it is pedantry to talk sense, and from whom he no more expects it than thistles from grapes. I have let you go on; I have put up with your presence in my house in season and out of season, but everything finally reaches its climax and comes to an end, and by ——! my patience is at last worn out."

"So is mine," said Long. "I will go."

He moved away without another glance. He found the door bolted, and while he was fumbling at the catch Roger called "Rex?"

Long turned. "Well, say on."

He saw that his cousin had thrown himself into a chair.

"I was a brute," he said, in a tone of dejection. "I was tempted of the devil."

"I know you were. I was more sorry for you than hurt," said Long. "It makes no particular difference to me that you pour out the wildest folly, but I don't like the signs and indications. A child could see that you had been drinking, Roger. It is an abominable pity."

Long had turned on his steps, drawn a chair to the office table opposite Roger, and the two looked at each other.

"I don't often take anything in the morning," said Roger, "but I found myself confoundedly nervous."

"Nervous about what? What is going wrong with you?"

"Everything," said Roger moodily. "Nothing ever goes right with me. Nothing has ever gone right with me. It has been a simple progression from bad to worse."

"Do you mean business, or do you allude to your private affairs?"

"It is all of a piece," said Roger, in a tone of utter despondency.

"I thought trade was booming."

"That is just my usual luck. Spencer was just telling me when you came in that a strike is ordered all through this region. Our men will go out with the rest next Tuesday."

"How does Spencer happen to know?"

"He has a finger in every pie."

"Will it hurt you?"

"That remains to be seen. We cannot pay more wages, and that is what they are after. For myself, I don't care," Roger pursued with heat. "I 'm sick of the Rexford Manufacturing Company. Every man has his Russian campaign, and this is mine, only it has lasted seven years. For all I shall object, they may burn up the works, bury the entire plant deep in ruins. This place simply represents to me what I hate. I sold my soul for this infernal fraud and have never enjoyed a moment's freedom since. If I go away I am dragging a chain; if I stay here I look up at a sword hanging over me. Let them do their worst, I say. I have had no luck out of it and expect none."

The tone and look as much as the words deepened Long's impression that Roger was half out of his mind.

"I cannot believe your men are likely to go to any extremes," said he. "When I used to be here as a boy, I thought them no end of good fellows. It seemed all like one family."

· "They will have to do as they are bid," said Roger, with contemptuous emphasis. "They are under orders. Beresky is managing the strike, Spencer says. He is an out-and-outer. Let them begin at Rexford's, and tear the whole place down, I say, then perhaps I can get away and be free to breathe again."

"I wish you would be frank. Don't exaggerate. Tell me how you stand."

"How I stand? Unpleasantly near the edge of the precipice, and there I've stood for years."

"I don't ask for metaphors. Just give me a few facts."

"Oh, facts!" Roger pounded his clenched fist down on the table. "I can't look facts in the face; they would strike me dead."

· "I see how it is," said Rex. "You try to avoid unpleasant thoughts. You stupefy yourself to get away from the possibility of grasping actualities. I used to think, Roger, you were a brave man; you've got strength in you somewhere. I want you to get hold of yourself. Free confession is good for the soul. Tell me the whole story."

"The whole story?" said Roger uneasily. "There is no whole story." His cousin's kind, quiet glance and friendly tone began to tell upon him. His feeling that dogged endurance was necessary and that he must give way to no feebler instincts changed. There was clear sympathy in Long's manner, and he was suddenly smitten by a wish to yield to the comfort of it. But his mind was heavy, confused, inert. It fastened only on far-off thoughts and speculations; the near seemed distant, and the distant seemed near.

"Rex," he burst out suddenly, after a pause in which he had tried to grasp vanishing clews of thought and intention, " do you remember your class poem?"

"Well, yes," said Long. "What makes you think of that?"

"It suddenly came into my head how you looked when you delivered it. It impressed me then. I have always remembered it. The subject was the famous simile of the eagle stricken to death by an arrow feathered with one of his own plumes. You said that was the fate of most men. What ruined mortals was born with them, was part of them; grew with their growth and strengthened with their strength. I suppose you spoke out of fancy, not out of experience, but there is something in it. At least, my career proves it."

Long gazed at him expecting he would explain his meaning, but Roger sat drumming on the table, his restless eyes glancing from one object to another.

" I don't quite understand your allusion," said Rex.

" My allusion to what ? "

" To the simile of the eagle killed by his own plume."

" It is ambition that has killed me," said Roger with a short, bitter laugh, — " the belief that I had more brains than other men, greater powers of combination, and a knack of succeeding in all I undertook. Rex," — he leaned across the table and touched his cousin's arm, — " I had not been married forty-eight hours before I heard of the failure of a firm in New York by which I lost forty thousand dollars. I say *I* lost it. There were circumstances, — in short, I did not wish to saddle it on the company, for it had been a private venture of my own. I have never recovered from it. Since then I have always had something to dread, something to hide. It opened a gulf between me and safety and honor, and all I had in the world has been flung into it."

" But, Roger," interposed Long, " you have partners ; you have never had to stand alone."

" Partners ! " said Roger, — " I 've forked over dividends that cut me in two simply in order to keep Lowry from coming near me. I was determined not to be dictated to by a couple of mummies. After my father's death I got the control of the company and determined to keep it. And I had every right to keep it," Roger proceeded, throwing back his head in his old, proud, resolute way. " I should have been a millionaire to-day if the fates had not been against me. Rex," he cried out with anguish, " why is it that I have had disaster after disaster ? Have I sinned against the law of heaven and thus have to endure the penalty ? "

"Roger," said Rex, "I would not talk about fate. What we sow we reap, no doubt of that. Say you were ambitious, say you were impatient of dictation, wanted to initiate a new policy in the concern and make yourself a rich man in a few years; say you went into private speculations and lost money which you had no right to lose, and you have said enough to make it clear that you had to pay a penalty. But I cannot believe that financially you have ever stood in a position where you could not undo what you had done, retrieve your credit, and build up your house anew."

Roger seemed about to speak, then evidently changed his mind, set his lips, and remained silent. Long was in doubt what to say and what to leave unsaid. His cousin had put it wholly out of his power to allude to Evelyn or even to Bessy. That subject was ended. Long felt indeed at the moment that he wished never to see Evelyn again. Thus he felt all the natural outlets of advice and remonstrance closed against him.

"For one thing," he proceeded, ending the pause, "work with your partners. Don't trust yourself alone. Partners may be hinderers, but it is sometimes useful to be hindered. When the evil one wants to tempt any one he leads him into a solitude."

"Rex, you sometimes say a true thing," said Roger.

"Orrin Goodeve is in Europe, but Felix could come home and go into things with you."

"I 'm not alone nowadays," said Roger pointing his thumb over his shoulder. "Spencer is here."

"I know he is," said Long. "You had better get Felix Goodeve back."

"I don't care how things go," said Roger impatiently. "My heart is not in it, nor my conscience nowadays. I 'm callous. My only desire is to have done with it."

A knock came at the door.

"That's Spencer, I suppose," said Roger, drawing out his watch. "Come in." Spencer entered. "Are the men here? I'll be there in a moment. How is it, Rex? How long are you to be in Walford?"

"I shall take the 2.30 train," said Rex.

"Flaxman and some of the other manufacturers meet here, so I must go now. We are to talk over the situation."

"I hope some measures will be taken to avert the strike."

"It is sure to come sooner or later. Let it come, I say. It may cut some of the knots I have found insolvable. Well, good-by, Rex."

Deep, yearning emotion showed in his face as he met his cousin's glance. He gave a quick, short sigh.

"You 've known me a good many years, old fellow," he said. "Remember that I am harassed, besieged, tempted of the devil. I am not master of my acts. Good-by."

"Good-by, Roger," said Long, and the two parted with a grasp of the hand.

XXV.

MISS STANDISH and Mrs. Goodeve encountered in the street one day towards the end of November, and Amy turned and walked with the latter towards her house.

"Will you come in?" Mrs. Goodeve asked as they paused at the gate.

"Yes," said Amy, brightening beautifully. "I had been thinking of paying you a visit to-day."

Mrs. Goodeve ushered the girl in, feeling very proud of her. "I am going to make you take off your hat and wrap," she said. "You shall go up to my room and sit down with me while I sew, — just, my dear," here she kissed her, "as if you were my daughter."

"You have one daughter," said Amy.

"I have two; my daughter Edith, and then Mary, Orrin's wife. When Felix marries, I shall have three daughters."

They had gone up-stairs, and Mrs. Goodeve established her visitor opposite her at her work-table. A bright fire burned on the hearth, and the room was besides full of sunlight. Amy sank into the deep-cushioned easy-chair, with a somewhat heightened color.

"Is he going to be married?" she asked, trying to glance unconcernedly at her hostess, but failing, she lowered her eyes and her foot tapped the floor.

"Who, — Felix? He talks a good deal about it," said Mrs. Goodeve. She opened a box which stood on the table and produced a dozen or more photographs. "See these," she went on, handing them, one by one, to Amy.

They were all pictures of women, most of them handsome, not a few possessing remarkable good looks. There was one of a Spanish type who sat a horse magnificently; another had an exuberance of golden hair. Each card bore some inscription. Beneath the portrait of the equestrian was written "Mrs. Felix Goodeve, *Hem.*" On two or three of them was the question, "How should you like her for a daughter-in-law?" and others were inscribed, "Waiting for your approval."

"Who are they?" asked Amy in dismay.

"I hardly know who they are," said Mrs. Goodeve. "Every week or so Felix sends me one. You see, I have been for some time anxious that he should marry, and I suppose the poor boy is looking for a wife."

"He seems to have plenty of opportunity for choice," said Amy, flushing crimson. "And they are all very good-looking."

"To tell you the truth, my dear," said Mrs. Goodeve, confidentially, "I don't like any of them. I should be absolutely unhappy if Felix were to bring any single one of them home to me. I don't know, Amy, what you think of my boy. It may be a mother's partiality, but I feel as if he were worth a woman's falling in love with. I believe, too, that he deserves a good wife. I am a little ambitious for him. I want him to marry a really sweet girl, — a charming girl. I should hate to feel that he had not used his right of choice, that his real heart had not spoken; that he had simply taken up with somebody because he was tired and dispirited, — wanted somebody to make things seem home-like, or because she had made up her mind to marry him. Still, I dare say that some of these are very bright girls. Now, for example, what do you think of this dark-complexioned one on horseback? You see he actually calls her Mrs. Felix Goodeve. I am not sure but that she looks a little like you."

"I am not nearly so good-looking," said Amy, in a white heat of indignation.

"You have a sweeter and a nobler face," returned Mrs. Goodeve. "I do not like this young woman's attitude. I should not like her to turn my boy's head."

"I feel sure, Mrs. Goodeve, he would turn it away from her."

Felix's mother put the pictures aside, and began to talk to Amy. She spoke of her son, and told a great many little traits in his character; she illustrated them with anecdotes, and finally took out a bundle of his letters and read them aloud. Felix wrote very good letters; he had swift perceptions, described well, made rapid summaries, had a quick sense of the comic, and an aerial freedom of allusion to everything which was going on, at home and abroad. Occasionally he said, "Tell me about Miss Standish, — what she is doing nowadays."

When the letters were ended, Amy rose to go. As she put on her wide-brimmed hat, she looked at Mrs. Goodeve with so lovely a color, such bright eyes and such a soft smile that the latter said, suddenly drawing the girl to her : —

"Oh, my dear, you are such a beauty!"

"Is that the best thing you can say for me?" asked Amy, with a swift caress.

" I like girls to be pretty; I think that is partly what they are for," said Mrs. Goodeve. " But, Amy, I consider you simply perfect."

Amy, with a hand on each arm of the older woman, stood looking up into her face.

" Mrs. Goodeve," she said softly, " I came to ask you something."

" Ask me this moment."

" It is just a little hard to ask."

" I 'll give you anything I have in the world, my dear."

" I wish your son would come home."

" My dear, I have two sons."

" I mean Felix," said Amy.

" Oh, you mean Felix. Shall I write and tell him that you wish he would come home ? "

" Please do."

" Shall I give him any reason ? "

" I don't think you need."

" I shall just say then that Amy Standish wants him to come back to Walford."

" Yes."

" Shall I give him any promise ? "

" No."

" Perhaps he will take it as a promise; perhaps you are binding yourself to something. Men can be very foolishly illogical, but they are given to very clear deductions where the girl they are in love with is concerned."

Amy put her arms around Mrs. Goodeve's neck and looked into her face.

" Perhaps," she said, half laughing and half crying, " he has got over it."

"No, I do not think he has got over it," said Mrs. Goodeve.

Amy said no more. The two kissed each other, and the girl went her way, hardly knowing what forces had guided her irresistibly towards sending for Felix. But she had many a time remembered how once at her need she had stretched out her hand and found strength in him, and now, if he could come, it would be comfort and gain.

"He can be here in two or three weeks, I suppose," she said to herself. It was something to have a whole fortnight to make up her mind exactly how to meet him. The moment she had committed herself a reaction of feeling set in. She longed to take back her words. What had she meant, what had she wished? Mrs. Goodeve had observed that men could on occasion be very logical. Amy told herself, hanging her head and blushing with shame, that she felt hopelessly illogical. She wanted to see Felix, and had been ready to say that she was indifferent to consequences. But then she had not defined what the consequences might be.

A Benedict might observe with a touch of humor that when he once declared he should die a bachelor he had not supposed he should live to be married, but Amy knew not how to carry off her inconsistency humorously. Perhaps, too, Felix had by this time changed his mind, and she had vivid hurried images of the women whose pictures she had seen. It began to appear the very height of presumption and absurdity for her to have counted so assuredly upon his being in the same state of mind as on that April day seven or eight months before.

It was on the fifth morning after she had made her request to Mrs. Goodeve that Amy was sitting over the fire in the library, pondering the situation which, day by day, now became more trying to her. She was meditating some means of arresting the letter now on its way; failing that, she was thinking of flight, when she heard a voice in the hall saying, "I want to see your sister Amy first." At the same instant Evelyn's arch face appeared at the portière; she ushered some one in, then closed the door.

Amy looked up, and her heart gave a great leap. She rose, although she felt unable to stand. It was Felix.

He was already close beside her; he had taken her hand.

"You sent for me," he said.

"I did not suppose you could be here for a fortnight yet," she faltered.

"Am I too soon? Did I come too swiftly?"

"No."

"Don't you want to see me after all?"

"I counted the days it would take a letter to reach you," she murmured, by turns pale as death and consumed with blushes, unable to lift her eyes, "and I supposed you could not possibly receive it until the day after to-morrow, possibly not until Monday."

He still held her hand, and now, looking down into her face with a flush and a smile on his own, and with a half-sigh, too, born we will not say of what sweet impatience, he lifted it, put it to his cheek, his temple, his eyes, for a moment against his lips. Even then he did not let it go, but pressed it to his breast.

"There is such an invention as the telegraph," he remarked.

" Did Mrs. Goodeve telegraph you to come ? " said Amy aghast. " I never supposed such things could be telegraphed."

" Such things are what a telegraph is for. Bad news travels fast enough, no matter how slowly it goes. I came on the instant, Amy, that I heard you had asked for me. Here I am."

She looked up. What she saw in his eyes reassured her. Their glance might well have puzzled and tormented ; they might have laughed at her, triumphed over her, half-threatened her ; instead they were friendly, caressing, joyous.

" Yes, I see you," she said.

" You are sure you wanted me to come ? "

" Absolutely sure."

" Tell me are you glad to see me."

" Yes. I am glad. Things are going badly. I felt as if you might put them right."

" What things are going badly? "

" Sit down," she said, attempting to draw her hand from him. " We will talk matters over."

" I am afraid to let go my clasp lest you should vanish into space," he said.

Their eyes met a moment.

" You don't mean to send me away again ? " he said.

" I know that you are a busy man," she returned. " Felix, I hope you found it convenient to come."

" I found it most particularly convenient to come when you invited me."

" I hope you wanted to come."

" Did n't I just ? "

" You remembered me? "

" Well, rather."

"But I saw all those photographs you sent your mother."

"Oh, did you?" The old twinkle was in his eye.

"Are the originals very particular friends of yours?"

"Not all. Half of them I never set eyes on."

"Sit down, and I will tell you why I needed you."

He led her to the sofa, established her there and himself leaned over the arm and looked into her face.

"Business first," said he. "What is it?"

He had, it seemed to her, grown older. He was at least thinner, and some of the boyishness had gone out of his face, which had gained in expression. He looked so kind, so strong, so ready, that she gazed at him with a sudden evaporation of all her doubts and dilemmas.

She put her hand on his coat-sleeve a moment.

"By the way," she asked, "did I tell you I was glad to see you?"

"Not so eloquently as I should like to have you tell me," said he. "Not altogether so sweetly as I fully intend that you shall tell me when we have a little leisure."

"You see," she exclaimed, "I have felt such a longing to put out my hand and find a friend, a real friend."

"Here he is. What shall he do for you?"

"Have you heard that the strike has begun?"

"It was the first news that greeted me. I think there is no occasion for alarm. I know Walford men, and I cannot believe there will be any real trouble."

"It was not that sort of trouble I dreaded."

"No. Had it anything to do with Spencer?"

She nodded. "Roger has been here, pressing me to accept him."

" Roger Rexford ? "

" More than that," whispered Amy; " Mr. Spencer
has told me that he has it in his power to ruin Roger ;
that the safest way for us all is for me to marry him."

" Oh, the scoundrel ! " Felix drew himself to his full
height a moment and seemed to reflect. " Tell me
exactly how you stand with Spencer," he said then, —
" that is, if you are willing."

" I told you how it was last spring," she said.

" Have matters remained unchanged ? "

" No." She looked up at him with a half smile.
" Please sit down," she said. " You look so tall — so
— far off — as if — " He had taken a seat at the end
of the sofa, and she slid towards him. " Don't be angry," she whispered.

" Well, no, not raging, not furious. Go on ; tell me
everything."

" When I first came to Walford," she said, " I felt
anxious to help Mr. Spencer. He interested me. It
was not for a long time that it ever occurred to me he
could — could — "

" Fall in love with you ; but I will answer for him
that he did the first moment he laid eyes on you," said
Felix. " The impertinent puppy. I long to get hold
of him."

" I don't think he is very much in love with me," she
said eagerly. " I am sure I should have suspected it
if he had deeply and truly cared."

" Come now, did you not know *I* was in love with
you from the time we met in the vestry to baptize Sam
Porter's baby ? "

She looked at him as if trying to remember.

" That was different," she said with a little nod. " I

was always, as it were, conscious of you. But I never thought of anybody's being in love. In love! I hated the phrase! Indeed I hate it now."

"What's in a name?" said Felix. "Call it natural selection if that sounds more scientific, call it a blind principle of evolution if that is better, only — only — accept the clear hypothesis that the moment a man looks at you, Amy, the most beautiful domestic ideas begin to form in his mind, he — However, we are at present discussing matters of business. I want to be rid of that upstart, Spencer. Just as I left Eagle's Creek there was a man named Leary who wanted to get hold of a certain Colonel Noble. Colonel Noble equally wanted to get hold of Leary ; each had started out after the other with a couple of revolvers and a bowie-knife, but they went in opposite directions. That is the way Spencer and I have felt about each other ; we want to get hold of each other bad ; but there has hitherto been a certain inconvenience in meeting face to face."

"I don't want you to be angry with Mr. Spencer," said Amy earnestly. "It was really all my fault. It never occurred to me I had encouraged him, until he began to talk about my marrying him. It seemed to me absolute nonsense. When I finally promised to marry him if I ever married anybody," she went on with a sort of childish petulance, "it was as if I said ' If I ever go to live in the moon I will marry you.' "

Felix's bright glance was fixed on her. He said nothing.

"I knew that human beings cannot live in the moon," she proceeded, as if anxious to establish her premises irrefutably. "And I was also certain that under no

circumstances should I be willing to marry anybody."
He caught her hand and detained it.

"Of course I was wrong," she said, with admirable
candor.

"Of course you were absurd," said Felix.

"I had told him, over and over again, nothing could
ever induce me to marry," she went on, "and finally I
only yielded because it seemed not to matter in the
least." They looked at each other like two children in
doubt. "Last June," she proceeded, "I took back my
promise. I told him I must be free."

"Last June?" repeated Felix. "Why did you not
send for me then?"

As she felt the sweetness of his smile and understood the sudden gladness in his voice, she felt wholly
dominated, but she forced herself to go on.

"Mr. Spencer said," she continued, "that I could
not take back my promise. He insists that — "

"Amy," Felix burst out, "don't think again about
that fellow. I will settle him. I was ready to tell you
last spring that I could free you from him; but I could
– not – help – fearing – you – liked – him – a little."

"Liked him?" She looked up with a sort of shudder. "I never really liked him. Now I detest him."

"He has troubled you?"

"He has persisted. He still persists, and as I said
before, he seems to threaten that he can ruin Roger.
And Roger is not himself; there is a strange reckless-
ness about him; and Evelyn is not happy; and, Felix,
I sent for you."

She raised her eyes; there were tears in them.

"Don't think of Spencer again," said Felix. "Oh,
my poor little girl, to realize that you have been suffer-

ing annoyance from that cur, while I stayed away eating my heart out in jealous pain and grief when I might have been here looking after you. Come now, is there any more trouble ? "

" There are a good many little troubles in these great ones."

" I must go find out what is going on," said Felix, " only first there is just one little matter I should like to settle."

She saw a glimmer of a smile in his eyes.

" I suppose," he went on demurely, " we are engaged."

" Oh, is that important ? " she tried to answer archly, but the thrill of feeling which stirred her under his clasp and glance ran into her speech.

" No, not between you and me, of course," said Felix. " But outsiders are always curious. My mother, for example, will be anxious to know if we are engaged. I suppose I may as well tell her that we are."

" I fancy she will know without asking," said Amy.

!

XXVI.

ALONZO SLOPER'S GREAT OPPORTUNITY.

As Amy had told Felix, the strike had begun. Flaxman's men had taken the initial step, and gradually all
the manufacturers in Walford had had to shut down.
At Rexford's a few of the steel workers were still in
their usual places. These were Walford men, New
Englanders, who did not belong to any trade-league and
who resented any jurisdiction outside of Rexford &
Company. Whether this nucleus would have the effect
of drawing to itself all the better elements among the
mass of men now tasting the sweets of liberty and in-
action at the street corners and in the saloons, or
whether it would become a source of danger to Rexford's remained to be seen. So far, the whistles
sounded in their usual way, and one of the tall chim-
neys still belched out columns of smoke to the sky.

When Felix Goodeve arrived on the scene, he found
Roger Rexford and Spencer sitting in their office as if
things were going on as usual. The men he had met
in the streets had greeted him with enthusiastic good-
nature, and it was hard to believe that any serious
danger was brewing. But Roger and Spencer both
rose with a look of such surprise as he came in, that it
was not easy to decide whether to put a construction
upon their dismay unflattering to himself, or to impute
it to the state of affairs in general.

Felix told them his mother had desired him to come home and he had arrived apparently in the nick of time. He sat down, asked for an enumeration of the existing complications and listened, while Spencer, who had quickly regained his equipoise, gave himself free play in setting forth the situation, which he was inclined to consider a grave one. He had a mind of a far-reaching order, and was quick to perceive the advantage of having one of the Goodeves to depend on in these straits. Spencer said that Flaxman's men had begun the mischief; they were chiefly foreigners; not a few of them were of the fiery haranguing sort, and they had led their followers on from place to place, stopping work and gaining adherents. But when they came to Rexford's they found only part of the men ready to join them. The older ones, of a sturdier sort, had ordered out the strikers and kept on at their posts, influencing all that they could to stay with them. The advantage of this, Spencer considered doubtful. It made those who had gone out suspicious and resentful. There were already threats that the men would be hindered from continuing their work, and his advice was, that the place should be shut up until some terms were agreed upon.

Roger, feeling sure that his side would have an adherent in Felix, confessed that he differed widely from Spencer. Their own men who had gone out made no threats, and he believed in them sufficiently to feel sure they would stand by Rexford's if it came to having a choice thrust upon them. They were run away with by the novelty of the situation, but they would soon see that this system of war against old and tried employers was fatal from every point of view. Americans and Americanized men did not like to be dictated to by a man like Beresky, whom they would heartily despise a little later, when they saw what his teachings led to. In a day or two, the worst elements in the mob would get uppermost; somebody would fall to and break somebody else's head. By that time the men who were good for anything would have got sick of this aimless Donnybrook fair enterprise and would be glad enough to come back. Hence the imperative necessity of standing by the employees who still stood by him. He would keep Rexford's whistles going so long as one man kept his place.

"That is what exasperates the fellows who are out," said Spencer. "Suppose they make a nasty riot and come and burn down the works. They are sure to do something before they get through."

"I mean to trust to my own judgment in this matter," said Roger.

"Trusting to your own judgment has got you into trouble before now," remarked Spencer, whose irritation was growing every moment. "When it is just too late, you will give way and wish you had taken my advice, as you have done before now."

"I ought to know something about our men," said Roger.

"You never knew anything about a mob in all your respectable life," retorted Spencer.

"What do you think, Goodeve?" inquired Roger, feeling the need of an auxiliary.

"I am with you," returned Felix, briefly. "It seems to me that Mr. Spencer is frightened."

"I am not at all frightened," said Spencer with some bluster. "But I have watched the trouble take shape and gather force before my eyes."

"However," said Felix, "it is the company's affair, and luckily you are still outside the risks of the Rexford Manufacturing Company, Mr. Spencer."

"I 've had plenty of the responsibility, sir," replied Spencer.

"Plenty," said Felix, with a decisive nod. "I admit all that. You have had plenty of the responsibility."

"You seem to speak as if I had had too much," said Spencer, with exasperation. "If the Rexford Manufacturing Company has had an interval of success of late, it has to thank me for it."

"You have apparently brought us to this," said Felix, "which is almost too good a pace."

Spencer laughed, but his laugh suggested no amusement.

"You mean, evidently, Mr. Goodeve," said he, "to show me that it is not my business to meddle. Interfering with other people's folly is always thankless work."

"Exactly. I advise you to wash your hands of us," said Felix. "You and I will stick by the old concern, Roger. We are brothers. I have not told you yet, but I have the honor to be engaged to Miss Standish. Thus our interests are incorporated, identical, individual, one and the same. We will live or die, sink or swim, together."

Felix had made this announcement lightly, as if it were nothing particular, and looked at neither of his auditors. There was a moment's silence ; then Roger said : —

"I am utterly taken by surprise. How long has this been going on ? "

"As far as I am concerned," said Felix, " I am quite willing to say it has been going on ever since we met. It is only lately, however, that Miss Standish has made up her mind that it was within the limits of possibility for her to accept any man."

Spencer uttered some inarticulate sound. He had turned pale at Felix's first announcement, but now grew positively ghastly and seemed to be struggling to assert himself against some insuperable obstacle.

"Did you speak?" asked Felix, looking at him with a stern glance, and the other quailed before it. His eyes seemed to sink beneath his brows; his whole face shrunk. It would have been some satisfaction if he could have brazened out the situation and established some claim over Miss Standish — at least to have made a parade of indifference. He could do neither. He knew by instinct that Felix had been made aware of all the means he had taken to influence the girl he coveted. He had felt, even while he used them, that he was acting a cold-blooded, mean, dishonorable part, and now he dreaded lest he should be taken to task for it. He could bear no more. He flung himself out of the office, turned into his own, and sat down, feeling as if physically shattered. Tears actually gushed from his eyes, as he sat feeling helpless and beaten. It was not at first that the worthlessness of his dreams, the nothingness of his chimeras, broke sadly on his mind; but that he felt the degradation and misery of being spoken to like a cur who had stolen a cake. He pitied himself; he felt the old bitterness, which he had thought forever swallowed, rise again in his throat, and realized that there are some shames which last all one's life and assert themselves against the boldest and cleverest devices. He seemed to feel himself again the little ill-fed, undersized lad he had been on entering Rexford's ; glad to fetch and carry like a dog, snapping, too, like a dog at anything which satisfied hunger or thirst, and finally tamed and developed by the example of something nobler into a better boy, indeed a promising boy, with the makings of a man in him. He hated Felix Goodeve with unquenchable rancor as he remembered how he had spoken and how he had looked. He had not been in any degree authorized to come back thousands of miles and walk into Rexford's, as if he was easily master of everything, and assert his own views. The very absence of authorization made the insult rankle deeper in Spencer's breast, since he was so instantly made to feel that he was superfluous ; he, who had of late been counting with assurance on being the one important man in the company. Stung, dejected, hopeless, Spencer, for a time, as he sat overwhelmed by the conflux of opposing thoughts and emotions within him, was ready to hope that the worst the strikers could inflict upon the works would come to pass. It seemed as if he could not go on existing, while other men were happy and prosperous. He thought of Felix Goodeve, flushed and smiling, as he announced his engagement to Miss Standish, and as his imagination suggested what must have taken place between the two, how the sweetness which had only mocked himself had been freely yielded to this lover, how instead of eternally denying she must now have been complying, a muffled cry of anguish again burst from his breast. He jumped up and strode about the room, striking his forehead with his clenched fists. Distracted, shuddering, he felt as if his anger must find some outlet ; he longed to have somebody or something at his mercy. Nothing, it seemed to him, except crushing and trampling upon something, could be an antidote to the rage and disgust and bitterness which swelled his heart. He pounded his fist upon the table and made it ring with his blows; he smashed a chair against the fireplace; then, as the echoes of his violence came back, he felt as if his own folly mocked and derided him. He began to experience a reaction, and instead of wishing that the strikers might come on and burn the place, annihilate Felix Goodeve at a breath, inflict indignity upon Roger Rexford, he began to look at the situation more sanely, and to reflect that such excesses were sure to be his own destruction.

He had spent the hour from twelve to one in brooding over his troubles. Looking out of his window he could see Roger Rexford and Felix Goodeve talking with the men who were eating their dinners in the quadrangle. It showed Spencer's deep-rooted instinct of belief in and homage toward Felix Goodeve, that, bitter although his personal feelings were against the man, his presence yet helped to lighten the situation. It was likely to promote good feeling and check trouble. Instead of, as before, devising punishments and tortures for Felix, Spencer now began to think how he might be turned to account. His nerves had had their paroxysm, and now reason began to assume its usual sway. His ruling passion had always been to make the most of whatever opportunity presented itself; in spite of his ambitious dreams he had always lived in close relations to facts, generally finding them pliant to his will. He was no man to fight windmills, or to measure himself against obstacles that he was powerless to overcome. He had heroically combated his poverty and insignificance, and by means of zeal, patience, obstinacy, and cunning had advanced miraculously; but he had never demanded what he considered impossibilities. Even when he had fallen in love with Miss Standish, she had, as he believed, given him great encouragement; thinking over each detail of his interviews with her with unwearied satisfaction, repeating her words to him and dwelling on her looks, it had always been easy to decide that she was interested in him. No shadow of a doubt was possible that he was right in claiming all she would yield him. He had not been the sport of illusions ; he had not been presumptuous. He had simply made up his mind to lose nothing by not putting out his hand to seize it.

He tried to put away all thoughts of Amy. It made him grind his teeth to think, with a rage of impotent longing, how she had used him. Words he had uttered in his infatuation, exaggerations of speech and action permissible to happy lovers, but absurd when they disclose the far sweep of curve a man's imagination can take, when he does not accept palpable and existing facts, came back to his memory and overpowered him with shame and confusion. And now she was engaged to Felix Goodeve, and he hated her. It was characteristic of her blundering feminine logic that she should airily deny the possibility of marriage and dismiss such relations to the region of the impossible, then find it convenient after all to have a husband, and affirm all she had hitherto denied.

Now that the tide of his confidence had ebbed Spencer felt that he had always grazed bottom, — had always had to go warily ; but this conviction did not make him more contented to accept the sight of Felix Goodeve sailing into port with all his canvas set, having met the flood which bears men on to success.

However, all disappointment about his love affairs must be set aside for the present; feelings must be subordinate to facts. Spencer decided to postpone any personal action. Felix Goodeve had suggested that he was badly frightened, and that as he had no personal risks, he might easily cut and run to a place of safety. This was beastly ingratitude; but, after all, Spencer said to himself, he was glad he had no more at stake. He felt an awe of the unmanageable force of the mob. Since others assumed the responsibility, let them have all the responsibility. He himself could decide on no better plan of action than silently to resume his usual afternoon work. He would suggest nothing, invent no schemes, but listen and watch, absorb all that he might, and use his knowledge at the right moment. Accordingly he took half-a-dozen letters which had arrived that morning, and went to Roger Rexford for instructions, precisely as if nothing had happened between them. Felix Goodeve was still sitting in the office.

"You had better wait until to-morrow before writing, Spencer," Roger said. " Either things will be better to-morrow, or they will be worse. The situation begins to resolve itself. At Flaxman's they are glad to have a quiet interval to take stock and settle affairs generally; they are willing that the strikers should hold out till the first of January; but at Jones's they are pushed with work, have orders to fill by December fifteenth, or they will lose confoundedly."

" You have had news," remarked Spencer.

"Goodeve went out," said Roger. "He asked our men what they were striking for; that we had always been willing to make prices right. They replied they did not like our keeping the non-union men."

Spencer's face lighted up, but he refrained from saying, " I told you that was the mainspring of trouble." What he did observe was, " The leaders will want to put the screw on Jones."

" Of course. Sit down, won't you ? "

Roger saw something to pity in Spencer's pinched white face, which showed traces of the struggle he had gone through. Even Felix was sorry for the man, whose whole aspect expressed the fact that he had lost the exultant feeling he had lately enjoyed and acknowledged himself beaten ; and he at once included him in their conversation. Abashed by such politeness, Spencer felt his ease and self-possession desert him. His usually intelligent judgment seemed to lose all its force the moment he tried to express himself ; and to his mortification he found his remarks, which fell wide of the mark, accepted as if they were worth consideration. He would rather have met the scorn and contempt shown him three hours before. As it was, he looked about him uneasily, and was glad of a chance afforded him for escape.

It is a truism that each of us flourishes at the expense of another. Felix Goodeve, with the thrilling and delicious certainty at his heart that, in spite of the tedious and dispiriting interval of trouble, he still had won Amy, tried hard not to show his triumph over Spencer, who had had to bear disenchantment and failure. It was easy enough to perceive, however, that the happy lover was secretly exulting with the joy of a

man who after long waiting gains what he has striven
for. Spencer was glad to get away. It did not occur
to him, as he struggled with his offended pride, that he
himself had inflicted pangs more cruel than those which
he now suffered. He was soon to be reminded of it.

He had himself suggested that he should go down to
see Jones and talk matters over with him. He had
heard that the strikers were on the main street, in and
about Chester's. Nothing could be easier than taking
the other road to the Corner, which would enable him
to reach Jones' without any encounter. As soon as he
was outside the works, and beyond the buzz and thud
of the machinery still in operation, he could hear the
sound of high-pitched voices and shouts. Evidently
somebody had been making a speech in the open air, and
had gained applause. It was a calm, late November
afternoon; the placid, far-off sky showed that the Indian summer still had a day or two to reign. The hills
lying about Walford were touched with haze, and a
mellow atmosphere harmonized all the brown and sere
herbage which still lingered. No scene could be more
peaceful; but the moment he was alone, Spencer was
conscious of nothing but irritation. The sound of the
excited voices brought back his alarms of the morning,
when the strikers visited the works and only moved on
because at the moment some errand called them elsewhere. For a time he had been so galled by his own
crowd of stinging, exasperating thoughts that he had
almost forgotten other difficulties and dangers. But
no sooner had he heard that babel of confused voices
than he once more felt the oppression of the stormy
and passion-laden atmosphere which hung over Walford.

He strode on, anxious to gain shelter. He had cast about in his mind for a peg on which to hang a plausible reason for getting away from Felix Goodeve ; but now that he realized the danger of being out alone, he wished he had not come. There are dangers and dangers ; it was unpleasant to meet Felix Goodeve's look, good-natured but slightly disdainful ; but clearly such an ordeal was easier to bear than having to contend with the electric and fevered currents which ran through the veins of a crowd of dangerous men, breathing fire and vengeance. For it was not reassuring to hear at intervals a shout sometimes inarticulate, then again defining itself into some clear exclamation like, — "Go on !" "Give it to 'em !" "Hit 'em agin !" The air was so quiet, it carried vibrations of sound to a great distance ; that was Spencer's way of reassuring himself. But evidently something was going on, and it was nothing in the way of good. He distinctly heard a drum and a fife playing; then there came a hush.

As he turned a corner, a sudden clamor broke out ; and just too late he discovered that he had inadvertently turned towards at least a score of men, advancing by twos and threes, or breaking their ranks by falling into groups of half-a-dozen. At the sight, Spencer looked about him uneasily, as if hoping for some means of passing them, or at least retreating from them unseen. Then submitting to the inevitable, and feeling himself at their mercy, he slightly slackened his pace and tried to meet them with dignity.

He had at first supposed it to be the advance guard of the mob he dreaded. Thus it was with a sensation of relief that he recognized in this detachment a group of loafers, no doubt summarily ejected from the better class of strikers, who had, so far, principles to act up to and work to do. The column was headed by Alonzo Sloper and Sam Porter walking arm-in-arm, followed by McCann, Green, Simms and Cole, congenial spirits all. The remainder of the party was composed of riff-raff, chiefly boys, eager for some share in what was going on. Alonzo and his followers had had a great deal to make them happy all day; no work to do, all they wanted to eat, and far more than they needed to drink; all at the expense of higher powers who called this sort of picnic a righteous cause, swore by it, and preached a crusade.

Not that it offered a wholly new experience to Alonzo Sloper; indeed, it was the career he had been embarked on for years, but only now with high intentions and a lofty sense of doing his whole duty. Hitherto, this course of conduct had met with reprobation. To-day, he felt like an apostle.

When Spencer perceived what sort of foe he was to encounter, he was annoyed, but felt that he could at least dismiss his fears. He knew very well what stuff these men were made of. He failed to realize the inner tempest of crushed hopes, the consciousness of unavenged insults, which had of late been swaying Alonzo Sloper. Nor did he recognize the fact that the present opportunity added flame to fuel; nor that Alonzo had all day experienced a burning anxiety to lead on his followers to achieve some heroic exploit. Catching sight of Spencer he called authoritatively, "Halt!" and bringing himself up heavily, he interposed a solid obstacle to the advancing corps, which tumbled back unsteadily. He also offered a barrier to the man who was approaching.

"Stand," said Alonzo, thrilled with a sense of power, his purple face assuming a deeper dye.

"What do you mean? Get out of my way," said Spencer angrily. He carried a light cane, and he tried to parry the ponderous arm which was stretched across the sidewalk.

"No, Mr. Spencer," said Sloper magisterially, "I shall not get out of your way. Take care, boys, that he does not cut and run. Block up his lines of retreat. I have got a few questions to put to this gentleman."

"You are drunk," said Spencer with unutterable disgust. "You are all drunk. Sam Porter, I'm sorry to see you in such bad company. I thought better of you."

"Bad company!" said Alonzo Sloper, swelling with offended dignity, and feeling that he must not lose sight of the great principles which actuated him. "We're a band of brothers. An injury to one of us is an injury to all; we are — "

"Shut up your nonsense," said Spencer. "Let me pass."

"Not yet," said Mr. Sloper, enough of a strategist to perceive that the other was by this time quite at his mercy, being completely hemmed in by the crowd. "I am going to ask you a few questions, Mr. Harry Spencer, which I want you to answer before witnesses. When are you going to marry my daughter?"

"Yes, Mr. Spencer," called Michael McCann, whom Spencer had turned out of Rexford's six months before, — "when are you goin' to marry Miss Leo Sloper?"

The whole crowd took up the cry jeeringly, — "When are you going to marry Miss Leo Sloper?"

"You may well ask it of him, gentlemen," said Alonzo plaintively. "He swore to be a husband to her, — a son to me. There's no sacrifice I have n't made for him. But now he turns round and wants to sell my own home from over my head."

"The villain!" shouted McCann. "That's the way he gets on in the world, usin' us when he finds it convanient, and then dismissin' us to perdition, the heartless, perjured raskill that he is!"

"It's a shame," said Green. "Such a pretty girl, too."

"A lady, if there ever was one," said Mr. Sloper. "Nothing in my house was ever good enough for her."

Meanwhile, Spencer, humiliated and disgusted by this treatment, was anything but passive under it. He appealed to each man in turn; then, met by jeers, called them individually and collectively every name he could think of. Twice he tried to make a dash and escape from the trap, but each time met wily opponents who detained him, tripped him up and laughed at him.

"I'll not be treated so," he cried, lashed into fury, and began using his fists. His efforts were wholly ineffective, since, whichever way he wheeled about, he met half-a-dozen adversaries. "Let me go. You have no right to keep me here. Let me go."

"Not until you promise to marry Miss Leo Sloper," said one of the boys.

"And be a son to Alonzo's old age, ye black ingrate!" put in McCann.

Not a few changes were rung on this theme. It seemed to Spencer, indeed, as if the air were thick with swiftly flying arrows, which came from every direction threatening to pierce him. Angry, maddened, and desperate, he struck out again, with the intention of breaking down his enemies and rushing over them.

"He's dangerous, the desateful dog!" cried Mc-Cann. "Walt, you know the trick; just let him down aisy. Be affable, don't hurt him, — we don't want no felonies."

A cry of triumph went up as Spencer was laid flat in the dust.

"Don't ye move a hand or foot, Mr. Spencer," said McCann. "We've got ye now an' we intend to kape you. It was you struck the first blow. Twinty men'll swear to that — "

"Nonsense," put in Green. "What do you want to do with him? Let him go, and a good riddance."

"Not yet," said McCann. "Not till he has expiated some of his sins. Why not tie him hand and foot?"

"Who wants him?" argued Green, not loving a fray as well as McCann did.

"I'll tell you who wants him," spoke up one of the crowd. "Miss Leo Sloper wants him bad. Let's take him to her."

This suggestion was received with cheers. It suited even Alonzo, who recognized the poetic justice of such a revenge. The others chuckled with delight at the novel idea of carrying a man by force to the feet of his true sweetheart.

"You'd better kape quiet," said McCann, as Spencer struggled again and again, and tried to rise in spite of the odds overmastering him. "You're a drivin' us to violence, sure. I tell you it's you yourself as is makin' us tie you. It's lambs we are. It's only your own good we're after, Mr. Spencer. That'll do, boys, that'll do. Now lift him, lift him high and sure, like a basket of eggs."

Just as the victim felt the ground drop from beneath him, as he bounded into air, there came a diversion. A whirl of dust, a rumble, — and a pony-cart stopped within three feet of the crowd, and the men laid down the burden.

"What is it?" cried a clear, fresh voice. "What are you men doing? Is anybody hurt?"

"Nobody at all, at all," said McCann. "It is just simply a sloight accident, an' we'll rimedy it without loss of toime. You'd best drive on, Miss. We might scare your horse."

"What has happened?" demanded Miss Standish, for it was she who, with Bessy Rexford beside her, had come upon the scene. "Mr. Sloper, I beg you to tell me who is on the ground? If there has really been an accident, I could take the hurt man home."

"He is simply a dangerous individual that we are bindin' over to kape the pace," said Michael. "He was for assaultin' us."

"Mr. Sloper," persisted Amy, "I appeal to you. Who is it?"

"Miss Standish," said Alonzo, raising his heavy arm with an impressive gesture, "this is a m–m–movement of a united b–b–brotherhood."

"Sam Porter!" cried Amy authoritatively, her eye fastening on her special protégé, who had been skulking behind the group, hoping that his presence might not be detected. "Come here this instant!" Sam tottered along the gutter towards his benefactress, in a manner which suggested that he was at the end of his strength.

"Oh, Sam!" said Amy in a voice with a sob in it. "You've been drinking again, and your two dear little children sick at home with scarlet fever and your poor wife quite worn out with trouble!"

He had brought himself to the wheel of the carriage, and fixing his glassy eye on Amy, he swayed about for a few moments silently; then, seizing an idea, he said with intense solemnity : —

"You may think I've been drinking, Miss Standish, but appearances is often deceitful; it's me feelings that overcome me."

Having thus cleared himself of the accusation, with a view perhaps to showing the mastery of his finer sentiments, he sat down in a loose heap on the curb-stone.

"Get up, Sam, and go home," said Amy reproachfully.

"Get up this minute!" put in Bessy, who was thrilled with excitement. "I won't have any disobelience!"

Spencer, meanwhile, had been torn in two by conflicting feelings. He was afraid of the men, who had grown rougher and more brutal each moment, but his first impulse had been to dread even more having Miss Standish a witness of his discomfiture. When he recognized her voice, he said within himself that he would rather die than that she should come to his aid and extricate him from this ignominious position. But there was an unaffected reality about his discomfort which had by this time quieted his scruple of pride or vanity, and now he called with all the force of his lungs : —

"Miss Standish, Miss Standish, it is I! Make them let me go. They have bound me hand and foot."

"Who is it?" said Amy, horror-stricken. She stood up whip in hand and spoke imperiously.

"It's jist nobody at all, Miss," said McCann.

"Mr. Sloper," said Amy, "I insist that you shall let

the man go at once. Who is it ? I seem to know the voice."

"It 's the voice of a perjured villain who is gettin' his just deserts, sure," said McCann, for Alonzo Sloper stood regarding the young lady in a dazed sort of way, struck dumb between a sense of the high principles he was contending for and a chivalrous feeling that Miss Standish ought to be obeyed.

Bessy had flown to the rescue. She had clambered out of the dog-cart, and, with an imperious gesture motioning aside the crowd clustered about their victim, had gained the side of the prostrate man, who lay livid and gasping.

"Aunt Amy," she said, "it 's Mr. Spencer !"

"Mr. Spencer !" echoed Amy.

"He is tied up," said Bessy indignantly. She turned to the group, who had fallen off and were looking on grinning. "Untie him !" she ordered, stamping her foot. "It is very naughty of you to tie him up in that way. Let him go this minute !"

The men obeyed orders, laughing, cutting the cords with looks and gestures of amusement and contempt, which Spencer felt like a slap on the face. He was unable to resent their impertinence, or to thank his deliverer. He was exhausted with his tussle and with his still unspent fury, and could hardly move. When he did contrive by Bessy's help to rise to his feet, and stood up choking with shame and wrath, he made a sorry spectacle. His clothes were torn ; his hair was matted with dust ; his face, by turns ashy gray and crimson, was begrimed with clay and mire.

"Oh, Mr. Spencer," murmured Amy, " this is dreadful ! What were they doing to you ?"

"We was simply havin' our bit o' fun, Miss," said McCann. "He's not hurt. He loikes it. We was practessin' on him, jist in order to show what we could do when our blood gets up. We was avingin' the cause of his lady-love too. We was goin' to carry him to Miss Leo Sloper. He's goin' to be a man hencefor- ward and marry Miss Leo Sloper as he ought to ha' done long ago, an' be a son to Alonzo in his old age. But since you insist on it, we 'll let him go."

Bessy had led Spencer up to the dog-cart.

"Get up behind," said Amy to him in a low voice, as she lifted the child to her seat. Spencer, white as chalk, his knees breaking under him and a roaring in his head which deafened and blinded him, clambered up gratefully. "Sam Porter," pursued Amy, "I shall take you home to your wife. Get up and sit beside Mr. Spencer; I am ashamed of you."

Sam looked up and smiled vacantly.

"Can't," said he, "can't do it, Miss Standish. Very partic'lar reasons. I 've struck. They would n't let me go back. If I was to be cut in two I 'd have to stay out as long as I 'm bid."

"Nonsense," said Amy. "You must do what I bid you. Mr. McCann, just put Sam Porter up."

"Come this minute!" Bessy struck in. "I won't have any disobelience!"

The men burst into a roar of applause as Amy drove away, with the two men huddled on the back seat of the dog-cart.

"God ha' mercy on us," said McCann, "but a mere man can't stand up against a woman!"

"It was an unfort'nate int'ruption," said Alonzo, who under the influence of his conflicting emotions found himself hopelessly fuddled. He felt that a good opportunity had slipped out of his hands. His great opportunities had always been of a slippery description. A tear rose to his eye and ran down his crimson cheek.

" We 'll do it next time," said McCann, consolingly.

XXVII

FATE CUTS THE KNOT.

" SURELY, Roger, you are not going out again to-night," Evelyn said anxiously, as she saw her husband looking for the second time at his watch.

"I must be at the office at half-past eight."

" But why ? "

" Felix and I have talked the matter over," said Roger, " and we have decided that it will be best for us to stay there, to-night. There are four watchmen, and we are to watch the watchmen."

He laughed as he spoke, but Evelyn was not convinced or reassured.

" Do you expect the strikers to go there ? " she asked.

"No," said Roger. " It is not at all probable. Still, we have decided to stay. I shall relieve Felix, and he can spend an hour or two with Amy; then he will join me and we shall take turns of sleeping on the lounge. You need have no apprehension, Evelyn. To begin with, the men are not likely to come near us; and if they should come they are not at all violent. According to Amy, a little child can lead them."

The two were sitting together in the library. The trouble among the men had roused Roger's slumbering forces, and he had been for the past three days almost his old self. The weary, moody expression had left his face ; his eyes were clear, his motions were more alert.

It seemed to Evelyn, indeed, that the old Roger had
come back. She hardly realized that it was danger
which had been a summons to his best powers. She
was ready to believe that all her efforts to restore happiness and peace between them were to be answered. She
had resolutely put aside every thought of late, except of
pleasing Roger. What other duty existed? What other
duty so palpable could exist? One might have believed
that she was trying to make her husband fall in love
with her over again. She had put on toilets to please
him; had met him at the door, hung about him,
swiftly divined his every need. If he looked up from
any occupation with a seeming wish, she flew to him
eagerly demanding what it was. Amy was delighted
with her sister, whom she now saw almost for the first
time bright, arch, and gay, talking without monotony,
with many delicate and shrewd observations, phrases
which suggested witticisms, and looks and tones to kin-
dle joy. It had pained the girl, sometimes, to see Roger
turn his eyes on his wife with a long stare as if he wondered at her, for at such a sign of coldness Evelyn's
face would change; she seemed to be trying not to
weep, and more than once a tear trembled on the lashes
of her brown eyes. In general, however, Roger had
been, even if quiet, at least gentle and considerate.
He was preoccupied, and had made it clear that he was
preoccupied. If Evelyn felt at times that her small
feminine efforts had no charm or cheer for him, that
perhaps they stung his loneliness and despair, that the
joys she offered were no release, only made his apathy
the clearer to him, — she had not relaxed her effort to
please him, and for these three days she at last found
an answer in his glance, in his words, and in his caressing touch.

"I must go," Roger said, with a laugh. "You must reflect that Amy wants to see Felix. How long do you suppose she has been in love with him, Evelyn?"

"She confessed to me that it had been going on a long time, but that at first she did not understand the feeling nor investigate its origin," said Evelyn lightly. "It is now classified. She knows precisely what its ingredients are composed of. She never expected to be in love, because she had never supposed that there was on the face of the earth a man like Felix. She says he is so wholly unlike other men; and when I laughed and told her I never saw anybody so much in love in all my life as she is, she said quite soberly that it was because he was stronger, sweeter, wiser, and dearer than the poor creatures other girls had to take up with. She says there is something absolutely wonderful in the effect he has on her; when he came in and took her hand to-day, she felt as if she had escaped earthquake or shipwreck, and henceforth could be happy and grateful simply to sit looking at him and reflecting that he would henceforth take care of her."

Roger had risen. He sighed instead of answering Evelyn's laugh. He drew her to him. "Poor little wife," said he, "that was not the sort of husband you were so lucky as to get."

"I love my husband with all my heart," she said, soberly.

"Well, I think you do," he answered. "You love him far better than he has seemed to deserve." He was silent a moment, then added, "I like Felix. Sitting side by side with him to-day, and taking counsel together as we did, I could not help saying to myself, 'As soon as we are out of this mess I will tell this good sensible fellow the whole story of my troubles.'"

Their eyes met; there came a flash of something like joy from hers.

"Evelyn, keep me to it," he said. "Don't let me fall below my good resolution."

"I will try to do all I can," she said softly.

"I don't wonder you have a little doubt of me."

"No, I have no doubt," she said. "I am so glad you thought of telling him. That will be best."

"If daylight can shine through the blackness, it shall shine through," said Roger. "We will not mind any consequences, Evelyn?"

"No," she said, and something in her uplifted eyes showed that she was forbidding tears, glad tears of relief and hope.

"Then, perhaps," said Roger, "we can begin once more to live."

She put her arms round his neck and let all the soft flood of her tenderness sweep over him. The caresses unnerved him. He kissed the soft, beseeching face, then put it away.

"I must go," he said.

"Oh, do not go. I beg you not to go," she pleaded.

"You don't think of Amy, Evelyn. You don't reflect what it is to be just engaged with none of the bloom rubbed off the sweetness of it."

As he spoke it was evident that a new idea suddenly entered his mind. He crossed the room to a cabinet, unlocked a drawer, and took out a pair of pistols.

The sight brought Evelyn a clearer realization of what was going on outside, in the streets of Walford. She uttered a little cry and again implored him not to go out; he could send for Felix; it was best for them both to be here. Something terrible was sure to happen at the works.

He was looking the weapons over with an experienced eye.

"I have not the faintest idea that there will be any need of using them," he said. " Certainly I do not.intend to shoot anybody, and I hardly think any man in Walford will try to shoot me. But it is better to have them with me in case of emergency."

As he spoke she was conscious that he was a strong man and could face danger without nervous panic. She admired him. He was absorbed in the immediate facts of his position, which required all his prevision and all his energy. The real significance of the contrast between his state of mind and hers at that moment lay in the fact not that he was strong while she was weak, but that a subtle stirring of conscience made her shrink from flying to him for refuge. She gave a convulsive sob.

"What is it?" he said, startled, raising his eyes from the pistols. He was thinking to himself that the action of the catch of one of them was too easy.

"I don't know," she replied. "It is only that you seem so far off ; that I want to speak to you, yet cannot make you hear ; that I want to reach you, but my arms are too short."

He smiled, put the weapons in his pocket and came towards her. He was moved ; her words seemed to make it clear that she loved him, just as she had always loved him. He spoke, however, with perfect self-command.

"The pistols frightened you," said he. "Women always suspect that fire-arms will go off of themselves. I supposed you would be glad to know I had them with me, and that I know how to use them. Come

now, good-by. Of course, you will give Felix some
supper when he comes in ; nectar and ambrosia are not
enough for such a big fellow."

He drew his wife to him and kissed her.

" I don't see," he said, with the flicker of a smile on
his grave, handsome face, " that we are, after all, so
very far from each other."

She flashed from tears to laughter one moment, as
she nestled against him, but his mood deepened instead
of lightened.   Perhaps, even while he spoke, he was
not free from some foreboding, and even her beautiful
upturned face could not hinder rushing images of
possible violence and trouble to come.   He kissed her
passionately again and again ; then, refusing to let her
go even into the hall with him, he shut the door of the
library upon her, took his hat and overcoat and went
out alone.

The moment he was outside, Lewis, the coachman,
and Birdsey, the gardener, came up to him with O'Fee,
who was telling them the news.   He had been on the
street, where Beresky was haranguing the men and they
were talking back at him.

" You can't hear yourself spake," said O'Fee, " an'
me privit imprisshin is that the min is all tired to death
of talkin', and longs to begin fightin'.' "

" Whom do they want to fight ? " said Roger.   " Each
other, I suppose.   Two-thirds of them have been drinking too much and feel quarrelsome."

" They are all talkin' of the dimonstrashin against
Mr. Spincer," said O'Fee.   " The min who was in it
are proud and consequenshil as if it was a foine act
they was guilty of.   They had 'im down in the dust an'
quoite at their mercy.   An' they loiked the feelin' of 't.

They're simply a hungerin' an' a thirstin' to rub some-body else in the moire."

Birdsey and Lewis both had some testimony to the effect that the crowd was lively and mischievous and, if not bent on actually dangerous enterprise, would be only too glad to have something occur which should give the necessary spark of fire to their inflammable impulse.

Roger spoke reassuringly to the three men. O'Fee was Birdsey's brother-in-law, and was to stay on the place for the night. Roger gave explicit directions what they should say and do, if the rioters appeared to be coming in their direction. Then he walked rapidly on to his office, at the works, where Felix Goodeve was waiting, with more or less impatience, to be relieved.

"Suppose, Felix," Roger said to him as he was about to leave the office, "you should stop at the station and telegraph to Rex Long to come up if he can. Rex has helped me out of many a trouble, and he will be glad to stand by us now."

Then Roger was left alone. There were two watch-men inside the works and two outside, each of whom was ordered to report every half hour to McDougal, who was in charge of the main building. Roger had spoken to Jimmy McCann, the brother of Michael, as he came in. Jimmy had the front patrol. He had told Roger that no danger was to be apprehended that night, at all events. He had heard that next day, if the steel-cutters came back to their work, the strikers would march in and order them to suspend, and that then, if they did not obey, there might be a show of violence.

Roger sat down and thought over what was likely to happen on the morrow, and what this show of violence might prove to mean. He remembered his pistols, took them out of his pocket, loaded them carefully, and laid them on his table, putting a newspaper over them lest they should have too threatening an aspect, if anybody came in.

The office was brightly lighted, and Felix had been passing the time in reading. Roger felt no inclination even to glance at the evening papers, but sat, his hands thrust into his pockets and his gaze fixed on the floor. He was still conscious of the deep emotion Evelyn's tenderness had roused in him. Half his feeling had at first been pain, but now he experienced a sensation of comfort; some trouble seemed to lift from his heart. It was evident that her love had survived all the strain put upon it. Of late he had constantly said to himself with half-bitter irony, "Poor little soul, she is trying to do her duty." But after all she loved him with the same love which had vibrated from the beginning.

And he reflected that they were both young. He was thirty-five and she ten years and more younger. They had a long life before them, and they might as well try to get happiness out of it. He realized now that he had made a mistake in believing that he must stand alone. He had not after all stood alone, but had had Spencer, who had constantly given him rotten planks to mend the bridge which he must pass in order to get over his difficulties. He must take his pride in his two hands, get the better of it and ask counsel of Felix Goodeve and Rexford Long. The complications in his position were tortuous, but they were not necessarily hopeless if he had strong backers. It would be an abhorrent ordeal; it would be like undergoing some physical operation of which the pain is frightful and the danger appalling. Still, not a day passes that men, and women too, do not nerve themselves to bear what freezes flesh and blood with terror to think of ; later, when the disease which has been poisoning their fount of life is arrested, they are ready to speak of the experience as something to rejoice over. He, too, must somewhere within him have the requisite force which should enable him to brace himself up and bear the agony of confession which would cut his manhood in two. Yet afterwards he could live again and be able to think of something besides the humiliation of being found out.

" Then I shall begin once more to live," he muttered to himself. But even while he planned a way of escape from his long bondage, a way wise, honorable, and easy for himself, his nerves began to betray him. He felt restless, ill at ease ; fresh difficulties and dangers confronted him. He began to say to himself that this would happen, and the other thing must come to pass. The possibilities contingent upon a clear illumination of the dark and devious places of his life seemed to open like lightnings out of the black heavens, flashing upon him like flames, making him quiver under the whip-lash of fire they wielded. He knew how he could suffer under these goads ; he had borne them only too often. It would not do for him to become unmanned and trembling to-night. Just to restore his self-command, to afford himself relief from the oppressions and anxieties which must be postponed until the present danger was passed, he went to the closet and poured out a few drops of a liquid which, he well knew, could soothe needless disquiet and suspend the ache of over-vivid thought. By this time it was half-past nine. He lay down on the lounge, thinking it as well to rest until there should be some summons to action.

It was ten minutes later that Jimmy McCann, walking up and down outside, saw a small squad of men coming up the street. They halted at the corner, some two hundred feet below his beat.

" Who be 's ye ? " he called out.

" Hist ! " said a familiar voice, and a figure familiar even in gloom started out from the group.

" Is that you, Mike ? " called Jimmy. " An' what, I should like to be informed, are ye doin' round these primises ? "

" What are ye doin' yerself ? " returned Michael McCann. " You 'd much better be afther j'inin' yer frinds."

" As soon as I find bitter frinds, I 'll be afther j'inin' them," said Jimmy. " I 'll be lavin' off sarvin' me inimies. I 'm waitin' to secure the very bist advantages, sure."

Jimmy had by this time approached the group, which he found to consist of his brother, Alonzo Sloper, and half-a-dozen others.

" Ye 're kapin' watch ? " asked Michael. " I see a light in the wurruks. Is anybody there ? "

" An' why not ? " said Jimmy.

" Who is it ? " demanded Michael.

" Who should it be thin ? " said Jimmy, who felt his own importance and knew that it was not well at any time for a man to part too easily with all he knows.

" Is it Mr. Henry Spencer ? " inquired Alonzo Sloper in an anxious voice.

" Why should n't it be Mr. Henry Spencer ? " said Jimmy. " He 's the manager of the wurruks an' often writes letters till midnight in the office."

" We want to spake to Mr. Henry Spencer," said Michael.

"Spake away," said Jimmy.

"Can we go in and find him?"

"Not if I 'm 'round," returned Jimmy. "Me orders is impiritive. I am to walk up and down here, ask any man who comes what his business is and report him to Mr. McDougal inside."

"What is Mr. McDougal doing inside?"

"Mr. McDougal walks up and down the main buildin'," said Jimmy, "and every half hour he comes out to the office door, calls me an' asks what 's up."

"Mr. Sloper is after wishin' most particular to spake to Mr. Spencer," explained Michael.

"What about?" demanded Jimmy, feeling that he was the pivot on which great events turned. "Mr. Spencer has got nothing to do with the stroike."

"This is n't about the stroike. It 's private business. It 's a breach of promise case, an' he wants to addriss a word of admonition to the raskill who has been triflin' with his daughter's affictions. Could n't ye arrange it for us, Jimmy, to let us in quietly?"

"No, I could n't," said Jimmy. "I 've had me impiritive orders, an' I am a man who does his duty."

"Nobody better. But ef ye could go in an' kape old McDougal in conversation for five minutes while we cript up the office stairs?"

"Nothin' of the sort," returned Jimmy, chuckling. "I 've got me honor an' me conscience."

"An' what are ye goin' to do with thim vallooables?" inquired Michael, with fine irony.

"It 's toime Mr. McDougal was comin' to the door of the office," said Jimmy, drily, "an' accordingly I shall go to the door of the office an' report."

"An' what shall ye report?"

"That all's as still as a mouse," said Jimmy. "I shouldn't take up his attintion with troiflin' interruptions loike these."

"An' what shall ye do thin?"

"Walk to the other ind of me beat, sure, as me duty is," said Jimmy.

This plan he followed out to the letter. He reported to McDougal that all was tranquil; then, turning on his beat, walked as far to the north of the works as the group of men had been lurking in the shadows to the south. It was a neat trick to allow them to believe they had Mr. Spencer within reach. They would soon find out their mistake, and the humor of the situation was far from being lost upon Jimmy. Meanwhile Michael McCann and Alonzo Sloper, followed by the others, had moved noiselessly on towards the doorway of the works. They had listened to McDougal's brief colloquy with Jimmy, then waited, until five minutes later they heard the Scotchman's voice at the other side of the building. Michael felt that it was now safe to attempt their enterprise. Ever since the afternoon they had been reveling in recollections of their triumph over Spencer, and had been swearing at each other for allowing their victim to escape. Mr. Sloper, with tears in his eyes, had recounted his wrongs, that is, as long as he retained the power to utter coherent words. By this time, he was speechless; but a dull arabesque of expectation still kept awake the heavy tissues of his brain, and he was eager to see Michael again handling the enemy and getting a little fun out of him. All sorts of rumors were afloat, one being that Spencer was to have them all arrested on the morrow. It needed just this challenge to make Michael eager for the fray.

Alonzo declared that Mr. Spencer was always at the works in the evening ; so they had come.

Michael tried the outer door, which was, as he expected, bolted. He knew the place and remembered the low window at the side. Two bars of iron protected it, but he was a powerful fellow, and soon wrenched them out of the board. In another instant he was inside, had unfastened the bolts, and unlocked the door.

" Softly, softly," said he as he opened it. " None of yer trampin' here. Stale up like ye was shod in velvet."

He himself led the way up the broad, shallow stairs. The office door was open, the light shone out, and the hush of the place roused a half apprehension. Michael began to wish himself through the business, but it was too late to retreat. He pushed forward Alonzo Sloper, who was shaking like a jelly.

Roger Rexford still lay on the lounge, half conscious and half dozing, in a mood for seeing visions and dreaming dreams. He had a confused sense that some one had entered, but was reluctant to rouse himself. Coerced, however, by a vague, gathering sense of the necessity for being up and alert, he asked, —

" Is that you, Felix ? "

" Why, it 's Mr. Rexford ! " was the exclamation which brought him to himself, at least roused him to the point of starting to his feet, to gaze horror-stricken at what seemed to him a threatening band of men stealing towards him.

" You rascals ! you scoundrels ! " he cried, with a swift movement towards the table, to get hold of his pistols.

The intruders understood the gesture ; they wheeled

about, getting in each other's way. There was a sort of scuffle. Alonzo Sloper fell down in sheer fright and cried aloud for help ; the table was overturned. At the same instant a pistol shot rang out keen and sharp.

The alarm was general. Within five minutes all the watchmen about the building had gathered. McDougal was the first to enter. The office was empty except for the master of it, who lay across a chair just as he had fallen, with a bullet through his temple, dead.

XXVIII.

IT was not clearly known for some little time after-
ward just how Roger Rexford had been killed. It was
at first supposed that some one of the strikers had been
the murderer, and a thrill of horror and execration of
such a deed ran through the whole body of men who
had gone out.

The next morning, every man who belonged to the
works was in his place. All Walford loved Roger
Rexford, had known him from his birth and was proud
of him, and now mourned him. To this day, when the
final act of the tragedy is talked over among the men
who gather at the post-office and street corners, not a
few of them are heard to declare solemnly that the real
truth of Roger Rexford's death had never been told;
that nobody had plucked out the heart of the mystery.
· For it was not reasonable to suppose that an all-round
man like Roger Rexford, calm, strong, sure of himself
and of his influence on all who approached him, should
have been killed in a scuffle by a chance bullet from his
own exploded pistol.

Yet, had Roger Rexford himself foreseen just how he
was to die, he would have said it was but the final knot
in the tangled skein of his life, that it ended the miserable web in just the way he might have expected. It
had for years been his grievance that he was always at

the mercy of accident, of events set in motion by no adequate cause.　He had felt himself borne round and round in the eddies of a whirlpool ; had had to submit to whatever happened ; had never, by any chance, been able to choose his own path, or use his intellect in shaping circumstances to his own will.

Rexford Long had received the telegram which Felix Goodeve had sent at Roger's request, and was in Walford next day, before he had heard the news of what had happened.　Rex had said to himself a few weeks before that he should probably never see the place again nor Evelyn ; yet here he was.

When he was once more face to face with his cousin, Roger was lying on his side and looked as if asleep. He had been in life a handsome man ; in death he was singularly beautiful.

If anything rankled in Long's memory it was forgiven.　A wave of love and pity broke over him as he stood and gazed.　This was a man who had begun with lofty dreams, who had conceived great enterprises, sure of his strength to carry them out.　Let others who had with equal ambition schemed, then bravely borne the full strain and stress and fully executed, judge him for his failure ; Long felt that he himself had known in all his life nothing but selfish ease, compared with the man who lay before him with a look on his face as if quaffing thirstily of the long-craved boon of rest.

Both Long and Felix Goodeve had months before them of arduous work in following up the clews of the labyrinth of mismanagement Roger's affairs disclosed, but there was never a word uttered by either in dispraise of the dead master of Rexford's.

"There is no need of Evelyn's knowing," Felix had remarked to Long.

"I wanted to say to you that somehow we must contrive that she shall never know," Rex had answered.

"What Madam Van left must be given to the hospital," Felix added.

"Every cent of it," said Rex. "When Evelyn is stronger that will be her first wish."

The blow had for the time crushed Evelyn. Her mind had been rushing with impetuous current towards every possibility of change at the very moment that her husband was brought in dead.

He had parted with her in a way which had allowed her to miss little of his old tenderness. That final embrace had rent her in two, but it had renewed the old inward bond of love. She sat by Roger all that night, and memory took her back to the time of perfect trust when Roger's very presence had made her happy. Such a surge of sweet poignant recollections broke over her, as she watched, that they helped her to evade the implacable reality of the present. The marble-like rigidity did not repel her. The yearning she felt to be once more all she had ever been to her husband was enough almost to turn dust into sentient flesh and blood.

Indeed, to most of us the shock of death of a dear one brings with it a wonderfully vivid sense of the old life at its fullest. Voices speak again; the sound of happy laughter comes back; old memories rise and make past joys thrill and vibrate anew.

It was only when Evelyn was separated from her husband that she realized the inexorableness of the parting, and as she realized it all motive seemed to slip from her. "Try to live," everybody said; but it must

be, she felt, a perfidy to the dead to live on; to put one
foot before the other; to appoint any sort of goal for
herself.   The outward symbols which served to express
that the tie which had made her outward identity was
broken brought a new train of thought.   Happy memories had had their time while Roger was yet within
reach.   Now that he was remote, forever silent, bitter
recollections asserted themselves with cruel force and
threatened to exclude everything else.   Heart-cutting
thoughts of her alienation from him came.   She felt
again the horror of his recoil when instead of a trusting
wife he had found an accuser.   She said to herself that
she had been wicked, and her irredeemable offense
weighed upon her.

This was the darkness that Evelyn sat in for days.
She saw no ray of light through it.   Her boy was
brought to her and taken away; Bessy's prattle and
caresses fell on deaf ears and unanswering lips.   She
dared to know no solace.   Anything which could
suggest that she had a life of her own to lead with
fresh interests, hopes, and consolations was a vision from
which she turned shudderingly away.

Then all at once Bessy sickened with scarlet fever.

XXIX.

Two of the Porter children had been very ill of scarlet fever at the time that Amy brought their father
home in the dog-cart; Bessy, it was to be presumed,
had thus taken the infection.

For the first five days the case promised to be of the
mildest character. It was, however, the first ailment
the little girl had ever been known to have, and the
slight illness roused a painful revolution of feeling in
Evelyn. Her whole mind was tinged by presentiments
of danger. Since her husband's death she had seemed
to lookers-on to be stunned. The rush of thoughts
within had made her feel dead to outside impressions,
and if she experienced any personal longing it was to
nestle, bruised and desolated as she was, into some quiet
place and have everything ended. But the moment
Amy told her that Bessy had symptoms of scarlatina
she rose with a great cry. She gathered the child into
her arms, and seemed to be defying an enemy. Not
even the light aspect of the disease reassured her.
Mrs. Goodeve and Amy, looking on, could hardly fathom
the meaning of Evelyn's deadly terror. Although for
the sake of her baby she tried to save her strength, it
was a wrench like that of parting body and soul for her
to separate herself from Bessy. It was a bitter anguish
for her to resign the least of a nurse's duties to Amy.

Bessy herself enjoyed the first few days of her illness. There was clear comfort in being made much of by her mother, who had of late kept apart ; she liked to be held in Evelyn's arms, to listen to soft, cooing lullabies, to be fed with milk and broth, and promised jellies, poached eggs, and chickens, as soon as she should be well enough.

But the fifth day the child's eyes showed a change ; there was a slight wandering of mind, and towards night convulsions. Evelyn was shut out of the room.

"Take care of her," Amy said to Felix. "She is almost out of her mind. She frightens me more than Bessy's case does. She must not come into the room again until the child is better."

Felix carried Evelyn down-stairs. Rexford Long was sitting there in anguished suspense, and he rose and helped to lead her in.

"She is dying," Evelyn said to him in a hard, dry voice. "From the first I knew that she must die. It is of no use. They are trying all sorts of remedies and there are three doctors. But she is dying all the same. Nothing can save her. She was certain to die."

The two men had put her into a chair. They could only gaze at her helplessly. Each felt that he should never have known that it was Evelyn's face looking up at them. The features were distorted with anguish.

" Dr. Cowdry declares that many a child has been far worse and pulled through," said Felix. "Come now, — my mother tells me Bessy is as likely to live as to die."

"You see they don't know," Evelyn whispered. "We have broken man's laws and God's laws. Her death will put things right. Besides, our sin finds us out ; the guilty must suffer."

"You are not guilty, Evelyn," said Long, his heart quaking with hers, in presentiment.

"I am guilty," she said in a voice born of pain. "I have known for months that she was not really my own Bessy, and that all that money ought to have gone to the children's hospital. It is being visited on me now. Her death will put things right. We would not do our duty, and now it is being done for us."

"Evelyn," said Long, "Felix and I have talked over that matter about Madam Van's will. I told him you had more than a grain of doubt about Bessy's identity, and he said at once that the thing to do was to give up the money. It is going to be done. It is already being done. Now it shall be done at once."

"You see," said Felix, "we did not like to throw any suspicion upon the dear little creature's belonging to us. Now, don't you see, this illness offers an occasion. Madam Van's property shall go to the hospital as your thank-offering for her recovery."

"Can it go? Can it be paid over?" asked Evelyn, with evident doubt. "I was afraid some of it had been used."

"It shall be paid over, principal and interest," said Felix. "It is going to be paid over. When I found out that you had had such a cause of trouble, I told Rex that the legal dilemma should no longer exist. We are all one family. I want to look at Bessy without a doubt that she is in her rightful place."

"If the money could go where it belongs," faltered Evelyn in a pitiful voice, "perhaps I might hope. Oh, let it go. Sell this place, — sell everything. That last night Roger told me that he was going to have daylight in his affairs, and asked if I should be willing to take the consequences. Perhaps he meant whether I should mind being poorer. I would rather be poor. I should be glad to be poor, if I could only have Bessy —" She started up. "Some one is on the stairs," she whispered.

It was Dr. Cowdry. He brought the news that the child had come safely out of the paroxysm. It had been caused by a slight complication, which he trusted and believed was removed. Even if it should return, Miss Standish understood very well how to treat it.

Evelyn accepted this reprieve like a direct sign from heaven. She was no longer pierced by the presentiment that Bessy's life was to pay the forfeit of the wrong others had done.

The child soon surmounted the dangers of the disease. Evelyn had the whole winter to devote to the task of nursing her, and bringing her back to complete health. The money was given over, — nobody except Felix Goodeve and Rexford Long were ever to know at what sacrifice, — for the children's hospital as a thank-offering.

Evelyn saw nothing in her husband's course which any one could blame. He too had wished the property to belong to its rightful owners. She never ceased to condemn herself for having, in ignorance of the problems which confronted him, been arrogant, unjust and cruel. There must always remain that little sting at her heart. But she believes that before the end came he had forgiven and reinstated her.

Felix and Amy were quietly married the following Easter. They have continued to live in Walford, for Felix is at the head of the Rexford Manufacturing

Company. Amy's activities have widened, not narrowed; the fire of her soul has not lessened, but has
turned into tenderness and self-abnegation. For she
still believes that her happiness is something excep-
tional. She finds perpetual comfort in her husband,
although she sometimes says, "Felix, I never feel absolutely sure you are not laughing at me, ever so little."

"I laugh that I may not cry," he returns, "for I 'm
so running over with pride in you and joy in you."

Spencer, cruelly humiliated and hopelessly defeated
in all his dearest objects as for the time he had felt
himself to be, was destined nevertheless to re-trick his
beams. He had had some very curious and unpleasant sensations, while he believed himself to be in danger; and for a long time afterwards the experience
humbled him. Roger Rexford's death gave a terrible
shock to his sensibilities; all the more because it was,
after a little investigation, discovered that the men who
broke into the works were in search of himself. Spencer thus could not help realizing with a shudder what
might have been his own fate. Roger's death deprived
him of his best friend, and he was at first in despair
about his own future. The Goodeves, however, were
always staunch friends and did not easily let go their
grip upon any one who had shown any signs of faithfulness. And Spencer had been, in many ways, faithful.
Felix had a talk with him. Spencer had been a little run
away with by his belief in his own surpassing cleverness,
also by an ambition which events had relentlessly
curbed. When he was offered a good place in the
Western branch, he now accepted it gratefully. He was
glad to leave Walford. It may, however, be of interest
to relate, that eighteen months later he returned, and

happening to encounter Miss Leo Sloper, he found her
so pretty, so much developed, so exactly what he admired, that he at once returned to his old allegiance.
Mrs. Felix Goodeve had done all she could for Leo,
who had also done all she could for herself. Alonzo
Sloper had by this time paid the penalty of his consistent habits of dissipation, and had been cut off in the
very vigor of his middle age. His nerves had, it is to
be feared, been shaken by the terrible accident which
ended the Walford strike, and henceforth it was his way,
whenever the painful recollection rose to his thoughts,
to reach out his shaking hand for a fresh glass of something to reassure him.

And do we need to say any more of Evelyn? She is
living with her two children in the place by the river,
and if not completely happy, it is because along with a
feeling of complete happiness comes a pang of conviction that perhaps she ought not to be too happy. She
keeps very busy, for Bessy's mind grows with her
growth and strengthens with her strength, and her activities are boundless. Evelyn endeavors to hold a loving
curb over the bright little girl ; she tries to teach both
children, although Theodore is still too young to take
to philosophy, that we must choose always to do
what we know to be exactly right ; that pleasure is
nothing, that rewards are nothing, so long as it is our
own narrow advantage we seek ; that we must be true,
and honest, and open, and pure of heart, and each day
let God's own sunlight shine through our most hidden
thoughts.

Rexford Long is often in Walford. He has never
yet spoken a word of love to Evelyn. The three years

of her mourning for Roger will soon be over, and then, he tells himself, he may dare to end the long silence. But he also tells himself that he dares hope nothing; that it is a bliss beyond his deserts to think of gaining Evelyn for a nearer relation, and that rather than cause her a moment's pain he would go on lonely to the end. Yet all the time he is impatient, perhaps the more so that Evelyn is sometimes a little shy of him, for she remembers, — she cannot help remembering, — certain words of Roger's. Felix Goodeve looks on with an occasional twinkle of the eye when he sees the two together, but all he has ever said on the subject was when he asked Rex if he had ever told Evelyn the story of her own little Bessy's end.

"No, not yet," Rex had answered. "I sometimes feel as if I never should dare to tell her."

Felix put his hand on his cousin's shoulder : —

"Yes," he said, softly. "Years hence, perhaps, when Evelyn has been your own wife a long time, and when she is perfectly happy again, tell her. By that day it will be rest and peace for her to know. For she must often wonder about it."

Rex turned all colors as Felix said this, but did not answer. Perhaps such encouragement made him all the more impatient for the appointed limit to be reached. Then he will speak, and speak, we can fancy, — quiet, silent fellow although he is,— with an eloquence born of his long repression. It is not probable that Evelyn will hear him without a shock of strong emotion; without cruel pain and a feeling of repugnance. For the memory will return, with cruel vividness, of those words which hurt her long ago, to which this full confession will give a meaning they did not at first hold ; her husband's jealousy of Rex will seem to her a prohibition. With the first imperious force of her conviction that she ought always to be true to Roger, she will perhaps send Rex away, almost with bitter words. But she knows well, even by this time, that she cannot live without him ; that she depends at every turn upon his decision, his companionship. Her children love him so well, they will be his avengers. If he goes away at her bidding with sorrow he is likely to return in joy.

Evelyn is not a woman of theories. She only feels strong in the strength and security of her affections. With all our love for her absolute consistency of character from first to last, we can imagine her saying some time, perhaps years, hence : —

"I see it all now, Rex. I always loved you, that is, with the real love of my life. I was a child when I married Roger."

And Bessy? Shall we say anything more of her? The gift for the hospital went in her name and Madam Van's. She has, as it were, expiated the unconscious offense of her happy little life.

FINIS.